D1648075

The SECRET *of* PEMBROOKE PARK

Books by Julie Klassen

The SECRET of PEMBROOKE PARK

JULIE KLASSEN

BETHANYHOUSE
a division of Baker Publishing Group
Minneapolis, Minnesota

© 2014 by Julie Klassen

Published by Bethany House Publishers
11400 Hampshire Avenue South
Bloomington, Minnesota 55438
www.bethanyhouse.com

Bethany House Publishers is a division of
Baker Publishing Group, Grand Rapids, Michigan

Printed in the United States of America

Library of Congress Cataloging-in-Publication Data
Klassen, Julie.
    The secret of Pembrooke Park / Julie Klassen.
        pages ; cm
    Summary: "In Regency-era England, secrets come to light at the abandoned manor house Pembrooke Park. Will Abigail find the hidden treasure and love she seeks . . . or very real danger?"— Provided by publisher.
    ISBN 978-0-7642-1278-9 (hardcover : acid-free paper)
    ISBN 978-0-7642-1071-6 (softcover)
    1. Single women—England—Fiction. I.Title.
PS3611.L37S43 2014
813'.6—dc23   2014029252

Unless otherwise noted, Scripture quotations are from the King James Version of the Bible.

Scripture quotations identified GNV are from the Geneva Bible, 1599 Edition. Published by Tolle Lege Press. All rights reserved.

Cover photography by Mike Habermann Photography, LLC
Cover design by Jennifer Parker

Author represented by Books & Such Literary Agency

14 15 16 17 18 19 20   7 6 5 4 3 2 1

With love
to my brothers,
Bud & Dan

For nothing is secret,
that shall not be evident:
neither anything hid,
that shall not be known,
and come to light.

—Luke 8:17 GNV

Prologue

J sat across the table from the man I most admired, feeling self-conscious. How I wished I'd taken more time with my appearance. But my meeting with the housekeeper had run long, allowing me barely enough time to wash my face and repin my hair in a simple coil. I had planned to wear a new evening dress—golden satin with red roses embroidered throughout the bodice—but instead I'd slipped into the plain ivory gown I usually wore. It had far fewer fastenings.

I glanced over at my beautiful younger sister, her hair curled and styled by Mamma's lady's maid. Louisa wore the emerald necklace I had planned to wear, declaring it looked so well with her new dress. She'd said, *"You know you don't care a fig about fashion, Abigail, so don't fuss. You can wear my coral. It will look fine with the gown you always wear."*

I reminded myself it didn't really matter how well I looked. Gilbert Scott and I had known each other since we were children. He knew what I looked like without a hint of powder, skin clear or with eruptions, with hair up or down or in need of a good brushing. We grew up as friends and neighbors through the awkward stages of adolescence and into adulthood. The time for first impressions had long past.

Even so, this was his going-away party. The last time I would see him for a year. And I'd wanted his final memory of me to be a good one. For I cherished a secret hope. Perhaps when Gilbert returned from studying abroad he would finally ask me to marry him.

For more than an hour, our two families enjoyed a lovely meal of several courses in the Scotts' dining room. Warm and friendly conversation flowed easily around the table. But I barely noticed what I ate.

I turned to Gilbert's sister and asked, "How goes the magazine?"

"Very well, I think." Susan smiled, then looked at her brother. "Bertie, you ought to write an account of your travels while you're away."

"Capital notion, my love," Susan's husband said, adding his approval. "Send us a few sketches to accompany the piece and we'll publish it."

Gilbert shook his head. "I shall have my hands full with my studies, Edward, but thank you just the same. Susan's the writer in the family, not I."

Gilbert's father spoke up from the head of the table. "But you will write to us, my boy, won't you? You know I . . . your Mamma will worry otherwise."

Humor shone in Mrs. Scott's eyes. "That's right, my dear. *I* shall worry. But not you?"

"Well, perhaps a bit. . . ." He gestured for the butler to refill his wine. Again.

Over my glass, I met Gilbert's gaze, and we shared a private smile.

Mr. Scott addressed my father. "I say, Foster, did you not invest in that bank mentioned in the newspaper today—the one having some sort of trouble?"

"We . . . did, yes. My brother-in-law is one of the partners. But he assures us it's only a minor setback. All will be well."

Father sent me a guarded look, and I forced a reassuring smile.

This wasn't the time or place to discuss finances. Nor did I wish to cast a pall over Gilbert's send-off.

When the meal concluded, the men remained behind to smoke and sip port, while the ladies retired to the drawing room.

Gilbert, however, did not remain with the other gentlemen. Instead, he asked me to join him in the library.

I did so, my heart tripping a little faster with each step.

Alone with Gilbert inside the candlelit room, I reminded myself to breathe normally. We stood very near each other at the high library table, necks bent to study the measured drawing of a church façade in classical style. Gilbert had won the Royal Academy's silver medal for the drawing. And a gold medal for his design of a guildhall. For his achievements, Gilbert had received a traveling scholarship from the academy to study architecture in Italy. I was so proud of him.

"In the end, I altered the design to create a grander façade," Gilbert explained. "With a Corinthian portico six columns wide, based on the Pantheon in Rome. And notice the steeple here? I designed its top stage to resemble a miniature temple. . . ."

He spoke with enthusiasm, but for once I wasn't really listening. My interest had strayed from the drawing to the man himself. With his eyes on his prize-winning design, I felt at liberty to study his profile, to linger on his features—his jaw more defined than I had noticed before, his cheekbone framed by long, stylish side-whiskers, his lips thin but expressive as he spoke. I thought I might try to sketch him, though doubted my ability to do him justice. And he smelled good too. Bay rum cologne, I thought. And mint.

As he reached over to point to some detail of the drawing, his broad shoulder, elegant in evening wear, pressed against mine. I felt the warmth of it through my thin muslin and closed my eyes to savor the sensation.

"What do you think?"

"Hmm?" I opened my eyes, chagrined to be caught not listening. "About the steeple?"

Personally I thought it a bit much but held my tongue. In the past, I had often offered my opinion or a suggestion, but as the design had already won a medal from the Royal Academy, who was I to disagree?

"Lovely," I murmured. It was an innocuous, uninformed, feminine remark. Something Louisa might have said. But in his flush of triumph, he did not seem to notice.

I glanced over my shoulder. Through the open library door, I could see into the Scotts' drawing room. There Susan slipped her arm through her husband's as they stood talking to my mother. My parents lived very separate lives—Father occupied with his club and investments. Mother with her social calls, charities, and husband hunting for Louisa. No, I didn't want a marriage like my parents'. But a life like Susan's, working side by side with the one you loved . . . Yes, that seemed ideal.

With that hope, I glanced up at Gilbert. He had followed my gaze toward his newly married sister. He briefly met my eyes, then looked down, his Adam's apple convulsing, his fingers distractedly rolling the corner of his plan.

Noticing his nervous hesitation, my heart beat hard. Had the moment come? Was he about to propose?

He began, "You know you mean a great deal to me, Abby. And I realize you might be expecting . . ."

His words trailed away, and he swallowed. Had he guessed my presumptuous thoughts?

"No, no. I am not expecting anything," I reassured him, adding to myself, *Not yet.*

He nodded but did not meet my eyes. "We have been friends a long time, you and I, but you need to know that I . . . That with all the chances involved in the coming year away, I don't think either of us should shackle ourselves with promises."

"Oh." I blinked, stomach plummeting. Perhaps he was merely trying to protect me, I told myself. He no doubt had my best interests at heart. I forced a smile. "Yes, you are perfectly right, Gilbert. Very practical."

Gilbert's mother stepped into the room. "Thought I would find the two of you in here," she said. "Come through. We're serving coffee, and your father needs a great deal of it." Mrs. Scott patted her son's arm. "He's terribly proud . . . but so sorry to see you go."

Me too, I thought.

Later, when the evening began winding down and my parents were thanking Mr. and Mrs. Scott for dinner, I went in search of Gilbert, hoping to say my good-byes to him in private. Instead I found Gilbert and my sister ensconced in the vestibule, alone.

With sinking heart, I saw Louisa hand something to Gilbert. She said, "To remember me by."

He slipped it into his pocketbook and tucked it away, his gaze lingering on her lovely face all the while. Then he smiled and squeezed Louisa's hand.

Feeling light-headed, I turned away, not waiting to hear his reply.

What had Louisa given him? A miniature? A lover's eye? A lock of hair set in a ring? I had not seen Gilbert place anything on his finger, only in his pocketbook. Surely it had been nothing of such import—nothing that indicated a courtship or engagement. Even if Louisa had developed a schoolgirl affection for our neighbor, that did not mean Gilbert returned her feelings. He was likely too polite to refuse her gift, whatever it was.

Even so, it was all I could do to smile and feign normalcy a short while later, when everyone gathered at the door to say farewell and wish Gilbert success and safe travels.

Gilbert took my hand, the old brotherly tenderness coming back into his expression. "Abby. You won't forget me, I know. And I shall never forget you. Your father has given me permission to correspond with you and your sister. Will you write to me?"

"If you like."

He pressed my hand warmly and then turned to shake Father's hand and made Mother blush by kissing her cheek. He hesitated when he came to Louisa, her head demurely bowed. He made do with a bow and a murmured, "Miss Louisa."

She looked up at him from beneath long lashes, and I saw the telltale sparkle in her eye even if no one else did.

When did things change between them? I wondered. Louisa had always been the pesky little sister, someone to tease or avoid. Someone with a plait of hair to be tugged—not presented as a lover's gift.

I had wanted Gilbert's year away to fly quickly past. Now I wasn't so sure.

I had looked forward to life after his return—a life in which he played a significant role.

Suddenly the future seemed far less certain.

Chapter 1

The jewel case lay open on the desk between them, the evergreen emeralds glittering against the black velvet lining. The necklace and matching bracelet had been passed down through the Foster side of the family. Her mother's family had no precious gems to pass down. And soon neither side would.

Her father snapped the case shut, and Abigail winced as though she'd been slapped.

"Say good-bye to the family jewels," he said. "I suppose I shall have to sell these along with the house."

Standing before her father's desk, Abigail gripped her hands. "No, Papa, not the jewels. There must be another way. . . ."

Nearly a year had passed since Gilbert left England, and with it Abigail's twenty-third birthday. When she had predicted an uncertain future on the eve of his departure, she'd been more accurate than she would have guessed.

What had she been thinking? Just because she could run a large home and staff did not mean she knew anything about investments. She was the type of person who usually considered things carefully, investigated thoroughly before acting—whether it was selecting a new dressmaker or hiring a new housemaid. Abigail was the practical, behind-the-scenes daughter and had long prided herself on making sound, rational decisions. That was why her mother left much of the household management to her. Even her father had come to depend on her opinion.

Now they were facing financial ruin—and it was her fault. Little more than a year ago, she had encouraged her father to invest in Uncle Vincent's new bank. Her mother's brother was her only uncle, and Abigail had always been fond of him. He was charming, enthusiastic, and eternally optimistic. He and his partners, Mr. Austen and Mr. Gray, owned two country banks and had wished to open a third. Uncle Vincent had asked her father to post a large bond of guarantee, and under Abigail's influence, he agreed.

The banks were at first successful. However, the partners made excessive, unwise loans, sometimes lending to each other. They sold one bank but struggled to keep the others afloat. The new bank had stopped business in November, and a week ago the original bank failed and the partners declared bankruptcy.

Abigail could still hardly believe it. Her uncle had been so sure the banks would thrive and had made Abigail believe it as well.

Seated at his desk, her father set aside the jewelry case and ran his finger down the accounts ledger.

Abigail awaited his verdict, palms damp, heart beating dully.

"How bad is it?" she asked, twisting her hands.

"Bad. We are not destitute, and you and Louisa still have your dowries. But the lion's share of my capital is gone and with it the interest."

Abigail's stomach cramped. "Again, I am sorry, Papa. Truly," she said. "I honestly thought Uncle Vincent and his partners would be successful."

He ran a weary hand over his thin, handsome face. "I should not have allowed myself to be swayed by the two of you. I have seen his other ventures fail in the past. But you have always had a good head on your shoulders, Abigail. I thought I could trust your judgment. No, now, I don't say this is entirely your fault. I blame myself as well. And Vincent, of course."

Seeing her father so deeply disappointed and disillusioned—with her and with life—left her feeling sick with guilt and regret. Uncle Vincent blamed his partners and their risky loans. But in the end, regardless of who was to blame, the fact was that Charles Foster had agreed to act as guarantor. He was not the only person who lost money when the banks failed, but he lost the most.

Her father shook his head, a bitter twist to his lips. "I don't know how I shall break it to Louisa that she is not to have her season after all. She and her mother have their hearts set on it."

Abigail nodded in silent agreement. The London season was well-known hunting grounds for wealthy husbands. She hoped Louisa's eagerness to participate meant she was not waiting for Gilbert Scott. If Louisa and Gilbert *did* have an understanding, Louisa had clearly kept it a secret from her mother, who was determined to give her youngest a spectacular season. At nineteen Louisa was at the peak of her beauty—or so their mother declared, insisting it was the perfect time to find her an advantageous match.

Her father leaned back in his chair with a defeated sigh. "If only we could avoid selling the house, but as much as we all love it, it is too large and too expensive. The price of being fashionable, I suppose."

Not to mention the cost of maintaining a Grosvenor Square–style of living—behaving like nobility, though in reality they were only genteel, with no title or land. As a gentleman, her father had never in his life had to work. The family had lived on the interest from his inheritance. Money he had invested wisely—until now.

Once again, Gilbert's suggestion that they not *"shackle ourselves with promises"* echoed through Abigail's mind, and she straightened her shoulders in resolve. "Yes, Papa. We shall have to sell the house, but not the family jewels. Not while there is another option. . . ."

A short while later, Father asked Mamma and Louisa to join them in the study, and attempted to explain the situation. He did not assign any blame to her, Abigail noticed, but knowing he held her partially responsible for their predicament was enough to make her miserable.

When he had finished, Anne Foster protested, "Sell our house?"

"You know, Mamma, that might not be so bad," Louisa said. Grosvenor Square isn't as fashionable as it once was. I saw some lovely houses in Curzon Street that would do us very well."

"Curzon Street?" Father echoed. "That will not be possible, my dear."

"I think it would be wisest to retrench elsewhere," Abigail said. "In a smaller city or even in the country, where the pressure to have an army of servants, large dinners, and the latest gowns would be far less."

"The country?" Louisa's pretty face puckered as though she'd found a mouse in her soup. "Unless you are talking about a great country estate, with house parties, and fox hunting, and hedge mazes . . ."

"No, Louisa, I am afraid not. Something smaller."

"Oh, why did this have to happen?" Mamma moaned. "What about Louisa's season? Her dowry? Is it all gone? Is our youngest daughter not to have her chance, after all?"

"I didn't say that. No. Louisa is to have her season." Father sent an uneasy glance toward Abigail, then quickly looked away. "We will muster enough for Louisa's gowns and things. I trust your aunt Bess will allow us to stay with her for a few months?"

"Of course she will. But . . . I don't understand. I thought you said there would not be enough money."

With another glance at Abigail, Father began, "Abigail has kindly—"

But she interrupted him. "I have helped Papa find a few ways to economize. Some funds we had set aside for a . . . rainy day. And a few things we can sell—"

"Not your father's emeralds!"

Abigail shook her head. "No, not the emeralds."

Her mother firmly nodded. "Good. Louisa must have her chance to wear them, as you did."

Abigail noticed with relief that her mother refrained from adding, *"for as much good as it did you,"* or something of that sort.

Abigail forced a smile. "We shall scrape together enough to give Louisa a wonderful season. The season she deserves."

For a moment her mother stared at her as if she spoke a foreign language. Abigail feared she would probe further into the source of the money—perhaps even suggest Abigail's dowry could be used for additional funds, since *she* no longer needed one. It was one thing to offer it up quietly, willingly—as Abigail had done privately to her father—but quite a different, humiliating thing to be told a dowry was wasted on her.

Mollified, her mother only nodded. "As it should be." She pressed Louisa's hand. "You see, my dear, you are to have your season after all. What did I tell you? You shall meet the most handsome, best connected, and wealthiest young man this year. I just know it!"

And so, while Mrs. Foster and Louisa attended dress fittings, Abigail began helping her disillusioned and disappointed father find a more affordable place to live.

Abigail contacted a property agent and made inquiries for a suitable dwelling. But she heard of no situation that answered her mother's notions of spacious comfort *and* suited Abigail's prudence. She had rejected several houses as too large for their income.

One afternoon, among the correspondence about properties, Abigail received a letter from Gilbert Scott, postmarked *Roma*. Her heart gave a little foolish leap, as it always did when seeing her name in his neat hand. Over the preceding months, Gilbert had sent letters to both her and Louisa. Abigail always read his descriptions of his studies and the architecture of Italy—sometimes with sketches in the margins—with absorption and dutifully wrote back. She did not know what sort of letters Gilbert wrote to Louisa. Abigail feared they might be of a more romantic nature than those she received but hoped she was wrong.

She retreated to her bedchamber to read Gilbert's letter in private.

My dear Abby,

Hello, old friend. How is life in London? I imagine you are bored without me there to tease you and drag you about the city to see St. Paul's, or the construction at Bethlehem Hospital, or to hear some lecture or other. Italy is amazing, and you would love it. But I shan't overwhelm you with details in this letter, for fear of making you jealous and risk your not writing back.

You have been very good about answering my letters, Abby. I appreciate it more than you know. As much as I enjoy Italy and my studies, I don't mind confessing to you—since you know me so well—that I do feel lonely now and again. How I would love to walk with you along the Piazza Venezia and show you the Roman Forum!

I have not heard from Louisa in some time. Like you, she was prompt in writing back when I first began my travels. But her letters have trickled off of late. I hope she is in good health—as well as you and your parents, of course. Perhaps I have done something to vex her. If I have, it was unintentional. Please tell her I said so. If only all women were as easygoing and forgiving as you, Abby.

You asked in your last letter which building I most admired here. I seem to find a new favorite every day. Which reminds me, I had better sign off for now. We're soon to leave to visit the Basilica di Santa Maria del Fiore in Florence. Perhaps I shall find a new favorite.

Fondly,
Gilbert

Abigail folded the letter and for a moment held it to her chest, imagining Gilbert's handsome, earnest face as he wrote it, the ink on his fingers, and the tip of his tongue protruding as it always did when he concentrated on a task. Then she imagined walking arm in arm with him through Rome. . . .

"What has you smiling?" Louisa asked, pausing in her bed-chamber doorway.

"Only a letter from Gilbert."

"And what has he to say this time? More lengthy descriptions of columns and cupolas, I suppose?"

"You may read it if you like," Abigail held it forth to show she had nothing to hide, hoping Louisa might return the favor. Not that Louisa ever exhibited any sign of being jealous of her older sister.

Louisa waved away the offer. "Maybe later."

"He asks why you have not written to him lately," Abigail said. "He's afraid he has vexed you."

Louisa lifted a delicate shrug. "Oh, nothing of that sort. I've just been so busy answering invitations and attending fittings and the like. And now that Easter is over and the season has begun . . . Well, you remember how it is. Up late every night, sleeping in every morning, and every afternoon given to calls. . . ."

Abigail had never told Louisa that she had witnessed her private tête-à-tête with Gilbert, nor asked what she had given him as a parting gift. Perhaps it was time she did.

"Louisa, I know you gave Gilbert something before he left. Is it a secret, or . . . ?"

Louisa blinked at her in surprise. "Did Gilbert tell you that, in his letter? I . . . gave him a lock of my hair. You don't mind, do you? For you've always insisted you and Gilbert were just friends."

Had she? Abigail swallowed. "Well, yes. Good friends."

Had Gilbert *asked* for a lock of Louisa's hair? Did he even now wear it in a ring? Her stomach cramped at the thought, and she couldn't bring herself to ask. She wasn't sure she wanted to know.

Instead, she made do with a sisterly "It's impolite not to answer letters promptly, Louisa. Surely you might manage a few lines at least? To assure him all is well and you are still . . . friends?"

Louisa flopped into an armchair, her usual concern for posture and poise neglected in only her sister's presence. "Oh, very well."

Then she grinned sweetly at Abigail, a teasing light in her fair eyes. "Or might you not tell him so for me when you write back? For I know your reply shall be in tomorrow's post."

Soon they began receiving offers on their house—the best price contingent on keeping the majority of furnishings in place. They were relieved to receive such a good offer, but even so, once her father finished paying off the bond, there would be little left to spend on new lodgings. Although tireless in her efforts, Abigail began to despair of ever finding a house that would suit them all.

Early in April, while Abigail met with the housekeeper about more modest menus and other economizing measures, a footman came to find her.

"Your father asks that you join him in the study, miss," he said.

"Oh? I thought he had a caller."

"Indeed he does." The servant bowed and backed away without further explanation.

Abigail thanked the housekeeper, made her way to the study, and let herself in.

Her father sat at his desk. A man in black stood to one side, framed by one of the windows.

With an uncertain glance at the man, Abigail began, "You asked for me, Father?"

"Actually, this gentleman requested you join us." Mr. Foster gestured to the visitor—a man of about sixty years, she guessed. Not tall, but a distinguished figure in his black frock coat and charcoal-grey waistcoat. His high white shirt collar framed an arresting face—deep hooded eyes under heavy arched eyebrows as black as a bat's wings. Deep grooves ran from either side of a straight nose to the corners of his mouth. He wore a small mustache and beard trimmed in the Van Dyke style—his cheeks cleanly shaven. His hair and beard were black edged with silver. But it was his eyes that drew her back. Keen and calculating. Knowing and judging.

She was quite certain she had never seen him before. She would surely have remembered him. Why then had he requested her presence?

"Have we met before, sir?" she asked.

"No, miss. I have not had that pleasure," he replied, displaying no pleasure in meeting her even now.

Her father made belated introductions. "My elder daughter, Miss Abigail Foster. Abigail, this is Mr. Arbeau. A solicitor."

Abigail's stomach tightened. Was her father in more trouble because of Uncle Vincent's failed bank? Was he there to announce they were responsible for yet more money? Abigail fisted her hand. They had lost too much already.

Mr. Arbeau cut a crisp bow, then straightened, folding his arms behind his back. He was an intimidating presence with all his dour elegance.

He looked somewhere over her father's head, then began, "Mr. Foster, I gather that you are facing a financial crisis, and the offer of a commodious abode at a low rate would not be unwelcome at this time?"

Her father's face darkened. "I do not appreciate my private affairs being bandied about by strangers, Mr. Arbeau."

"Then I advise you not read the papers, sir." The man waved a graceful hand, and Abigail noticed the gold ring on his little finger. "Yes, yes. You are a proud man, I understand. But not too proud, I hope, to at least consider the offer I am prepared to make."

Her father's eyes narrowed. "What offer? I suppose you have a *commodious abode* to let?"

"Not I, no. But a client of mine possesses an old manor house, and has instructed me to offer it to you on very easy terms."

"And who is your client?" Father asked.

The man pursed his lips. "A distant relation of yours, from a family of consequence and property in western Berkshire. That is all I am at liberty to say."

"If he is a relative, why the secrecy?"

The man held his gaze but offered no reply.

Her father looked up in thought. "I do have antecedents in Berkshire, now that I think of it. May I know the name or location of this property?"

"Pembrooke Park. Spelt with two *o*'s."

"Ah." Father's eyes lit. "My maternal grandmother was a Pembrooke."

The man continued to regard him evenly but neither confirmed nor denied the connection.

Instead Mr. Arbeau said, "Please understand that you are not *inheriting* said property, as closer heirs still live and the will is held up in probate over some question of ownership. However, the current executor of the estate lives elsewhere and wishes the property to be inhabited—and by deserving relatives if at all possible."

"I see . . ." Her father tented his fingers, and Abigail saw his mind working, considering whether to be flattered or further insulted to be considered a *deserving* relation.

Mr. Arbeau went on, "The house has two main levels and five bedchambers. As well as attic servants' quarters, and kitchens and workrooms belowstairs. Church, stables, and outbuildings. Nine acres of parkland, ponds, orchards, and gardens, though uncultivated for years."

"But an estate so large," Abigail interjected. "I am afraid it would be beyond our . . . needs."

The man withdrew a card from an inner pocket upon which was written a figure. He handed it to Mr. Foster, who in turn handed it to Abigail. Glancing at it, Abigail felt her brows rise in astonishment. Curious, she flipped it over. The other side was a simple calling card printed with only *Henri Arbeau, Solicitor*.

"That is an uncommonly reasonable and indeed generous offer," Abigail conceded. "But I'm afraid the staff and expense to manage such a place would be beyond our means."

The solicitor eyed her shrewdly and addressed his reply to her. "My client was right, I see, in wishing you present during this meeting, Miss Foster." He pulled a second slip of paper from his pocket. "I am authorized to engage and pay basic staff, though my commission does not extend to French chefs or a tribe of liveried footmen." He glanced at the list on the paper. "You are to be provided with a cook-housekeeper, kitchen maid, manservant, and two housemaids. Personal servants—valet, lady's maid, and the like—must be provided by yourselves. If that is agreeable."

Abigail opened her mouth to utter some incredulous comment, but before she could fashion one, Mr. Arbeau held up his palm.

"Now, before you credit me or my client with an overly 'generous' offer, I must ask you to moderate your expectations and your gratitude. The house has been boarded up for eighteen years."

Abigail gaped. She dragged her gaze away from the stranger to her father to gauge his reaction. Did his heart sink as hers did? Why would anyone abandon a house for nearly two decades? What condition would it be in?

Her father said, "May I ask why it has been allowed to sit empty for so long?"

"It is not my place to judge my client's past decision in this regard. Suffice it to say, neither my client nor anyone else in that family has been able or willing to live there."

"And it has not been let before?"

"No." Mr. Arbeau drew an impatient breath. "See here. My client apprehends that your family is in need of a dwelling and wishes to fill that need. Be assured that everything shall be done to render it habitable. I will escort you there myself, and you and your daughter may judge for yourselves whether Pembrooke Park might, by any alteration, be made suitable. And if you are willing to inhabit the place for at least a twelvemonth to make the investment worthwhile, my client will bear the expense of repairs, cleaning, and a staff of five to keep you reasonably comfortable."

Abigail stared blindly as her mind struggled to tally the sizeable expense his client was willing to bear, compared to the modest rent requested. She blinked at the disparity. A pinch of disquiet, of suspicion, unsettled her stomach. Had the business with Uncle Vincent not taught her that anything that sounded too good to be true usually was? But they could ill afford to pass up such an opportunity.

Her father seemed less aware of the astounding nature of the offer, or simply took it as his due. He said, "I assume the servants will prepare the place ahead of our arrival?"

"You assume wrong," Mr. Arbeau replied crisply. "My client is most insistent on that point. You and Miss Foster are to be present with me when the house is unlocked and opened for the first time since 1800."

It was her father's turn to gape. "But . . . why?"

"Because that is my client's wish and stipulation." His tone did not invite further inquiry.

Her father ducked his head to consider the matter, his furrowed brow indicating bewilderment.

The mantel clock ticked.

Mr. Arbeau consulted his list again, then refolded it. "There is an inn not terribly distant from the manor. If we discover that the house is uninhabitable as is, you are welcome to sleep at said inn for a period of up to a fortnight—as long as you return to the house each day to oversee the servants' preparations."

He returned the list to his pocket and said in a patronizing, nearly mocking, tone, "*If* that meets with your approval?"

Abigail stole a glance at her father and found his face growing florid. Fearing he might send the man away with a sharp setdown, she quickly spoke up. "Again, that is very generous, Mr. Arbeau. I can find no objection to at least visiting Pembrooke Park. Can you, Papa?"

He hesitated, taking in her pleading expression. "I suppose not."

Abigail ventured, "Is the place furnished, or would we bring our own things?" She remembered the highest offer on their own house, contingent on leaving the furnishings behind.

"Fully furnished, yes," Mr. Arbeau said. "I have never been inside, but my client assures me you will find Pembrooke Park already fitted up when you take it. Beneath the inevitable dust, that is." His eyes glittered wryly.

Might this be her chance to help improve her family's circumstances and regain her father's trust?

Abigail prayed she wasn't leading her father astray once again. She squared her shoulders and forced a smile. "Well, we are not afraid of a little dust, are we, Papa?"

When they had agreed on a date to visit Pembrooke Park, Mr. Arbeau took his leave. It was a relief when the officious man and his astounding offer departed.

Chapter 2

Abigail and her father rode with the somber solicitor in a well-sprung post chaise hired for the occasion. They traveled for most of the day, on turnpikes and through toll gates, stopping to change horses and postilion riders at regular intervals, or to take a hurried meal at a coaching inn.

Finally, they reached western Berkshire, its rolling hills and woodlands giving way to farms and chalk downs near its border with Wiltshire. They passed through the village of Caldwell, with a fine church, cloth mill, and the Black Swan, which Mr. Arbeau pointed out as the nearest inn where they might sleep until they deemed the manor house habitable. A few minutes later, they reached Easton—a small cluster of shops and thatched cottages—near Pembrooke Park.

Abigail felt her pulse quicken. *Please, God, don't let the manor be an utter ruin. . . . Not when I advised Father to come. I cannot stand to disappoint him again.*

Leaving the hamlet behind, they turned down a narrow, tree-lined lane. Bumping down the long drive, the coach came to a jarring halt.

Mr. Arbeau's black eyes flashed. "What the devil . . . ?"

Abigail lifted her chin, trying to see out the window.

The groom opened the door. "Way's blocked, sir. This is as far as we can go in this big ol' girl."

"What do you mean, the way is blocked?"

"Come and see, sir."

Taking his tall beaver hat with him, Mr. Arbeau alighted, the carriage lurching under his weight. Abigail took the groom's offered hand and stepped down as well. Her father followed.

Abigail was instantly surrounded by the lush smell of pines and rich earth. Ahead a stone bridge crossed a narrow river. But the bridge was blocked by stout barrels heaped with rocks. The barrels were placed at intervals, allowing pedestrians or single horses to pass but not carriages.

Mr. Arbeau muttered over the barricade and began discussing the situation with the groom and postilion rider. But Abigail's gaze was drawn beyond the bridge to the manor on its other side—a large house constructed of rubble stone in warm hues of buff gold and grey, with a tile roof and steeply pitched gables. It faced a central courtyard, with stables on one side and a small church on the other, the whole surrounded by a low stone wall and approached through a gate beyond the bridge.

Beside her, her father said, "That's it, ey? Pembrooke Park?"

"Yes."

She glanced at him to gauge his reaction, but it was difficult to tell what he was thinking.

Mr. Arbeau stepped nearer, addressing them both. "My client did not mention any such barricade. It must have been erected in recent years without my client's knowledge." Mr. Arbeau tugged on his cuffs. "Come. We shall walk from here."

He employed a gold-headed walking stick as he strode off. Abigail and her father exchanged uncertain looks but followed the solicitor through the barrels and across the bridge.

On the other side, they passed through the gate in the stone wall and crossed the courtyard, their shoes crunching over the pea-gravel drive, where patches of weeds had grown up here and there from disuse.

Nearer now, Abigail noticed the manor's windows were of different styles and eras. Some were arched, others square casement, and there were even two lovely projecting oriel bays. The front door was recessed under an arched porch. To Abigail it looked like a gaped mouth, and the windows above like frightened eyes. She blinked away the fanciful image.

A chain and padlock bound the double doors closed. Abigail and her father paused as Mr. Arbeau fished an old key on a black ribbon from his pocket. He lifted the padlock and inserted the key.

Suddenly a dog barked viciously and bounded across the drive toward them. Abigail stiffened and looked about for a weapon, ready to grab Mr. Arbeau's walking stick if he didn't think to use it. The muscular, square-headed mastiff lurched to a halt a few yards away, body coiled, teeth bared as its warning barks lowered to ominous growls.

Crack! A shot rang out, making Abigail jump and whirl around with a cry.

Her father stretched out an arm as though to shield her, the act touching if futile. Mr. Arbeau slowly turned in the direction of the shot.

There at the corner of the house some twenty yards away, a man held a smoking double-barrel flintlock, pointed up in the air. He was a tall, lean man of perhaps fifty years with faded red hair and trimmed beard, his legs spread in confident stance.

He lowered the gun, leveling it at them. "Next time I'll na' aim over yer heads."

Her father raised his hands.

Mr. Arbeau regarded the man, hooded eyes revealing neither fear nor noticeable surprise.

A second, younger man ran onto the scene. "Pa!" His voice rose on a warning note. "Pa, don't." The man was in his midtwenties, with red hair as well.

He flicked a glance in their direction. "Put the gun down, Pa. And call off Brutus. These good people mean no harm, I'm sure. They don't look like thieves to me."

For a moment the older man remained poised as he was, sharp eyes darting from Mr. Arbeau, to her father, and at last to her.

The younger man reached out and lowered the barrel of the gun. "There now. That's better."

The older man kept his eyes locked on them and demanded, "Who are ye, and what's yer business here?" His low voice betrayed a faint Scottish lilt. His long, thin nose and high, defined cheekbones gave him the look of an ascetic or aristocrat, though his clothes were less refined than his features.

Mr. Arbeau stepped down from the porch, reaching into his pocket as he did so.

The gun snapped up again in response.

"My card," the solicitor explained, his hands wide in supplication. "The name is Arbeau. And we have every right to be here, I assure you."

"I'll be the judge of that."

Mr. Arbeau offered his card. "I represent the executor of the estate."

Tucking the gun under his arm, the man snatched the card and glowered down at it.

Mr. Arbeau's hooded eyes roved the taller man's face with calculating interest. "You, I take it, are Mac Chapman."

The man's head snapped up, eyes flashing. "And how is it ye know my name, when I have'na laid eyes on ye in my life?"

The younger man gave them an apologetic look, an ironic smile tugging his mouth. "No doubt your reputation precedes you, Papa. Or certainly will, after this."

The humor was lost on the elder Mr. Chapman. He lifted his red-bearded chin toward Abigail and her father. "Who are these people? And why do they trespass here?"

Mr. Arbeau sent them a sidelong glance, likely considering how best to disarm the man—quite literally. "Miss Foster and her father have come all the way from London to see Pembrooke Park."

Her father stepped forward, arms still raised but flagging to waist level. "I am Charles Foster. My maternal grandmother was Mary Catharine Pembrooke, daughter of Alexander Pembrooke."

Abigail felt a flush of embarrassment on her father's behalf.

She had never heard him speak those names before. He must have been studying the family tree since the solicitor's first call. His pride in his distant relationship to an old family they barely knew left her uneasy.

Mr. Chapman seemed to consider her father's words with sincere interest, his eyes lifting to the sky as he searched his memory. "Mary Catharine Pembrooke . . ." he echoed. "Oh, aye. She would have been Robert Pembrooke's great-aunt."

"I . . ." Her father hesitated. Like her, he probably had no idea who Robert Pembrooke was.

The man continued to search his memory. "She married a Mr. Fox, I believe."

Father's head reared back in surprise. "That's right. My grand-father. But how did you know?"

The younger man clapped his father's shoulder. "My father served as Pembrooke Park's steward for many years. He took great pride in his work, and the family he represented."

"Apparently, he still does." Mr. Arbeau drew back his shoulders. "Well, if we are finished with our genealogy lesson, I think it is time we went in." He turned toward the door.

Mac Chapman stiffened and scowled. "Go in? Whatever for?"

"Why, to show Mr. and Miss Foster around the house. My client has offered to let the place to them for a twelvemonth, if it meets with their approval."

Abigail did not miss the stunned look father and son exchanged. They were certainly not happy to learn people might be moving into the abandoned house.

Mr. Arbeau returned his attention to the padlock, struggling to unlock the rusted old thing. But Mr. Chapman handed his son the gun and strode forward, pulling a tangle of keys from his coat pocket.

"Allow me," Chapman said. "That key ye have is for the door itself."

Mr. Arbeau stepped aside, offense sparking in his dark eyes. "By all means." Noticing a rusty orange-brown smear on his silky black palm, he wiped his gloved hands on a handkerchief.

Mr. Chapman employed one of his keys, and the padlock gave way. He unhooked it from the heavy chain and pulled the links from between the door handles.

The son offered, "My father has kept the roof and exterior in good repair over the years, as I believe you will see."

Mr. Arbeau surveyed man, dog, and gun. "And taken it upon himself to padlock the place and act as self-appointed guard?" he suggested, black eyebrows raised high.

"What of it?" Chapman said, setting the chain aside.

"I suppose it is you we have to thank for the barricade on the bridge?"

"There have been attempted break-ins in the past."

Her father said, "Youthful dares and vandals, I'd guess?"

"No, sir. Ye guess wrong. Treasure hunters. Thieves."

"Treasure hunters?" Abigail asked sharply.

Mac Chapman looked at her directly, and at such close range, she was struck by his intense green eyes. "Aye, miss. Brought on by old rumors of treasure hidden in the house. In a secret room." His eyes glinted. "Stuff and nonsense, of course."

"Of course," she echoed faintly. *Treasure?* Abigail wondered. *Could it be?*

He inserted a second key into the door lock. "Stuck eighteen years ago, and I doubt disuse has helped matters." He butted his shoulder against the wood while pressing the latch. The door released with a shudder, then creaked open.

"Well, Mr. Chapman," the solicitor said, "would you like to do the honors of giving us the tour?"

"It's just Mac, if ye please. And no thank ye."

His son said, "I wouldn't mind seeing it, Pa. I haven't been inside since I was a boy."

Mac gave him a pointed look. "I am sure ye have important duties to attend to."

He met his father's steely gaze. "Ah. Yes, I suppose I do."

Movement caught Abigail's eye. She looked over her shoulder and saw a young woman step through the gate, accompanied by a girl of eleven or twelve. They crossed the courtyard, then stopped in their tracks at the sight of the visitors.

Mac Chapman tensed. "Will," he said under his breath, "take Leah home, please. Kitty too."

The young man looked up sharply at something in his father's tone. "Very well." He gave a general bow in their direction, then turned and strode quickly away in a long-legged stride. He put an arm around the pretty woman and took the girl's hand.

His wife and child, perhaps? Whoever they were, the young man gently turned them, leading them past the stable and out of view.

"Are you sure you won't accompany us, Mac?" Mr. Arbeau asked again, adding dryly, "Make sure we don't steal anything?"

Mac looked through the open door and into the hall beyond with an expression riddled with . . . what? Longing? Memories? Regrets? Abigail wasn't sure.

"No. I'll wait here and lock up after ye leave."

The stale, musty odor of dampness met them inside a soaring hall. Some small creature skittered out of sight as they entered, and Abigail shivered. Cobwebs crisscrossed the balustrades of a grand staircase and draped the corners of portraits on the walls. Dust had settled into the folds of draperies covering the windows and into the seams of the faded sofa beside the door. A long-case clock stood like a silent sentry across the room.

Mr. Arbeau pulled a note from his pocket and read from it. "Here on the main floor are the hall, morning room, dining room, drawing room, salon, and library. Shall we begin?"

Their tentative steps across the hall left footprints on the dust-covered floor. They walked into the first room they came to—it appeared to be the morning room. Through it, they entered the dining room, with a long table and candle chandelier strung with crystals and cobwebs. The table held the remnants of a centerpiece—flowers and willow tails and perhaps . . . a pineapple? The arrangement had dried to a brittle brown cluster of twisted twigs and husks.

Next came the drawing room, and Abigail stared in surprise.

It appeared as though the occupants had just been called away. A tea set sat on the round table, cups encrusted with dry tea. A book lay open over the arm of the sofa. A needlework project, nearly finished, lay trapped under an overturned chair.

What had happened here? Why had the family left so abruptly, and why had the rooms been entombed for almost two decades?

Her father righted the chair. Abigail lifted the upturned needlework basket, only to discover a scattering of seedlike mouse droppings beneath. She wrinkled her nose.

Her father posed her unasked question. "Why did the former occupants leave so suddenly?"

Arms behind his back, Mr. Arbeau continued his survey of the room. "I could not say, sir."

Could not, or would not? Abigail wondered, but she kept silent.

They looked briefly in the shuttered salon and dim library, its floor-to-ceiling shelves crammed with abandoned books. Then they slowly mounted the grand stairway and rounded the gallery rail. They looked into the bedchambers, one by one. In the largest two they found carefully made beds, tied-back bed-curtains, moth-eaten clothes lying listless in wardrobes, and bonnets and hats on their pegs. In the other rooms, they found beds left unmade, bedclothes in disarray and bed-curtains hastily thrown back. In one of these rooms, a chess set waited for someone to take the next turn, as though abandoned midgame. In another room stood a dolls' house, miniature pieces neatly arranged; clearly a cherished possession. Abigail's gaze was arrested by a small blue frock hanging lifeless and limp from a peg on the wall.

Again, she shivered. Where was the girl who once wore it now, eighteen years later?

She asked, "What became of them—the family who lived here?"

"I am not at liberty to say," Mr. Arbeau replied.

She and her father exchanged a raised-brow look at that but did not press him. They made their way back downstairs to the hall.

"Well?" Mr. Arbeau asked, with an impatient look at his pocket watch.

The house, beneath its layers of cobwebs and mystery, was beautiful. Once cleaned, it would be a privilege to live in such a place. She looked at her father as he surveyed the hall once more with a pinched expression.

"It will require a great deal of work . . ." he said.

"Yes," Mr. Arbeau allowed. "But work you will not personally be required to perform. I shall ask Mac Chapman to recommend qualified staff to ready the house, if that meets with your approval?" Again that condescending glint.

But staring up at the formal portraits of his distant ancestors, her father didn't reply. In his stead, Abigail answered, "If Mac is willing, yes. I think that an excellent idea."

"So you will take the place for a twelvemonth, at least? And sign an agreement to that effect?"

Abigail looked at her father. Would he accept her advice after she had failed him before? She wasn't sure but gently urged, "I think we should, Papa. If you agree."

Charles Foster nodded as though toward a painted gentleman in Tudor attire. "I think we must."

They spoke with Mac Chapman before they left, and he assented to engage a trustworthy cook-housekeeper, manservant, kitchen maid, and two housemaids, as requested.

"Give me a few days to interview folks and investigate their characters," he said, looking uneasily at the dim, blind windows of the upper story as he said the words. "Can't hire just anyone, you know—not to work here."

Abigail and her father thanked the man and said they would see him soon.

As they took their leave of him, Mac cautioned Abigail, "Now you've taken the place, yer sure to hear gossip. Pay it no mind."

"Gossip?" she asked. "About the supposed treasure, you mean?"

"Aye." His green eyes glinted. "And other rumors far worse."

Chapter 3

They returned home, told Mamma and Louisa all about their new lodgings, and accepted the highest offer on their London house. The buyer, having recently returned from the West Indies, desired to take possession immediately, so Abigail launched herself into preparations to vacate the premises.

Some of the art was to be sold separately, and a few special pieces of china and linen taken with them, but the rest would remain with the house. Abigail oversaw the packing of trunks but left the negotiations with the art dealer to her father.

She felt nostalgic as she packed things from the bedchamber she had occupied for most of her life. How strange to leave the furniture and bedclothes for someone new to sleep in. She hoped he or she would appreciate them. She packed away her own clothes, sorting between those she would take in her valise for immediate use and those she would pack away in her trunk to be sent down later. She packed her favorite books—books of house plans, landscaping essays by Capability Brown, and a few novels.

Because the new owner was willing to retain the household staff, the Fosters decided they would take only the lady's maid, Marcel, though she would remain behind in London with Mamma and Louisa for the time being. Her father's valet refused to leave

London and requested a character reference to use in seeking another situation.

The horses were sold, as well as the town coach. They would hire a post chaise for travel.

A fortnight later, everything was settled, allowing Abigail and her father to return to Pembrooke Park. Meanwhile, Mrs. Foster and Louisa removed to Aunt Bess's home, planning to join them in Berkshire after the season.

The night before they left, Abigail finished packing her remaining personal belongings, checking to be sure she had everything she would need for a week or so in her hand luggage—nightclothes, a clean shift, toiletries, the novel she was currently reading. She went through her desk drawer, looking for a drawing pad and pencils to take along. She spied a tube of paper and unrolled it, her heart aching as she recognized the house plans she and Gilbert had drawn up long ago. After much discussion and many revisions, here was their ideal house.

Perhaps it had only been a game to him. An exercise. But for her it had been very real. She had imagined living in those rooms. Filling those bedchambers with their children. Eating their meals together in that dining room with its bow window overlooking a landscaped garden through which she and Gilbert would stroll arm in arm. . . .

She blinked away the foolish images and the tears that accompanied them. They had been adolescents. He probably didn't even remember drawing these plans with her and would likely be chagrined to know she had kept them. She was tempted to tear them up, or burn them, but in the end, she couldn't bear to do so. Although it was not very practical to go to the trouble of transporting them to their new home, she rolled the plans carefully and laid them in her trunk—keeping alive a dream probably better relinquished once and for all.

On the appointed day, Abigail and her father traveled by post chaise back to Pembrooke Park. A line of newly hired servants stood shoulder to shoulder at the entrance awaiting their arrival.

Mac Chapman was there to greet them. "Good morning, Miss Foster. Mr. Foster. May I introduce Mrs. Walsh, your new cook-housekeeper."

The thick-waisted, kind-looking woman bowed her head respectfully. "Sir. Miss."

"Her kitchen maid, Jemima."

A thin girl of no more than fifteen giggled shyly, then bobbed a curtsy.

"And these are Polly and Molly. Sisters, as you may have guessed. They will be your housemaids."

The two dipped curtsies and smiled warmly. The pair of pretty girls were perhaps eighteen and nineteen, one with dark blond hair and the other a light brown.

Abigail smiled in return.

Mac turned to the lone male among the new hires. "And this is Duncan. He's to be your manservant, odd job man, haul and carry—whatever you need."

The man with sandy brown hair was in his late twenties with broad shoulders and brawny arms. He certainly looked as if he could haul and carry.

He bowed perfunctorily but offered no smile as the others had done.

Her father said to the former steward, "Thank you, Mr. Chap—"

"Mac," he reminded them.

"Mac. Well . . . Welcome, everyone."

Abigail added, "We are glad you are here. Shall we get started?"

After consulting with Mac and Mrs. Walsh, they decided they would begin with the kitchen, scullery, servants' hall, and sleeping quarters—so the staff could eat and sleep in the manor—and then move on to preparing bedchambers for the Fosters. Mrs. Walsh would occupy the housekeeper's parlor and Duncan the former butler's room belowstairs, while the young maids would sleep in bedchambers in the attic.

For several days, while her father primarily remained at the Black

Swan, Abigail oversaw the servants' work each day, returning to the inn at night. She answered the servants' questions as they cleaned and aired the house room by room.

Abigail's father insisted she pick whichever bedchamber she wanted for herself—her small reward for coming early and preparing the house. It was kind of him, the first kind words he'd spoken to her since the disastrous bank failure, and she treasured them—though her practical, skeptical mind told her he'd only said it to assuage his guilt for leaving her to oversee the work alone.

Whatever his reasons, Abigail did not choose either of the largest rooms—the master's and mistress's bedchambers in the past, she guessed. Nor did she pick the newest—the one in the later addition over the drawing room with its big sunny windows and lofty half tester bed.

Instead, she picked the modest-sized room with the dolls' house. She was drawn to the little window seat overlooking a walled garden and pond with the river beyond. She was drawn to the cherished dolls' house and the small blue frock hanging on its peg. She was drawn to the secrets she sensed in this room and wanted them for herself.

She personally helped clean the chamber, assisting the maids in taking down the draperies and bed-curtains to wash, and removing the carpets for cleaning. Polly scrubbed down the walls, mopped the floors, and washed the windows. But Abigail herself dusted the books and toys and every tiny piece of furniture in the dolls' house, returning each precisely where she'd found it. She didn't know why, exactly. It would be far more practical to box up all the playthings, far easier to clean without them than around them. Mr. Arbeau had asked them not to dispose of anything, but she could have asked Duncan to haul it up to the attic storeroom. She did not.

The dolls' house—or "baby house," as she'd sometimes heard them called—was impressive indeed. The structure stood atop a cabinet to raise it from the floor. The exterior of the house had been built as a scale model of Pembrooke Park itself, with paned-glass windows and tiny shingles. The three-story interior, with a central staircase hall complete with oak rails and balustrades, had been somewhat simplified, she realized, so that all of the major rooms were accessible from its open back.

The rooms themselves were fashioned with intricate details, like moulded cornices, paneled doors, and real wallpaper. Bedchambers were furnished with mantelpieces, four-poster beds, and washstands with basins and pitchers no bigger than thimbles. In the dining room, a crystal chandelier hung over a table set with farthing-size porcelain plates and tiny glass goblets. The drawing room held small woven baskets, a silver tea set, and miniature books with real pages. The kitchen—shown on the same level as the dining room, though in reality belowstairs—contained a miniature meat jack, a hearth with spit, tiny copper kettles, and jelly moulds.

To buy all these miniatures or have them created by craftsmen would have made for an extremely expensive hobby. Abigail guessed this dolls' house had at first been some wealthy woman's pastime, before it had become a child's plaything.

Abigail pulled out the drawer of the cabinet and found a family of dolls with porcelain faces and soft bodies dressed in costumes of decades past: mother, father, and two sons. At least she assumed they were boys from their attire, though one body was missing its head. She wondered where the daughters were.

While dusting the small dining room, she admired the miniature silver serving platter on the table, complete with a domed lid. Curious, she reached in and lifted the lid. There on the platter was the severed head of the second boy doll, with dark embroidery-floss hair and stuffing stringing out from its neck.

Abigail shivered. The work of some nasty little boy, she told herself. How he must have vexed his sister, whoever she was, with his destructive mischief. Abigail put the head in the drawer with its body, determined to repair it someday when she had time. But at the moment, it was time to get back to work.

Chapter 4

O n her third day working in the manor, Abigail helped herself
to a cup of tea and stepped out onto the small front porch
for a respite. It was a fine spring morning, and she drew
in a deep breath of fresh air. She looked forward to exploring the
gardens and grounds soon, but the house came first. The work
was going well, she judged. Mrs. Walsh was an even-tempered, no-
nonsense leader who ruled with a gentle hand and an encouraging
reprimand. *"Now, girls, I know ya can do better than that. . . ."*

She cheerfully met with Abigail regularly in her parlor to discuss progress, plans, and purchases. She had made it clear early
on, however, that the kitchen was her domain and she would not
appreciate the lady of the house interrupting her work there. So
Abigail did not often see the kitchen maid, Jemima.

She saw a great deal, however, of Polly and Molly. Especially
Polly, the elder sister, who had volunteered to serve as Abigail's
personal maid—helping her dress and so on—along with her
other duties as upper housemaid. Both were pleasant, hardworking girls, daughters of a local farmer, who found even heavy
housework far lighter than the chores they were accustomed to
on their father's farm.

Duncan worked hard those first few days as well, even offering to help the maids carry cans of water and other heavy loads. Now and again Abigail saw him glance at Polly to see if she noticed his efforts. Abigail hoped she would not have a staff romance on her hands—though Polly, nearly ten years younger than Duncan, did not exhibit anything but friendly politeness in return, so perhaps all would be well.

Abigail had quickly discovered, despite the friendliness of the staff, that all were tight-lipped about the past and the former residents. When she'd asked Mrs. Walsh about the Pembrookes, the woman shook her head, eyes wary. "No, miss. We're not to talk about that."

"Why not?"

"No good can come of it, Mac says. It's too dangerous."

"Dangerous? How?"

But she only shook her head once more, lips cinched as tight as a drawstring reticule.

When Abigail asked Polly what she knew about the former residents, the young woman had shrugged. "Not a thing, miss. I was only a babe when they left, wasn't I?"

"But surely you've heard rumors."

"Aye, miss. But rumors is all it is. I don't want to lose my place for gossipin', do I?"

Clearly Mac had laid down the law when he'd hired the servants.

So Abigail set aside her questions for the time being and lost herself in sorting, cleaning, and organizing, as well as writing up lists of needed repairs and orders for the larder and supply cupboards.

Standing there now on the front stoop, sipping her tea, Abigail found her gaze drawn across the courtyard to the church within the estate's walled grounds.

Mac passed by in a long Carrick coat, leather breeches, and knee-high boots, his dog at his heels. He wore a greenish-brown Harris-tweed cap in honor, she'd heard, of his Scottish mother. The strap of a game bag crossed his chest, and he carried a veterinary case in one hand and a fowling piece in the other.

She had learned Mac Chapman was not only the former steward and protector of Pembrooke Park. He also served as land agent for Hunts Hall, an estate owned by a family of gentry on the other side of Easton.

Seeing her standing in the doorway, he tipped his hat to her. "Miss."

"Good morning, Mac. What are you about today?"

"Oh, off to try a new remedy on an ailing cow, and to check a new drainage ditch while I'm out there."

"And the gun?"

"In case my doctorin' fails."

She looked up in alarm.

"Only teasing you, lass," he said. "Often carry a gun when I walk about on my duties. Never know when a wild dog or mangy badger might decide to harass me or the livestock."

"Or a trespasser?" she suggested wryly.

He frowned. "That's no joking matter, lass. As you may discover for yourself."

She changed the subject. "May I ask about the church, Mac? Has it been locked up like the house?"

He paused to follow the direction of her gaze. "Not at all. It's the parish church, along with the church in Caldwell, and the chapel of ease in Ham Green. Services every Sunday and on feast days."

"May I peek inside?"

"Aye. It's always open. The parson's a good man, if I do say so myself." His mouth quirked in a grin. How different he appeared now compared to the fierce stranger who'd given them such an inhospitable welcome not long ago.

Later, while the servants ate a light midday meal, Abigail walked across the gravel drive toward the churchyard. Stepping onto the spongy grass verge, she passed through the opening in the low wall. She glanced around the well-kept graveyard and then looked up at the narrow church itself. The front door was sheltered by a hooded porch—a later addition to the original building, she guessed. Above was an arched window, and a square bell cote topped by a crocketed spire. She stepped into the porch, pushed open the old wooden door, and entered the cool interior.

It took a moment for her eyes to adjust to the light—dim compared to the sunny day, yet surprisingly well lit from a large window on either end. Her mind quickly identified a fifteenth-century stone screen dividing chapel and long narrow nave. Paneled walls and wagon roof. Box pews, communion rail, and canopied pulpit—all of oak. Even Gilbert would have approved.

In the central aisle, a ladder stood empty beneath a high brass chandelier. She wondered where the workman was.

She stepped nearer the back wall to study a series of old paintings.

As she stood there in the shadows, a man entered from the vestry in plain waistcoat and rolled up shirtsleeves, a box under his arm. He climbed the ladder and began removing the spent tapers. Humming to himself while he worked, he'd obviously not noticed her there.

Not wishing to startle him, she cleared her throat and softly greeted, "Good afternoon."

He looked in her direction. "Oh! Sorry. Didn't see you there."

It was the younger man she'd seen with Mac—his grown son, she assumed, though they'd not been introduced.

She walked slowly up the aisle. "If you are ever looking for more work," she said, "we've no end of it at Pembrooke Park."

He chuckled and readjusted the box under his arm. "I imagine so, but as you can see, I have my hands full here."

She nodded. "Keeping the church in good repair the way your father does the house?"

"In a matter of speaking."

"I am surprised your father did not hire you officially."

He grinned and said fondly, "He is accustomed to assigning me chores without having to pay me. Family privilege and all that." He pulled out another stub and tossed it in the box.

Watching him struggle to balance ladder, box, and tapers, she said, "That high chandelier doesn't strike me as terribly practical."

He glanced down at her, then returned his focus to his task. "I suppose it isn't. Wall sconces would be easier to refill and maintain. But I like this impractical thing. I think it's beautiful. An endowment from the lady of the manor long ago."

He descended the ladder and nodded toward the paintings she'd been studying. "That's Catherine of Alexandria, the Martyr. Many paintings of saints were destroyed after the Reformation. But the artwork in our little church here was spared."

He set down the box and wiped his hands on a handkerchief. "We haven't been formally introduced. If you will allow the liberty, I shall introduce myself." He tucked away the cloth and bowed before her. "William Chapman. And you, I believe, are Miss Foster."

"Yes. How do you do," she said, and dipped the barest curtsy, not sure whether a land agent's son would expect such a courtesy or think it out of place.

At the sound of footsteps, Abigail turned. A woman entered the church behind them, head bowed over a box in her arms. "I've found more tapers," she called, glancing up. She drew up short at the sight of Abigail.

It was the woman Abigail had seen with the young girl the day she and her father first arrived. Seeing her more closely now, Abigail guessed the woman was in her mid to late twenties. Her pretty brown eyes and golden-brown hair well compensated for her plain day dress and unadorned bonnet. Was this the man's wife?

"It's all right, Leah," William Chapman said. "This is our new neighbor. She and her family come from London. Distant relations to the Pembrooke family. Very distant."

"Yes, Papa told me. Miss Foster, I believe?"

"Forgive me," Mr. Chapman said, turning to her. "Miss Foster, may I present Miss Leah Chapman, my sister."

Sister . . . She would not have guessed. "How do you do."

Mr. Chapman added, "My sister is a great help to me."

"In your . . . work, do you mean?" Abigail asked.

"Yes."

"Your father mentioned the parson is a good man."

"Did he?"

Leah smiled. "Father is biased. But in this instance, he is perfectly right."

William grinned at his sister. "Not that you're an impartial judge or anything."

Abigail felt left out of a private joke but said, "Then I shall look forward to meeting him."

They both turned to stare at her.

"But . . . you already have," Miss Chapman said, a little wrinkle between her brows. "My brother here is our curate. Recently ordained and our parson for all intents and purposes."

"Oh . . ." Abigail breathed, taken aback. She knew that curates occupied the lowest rung of the church hierarchy—assistant clergymen without a living of their own.

"Perhaps you refer to Mr. Morris, our rector," William added kindly. "He does visit from time to time."

"Not often enough," Leah said with a sniff. "He leaves far too much on your shoulders, William. And pays you far too little."

Abigail felt her cheeks heat. "I am sorry. I didn't realize. I mistook you for a . . ."

His eyes twinkled. "A manservant? Groundskeeper? Churchwarden? Yes, I answer to all of the above. No offense taken, Miss Foster. We are a small parish. I do whatever needs doing."

Leah said, "You do too much, if you ask me."

"Well, thankfully, I have you to help me. I dread the day you up and marry and leave me to my own devices."

Leah's eyes dulled, and she darted a glance at Abigail. "Small chance of that, you know."

"I know no such thing."

Uncomfortable, Abigail said, "I was rather surprised to find the church in use and left unlocked, when . . ."

"When we guard the manor so closely?" Mr. Chapman gamely supplied. "Papa is only adamant about keeping people out of the house. The house of God is open to one and all. I hope you will join us on Sunday?"

Abigail smiled but said noncommittally, "Perhaps."

The next night, Abigail left the inn and slept for the first time at Pembrooke Park. Her room was cleaned and ready, as were the kitchen and servants' bedchambers. Her father's room had been aired and was to be cleaned next—though there was little hurry, since he had been summoned back to Town to review some final details for the sale of the house and sign over the deed. He said he was comfortable leaving her, now that she had a maid and the other servants to attend her. Abigail had swallowed her disappointment, telling herself she should be proud her father had regained some of his confidence in her.

Polly came up to help her undress. Afterward, she thanked the young woman and bid her good-night. Abigail certainly hoped it would be good. She always had difficulty sleeping in a strange place. After she blew out her bedside candle, she lay awake for what seemed like hours, hearing every groan of wind through the windows, and every creak the old house made. Even after she fell asleep, she awoke often, not sure what had disturbed her and forgetting where she was. She reminded herself she was not alone in the house. There was no need to be frightened—the servants were there.

Why did that thought bring little comfort?

She was about to drift off again when she heard something. A whirring rise and fall, like a warbling brook or garbled, distant voices. Mrs. Walsh and Duncan had rooms belowstairs. Their voices wouldn't carry all the way from there. Though voices might carry from the attic above. Perhaps her room was under the sisters' room and she was hearing their conversation. Abigail could not identify any particular voice, or even its gender. In fact she wasn't certain it was a voice at all. It could be a trick of the wind, winnowing through the chimneys.

As Abigail listened, she suddenly heard a ghostly moan, "All alone. All alonnnnne . . ."

She gasped and lay still, listening hard. But all she heard was the wind. Surely she had imagined the voice. Yes, of course, she told herself, long into the night. It had only been the wind.

In the morning, Abigail stayed in bed later than usual, having slept poorly. It was Sunday, but Abigail decided against attending church. She wasn't ready to meet all those strangers, to feel their stares as she, the newcomer, entered. And what if they did things differently in the country? She would feel uncomfortable and uncertain what to do. Her family had attended divine services only sporadically in London, when they had not been out too late the night before, or when her mother decided they ought to show up for appearances' sake, especially if a prospective suitor was known to be devout. Besides, Abigail had several letters to write, and she would finally have the time to do so.

Polly brought up a breakfast tray and helped her dress before leaving to attend church herself. Mac had strongly suggested the servants be given a day of rest on the Sabbath, so they might attend church and visit their families. Abigail had agreed, wishing her own family were there so she would not be alone.

After breakfast, Abigail reread a letter she had received at the inn the day before from Gilbert's sister. Susan expressed regret that Abigail had left Town and concern over her family's new situation. She had also added a postscript:

You described Pembrooke Park as being a remote place near the tiny hamlet of Easton and the village of Caldwell. Interestingly enough, Edward and I have heard of Caldwell. One of the magazine's regular contributors lives there. What a small world it is!

Abigail idly wondered who it was. She dipped a quill in ink and began her reply, trying to sound optimistic about the change in their circumstances, to ward off her friend's pity or worry. She was fine. They were fine. She asked the name of the local writer, in case she encountered this person.

But she soon found herself distracted and rose and crossed the hall to her father's room. From his window, she saw a few wagons and gigs stopping on the other side of the bridge. The habit of leaving horses and vehicles was well ingrained, she saw, though Mac had finally agreed to removal of the barricade. Duncan had not enjoyed the task, she knew.

Other families came on foot from nearby Easton, greeting one another as they passed through the gate. The church bell rang, startling Abigail after the silence of the empty house. The last of the parishioners disappeared inside, and with a sigh Abigail returned to her letter.

Later, when the service ended, Abigail again rose to watch the congregation depart. As the small crowd diminished and trickled away over the bridge, she finally saw the Chapmans emerge—Mac, a middle-aged woman who must be his wife, William, Leah, the younger girl, and a red-haired boy as well. They talked and laughed as they walked across the courtyard on their way home. Mac's cottage was somewhere just beyond the estate grounds. William, she'd gathered, had recently moved into the small parsonage behind the church, though clearly he still spent time with his family.

The dog, so fierce when she'd first seen him, bounded over and joined the family with a lolling tongue and wagging tail. The tall red-haired boy of perhaps fifteen tossed a stick to him and then went chasing after the dog. His younger sister followed suit. Mac called some ireless admonishment after them, while his wife laughed and took his arm. Behind their parents, Leah took William's arm as well. The sweet picture of familiar affection caused a little ache in Abigail's heart. Her own family was not terribly affectionate. But she'd always secretly hoped that she and Gilbert would make up for it with their own children someday. Tears bit her eyes, and she blinked the painful thought away.

As though sensing he was being watched, William Chapman

glanced back, looking up at the house. Although she doubted he could see inside the dim room on the sunny day, she stepped away from his view.

Later that afternoon, Abigail buttoned a spencer over her day dress—preparing to go out for a walk—when someone knocked on the front door. Since the servants had not yet returned from their day off, Abigail jogged lightly down the stairs and answered it herself, hat and gloves in hand. She felt a momentary hesitation about opening the door to a stranger—or possible treasure hunter—while she was alone in the house, so she was relieved to recognize the caller as William Chapman, basket in arms. Nothing about his fashionable green coat, patterned waistcoat, or simple cravat marked him as a clergyman.

"Good afternoon," she said.

He glanced behind her toward the empty hall. "Servants abandon you already?" A wry glint shone in his boyish blue eyes.

"No," she assured him. "Not at all. They are enjoying a day of rest."

"That was generous of you."

"Your father's idea."

"Ah. Yes, he isn't shy about offering his ideas on how I ought to conduct things on Sundays either."

"Oh?"

"He is the parish clerk, after all. So . . ." He shrugged helplessly.

"You poor man," she teased. William Chapman was handsome, she decided. His hair was darker than his father's, more auburn than red. And he was nearly as tall. His features were pleasing—straight nose, broad mouth, and fair skin.

He held up his hand. "Don't get me wrong, I have the utmost respect for my father. But he can be a bit . . . overbearing at times. I wouldn't want you to think you were the only one on the receiving end of his . . . suggestions."

He smiled, causing vertical grooves to frame his mouth and his large eyes to crinkle at the corners. Abigail felt a flutter of attraction.

"Here, this is for you. A welcome basket from my sister." He held forth the basket, bulging with gifts: embroidered hand towels, homemade soap, tins of tea and jam, a loaf of bread, and a mound of muffins.

"My goodness. Did she make all this herself?"

"Most of it, yes—even the basket—though Kitty helps with the soap, Mamma is the baker, and my father is famous round the parish for his jams."

"No . . ."

"Oh yes. Walking about as land agent, he's discovered all the best patches of wild strawberries, gooseberries, and blackberries. Plus, he's long had the run of the Pembrooke orchards. I hope you shan't tell the new tenant. . . ." He winked.

"His secret is quite safe with me. Especially since he shared his jam. But . . . why didn't your sister come herself? I would have liked to thank her in person."

He grimaced as he considered his reply. "Leah is a bit . . . not shy exactly, but cautious around strangers."

"Oh. I see. I did wonder, when I saw you escorting her away the day we arrived. Actually, when I saw you with her and a younger girl too, I thought they were your wife and daughter. . . ."

"Ah." He crossed his arms behind his back and rocked on his heels. "No, I am not married. I have not had that privilege. Though I was—" He broke off, and she thought she saw pain flash across his eyes before he blinked it away. "You saw my two sisters, and I have a brother as well. Kitty looks young for her age, but she is twelve."

"I see." Abigail stood there awkwardly for a moment, unsure whether she ought to ask him in. "I would invite you in to share this with me, but as I am alone in the house, I . . ."

He waved away the offer. "No, no. I have no intention of begging an invitation and wouldn't dream of depriving you of a single bite. Though if you share the jam with Mrs. Walsh, you shall have a friend for life."

She smiled up at him. "Then I shall indeed."

Duty discharged, William Chapman knew he should excuse himself, but felt oddly reluctant to part ways with the lovely newcomer. He forced himself to say, "Well, I can see you are dressed to go out, so I shan't keep you."

"I was only going for a walk," Miss Foster said. "I have been indoors all day and haven't had a chance to explore the grounds yet, so . . ." Her words trailed away.

Was she hoping he would join her? Unlikely, yet there was only one way to find out.

"A beautiful day for it," William agreed. "Would you mind some company?"

"Not at all."

He smiled. "A walk is exactly what I need after Mamma's roast dinner."

She returned his smile with apparent relief. "Just let me set this inside and put on my things."

A few moments later, she joined him in the courtyard wearing gloves and a straw hat.

"After you." He gestured her toward the side of the house, and they walked around it. "Other than the church, everything I love is back here."

Behind the house, lush green vines with white flowers climbed the manor walls. In the rear courtyard, a terrace overlooked a neglected rose garden, overgrown topiaries, and a lily pond.

He said, "It isn't as beautiful as it once was, of course."

"Perhaps when the house is ready, I might give the gardens some attention."

"Mamma would be happy to help. She loves a garden. And Papa would be eager to offer you many suggestions of how to go about it."

The two shared another grin.

They passed a walled garden, potting shed, and orchard. William pointed toward a large pond beyond. "That's the fishpond. Robert Pembrooke left Papa the use of it, along with ownership of our cottage, in his will."

"Robert Pembrooke . . ." Miss Foster echoed. "Is that who lived here before us?"

"Not immediately before. He died twenty years ago."

William did not expand on his reply. His father didn't want him inviting questions about the manor's former occupants.

As if sensing his reserve, she asked instead, "Where is your family's cottage?"

"Come. I'll show you."

"I don't want to intrude."

"Then I'll just point it out to you. You should know where it is, in case you ever need anything, or if there is ever any . . . trouble." Lord willing, there would not be, William thought, though his father was full of dire predictions and warnings.

He led her past the former gamekeeper's lodge, then along a well-worn path through a grove of trees, carpeted with green-and-white wood anemones. Nestled in a clearing sat his family's white cottage with a thatched roof.

She paused to look at it from a polite distance. "How charming," she murmured.

He regarded the place fondly. "Yes, I suppose it is."

After a moment, she asked abruptly, "Is your family as happy as they seem?"

He considered her unexpected question, pursing his lips in thought. "Yes, for the most part we are a happy lot. Or perhaps *content* is the better word. We have our squabbles like any family, but woe to anyone who tries to harm a Chapman." He tried to smile but felt it falter. "If only Leah . . ."

She regarded him in concern. "If only Leah, what?"

Why had he said anything? "I am not criticizing," he hurried to assure her. "But Leah has struggled with anxiety for as long as I can remember. I wish I could help her. Scripture says fear not.

And perfect love casts out fear, but nothing I say—or pray—seems to make any difference."

"Love without fear . . ." Miss Foster murmured, considering the notion. "It doesn't sound very practical, I'm afraid. For the more one loves, the more one has to fear losing."

He looked at her, a grin tugging his mouth. "Impractical, maybe. Difficult, yes. But what a beautiful way to live."

He cocked his head to one side, allowing his gaze to roam her lovely face. "You value practicality, I take it, Miss Foster?"

"Yes, I do." She drew herself up. "Speaking of which, perhaps I ought to get back to the house and let you return to yours. I am certain you must be tired after services."

"A little weary, yes. But nothing a quick nap can't fix." He turned and gestured for her to lead the way back.

As they walked, she said tentatively, "Thank you for not pressing me about attending church."

"Wouldn't dream of it." He *had* been a bit disappointed when she hadn't come but had no intention of pressuring her. Instead, he sent her a sidelong glance and said wryly, "You'll come when you're ready. I hear the sermons are quite . . . interesting."

She shot him a puzzled look. Had he piqued her interest? He certainly hoped so.

Chapter 5

*T*hat night, Abigail went up to bed early, weary from sleeping so poorly the night before and hoping she would sleep better her second night at Pembrooke Park.

Polly helped her undress, cheerfully chatting about church—"Mr. Chapman preaches the shortest sermons. Witty too. Some folks don't appreciate it, but I do . . ."—and about the afternoon she and Molly had spent with her parents and brothers out on their family farm. She also mentioned Duncan had just returned from visiting his mother in Ham Green, several miles away. As Abigail listened to the girl's happy account, she was glad she had heeded Mac's advice and given the servants the day off.

After Polly left, Abigail crawled into bed with a book she'd found in the library—a history of the Pembrooke family and manor. But she'd read only a few pages before her eyelids began drooping. She set aside the book and blew out her bedside candle. Lying there, Abigail thought back on the day's conversation with Mr. Chapman. They had touched on so many topics—family and fear and church . . .

Engulfed in darkness, her ears focused sharply, trying to catalogue every sound. For once identified, she would no longer need to fret about it. That howl? The wind through the fireplace flue.

That rattle? A window shaken by the wind. Telling herself she would grow used to the sounds in time, she determinedly pulled the bedclothes to her chin, pressed her eyes closed, and willed sleep to come.

Then she heard something new. A creak, like a door opening nearby. Probably only Polly, she thought, checking to see if the windows in the master bedchamber had been shut after yesterday's airing.

Faint footsteps reached her ears. In the corridor outside her room? No—it sounded more muffled, like footsteps on carpet and not wood. Was it coming from the next room? The room on that side of the wall was to be Louisa's. Why would anyone be in there, when they hadn't even started cleaning it yet?

A scrape—like a chair leg across wood? She was probably imagining things. It was likely only a simple creak of the house, of damp, warped walls and floorboards. After all, it was well past working hours and a Sunday yet.

Sleep, she told herself, closing her eyes again. *Fear not.*

In the morning, Abigail was still sound asleep when Polly came in with hot water and a breakfast tray.

"Oh. Sorry, Polly. I intended to be up before you came." Abigail pushed back the bedclothes and hurried to the washstand. "I didn't sleep well last night. The house makes so many odd noises. Have you noticed?"

"What sort of noises?" Polly asked.

"Oh, you know. Creaks and groans. Though last night I heard footsteps, long after you had gone to bed."

"You likely imagined it." The girl's eyes twinkled. "Or perhaps the place is haunted, like the village children say it is."

"Haunted?" Abigail echoed, drying her face. "By whom? I suppose my father and I have angered some ghost of Pembrooke past by moving in here?"

"Well, someone did die here twenty years ago. Was killed some say. Probably his ghost what does the haunting."

"Who died here?" Abigail asked. "One of the Pembrooke family?" She recalled Mr. Chapman saying a Robert Pembrooke died twenty years ago.

Polly's mouth slackened, face growing pale. "No, miss. I never said a word about the Pembrookes, did I? Please don't tell anyone otherwise. I don't know anything about the family. How could I? I was talkin' about a servant—that's all."

Abigail regarded the young woman, surprised by her panic. Hoping to lighten the moment, she teased, "Which servant? A cheeky housemaid?"

But the girl did not smile. "No, miss. Robert Pembrooke's valet. Walter something, I heard his name was, but that's the last word I'll say on the subject. I've said too much already."

Abigail blinked. "Very well, Polly."

The housemaid stepped to the closet. "My mouth will be the death of me yet, and you don't want *me* hauntin' the place, flapping my ghostly lips all night. Now, let's get you dressed. . . ."

When Abigail left her bedchamber a short while later, she paused at the door of the room that would be Louisa's. The door was closed, as it had been the day before. She opened the latch and inched it open, the mounting creak familiar. Is that what she'd heard last night?

At first glance the room seemed undisturbed. But then, in the morning light slanting through the unshuttered windows, she saw something. She frowned and bent to look closer. Yes, unmistakable. Footprints in the dust, all the way to the wardrobe. She had not even bothered to look inside yet, but someone had. The footprints appeared notably larger than her small shoes. So probably not one of the housemaids checking the windows.

Might it have been their manservant, Duncan? She didn't like the idea of a man roaming about a lady's bedchamber at night. Though she supposed he might have checked the windows as a favor to Polly, whom he seemed eager to help. But what business had he opening a wardrobe in an unoccupied room at night?

Later that day, Polly surprised her by handing her a letter—the first to be delivered directly to the house. The letter was addressed to her, in care of Pembrooke Park. Abigail did not recognize the handwriting, nor the crest pressed into its wax seal. It bore a Bristol postmark, but she could not think of any acquaintance who lived there. She peeled away the seal and unfolded the outer page, revealing a second page within. Costly indeed.

The outer page bore only a single line: *I think you are the very person to read this. . . .*

The page within was of a smaller size. One edge was ragged, as though torn from a notebook.

When first I arrived at Pembrooke Park, I was chilled by the tomblike silence of the place, the unnatural stillness. I shall never forget the tea service, spread atop the cloth-covered table, as though the occupants had merely risen to look out the window at the arrival of an unexpected carriage but had been yanked from the house then and there, never to return. The tea was now a filmy residue at the bottom of bone china. The scones hard and dry. The milk soured. The kettle and cups abandoned in haste, like the house itself.

I asked the housekeeper why she had not cleaned the place, and she said she'd been told to leave everything as it was. I wondered if she meant, so the constable could search the house for evidence. After all, someone died there only a fortnight before—an accident, I'd been told. But it was clear she didn't believe that for a minute.

Abigail sucked in a breath—stunned by the words, the similarities to her own experience upon entering Pembrooke Park for the first time. No one had died there recently, as far as she knew. Though Polly had said a valet died there twenty years ago. She read it again. The timing seemed different—the writer describing entering the house abandoned for weeks, not years—yet eerily similar all the same.

Was it a page of an old journal, torn out and mailed to her? Or a recent work of fiction? Who had written it, and why?

The next day, Abigail saw Leah Chapman walking across the bridge and hurried to catch up with her.

"May I walk with you, Miss Chapman?"

The woman stiffened, then recovered, saying politely, "If you like."

"Where are you off to?"

"Taking a basket to Mrs. DeWitt, who is ailing again."

"Thank you for the basket you sent over for me," Abigail said. "I wish you had delivered it yourself. I would have asked you in for tea and shared those delicious muffins with you."

"My mother makes them. They are very good, yes," Miss Chapman replied, ignoring the implied invitation.

Abigail added, "I'm sure Mrs. DeWitt will enjoy them as well."

"Oh, for her there is broth and syllabub. Poor dear hasn't many teeth."

"I see. How thoughtful."

Leah shrugged. "It isn't much. William is the thoughtful one. He visits her every week."

"Has he lived in the parsonage long?"

She shook her head. "Only since he was ordained. Our rector, Mr. Morris has the living. But he resides in a much larger and newer house in Newbury."

"So far?"

She nodded. "One of the reasons he doesn't come here very often. William conducts most of the services, calls on the sick. When he returned after his ordination, Mr. Morris offered him the use of the parsonage. Likely eases the man's conscience for paying him so poorly. And he knows William will keep the place in better repair than if it remained empty."

"Yes. I can well imagine."

Leah slanted her an empathetic look. "Is the manor in very bad condition?"

"Come and see for yourself."

"No, thank you."

"I don't blame you."

"Oh?" The woman's caramel-colored eyes widened. "Why would you say that?"

"I've heard the rumors."

Leah stopped and looked at her askance. "What rumors?"

"Take your pick: that someone was killed there, that the house is haunted—not to mention the threat of treasure hunters and thieves . . ."

"Ah, those rumors." Leah nodded and walked on. "And do you believe them?"

"Not all of them. But the house does make strange sounds at night. Probably round the clock, but I only hear them at night." Abigail forced a little chuckle. "I don't suppose you would come and spend the nights with me until my father returns?"

"I'm afraid that would be quite impossible," Leah said, lips tight.

"I was only joking," Abigail defended. "Or mostly joking." Again she forced a little chuckle, taken aback by the woman's adamant refusal. It was on the tip of Abigail's tongue to tell Miss Chapman about the letter she'd received, apparently confirming at least one of the rumors—about someone dying there—but seeing the woman's wary expression, Abigail decided to keep it to herself.

Abigail bid Miss Chapman farewell at the door of Mrs. DeWitt's cottage, and returned to Pembrooke Park alone. As she approached, she was surprised to see a man disappear around the side of the house. Her heart gave a little lurch. Torn between locking herself inside the manor and seeing who it was, she crept to the corner of the house and peered around it. There, where a chimney stack jutted from the wall, a man stood, staring up at the windows, hands behind his back. Was this one of the treasure hunters?

She swallowed and cleared her throat. "May I help you?"

The man turned, and she was both relieved and disappointed to recognize William Chapman.

He glanced over at her sheepishly. "Ah . . . Miss Foster. Good day."

Was he embarrassed to have been caught snooping, or guilty of worse? Surely he was not one of the treasure hunters, looking for a way to sneak inside without being seen?

"Are you looking for something?" She glanced up in the direction he'd been staring.

He shrugged. "Just wondering which room they'd put you in."

She looked at him askance. "And why should you want to know that?"

Had he been hoping for a glimpse of her through her bedchamber window—and him a clergyman . . . ?

"Only curious."

She said, "Father insisted I choose whichever room I liked for myself."

"And which did you choose?"

"I hardly think it would mean anything to you even if I told you. Unless . . . are you more familiar with the house than you let on?"

"I haven't been inside since I was a boy."

She decided to come right out with her suspicion. "Coming upon you just now, I confess I thought you might be one of the treasure hunters your father warned me about, looking for a way to break in."

He looked at her in astonishment. "Are you serious?" He gave a little bark of laughter. "I assure you, Miss Foster. Had I wanted to get inside Pembrooke Park, I could have done so at any time."

"Because your father has the key, do you mean?"

"No, that is not what I mean."

She waited for him to explain, but instead he ran a hand over his jaw and said, "I promise you, Miss Foster, I shall not *break in* to Pembrooke Park. But . . . if you are willing to give me a tour sometime, I would like to see the old place again. See what all the fuss is about."

"Would your father approve?"

"Not likely. But I can't see any harm in it."

She hesitated. "Very well."

"Thank you. I can't now," he said. "I'm off to read the newspaper to Mr. Sinclair. But perhaps tomorrow?"

"If you like," Abigail agreed, wondering if she ought to have put him off until her father returned. And propriety was *not* what most worried her.

Chapter 6

*T*he next afternoon, Duncan found Abigail in the library and announced that she had callers. "Will Chapman and his sister," he said, a slight curl to his lip.

She rose. "Oh yes, he mentioned wanting to see the house. Though I am surprised Miss Chapman came along."

"It's not Miss Leah. It's the younger girl."

"I see." She supposed Mr. Chapman brought his sister along as a chaperone of sorts and wondered if he was concerned about propriety more for her sake or his. "Will you let them know I shall be there in just a few minutes? I need to get this letter in today's post."

He stiffened, then said, "Very well, miss."

"Where have you put them?" Abigail asked, dipping her quill.

"I left them in the hall. Only a curate, isn't he? Not so high and mighty, whatever he or his father might think."

Abigail was taken aback by the servant's bitter words, but he had already turned on his heel and left the room before she could fashion a suitable reply. She quickly finished her letter, put it with the rest of the day's outgoing post, and hurried into the hall.

Mr. Chapman and Duncan stood talking in terse tones, while Kitty sat on the sofa beside the door several feet away, idly flipping through a magazine. As Abigail neared, Duncan turned and stalked toward the back stairs, avoiding her gaze as he passed.

She looked at William Chapman, her brows raised in question. "Is . . . anything the matter?"

He pulled a regretful face and stepped nearer to speak to her out of earshot of his sister. "Not really. Duncan isn't fond of me and did not enjoy having to wait on me like a servant."

"But he is a servant."

"Yours, yes, but not mine. At any rate, it's nothing you need be concerned about, Miss Foster. It's all in the past."

He drew himself up. "Now, enough of that. Here I am, ready for our tour. I've brought Kitty along. I hope you don't mind. I knew she would enjoy seeing the place."

"Not at all. She is most welcome."

His sister looked up at her words, and Abigail greeted her. "Hello."

"Kitty, this is Miss Foster," William said. "Miss Foster, my younger sister, Katherine."

The adolescent wrinkled her nose. "But I am only called Katherine when Mamma's vexed, so Kitty will do nicely, thank you."

Abigail smiled. "Kitty it is. Now, what would you like to see first?"

The girl rose eagerly. "Everything! You can't imagine how I've wondered about every room, walking by this place my entire life and never seeing inside."

"Then every room you shall see." Abigail squeezed her hand. And for a moment it was as if she were looking into Louisa's face at Kitty's age. A Louisa who had often looked up at her with fond affection, trust, and even admiration. Abigail's heart ached a little. Sometimes she missed those days. Missed their formerly close relationship. Missed *her*.

Abigail gave the two Chapmans the grandest of grand tours. Using information gleaned from the book of Pembrooke's history she'd found in the library, she described the house, its style, and the approximate ages of various additions with enthusiasm, incorporating architectural details she'd learned from Gilbert.

In the salon, Abigail noticed Kitty's attention stray. She cut short her monologue and instead gestured toward the old pianoforte, inviting Kitty to play the neglected instrument. The girl sat down and plunked out a few tentative notes.

Abigail became aware of Mr. Chapman's curious look. "Sorry," she said. "I got a little carried away."

"Not at all. I am only surprised by how much you know about architecture. Most impressive."

She shrugged, self-conscious under his admiring gaze. "It's nothing, really. I have always been fascinated by the subject."

"May I ask why?"

"I had a neighbor growing up, a boy named Gilbert. His father made his fortune in the building trade, and Gilbert planned to follow in his footsteps by becoming an architect. His enthusiasm was contagious, I suppose. I found myself borrowing his books, going with him to observe construction sites and the like."

"I see . . ." He studied her with measuring interest. "And where, may I ask, is this Gilbert now?"

She darted a glance at him, feeling her neck heat. She hoped she hadn't revealed her feelings—embarrassing feelings better kept hidden.

"In Italy. Studying with a master architect."

"Ah. And do you wish you were with him?"

"Me? Studying in Italy? Women don't do that sort of thing, as you know."

"I didn't mean studying," he clarified. "Though it's a shame you could not. I meant, do you wish you were with *him*?"

The burning flush crept from her neck into her cheeks, and she could not meet the man's blue eyes.

"I . . ." She hesitated. "Actually, I think it may be my sister he admires now." Agitated, she rushed on, "I don't know why we are talking about this. We are to be talking about Pembrooke Park." Abigail redirected her attention toward Kitty, walking closer to the pianoforte while the girl played a simple piece by rote.

Moving to stand at her elbow, Mr. Chapman said quietly, "Forgive me, Miss Foster. I should not have asked so personal a question. A professional tendency, I'm afraid."

She formed a vague smile but avoided his eyes. "I understand. Now . . . shall we continue?"

Kitty rose and asked to see her bedchamber. "You were given the pick of all the rooms, William told me. I want to see the one you chose."

"Then you shall. But I hope you won't be disappointed. I did not pick the grandest room."

"No?"

Abigail looked at the adolescent's wide, shining eyes. It wouldn't be long until Kitty raced toward womanhood, but for now, she was still in large part a little girl. "No. But when you see what's inside, I think you will approve my choice."

Abigail led the way upstairs.

At her door, William hesitated. "You two go ahead. I shall . . . wait here."

Another nod toward propriety, Abigail guessed. But as soon as she gestured Kitty into the room, she wished he had been there to witness his sister's delight.

"Oh, my goodness!" Kitty enthused over the dolls' house. "Look at this! It's wonderful."

"Yes, someone worked very hard on it and collected a great many pieces."

Kitty knelt before the open rooms, then looked back at Abigail over her shoulder. "I suppose I shouldn't touch anything?"

"You may touch whatever you like, but I would ask that you return everything to where you found it."

"I shall. I promise."

"There are dolls in the drawer below," Abigail offered.

Kitty eagerly opened the drawer. Her smile changed to a questioning frown as she slowly drew forth the headless doll.

"I found him that way," Abigail explained. "I haven't had a chance to repair it yet."

Kitty set it aside and began experimentally opening doors and cupboards, admiring all the tiny utensils and bowls in the kitchen.

She held up a miniature woven basket. "I have one very like this. Leah made it for me for my birthday."

"Yes, I have seen the fruits of her labors," Abigail said. "I hear I have you to thank for the sweet-smelling soap in my welcome basket."

Kitty shrugged. "I helped—that's all." She opened the door of a small wardrobe and extracted something. "Look, here's another doll."

Ah. The "sister" doll Abigail had wondered about had been hidden inside a miniature wardrobe. Another boy's prank, she guessed.

For a few minutes more, Abigail watched Kitty with pleasure. But then she remembered her brother waiting alone in the corridor. "I'll be right back," she said, and the girl gave a distracted nod without looking up from the dolls' house.

Abigail stepped back into the corridor and walked into the central staircase gallery. But she did not see William Chapman. Where had he wandered off to?

Across the gallery, she noticed an open door to one of the two large bedrooms—the one she'd chosen for her mother—and walked over to it. Inside, she found Mr. Chapman staring up at a portrait over the mantel.

He glanced over and noticed her there in the doorway. "I hope you don't mind. The door was open, and you left me to my own devices for quite some time."

Abigail did not remember the door being open but didn't press him.

"Kitty is investigating an old dolls' house."

"Ah. That explains it." He folded his hands behind his back and looked around the room. "Was this Robert Pembrooke's room, do you think?"

"I don't know. Why do you ask?"

"My father is forever talking about Robert Pembrooke. Robert Pembrooke this. Robert Pembrooke that. He was master of the place when Pa first came to work here."

66

"It might be. It's one of two large bedchambers facing the front of the house. So yes, I imagine one of them was the master's bedchamber. I suppose your father could tell us for certain."

Glancing around, Abigail noticed a drawer of the dressing chest left ajar and felt suspicion nip at her.

"Here you two are," Kitty said, stepping into the room. She followed her brother's gaze toward the framed oil painting over the mantel—a portrait of a gentleman in formal attire. "Who is it?" she asked.

"Robert Pembrooke," Mr. Chapman replied. "There's another portrait of him in the church, hung there to honor him, since he and his family were its primary benefactors. Miss Foster and I were just theorizing that this might have been his bedchamber when he lived here."

Kitty shook her head, gesturing about her. "But look at this flowery upholstery and those rose-colored drapes and bed-curtains. And that dressing table is a woman's, to be sure. I think this must have been where the lady of the manor slept, for she would more likely keep a portrait of her husband than he—unless he was a very vain man."

"Good point, Kitty," William said. "This does appear a feminine chamber, now you mention it." He looked at Abigail. "Does her portrait hang in the other large room, then?"

Abigail frowned in thought. "I don't think so. At least, I don't recall seeing it."

"Let's go look," Kitty said, whirling toward the door and setting off down the corridor.

"Kitty!" William mildly chastised, following behind.

Abigail laughed. "It's all right. I don't mind."

Kitty slowed when she reached the room, pushing open the door with apparent reverence. Abigail and William quietly followed her inside.

Sunlight shone through the tall oriel window, dust motes whirling in its angled rays. The second large chamber mirrored the first, with the bed, fireplace, and window in the same positions. They all looked expectantly over the mantel. There *was* a painting of a lady there—not a young woman, as they'd expected, but rather a matronly looking woman with wispy white hair and deep grooves framing her mouth and crossing her brow. The painting was not as large as that of Robert Pembrooke either. Odd, when everything else about the two rooms seemed symmetrical.

"That can't be the man's wife," Kitty said, clearly disappointed.

"Not unless his portrait was painted in his prime and hers in later years," Abigail suggested.

"She didn't live that long," William said.

Abigail turned to him in surprise. "What?"

He shrugged. "It's all supposition at this point anyway. That woman could be anyone."

Abigail said, "Perhaps I shall ask your father."

William hesitated. "I . . . wouldn't advise asking him more than necessary, Miss Foster. He doesn't like talking about the old place or his days here."

"I thought you said he talks about the occupants a great deal."

"Robert Pembrooke, yes. But . . . no one else."

"Why not?"

"I . . . don't think I ought to conjecture. Papa wouldn't like to find he'd been the subject of idle talk."

Abigail let the matter drop. "Well then. Have you two seen enough?"

Mr. Chapman chewed his lip, then said, "I would like to see the servants' hall belowstairs, if I might, and the workrooms."

She tilted her head to regard him. "May I ask why?"

"It's the only area I was allowed in as a boy, and I wonder if it's changed."

Abigail shrugged. "Very well. This way."

She led them downstairs, through the dining room and servery, and then navigated the steep stairs, warning Kitty to be careful.

Belowstairs, they walked along the main passage, with doors opening from it to the servants' hall, larders, kitchen, and scullery.

In the kitchen, Mrs. Walsh glanced up from her worktable,

frowning to discover unexpected visitors, but her frown melted away at the sight of Kitty.

"Kitty, my love, what a treat to see you. Speaking of treats, come be the first to try my new batch of ginger biscuits. I'm sure the mistress shan't mind." She gave Abigail a look sparkling with both humor and challenge.

"Indeed she won't mind," Abigail assured her with a grin.

"By the by, miss," Mrs. Walsh said. "Many thanks for sharing Mac's jam and Kate's muffins with us. We all enjoyed them a great deal. . . . Well, most of us."

"I am glad to hear it. I did as well."

"You're a lucky girl, my duckling," Mrs. Walsh tweaked Kitty's cheek. "Having two such fine cooks in your family."

"They've nothing on you, Mrs. Walsh," Kitty said around a bite of biscuit. "Mum's never tasted half so good."

Abigail glanced over her shoulder to share a smile with William Chapman, but the threshold where he'd stood was empty. She stepped to the door and peered around the doorjamb, surprised to see him lift a door latch at the end of the passage, only to find it locked.

"Looking for something?" she asked.

He glanced up, his fair complexion flushing. "Just wondered where this leads to. I used to play hide-and-seek here as a boy, but I can't remember . . ."

Abigail's stomach prickled with suspicion. First he'd disappeared while they were upstairs, opening doors and drawers and who knew what, and now poking about the cellar? She remembered again what Leah had said about William being paid very ill by the stingy rector. Was he tempted to supplement his meager income with treasure hunting?

Abigail hoped not. She had begun to think he might admire her. But perhaps he was only interested in the house and had feigned admiration to gain admittance. With a sinking feeling, Abigail considered the notion. It was far easier to believe an interest in treasure than an interest in her.

Certain she was right, Abigail said little as she walked them out. But then Mr. Chapman surprised her yet again.

He turned to her and said, "Miss Foster, will you dine with my family this evening, since you're on your own here?"

She hesitated, not sure how to refuse. "It isn't very much notice. Won't your family mind?"

"Not in the least. They shall be delighted, and heaven knows Mamma is used to me showing up with guests at mealtimes. I am no cook, and the parsonage kitchen is from the dark ages."

"Very true," Kitty said. "Yes, do come, Miss Foster."

William added, "Mother has been pestering Leah and me to bring you by. She wants to meet our new neighbor."

Seeing Kitty's hopeful smile, Abigail said, "In that case, I will happily accept. Thank you."

"Excellent. Will five o'clock be convenient? We eat unfashionably early here."

"I don't mind at all." She smiled and drew herself up. "Well, I had better go back down and let Mrs. Walsh know not to make up a tray for me."

They bid her farewell and turned to go. But then Kitty turned back once more. "Oh, I hear people in London dress up for dinner. But no need. We're informal at home."

Abigail looked to her brother for confirmation.

"Kitty is right. You are perfect as you are." He held her gaze as he said it.

Abigail felt her cheeks warm. Surely he was referring to what she was wearing—that's all.

Avoiding his eyes, Abigail addressed his sister. "Thank you, Kitty. That is good to know."

Kitty nodded and smiled. "We girls must stick together."

William walked his sister back home. He was glad he'd thought to invite Miss Foster to dinner. She had been alone too much of late.

And he hoped it would make up for his less than polite behavior during the tour. His curiosity was natural enough, but he ought to have restrained himself.

Beside him, Kitty pulled something from her pelisse pocket.

"What is that?" he asked.

"It's a basket. From the Pembrooke dolls' house."

William stopped in his tracks, stunned. "You took it?"

She rolled her eyes and scoffed, "I am not stealing it. Only borrowing it. I want to show Leah."

"Why?"

"It looks very much like the baskets she makes, does it not?"

He squinted at it but failed to be impressed. "Looks like any old basket to me. Did you ask if you could borrow it?"

"I meant to when I came and found the two of you. But then we began talking about the portrait and I quite forgot."

"You must give it back to Miss Foster. And apologize for taking it." He gave her his most withering look of clerical exhortation.

She screwed up her face. "Of course I will."

When they entered the cottage, there sat his mother and sister in their customary chairs in the sitting room, knitting.

Kitty hurried over to her sister. "Look at this."

Leah took the little basket in her fingers. "Is this the one I made for you?"

"No. That's why I wanted to show you. I found it in the dolls' house at Pembrooke Park. Did you give one to the girl who used to live there?"

Leah's brow furrowed as she looked from her sister to the basket, but before she could reply, their father came in from the next room, frowning.

"What were you doing in Pembrooke Park?" he asked.

Kitty said, "Miss Foster gave William and me a tour. I'll give the basket back—I just wanted to show it to Leah."

Leah said, "I'm sure Kitty meant no harm, Papa. But of course she must return it when she next calls."

"I don't want her going back there."

71

"Please don't be angry, Papa. I wanted to see inside. William did too."

"I have told you all that I don't want you going over there. I—"

"I don't see why not," Kitty protested. "Miss Foster is living there now, and she is perfectly amiable. William must think so too. For he invited her to have dinner with us tonight."

William felt his ears redden at the insinuation.

"Tonight?" his mother echoed. She raised her eyebrows and pierced him with a startled look. "Did he indeed?"

The Chapman cottage sat nestled in a wood bordering the estate grounds—on the same side of the river—which allowed Mac to guard the place from outsiders who had to cross the bridge to reach the house, unless they knew the back way through the wood. Abigail had seen the Chapman home from a distance on her walk with William Chapman, but approaching it now, cast in the golden late-afternoon sunlight filtered through a canopy of lime trees, Abigail thought it looked more charming than ever—like a painting in soft hues of gold, green, and ivory. Dark green shutters framed its windows, and tulips and daffodils crowned window boxes beneath. A low stone wall surrounded the cottage, the enclosed space filled with cheerful kitchen and flower gardens boasting blooming herbs and spring flowers. The only object marring the idyllic picture was a high-fenced dog kennel on one side—the dog within barking furiously as Abigail opened the gate.

She heard Mac Chapman's voice before she saw him stalking out from a side door, sternly chastising his dog. "Brutus. Quiet. Down!"

Drawn by the hubbub, a woman in mob cap and apron hurried out the front door. "Sorry about that. Don't worry. His bark is worse than his bite." She winked. "The dog's too."

The wink, the grin, the bright blue eyes identified the woman as William Chapman's mother.

"You must be Miss Foster," she said. "I'm Kate Chapman. A

pleasure to meet you. What a welcome! Your second inauspicious welcome at our hands! I am surprised you could be persuaded to join us. Come inside, my dear. The dog will calm down when he can't see you—the scary stranger."

Abigail returned the woman's smile, liking her immediately. Mrs. Chapman was a pretty woman in her early fifties with golden-brown hair and dancing blue eyes. Her teeth were a bit crooked but together formed a warm and welcoming smile. She showed none of her husband's suspicious nature nor her elder daughter's wary reserve.

"William would no doubt have escorted you over, but I've sent him to the Wilsons' for fresh cream. Should have done it earlier, I know, but I'm a bit scattered by the prospect of such august company!"

"Really—you oughtn't to have gone to any special trouble."

Mrs. Chapman opened the door for her. "Of course I must! And do be sure and notice Mac's collection of shooting trophies. Knowing you were joining us, he spent the last hour polishing them."

"Oh! I feel terrible. Your son assured me you would not mind—that you have guests all the time."

"He may have exaggerated just a bit, my dear. To put you at your ease, no doubt. And don't mistake me—I have been longing to meet you."

She took Abigail's arm and led her through the vestibule and down the passage. "Mary! Check the fish, if you please." She looked back at Abigail and explained, "We have a plain cook, and she is very plain indeed. We're attempting a fine dinner for you, my dear, but no guarantees."

"What may I do to help?" Abigail asked. "I'm afraid I haven't much experience, but I am happy to try."

"Oh, my dear—I like you already." She squeezed Abigail's arm. "Come back to the kitchen."

She followed the woman toward the back of the house and into a chaotic kitchen, with a worktable strewn with flour and mixing bowls and a stove covered with pots and stewing pans.

"Something smells good," Abigail said.

Leah looked up from where she sat, shelling peas. "Oh! Miss Foster. We are behind schedule, I'm afraid."

"I don't mind in the least. Give me something to do."

Mrs. Chapman snagged an apron from a peg on the wall, whisked it around Abigail, and tied the strings. "Look at that tiny waist! I had one of those once upon a time." She winked and plunked a bowl of glistening red strawberries on the table before her. "Stem these, if you wouldn't mind."

"I don't mind at all."

Mac Chapman came in, and drew up short at seeing her there at the worktable with his wife and daughter. "Miss Foster, you may wait in the sitting room, if you like, whilst we finish—"

"I am happy to help." She smiled at him.

He looked from her to his daughter, to his wife, and sadly shook his head. "It isn't right, my dear. Two such fine young women, working like kitchen maids, when they ought to be living like ladies."

"Mac . . ." Mrs. Chapman sent a meaningful glance toward Abigail.

"It's all right, Papa," Leah said. "Miss Foster has said she doesn't mind, and you know I don't. There is no place I'd rather be."

When Mac left the kitchen for more wood for the fire and Mrs. Chapman retreated into the scullery to consult with the cook about a sauce for the fish, Abigail leaned nearer to Miss Chapman and asked softly, "What did your father mean?"

Leah glanced toward the door, then whispered, "Oh, he thinks I should have married some wealthy gentleman by now." She ducked her head, self-consciously averting her gaze.

Why hadn't Leah Chapman married? Abigail wondered, looking at her lovely profile and thick golden-brown hair. She was certainly pretty enough. But she looked to be in her late twenties if not thirty. Was it too late for her? Was she destined to remain a spinster? Perhaps Leah and Abigail had that in common.

Kitty bounded into the kitchen, welcomed Abigail enthusiastically, and joined them at the table. She dug out a fistful of pea pods to help her sister, chatting happily all the while. Abigail decided to keep the rest of her questions to herself.

William hurried through the kitchen door, regretting how long he'd been away on what should have been a quick errand. But Mr. Wilson had talked on and on. . . .

He stilled right there in the threshold. Stopped so abruptly the cream sloshed over the edge of the pail. The scene that greeted him was as unexpected as it was delightful: Leah laughing at something their father said. Miss Foster—*Miss Foster*—sitting at their kitchen table as though one of the family, laughing right along with her.

Mac said, "No, now, you two will be thick as thieves in no time, I see, and I shall be in trouble."

How wonderful to see Leah smile—really smile, eyes and all. To laugh with ease in the presence of someone not of their immediate family. When had he last seen it?

His father glanced up. "There you are, Will. Milk the cow yourself and separate the cream?"

Kitty added, "You have been gone an age."

His mother ran her gaze over him. "You were supposed to *fetch* cream, my dear, not wear it. Good gracious, your shoes. Kitty, get a cloth, will you? And, Jacob, take that pail from your brother before he drops it. He seems dumbstruck."

William hadn't noticed Jacob at his elbow, waiting for him to move past the threshold so he might enter the kitchen as well. William surrendered the pail to his gangly brother and smiled sheepishly at his guest. "What a poor host I am, Miss Foster. To invite you and then be so tardy in joining you. I see you have already been initiated into the pack in my absence?"

"Yes. And happily."

"I am glad to hear it."

"Wash your hands, Jacob." His mother snatched the pail from him. "And then I need you to whip the cream with a little sugar."

"Let Will do it," the fifteen-year-old said sullenly. With his red hair, green eyes, and frown, he looked very like their father.

"Lazy bones," William gently chided him. "Tell you what. Half in two bowls and a race to see who can thicken his faster."

Jacob met his gaze with a gleam in his eye. "You're on." He turned to their father. "Care to place a wager, Pa? Me against William?"

"No, you know we Chapmans don't gamble," Mac said sternly. Then he winked at Kitty and whispered, "Sixpence on William."

She giggled and shook his hand.

"Oh, you two . . ." Mrs. Chapman sighed, but obliged with two mixing bowls and whisks. She poured even amounts of cream in each bowl and eyeballed a palmful of ground sugar. "Dinner will be at midnight at this rate."

William took up his whisk and readied for the challenge. "Ready. Steady. Go!"

"Back up, Miss Foster," his mother warned, "or you'll end up wearing your pudding."

He and his brother began whisking, now and again each looking at his rival to check his progress, only to grimace in effort once again.

"I don't want butter, mind," his mother said. "There, that's enough."

"Who won?"

His mother declared it a tie.

"May I taste?" Kitty blinked up at him.

"You may." William extended the whisk toward her, and she stuck out her tongue, but at the last moment, he tapped it to her nose instead, leaving a dollop of whipped cream on her small pert nose.

Taking the teasing in stride, Kitty fingered the cream from the tip of her nose to the tip of her tongue and pronounced it delicious.

After the filling meal, flavored with plenty of conversation around the table, William suggested a walk to stretch their legs. Miss Foster offered to help with the dishes but his mother refused, insisting both Leah and Abigail accompany him for a walk and leave the dishes to the rest of them, to the groans of Jacob and cheerful compliance of Kitty.

While the women collected their bonnets and wraps, William stepped outside to wait for them, drawing in a breath of cool evening air, refreshing after the warmth of the small house.

A man on horseback approached, causing Brutus to launch into ferocious barking.

"Brutus!" William hollered, but the dog paid little heed.

As the rider neared, William recognized Andrew Morgan. Seeing his old friend gladdened his heart. Andrew's father had recently inherited nearby Hunts Hall from a cousin, after the man's death. Before that, the two young men had become acquainted when Andrew's family visited Hunts Hall over the years. Later, they were at school together.

Andrew dismounted and tied the rein to the gate, the horse jigging a bit, clearly unsettled by the barking dog. His father came out and, to the horse's relief, quieted Brutus far more successfully than William had done.

Andrew came up the path, hand outstretched. "William, you old devil. Though I suppose I ought not call you a devil, your being a clergyman now. Good to see you, old man."

"You as well, Andrew. How are you?"

"Excellent. Enjoyed traveling about, but I'm glad to be back."

"I'm sure your parents are glad as well."

"Yes, Mother wants more grandchildren. Talks of little else."

"And do you mean to oblige her?"

Andrew cocked his head to one side. "Oh, I see how it is. Hoping for rich fees for performing the marriage and all those christenings, ey?" Andrew grinned. "What about you? Any progress in that area?"

William felt his smile falter. "No. I'm . . . afraid not."

Andrew sobered. "Sorry, Will. Have I brought up a sore subject? If it helps, last I saw Rebekah she was as big as a mother bear and half as cheerful. Though she has since been delivered of a strapping son."

"Yes, I heard." William shifted, and said awkwardly, "And I am not suffering in that regard, Andrew, I assure you. Though I was sorry to hear about her husband."

"Were you?"

"Of course."

The door opened behind him, and Leah and Miss Foster stepped out, wearing bonnets and pelisses and pulling on gloves as they came. William was struck again at Miss Foster's beauty. The bonnet framed her face and softened her angular features. Her dark eyes contrasted strikingly with her creamy skin. Beside him, Andrew Morgan stared as well. Had he imagined his friend's sharp intake of breath? He glanced over and found the man's gaze riveted on the ladies—or had one lady in particular caught his eye?

His sister stilled upon seeing his companion, her smile falling away, her features stiffening to the wary lines she always wore when confronted by a person not of close acquaintance.

"Leah, you remember Andrew Morgan, I trust?" William hastened to reassure her. She had met Andrew a few times in the past when he'd visited his father's cousin, though it had been more than a year since the two had seen one another.

Leah curtsied. "Yes. How do you do, Mr. Morgan."

Andrew bowed. "I am well, thank you, Miss Chapman. And you . . . you are in good health, I trust?"

"I am. Thank you."

William was surprised by the stilted greeting, especially on his gregarious friend's part.

Recalling his manners, William turned to Abigail. "Miss Foster, may I present my friend Andrew Morgan. Mr. Morgan, our new neighbor, Miss Foster."

"A pleasure to make your acquaintance, Miss Foster. It is a rare thing to have a new neighbor in this sleepy parish."

William explained, "Miss Foster and her family have let Pembrooke Park."

Andrew's eyebrows rose. "I had heard the old place was occupied at last, but I must admit I assumed by some undertaker or ghoul—not a lovely young lady like yourself. You are quite alive, I take it?"

Miss Foster shot him a bemused grin. "Quite alive, I assure you."

"Excellent. Well, welcome to the neighborhood."

William explained to her, "Andrew's parents live in Hunts Hall, on the other side of Easton. Papa is their agent. But Andrew here has been traveling abroad most of the twelvemonth since they moved in."

Abigail nodded her understanding. "Then you are a newcomer as well, Mr. Morgan."

"I suppose I am." Andrew smiled. "I say, what propitious timing. Mother is having a little dinner party in a fortnight to welcome me to Hunts Hall. She's inviting several relatives and friends of hers, and gave me leave to invite a few friends of my own. Why don't the three of you join us? Say you will, or I shall be bored to tears."

William hesitated, glancing at Leah to see how she would react.

She looked away from Andrew's eager face, clearly disconcerted, and demurred, "Surely your mother did not mean for you to invite just anyone you happened to meet."

"You are hardly just anyone. William and I were at Oxford together. And you are his sister. And—"

Miss Foster interjected, "Thank you, Mr. Morgan, but you needn't feel obligated to include me just because I happened to be here. But include Miss Chapman, by all means."

"Now, no more refusals or polite demurs, I beg of you. I shall have Mamma dash off official invitations as soon as I return home. No filling your social diaries with anything else in the meanwhile, hear?" He wagged a teasing finger.

"Oh yes, a busy social diary indeed," William agreed wryly. "We shall do our best to squeeze you in."

Later, after Mr. Morgan had taken his leave, William led the ladies around the gardens. When he suggested it was time to walk Miss Foster home, Leah begged off, leaving William the honor of walking Miss Foster home alone. He did not mind in the least.

As they strolled across the manor grounds, Miss Foster commented, "Your friend seems an amiable fellow."

"Indeed he is. And he seemed impressed with you, I noticed."

"Me? Hardly. He only had eyes for Leah."

William looked at her in surprise. "Did he?"

"Yes. I don't know how you failed to notice."

"Hm . . ." William considered her observation. On one hand, he was relieved to know that his handsome and wealthy friend had not already set his sights on Miss Foster, but he was disquieted by the thought of his being smitten with his sister. It would be interesting to see what happened now that Andrew had returned—apparently for good—with the intention of settling down and giving his mother grandchildren. He supposed everyone in Easton considered Leah Chapman, at eight and twenty, on the shelf and there to stay. Would Leah be able to overcome her reluctance and allow herself to be courted?

Whatever happened, William hoped Leah wouldn't be hurt. He himself knew what it felt like to be disappointed in romance. He had been rejected and lived to tell the tale, but his sister was so much more sensitive and isolated than he was. Nor was her faith the solid rock his had become, a faith that sustained him when disappointments came. He would pray for her. He would pray for them both.

Miss Foster began, "May I ask, Mr. Chapman, about Oxford. How did you . . . ?"

"Afford it?" he glibly supplied. "You may well wonder, considering my father's background. Even my mother's."

"I'm sorry. I meant no offense. I am only curious."

"You are a very curious creature—asking questions about many things, I have noticed."

"Forgive me, I—"

"In this instance, I don't mind in the least. As you know, my father was Robert Pembrooke's steward, and Mr. Pembrooke relied on him a great deal. It is a great matter of pride—of honor—to my father. A steward or servant who takes pride, reflected though it may be, from the honor or rank of the family he serves is nothing new. But Robert Pembrooke rewarded my father's faithful service with more than just words. Though not an old man when he died, Robert Pembrooke had already written his will.

"I previously mentioned he left my father the cottage and land it sits on, as well as use of the estate fishpond, but he also left him a tidy sum. Father might have invested that sum and lived off the interest fairly comfortably. Instead he invested that money in my education. I hope he doesn't regret the investment."

"Of course he doesn't," Miss Foster said. "His pride in you is perfectly obvious."

William shrugged. "Pride makes me uncomfortable, Miss Foster."

"I only wish my own father . . ." She stopped, allowing her sentence to trail away unfinished.

He glanced at her troubled profile. "Wish what?"

"Never mind," she said, avoiding his gaze.

They reached the front of the house and stood awkwardly at the door.

She glanced away across the courtyard, toward the gate and river beyond, and frowned. "Who's that?"

He turned to follow her gaze and saw a figure in a green cloak cross the bridge and disappear from view.

His stomach tightened. "I don't know. I only caught a glimpse."

But that one glimpse was enough to make him uneasy. It brought back a boyhood memory—lads telling ghost stories about a faceless man in a hooded cloak, coming to kill anyone who got in his way.

Chapter 7

*T*hat night, as Abigail went about her usual bedtime rou-
tine, she thought back to dinner with the Chapmans. She
realized that at some point during the cream whipping and
teasing and conversation between William Chapman and his family,
she had come to dismiss the fleeting suspicions she'd had about the
man. She liked him, and liked his family. And she missed her own.

She settled into bed with her sketch pad, attempting to draw
William Chapman's face. But it proved too difficult for her. She
idly sketched the Chapman cottage instead, the neat lines, shutters,
and charming thatched roof.

She wondered again what Mr. Chapman had meant when he
said, *"Had I wanted to get inside Pembrooke Park, I could have
done so at any time."* She still didn't know.

Abigail stopped, her drawing pencil pausing midstroke. What
had she just heard? Footsteps outside her bedchamber? She should
be used to servants going about their duties, she told herself. They'd
had even more servants in London, setting fires and answering
bells at all hours.

She set aside her drawing things and picked up an old novel
she'd found in the library. She read for several minutes, but the
account of an evil monk pursuing an innocent young lady chilled

her. Shutting the cover decisively, she laid the book on her bedside table and leaned over to blow out her candle. But at the last second she stopped and let it burn. Abigail settled under the bedclothes, the flickering light casting shadows on the papered walls. How she longed for her father's return. The dark house would seem less frightening once he was there.

She closed her eyes but, hearing a door whine open somewhere, abruptly opened them. *Polly*, she told herself and turned over.

Then she heard a muffled tapping sound. Tapping—at this hour? It was only a branch tapping against a window, she speculated. Or perhaps a woodpecker in a tree nearby, looking for insects. Did birds do so after dark? She had no idea. They must, she decided, and turned over yet again.

In the distance, something clanged like a tiny cymbal, brass upon brass. Abigail lurched upright, her heart in her throat. A water can—someone dropped a water can. Or kicked one, accidentally in the dark.

But it was no good. She knew she'd never sleep until she checked. She turned back the bedclothes and climbed from bed, wrapping a shawl around herself and wiggling her feet into slippers. Picking up her candle, she opened the door and listened. Silence. She tiptoed into the gallery, avoiding the many pairs of eyes glaring down at her from portraits of Pembrookes long dead.

She heard the faint sound of retreating footsteps padding down the stairs.

Heart pounding, she gingerly leaned forward and peered over the stair rail, her candle's light barely penetrating the darkness below. A hooded figure floated down the last few stairs. Stunned, she blinked. But when she looked again, the stairs were empty. She had probably only imagined the dark apparition.

With a shiver, she decided that was the last time she would read gothic fiction. It was back to architecture books for her.

She turned toward her room, but then changed course and crossed the gallery, lifting her candle to survey the closed doors until she spied one left ajar. There—the room that would be her mother's. The same room in which she had seen an open drawer when William Chapman toured the house.

She inched the door farther open and lifted her candle. The drawers were closed this time. But . . . there on the dressing table a hinged jewelry box stood open, and beside it lay a brass candle lamp, on its side. Heart pounding, she walked forward and felt the wick. Still warm.

Trembling, Abigail padded down the back stairs. She could have pulled her cord, but the bells rang in the servants' hall, and she preferred not to wake Mrs. Walsh. Nor was she eager to wait in the dark alone.

Reaching the former butler's room belowstairs, which Duncan had claimed for himself, Abigail knocked.

She heard a groan from within, followed by the creak of bed ropes, and then the door opened a few inches. There stood Duncan, hair tousled and chest bare. She hoped he wore something below but did not dare look down.

"What is it?" he grumbled.

"Sorry to disturb you. But I'd like you to check the house and make sure all the doors are locked."

"Already did. As I do every night."

"It's just . . . Mac warned me about intruders, and I thought I heard someone. Saw someone actually, and—"

"Saw what?"

"I . . . am not sure. But please check."

He smirked. "Had a nightmare, did ya? Shall I bring you some hot milk?"

Irritation flashed. "Will you check the doors or must I wake someone else to do your job for you?"

He frowned. "No need to wake the whole house. Not when you've already woken me."

She became aware then of the defensive way he held his door, only slightly ajar. She had at first thought he did so to shield his nakedness, but the longer he stood there without shirt *or* apparent modesty the more she doubted that was the real reason.

Good heavens! Had he brought some light-skirt into the house?

She narrowed her eyes. "Do you have someone in there with you?"

His head reared back in surprise. He looked over his shoulder into the room as if to ascertain the answer for himself, then opened the door wider. She saw clutter and mussed bedclothes, but no one else in the dim room.

He raised an arm over his head, leaning his elbow against the doorjamb, causing his bulky muscles to flex. He smiled down at her. "I'm flattered, miss. But no, I'm on my own. This time."

Anger now chased away her last remnants of fear. Better an apparition than a cheeky manservant who thought himself irresistible.

She drew back her shoulders. "Never mind. I shall check the house myself."

His smirk faded and he lowered his arm. "No, now, miss. Sorry." His demeanor softened. "Not used to young ladies coming to my room at night—that's all. Just give me one minute to put on a shirt. . . ."

Together, they checked the house and doors and found them all locked, just as Duncan had said. Upstairs, she showed him the candle lamp on its side.

"So that's where that lamp ended up," he said, righting it. "I wondered. Polly borrowed it from the lamp room the other day. She must have left it up here."

"But . . . what would she be doing in here?"

He shrugged. "Some errand or other." He pointed at the white covering on the dressing table. "Didn't you send her up with that cover when it came back from the lace repair woman?"

That's right, she had. She'd forgotten that. How foolish.

Had the wick been warm at all, or had it been a trick of her fevered imagination? She reached out a hand, now perfectly steady, and touched the wick again. Stone cold.

Definitely no more gothic novels for her.

The next day, when Molly brought her the day's post, Abigail took it eagerly, hoping for something from her family. Instead, she received a second letter with a Bristol postal mark in that unfamiliar hand. Enclosed was another journal page.

I heard footsteps outside my bedchamber last night. And then I heard the door to the linen cupboard open and some-one sifting through its contents. A housemaid, I told myself.

Then I heard the door across the gallery whine open. The guest room perhaps. But we have no houseguest at present. In fact, we never have guests here at sprawling Pembrooke Park, though we'd had them often enough when we lived in our few rooms in Portsmouth. Why would a servant be entering an unoccupied guest room at this hour? Especially when the housekeeper makes them rise and shine while it's still dark, to hear the maids tell it. Unless it wasn't a servant at all. . . .

Was one of my siblings trying to make me believe the house is haunted? I doubt either of them would dare risk Father's wrath by getting out of bed at such an hour.

Or was it Father himself? I felt a shiver pass over me at the thought of him prowling around in the dark, entering rooms unexpectedly. Was it not enough that he roamed about all day, opening cupboards and tapping walls, like some de-ranged woodpecker?

At that moment, my own door creaked open and I froze, my heart in my throat. But it was only the cat. Apparently, I'd failed to latch the door properly. The cat jumped up in bed with me. But for once the soft orange tabby proved little comfort.

Tonight I think I will lock my door.

With a little shiver, Abigail set the letter in her bedside table drawer with the first, then pulled on a pelisse to ward off the chill. At least the writer had found a cat to explain away the noises and doors opening, before she'd gone and made a fool of herself to a smug manservant. Abigail wished she had been as fortunate.

She left her room, crossed the gallery, and walked into her mother's room once more—this time in the light of day. Though Duncan had removed the brass candle lamp, the hinged jewelry box on the dressing table stood open as before.

Curious, Abigail leaned closer to inspect the box, and fingered through its contents. Brooches, a few strings of beads and another of coral. Her fingers hesitated on a pin, and she lifted it from a tangle of beads and chains. The brooch was made of gold in the shape of . . . an M, perhaps? She turned it over. Or a W? She replaced it, and inspected more colorful baubles and a few nicer pieces, but she found nothing of significant value. No "treasure." Though she supposed someone might have helped himself to anything valuable already, leaving her none the wiser. Perhaps she ought to have taken an inventory on their first day. But it was too late now.

On Sunday, Abigail looked through the gowns in her wardrobe, wondering what to wear to church, which she planned to attend for the first time that morning. In London, the soaring church they'd sporadically attended was immense and crowded, so few knew whether they attended or not, especially as Louisa was always slow getting ready and they often arrived so late that they'd had to sit in the back or, heaven forbid, in the gallery.

But here in rural Berkshire, with the small church located on her very doorstep, she felt she ought to attend. Her presence or absence would surely be noted by the small congregation. And by the Chapmans. She guessed Leah Chapman would be glad to see her there, and her neighbor's esteem seemed an elusive yet worthwhile goal. And yes, she admitted to herself, she was curious to see the Reverend Mr. Chapman in his clerical role.

At the bottom of the wardrobe, something caught Abigail's eye. She bent to look closer and was surprised to find a small doll pressed into the corner. Polly must not have noticed it when she'd put away her things. With a shrug, Abigail placed it in the dolls' house drawer with the others.

Polly entered, and with her help Abigail dressed in a printed muslin gown with modest fichu tucked into its neckline and a warm blue spencer. Then she tied a demure bonnet under her chin, tucked a prayer book under her arm, and set off across the drive. She had fussed too long with her appearance, and by the time she walked through the gate into the churchyard, the bell began to ring, signaling the beginning of the service.

Her heart beat a little harder than it should have for such a mundane excursion. Her palms within her gloves felt damp. Where was she to sit? Would it be presumptuous to sit in the Pembrooke box? What if she inadvertently took someone's regular seat? She dreaded the thought of all those eyes on her, judging her every move.

When she opened the door, she saw the congregants already seated and scanned the pews for an inconspicuous place to sit.

Mac appeared, his beard neatly trimmed, and dressed as dapper as any London gentleman in black coat, waistcoat, and trousers. "Miss Foster, good to see you. Allow me to show you to your seat."

Ah, that's right, Abigail thought. Mr. Chapman had mentioned his father served as parish clerk. He led her up the aisle, all the way to the front row. As Abigail feared, she felt many pairs of eyes upon her. Reaching the box on the right, Mac opened the low door for her.

"Are you sure I should sit here?" she whispered.

An odd wistfulness clouded his green eyes. "The residents of the manor have always sat here, lass. It's good to have someone sitting here again, even if it's not who it should be. The Lord giveth and the Lord taketh away."

With that dour benediction, Abigail took her seat. She noticed Andrew Morgan and an older couple seated across the aisle from her in the other place of honor.

A whisper hissed from a few rows back. "Miss Foster!"

Abigail looked over and saw Kitty Chapman, pretty in ivory frock and straw bonnet. The girl beamed and waved enthusiastically until her mother laid a gentle hand on hers and admonished her to sit quietly. Kate Chapman sent an apologetic smile Abigail's way, and Abigail smiled in return. Leah, beside her mother, nodded politely in her direction.

Abigail glanced up and saw the candles in the chandelier above her had been lit for the service. She wondered if William Chapman was even now in the vestry wiping the soot from his hands before donning his white surplice. She felt a grin quiver on her lips at the thought.

A moment later a side door opened and that very man entered. She blinked at the sight of ironic and playful William Chapman in white cleric's robe. Hands clasped, he beheld his congregation with a benign closed-lip smile before making his way to the altar. For a moment his gaze landed on her. Did a flicker of doubt cross his fair eyes? She hoped he was not sorry to see her, nor that he had guessed her secret motive for attending.

Mac, in his role as clerk, pronounced in a loud voice, "Let us sing to the praise and glory of God the forty-seventh psalm."

Abigail found it strangely affecting and edifying to hear the small clutch of congregants in this humble parish church raising their voices together in the praise of their Maker. In the soaring London church, there had been instruments and professional singers, but somehow the music here was all the sweeter for being performed by the peaceful and pious inhabitants of this rural village. The congregation sang and prayed alternately several times. The tunes of the psalms were lively and cheerful, though at the same time sufficiently reverent. William Chapman read the liturgy. The responses were all regularly led by his father, the clerk, the whole congregation joining in one voice.

Mr. Chapman looked at his father meaningfully, and Mac took his cue, rising to stand at the reading desk and positioning spectacles on his long, narrow nose. He traced his finger along the page of the book, already open on the stand, and read in a deep voice. "A reading from the first chapter of James, the last two verses. 'If any man among you seem to be religious, and bridleth not his tongue, but deceiveth his own heart, this man's religion is vain. Pure religion and undefiled before God and the Father is this, To visit the fatherless and widows in their affliction, and to keep himself unspotted from the world.'"

William Chapman nodded his thanks to his father and then climbed the stairs into the pulpit. "Good morning, everyone," he began informally, smiling at the congregation, looking from face to face. He turned his smile on Abigail. "And welcome, Miss Foster. We are pleased to have you among us. Those of you who have not yet met our new neighbor will wish to do so after the service."

He glanced down at his notes, cleared this throat, then began his sermon.

"A man I recently met told me that he was not interested in religion because religious people were a bore, not to mention hypocritical, pretending to be righteous while inwardly being as selfish and sinful as the next man. And during my years at St. John's College in Oxford, I heard many fellows and professors espousing that very view. Bemoaning the fact that Sunday services are often attended only for appearance sake, while our churches echo empty during the week on high days and holy days.

"Jesus himself clashed with the religious leaders of his day, namely the Pharisees, who were guided by their own tradition and man-made rules and less by love for God or their fellowman. Jesus wanted fellowship with them, but they were not willing to come to Him, nor to receive Him. Relying instead on their outward adherence to the law.

"Are you religious? Am I? If being 'religious' means following a set of rules so we can impress others, so that we can *appear* righteous—instead of cultivating a deep relationship with the Savior himself—then I agree with the detractors. I am not interested in that sort of religion. And, I suggest, neither is the Lord. Jesus offers forgiveness and love to all who truly seek Him, believe in Him, and worship Him. Regardless of which pew we sit in on a Sunday morning. Or our annual income. Or our family connections."

Abigail slid lower in her seat. Was that comment directed at her?

"He is waiting for you to come to Him," he continued. "To rely on His guidance and goodness. To listen and obey and serve. Are you listening—spending time reading His Word and seeking His guidance in prayer? Are you serving Him and your fellowman—the widows and orphans among you? I hope you will this week."

Did *she* spend time listening, obeying, and serving? Abigail asked herself. Not really. Not enough, at any rate.

"Let us pray . . ."

Abigail blinked as around her heads bowed and eyes closed and Mr. Chapman led them in prayer in preparation for the offering and Communion. She didn't recall ever hearing a sermon so brief and to the point. If she had, she might have attended more often. Around her the whole congregation joined in solemn prayer, and the sound of it touched Abigail's heart.

William had meant to go on to expound on several verses in Matthew 23 and John 5, but having Miss Foster there in the front box, staring at him with those keen dark eyes, had unsettled him, and he'd quite forgotten. His parishioners, especially the older ones, already gave him grief about his short sermons. And he would hear about this one, no doubt.

After the service concluded, he proceeded down the aisle to bid farewell to his parishioners at the door and to receive their comments. Although the title officially belonged to the rector, most called William *Parson* as a term of fond respect. But there was one exception.

"I must say, Mr. Chapman, that was an exceedingly short sermon today," Mrs. Peterman began. "Could you not be bothered to compose a longer one? I do wonder what we are paying you for."

"You pay him nothing, Mrs. Peterman," Leah tartly retorted, coming to stand near his elbow. "And the rector pays him a very small sum indeed."

Mrs. Peterman humphed. "Apparently you get what you pay for."

"You are correct, Mrs. Peterman," William admitted. "The sermon I delivered today was shorter than I intended, and I apologize. Did you have any concerns about the content itself, or only its brevity?"

"I didn't much care for the content either. I have half a mind to write to Mr. Morris and tell him his curate spends insufficient time in his duty. Perhaps you ought to spend less time fawning over pretty girls from the pulpit, and more time making sermons!"

"He only welcomed Miss Foster," Leah objected. "He certainly did not fawn over her."

William's mother joined the trio and, with a keen look at William, took the older woman's arm. "I would be happy to introduce you to Miss Foster, if you'd like, Mrs. Peterman," she offered. "A charming young woman."

Mrs. Peterman sniffed. "I think she's received more than enough attention for one day."

The woman's husband spoke up at last. "Now, my dear," Mr. Peterman soothed, "you overstate your case. Our good parson did nothing improper." He gave William an apologetic look. "And I for one appreciate short sermons." He winked.

William nodded. "I shall keep that in mind, sir."

"Don't listen to him," Mrs. Peterman protested. "The only saving grace of your short sermons is that my husband hasn't sufficient time to fall asleep and embarrass me."

The old man clucked and gently led his wife into the churchyard.

William glanced at his sister, eyebrows raised. He had never heard her speak so sharply to anyone.

"I am sorry, William. But she vexes me no end."

"I understand. And I appreciate your loyalty. But remember that she is one of my flock, and I am supposed to love and serve her."

"I know. But I cannot stand to hear her criticize you. I don't think she has any idea how hard you work and how much you do for your *flock*, as you call them."

"At least she has the courage to tell me what she thinks to my face."

"Unlike most of the sour tabbies who merely grumble and gossip behind your back?"

"Precisely." He grinned. "Though I wouldn't say it quite so . . . colorfully."

"I hate to see you ill used," Leah said. "You're easily twice the clergyman Mr. Morris is. Were it in my power, I would see you had the living in this place."

"Shh . . ." Mrs. Chapman said, eyes round in concern and laying a hand on her daughter's sleeve. "That's enough, my dear."

Leah glanced around at her mother's gentle warning, as if suddenly aware of the listening ears around her. "You're right. Forgive me. Like the Pharisees, I apparently need to learn to bridle my own tongue."

After the service, Andrew Morgan led his parents across the aisle toward Abigail and introduced them. Mr. Morgan senior was a rotund, handsome man with a smile as broad as his son's. Mrs. Morgan, a thin, sharp-featured woman, had shrewd eyes that instantly put Abigail on her guard.

"Ah yes. Miss Foster. I have heard of you."

Abigail smiled uncertainly. "Have you?"

"Yes. Well. A pleasure to meet you. Andrew tells us he has invited you to our little dinner party."

"Your son is exceedingly polite, Mrs. Morgan. But do not feel obligated—"

"I don't feel obligated—in this case. It is a pleasure to extend an invitation to you. Your father is in London, I understand?"

"Yes, but he should return soon."

"And your mother?"

"She remains in Town with my younger sister, guiding her through the season. They are staying with my great aunt in Mayfair but will be joining us at season's end."

"Mayfair, ey? Well. I shall include your father in the invitation as well. Tell him he is most welcome."

"Thank you, Mrs. Morgan. You are very kind."

The woman was impressed, Abigail saw. She was familiar with prestigious Mayfair but not, apparently, with her father's financial ruin. Her good opinion—and her invitation—would likely evaporate if she learned the truth.

After bidding the Morgans farewell, Abigail walked out of the church alone.

"Miss Foster!" Kate Chapman called a cheerful greeting and, leading William by the arm, walked over to join her. "I'm so glad you came today. Doesn't our William make excellent sermons?"

"Indeed he does," Abigail agreed sincerely, though she had not heard all that many.

"Short sermons, I think you mean, Mamma," William said good-naturedly.

"Brevity is a virtue in my view, yes," Abigail said. "But I also found the words convicting and to the point. Virtues as well."

"Not all would agree with you."

"Well, Miss Foster," Mrs. Chapman said, "you must join us for dinner later this afternoon. Cook has left us a roast of beef and several salads. I shall not even have to put you to work this time."

Abigail hesitated. "I would love to, truly. But Mrs. Walsh has left me a tray, and I don't think . . ."

Leah said, "You can save it for supper. Mrs. Walsh can't mind that."

"Actually, she could," Kate Chapman said with a little frown. "Tell you what. Join us next Sunday instead. That will give you plenty of time to give Mrs. Walsh notice—all right?"

"You *do* plan to attend church again next Sunday?" Leah asked.

Abigail hadn't meant to commit to every Sunday by attending once, but she found she didn't mind. She had enjoyed it, actually. "Yes, I do."

Leah smiled. "I am glad to hear it."

How pretty and young Leah Chapman looked when she smiled. Abigail thought attending church and gazing at Leah Chapman's brother every week would be a pleasant price to pay for the woman's approval. And hopefully her friendship.

Chapter 8

On Tuesday, the post brought the promised invitation from Mrs. Morgan, and a third letter from Bristol in that ornate feminine hand. Pulse accelerating, Abigail took the journal page into the library to read in private.

Her portrait is missing. How strange. I don't think anyone else has noticed. I suppose it's not surprising I had not noticed it earlier. For I have not dared to enter Father's bedchamber before today. But he has gone to London on some business or other related to his brother's will. So I felt safe in entering.

I have been in Mamma's rooms often enough. And over the mantelpiece in her bedchamber hangs a portrait of a handsome gentleman in formal dress. When I asked who it was, she said, "Robert Pembrooke," and we both stared up at it.

It was the first time I had laid eyes on my uncle Pembrooke's face. And considering he was dead, it was the only way I would ever see him.

"Did you ever meet him?" I asked.

"Once. Years ago," Mamma replied. "The day your father and I were married."

"Was this his wife's room, then?"

"Yes. So the housekeeper tells me."

My father had claimed Robert Pembrooke's room, but I know better than to think he'd done so in a nostalgic attempt to be close to his older brother after their long estrangement and his recent passing. No, I have heard him rail against the injustice of being a second son too often to think so.

I tiptoed into the master bedchamber, assuming I would see Elizabeth Pembrooke's portrait above the mantelpiece as I had seen Robert Pembrooke's over hers. I was wrong. The rooms are quite similar in other respects, though the furniture is heavier and the bedclothes more masculine. Had her portrait never been painted? Or had it been removed for some reason?

Whatever the case, in its place hangs a portrait of an elderly matron with drooping features and mob cap—someone's grandmother, perhaps.

I asked Mamma if she had ever seen Elizabeth Pembrooke. No, she had not.

"Why not?" I asked. "What happened between Uncle Pembrooke and Papa to cause such a rift between them?"

"It's the old story, I imagine," Mamma replied. "Rivalry and jealousy. But I don't know the details. He never told me. And I'm not sure I want to know."

A postscript had been added to the page in a darker ink color.

I found a portrait of a beautiful woman hidden away, and think it might be Elizabeth Pembrooke. I wonder who hid it. And why.

Where had she found it? Abigail wondered. And where was it now? Gooseflesh prickled over her as she reread the words. She felt as if someone had been watching them the day she, William, and Kitty looked for Mrs. Pembrooke's portrait and found the one of the old woman instead. Was someone secretly observing her movements and then sending journal pages related to her comings and goings?

Did the writer live nearby? Near enough to see her? But what about the Bristol postmark? Heaving a sigh she shook her head. She wasn't going to figure it out on her own.

Abigail went in search of Mac Chapman and found him oiling his guns in his woodshed.

"Mac, what can you tell me about the former residents of Pembrooke Park? Not Robert Pembrooke—I mean the people who lived here after his death. His brother's family, I believe."

He shot her a wary look, then returned his focus to his task. "What about them?"

"Their names, to begin with. And how long they lived here."

He began, "After Robert Pembrooke and his family died—"

She interrupted him to ask, "How did they die?"

Mac huffed a long-suffering sigh. "Mrs. Pembrooke and her wee daughter died during an outbreak of typhus, as did many that year. Robert Pembrooke was laid very low indeed and died the following year. A fortnight after his death, his brother, Clive, moved in with his family. But they were here only about two years."

"Why did they leave so soon after moving in—and so suddenly?"

"I don't know. I never pretended to understand Clive Pembrooke, and I cannot pretend I was sorry to see them go."

"Were you there when they left?"

Mac shrugged and re-oiled his cloth. "I showed up as usual one morning to meet with Clive Pembrooke, only to find the place deserted. The housekeeper at the time told me the missus had let all the servants go without notice, though she paid them their quarter's wages in full. We have'na seen the family since."

"So Mrs. Pembrooke knew in advance they were leaving? And that's why she sent the servants away?"

He turned to study her, eyes narrowing. "Why are you asking all these questions?"

"I . . . am only curious."

Should she tell him about the letters? Instead she asked, "Is there a portrait of Elizabeth Pembrooke somewhere? I've seen the one of Robert Pembrooke, but not his wife."

He frowned. "Why do you ask me that?"

She shrugged. "You were the steward—you knew the family. And the old woman in the portrait in the master bedchamber . . . Who is she?"

"Robert Pembrooke's old nurse, I believe. But again, why are you asking? Why do you care?"

"It's only natural I should care about what went on in the place I now live."

His green eyes glittered like glass. "You know what Shakespeare said about 'care,' Miss Foster?"

She nodded. "'Care killed a cat.'"

"Exactly." He tossed down his cloth. "Look. I don't want to talk about the Pembrookes or the past, Miss Foster. Not with you, nor with anyone. Let it lie."

Abigail held his gaze a moment, then turned to go.

Mac called her back. "Miss Foster . . . if Clive Pembrooke should ever show his face at the manor, promise me you'll let me know directly. I know it's unlikely. But, I never thought the house would be occupied again after all this time either, and here you are."

Abigail was surprised by the request but agreed. "Very well, I shall."

"He may not give his real name," he warned. "He might come under some guise or assumed name. . . ."

She frowned. "Then how will I know who he is? Is there a portrait of him somewhere, or has he some distinguishing feature?"

"No portrait that I know of. He did look something like his brother, though not as tall, and rather paunchy after two years of idleness, though who knows how the past eighteen years have changed him."

"That isn't terribly helpful," Abigail said.

Mac held up a finger as a memory struck him. "He always wore the same long cloak, left over from his navy days. With a deep hood for standing watch on deck in rough weather. It is unlikely he would still be wearing it after all these years, but if a man shows up at your door wearing such a thing, be on your guard."

In spite of herself, Abigail shivered. "I shall indeed." She remembered the hooded figure she thought she saw on the stairs—but she had only imagined that, hadn't she?

In spite of Mac's warnings, Abigail did not let the matter lie. Wondering if any of the former servants still lived in the area, she looked in the library, hoping to find the old household account books or staff records but finding nothing of the sort. Odd, she thought, unless such ledgers had been kept in the former butler's room or housekeeper's parlor. She asked Mrs. Walsh if she had come across any old staff records, but she had not.

"Were you acquainted with any of the former servants?" Abigail asked her.

"That was long before my time," Mrs. Walsh said. "I only moved to the area ten years back."

Abigail thanked the woman. As she left the housekeeper's parlor, Abigail paused at the former butler's room across the passage. Steeling herself, she knocked briskly. The door creaked open. She waited, but no one answered. Through the crack, she glimpsed a rumpled bed, a wad of faded green wool amid the bedclothes, and a pair of discarded trousers tossed on a chair. As mistress of the house, she had every right to look in a servant's room. Dared she? She placed her hand on the door and opened it a few inches more. . . .

"At my door again, miss?"

Abigail started and looked over her shoulder to find Duncan smirking down at her.

She drew herself up. "There you are. Good. I was looking for the old household account books, or staff records. Thought the butler might have kept them."

"And why do you want those?"

"Just curious about the former servants. If any of them still live in the area."

He crossed his arms and leaned against the wall. "Let's see . . . Not many, that I know of. One housemaid married and moved away, I understand. Another died. As did the old gamekeeper, last year."

Remembering something Mac had said, Abigail prompted, "Mac mentioned a former housekeeper . . . ?"

"Did he?" Duncan asked, brows high. "I am surprised he would."

"Do you know her?"

He nodded. "Mrs. Hayes. I am acquainted with her niece, Eliza Smith."

"Does Mrs. Hayes live nearby?"

"Yes. In Caldwell. She is all but blind now, Eliza says, and her mind isn't as sharp as it once was. Eliza takes care of her now."

Duncan obliged her by describing the house and where to find it, ending with, "Be sure and tell Miss Eliza I said hello."

"I shall." Abigail thanked him and went upstairs.

Donning hat and gloves, she set out for a chilly walk. The day was sunny, but the wind was brisk. As she crossed the bridge, a heron rose from the river and sailed over the wood, where the ash trees and some of the young sycamores were in full flower and leaf. She walked through nearby Easton and on to neighboring Caldwell, enjoying the sight of vivid bluebells among the trees.

Reaching Caldwell, she easily found the modest, well-kept house and knocked on its door. An intelligent-looking woman in a printed frock, fichu, and apron answered. She had reddish-gold hair, blue eyes, and a rather long nose, and was perhaps a few years older than Abigail.

"Hello. I am Miss Foster, new to Pembrooke Park. And you must be Eliza."

"That's right."

"Duncan asked me to say hello."

"Did he?" Eliza blushed and looked down awkwardly.

Abigail followed her gaze and noticed the woman's work-worn, ink-stained hands. She said, "I hoped to pay a call on your aunt. If she is . . . able to receive visitors?"

Eliza smiled, which made her somewhat plain features pretty. "How kind, Miss Foster. Come in." She stepped back, and Abigail followed her into the entryway.

"Auntie so rarely receives callers these days—except for Mac Chapman, kind man that he is."

Abigail hesitated. "William Chapman, do you mean?"

"No. His son used to come, but now his father comes in his stead."

"Oh." That surprised Abigail. She added, "And Miss Chapman, I suppose?"

"No. Just Mac," Eliza said. "He comes by every week at least. Helps us keep the house in good repair, and brings things for Auntie. But otherwise . . . it's as if people have forgot her."

Abigail wiped her feet on the mat. "It's kind of you to look after her."

Miss Smith shrugged. "She looked after me, when I was a girl. Raised me as her own after she left Pembrooke Park."

The young woman didn't mention her parents' fate, Abigail noticed, but decided not to ask.

Abigail's gaze rested on a brooch pinning together the ends of the linen fichu around the woman's neck. She'd seen something like it before. . . .

"Pretty brooch," she commented, admiring the letter E in gold, or perhaps brass.

The woman touched it self-consciously. "Thank you, it was a gift. I'd forgot I had it on. If you will wait here a moment, I will see if my aunt has awakened from her nap." She slipped into the next room.

While she waited, Abigail glanced idly around the entryway, noticing a bonnet and veiled hat on pegs near the door. Then she looked through the open door into a small kitchen. A pot of something sat simmering on the stove, sending savory aromas throughout the house. Upon the worktable lay writing paper, quill, and ink, and what appeared to be a stack of quarto-sized periodicals.

Eliza reappeared and said, "She's awake." She hesitated, then added, "I have to warn you, miss. Her memory isn't very keen. Or her mind. You can't take everything she says as fact. Or to heart."

Abigail nodded her understanding and followed the woman into the dim parlor.

"Auntie? There's someone here to see you. A Miss Foster. She lives at Pembrooke Park now and wanted to meet you." Eliza began opening the shutters for Abigail's benefit.

A diminutive white-haired woman sat hunched in an armchair, knitting needles clenched in her gnarled hands. She lifted her head and sightless eyes. "Pembrooke Park? No one's lived there for years."

Abigail stepped forward. "My family and I have only recently moved into the house."

"You live there? You're not her, are you?"

Abigail hesitated. "Not who, Mrs. Hayes?"

"The girl that used to live there?"

"No. I have only lived in Pembrooke Park for the last month or so."

"And not a Pembrooke, you say?"

Eliza sent her an apologetic glance. "No, Auntie. Remember, this is Miss Foster."

"Well, Miss Foster," Mrs. Hayes said tartly, "does she know you're living in her house?"

Abigail blinked. "Does who know, Mrs. Hayes?"

"You have to forgive us, Miss Foster," Eliza said. "It's a long time ago and we don't remember details so well."

"I remember perfectly well," her aunt snapped. "Miss Pembrooke. His daughter, of course."

Assuming she was speaking of Clive Pembrooke's daughter, Abigail said gently, "I have never met her. Do you know where she lives now, Mrs. Hayes?"

"Where who lives?"

Eliza winced in embarrassment.

Praying for patience, Abigail repeated, "Miss Pembrooke?"

"I haven't the foggiest notion. She told me to lock the house and not look back, and I haven't. Said she wouldn't look back either, not like Lot's wife. No matter what."

Abigail frowned, trying to follow. "Mrs. Pembrooke told you that, do you mean?"

"Not Miss Elizabeth. The other one."

"Are you talking about Clive Pembrooke's wife?"

The woman shuddered and crossed herself. "Don't say his name, miss. Not if you value your life."

"There, there, Auntie," Eliza soothed. She glanced up at Abigail. "If you will excuse me a moment, Miss Foster. I need to stir the soup. I'll make some tea as well."

After Eliza departed, Mrs. Hayes tsked and said, "Poor Eliza. Living here in this small house . . . waiting on me like a servant." She sighed. "How unfair life is."

"I think she is happy to do it," Abigail said. "She told me you took care of her after you left Pembrooke Park."

Mrs. Hayes nodded, expression distant. "Aye. Dark days them were. . . ."

When she said nothing more for several moments, Abigail asked, "Why did Clive Pembrooke's family leave, Mrs. Hayes? Did you see them go?"

She shook her head emphatically. "I was in my bed. Mindin' my own affairs. I saw nothing. Heard nothing. I was fast asleep all night."

The line *"The lady doth protest too much"* crossed Abigail's mind. But she said only, "I see. So you were in the house, but when you rose the next morning, they were gone? The whole family?"

Mrs. Hayes nodded. "I was sorry to see the missus go. Always decent to me she was."

"Had she planned to leave for some time? Mac said you'd all been paid through the end of the quarter and let go."

Again she nodded. "I think she feared what he would do to us if we were there when he discovered his family had left 'im. He was away hunting, you see. But he came home early and figured out

103

what she was plannin'—that's my guess. And tried to put a stop to it." She shook her head. "Poor Master Harold."

"Master Harold?" Abigail said. "What happened to him?"

"I don't know. I saw nothing."

"Mrs. Hayes, what do you *think* happened that night, if you were to guess?"

"I think he found her valise. Packed to leave. And her purse full of the money she'd been saving. Either that, or one of the boys gave it away. Not the girl. Not one for talkin', she weren't."

"And what did Clive Pembrooke do when he found out they were planning to leave him?"

"Don't know exactly. I may have heard a gunshot that night. Or maybe it was only a lightning strike. In the morning, after everyone had gone, I found blood on the hall floor."

Abigail sucked in a breath. "Blood? Whose blood?"

"Can't say for sure. I may have peeked, or I may have only dreamt it."

"Are you saying Clive Pembrooke shot someone?" Abigail asked in horror. "Someone of his own family . . . ?"

"I never said that. You didn't hear it from me. In the morning, everyone was gone. All gone! I saw the blood, see. But no body. So I must have dreamt it, hadn't I?" Her voice rose. "Don't tell a soul, miss! Not a soul! We don't want Master Clive to come back and exact vengeance, do we?"

Abigail swallowed and shook her head. She glanced through the open door into the kitchen to gauge Eliza's reaction. Eliza had gone to prepare tea, but at the moment she sat at the worktable writing something.

Abigail lowered her voice, trying not to rile Mrs. Hayes further. "Did they take the carriage? Were the horses gone?"

"Aye. The coach and carriage horses were gone. And Black Jack."

"But they took none of their belongings?"

"Oh aye, the mistress and the children took one valise each. But not one thing was missing from Clive Pembrooke's room. I even asked Tom to come in and look, to see if he agreed."

"Tom? Tom who?"

"Tom Green. The footman. Everyone knows that." The old woman frowned. "Now, what was your name again?"

Eliza came in with a tray, and Mrs. Hayes's attention was soon fully focused on her tea and toasted muffin. Abigail decided not to press the matter any further for the time being, and the conversation turned to more general topics of weather and parish life. When Eliza offered her more tea, Abigail noticed she no longer wore the brooch.

"Your brooch is gone," she said. "I hope you didn't lose it."

Eliza ducked her head. "No, I only took it off. Didn't want it falling into the soup."

"What? Who fell?" Mrs. Hayes asked. "He said Walter fell to his death, but I know better. He was pushed."

Walter? Was that the name of the valet who died in Pembrooke Park, Abigail wondered, trying to remember what Polly had told her.

"Hush, Auntie. Miss Foster admired my brooch—that's all."

Mrs. Hayes nodded over her teacup. "Ah. E for Eliza. That's right."

Later, as she walked home, Abigail reviewed what she'd learned from the letters, along with the information she'd gleaned from Duncan, Polly, Mac, and now Mrs. Hayes. Abigail wondered where Clive's family was now. The letter writer was apparently his daughter. The "Miss Pembrooke" Mrs. Hayes had mentioned. Abigail thought again of Eliza bent over quill and paper. She should have asked her what she was writing.

When she returned to Pembrooke Park, Abigail decided to do a little writing of her own. She went into the library, retrieved paper, quill, and ink, and wrote a letter to the solicitor.

Dear Mr. Arbeau,

I would like to ask the name of your client, the executor you mentioned of Pembrooke Park. I would also like an address so that I may write to this person. Or more accurately, so that I may write back in reply to her letters. You see, Mr. Arbeau, someone is writing to me here. Someone who has lived here before and is evidently female. I deduce the person must be Miss Pembrooke, though I suppose I may be wrong. In any case, would you please give me the name and direction of your client? Or if you prefer, ask your client if I may contact her?

Thank you for your assistance in this matter.

Sincerely,
Miss Abigail Foster

Molly knocked on the open library door and brought in the day's post—a letter from Mamma.

"Thank you, Molly." Abigail opened it and read.

Dear Abigail,

I hope this letter finds you in good health and spirits, and settling well into Pembrooke Park. Your father gives a good account of your efforts, but says it is well Louisa and I were not there to see it in its initial, neglected state. I know you will endeavor long and admirably to put it to rights for us before we arrive at the end of the season.

Speaking of the season, your sister has made quite an impression, I can tell you. Several well-connected gentlemen of means have expressed their admiration. She is enjoying herself tremendously, and you would be thoroughly proud of her. She sends her love, as does dear Aunt Bess, who has been the most gracious hostess during our stay here.

Your father asks me to tell you that he intends to return at month's end, but if you need him sooner for any reason, you are to write and let him know. He trusts you are well looked after by the servants and the protective former steward he told us about. I assured him you were more than capable of taking care of yourself, and with the maids to attend you, there should be no concern for propriety. Why, here in London Louisa ventures into Hyde Park with only one servant as escort, and there you have a staff of five! But if you are uneasy without your father there with you, do let us know.

Before I forget, I wanted to mention that Gilbert Scott has returned from Italy and accepted a position with an esteemed architect here in London. With his new polish and promising future, Gilbert is turning many heads, including our Louisa's. He has called at the house once or twice and sends his regards. I am still holding out for a title at present, but your sister could make a worse match.

Abigail's heart pounded. Gilbert . . . back in England. If only she were in London to see him. How she longed for her old friend's company—to hear all about his travels and see his latest drawings and plans. To see him smile at *her* . . . But was she fooling herself? If he had set his sights on pretty Louisa, he would be directing his smiles at her from now on. She recalled the letters Gilbert had written to her, in which he'd asked her why Louisa had not replied to his letters. Abigail had allowed herself to hope that Louisa's apparent interest in Gilbert Scott had faded. But now that he had returned more "polished and promising" than ever, had her hopes been dashed?

Abigail sighed and pulled forth another piece of paper. Ignoring the little stab of loneliness, she wrote back to assure her parents that she was just fine on her own.

After the Sunday service, the congregation waited until the clergyman and those in the front boxes exited before filing out behind them. So Abigail was the first to greet Mr. Chapman at the door and then step outside. As she walked toward the manor, she glimpsed movement in the churchyard and was surprised to see Eliza Smith turning from one of the graves. Abigail paused where she was while the young woman walked her way, wearing a pretty bonnet and blue overdress, her brooch peeking out from beneath her shawl.

Eliza looked up at her in surprise. "Church out already?"

"Yes, another short sermon today." Abigail wondered why Eliza and her aunt, apparently such favorites with Mac Chapman, had not attended church.

"And how is your aunt today?" Abigail asked politely.

"About the same. I don't bring her to church anymore. Never know what might come out of her mouth and disrupt the service."

"Oh. That's too bad—for you both."

Eliza shrugged. "I don't mind. I come on my own now and again. Sit in the back and slip out early. But today I had another destination in mind. . . ."

Visiting her parents' graves, Abigail guessed but did not say so.

Eliza glanced across the drive toward Pembrooke Park. Eyes on its windows, she asked, "Which room have they put you in, Miss Foster?

"I have a small bedchamber in the west wing."

"Ah. The one with the dolls' house. Miss Eleanor's old room."

Abigail hesitated. That was a name she had not heard before. It must be the given name of the Miss Pembrooke Mrs. Hayes had mentioned. "Um, yes, or so I assumed." She wondered why Eliza was familiar with the room. She asked, "You have been inside the house, I gather?"

"Oh, I . . ." Eliza ducked her head, suddenly self-conscious. "Well, a few times. Mamma died while Auntie still worked here. And now and again when our neighbor was unable to watch me, I would stay with Auntie belowstairs."

"I see. It must have been hard for you, after your mother died."

"Yes, and my father gone too . . ." Eliza's eyes misted over. "The happiest days of my childhood were those spent playing here. I snuck upstairs to explore once, but I slipped and fell. Mr. Pembrooke himself picked me up and patted my head. Instead of reprimanding me, he gave me a sweet."

"Which Mr. Pembrooke?" Abigail asked, doubting the kindness of the infamous Clive.

"Robert Pembrooke, of course."

Eliza inhaled a long breath and drew herself up. "Well, if you will excuse me." She turned to go.

"May I walk with you?" Abigail asked, knowing she had a few hours until her dinner with the Chapmans. "I long to stretch my legs after sitting on that hard bench."

"If you like."

The two young women walked companionably toward Easton, on the way to Caldwell. The warm May breeze felt good on Abigail's skin. Hawthorn blossoms dotted the hedgerows, and two whitethroats chased each other through its branches, singing all the while. The meadows beyond were yellow with cowslips, and the air smelled of apple blossoms.

Abigail drew in a deep, savoring breath. "Spring is so much more vibrant here than in London," she observed. "Have you been there?"

"No, not yet," the woman said wistfully. "Maybe someday."

"I imagine it's difficult to get away with your aunt needing someone to look after her."

"Yes, it would be."

As they passed the public house in Easton, Duncan swept out, then drew up short at the sight of his mistress. "Ah. Miss Foster."

"Hello."

"I saw Miss Eliza. And I hoped she might walk with me to Ham Green."

Abigail glanced at Eliza, saw the flush of pleasure she tried to hide.

"Then I shall leave you to it," Abigail said with a smile. "A good day to you both. And do greet your aunt for me."

"I shall, Miss Foster. Thank you."

Abigail continued her walk alone for a time, then turned and started back. As she strolled again down the tree-lined road, she remembered when she and her father had first arrived in Mr. Arbeau's carriage and were stopped by the former barricade. Now she crossed the bridge unimpeded, admiring the marsh marigolds and silvery white lady's smocks growing along the riverbank.

She looked ahead and was surprised to see two boys run through the churchyard. They threw open the church door, and from within she heard the hum of many voices before the door closed again, muffling the sound. Was there some special service she was unaware of?

Deciding to follow, Abigail entered the churchyard. As she did, she glanced over to where she'd seen Eliza standing earlier. Sure enough, flowers lay on one of the graves. She squinted, but the name on the headstone was not *Smith* as she'd expected. It was *Robert Pembrooke.*

She must have mistaken the spot Eliza had stood. Blinking away confusion, Abigail continued on to the church door. She quietly opened it and crossed the vestibule on the balls of her feet, to keep the heels of her half boots from disrupting the quiet within.

Inside she saw William Chapman sitting amidst several older boys and girls, their heads bowed over slates. Leah was sitting with a group of younger children, heads bent over books. William glanced up, and his quick smile at seeing her lightened her heart.

"Excuse me for a minute," he said to the children. "Colin, you're in charge."

The older boy nodded, and William walked over and joined Abigail at the back of the nave.

"Sorry," she whispered. "I didn't mean to interrupt."

"No problem."

"I saw a few children coming back to church and wondered what was going on. You must think me a terribly nosy neighbor. Are you teaching them the Scriptures, or . . . ?"

"We teach reading, writing, and ciphering, as well as the catechism, yes."

"Don't they go to school?"

"Our little Sunday school here is the only education some of these boys and girls will receive."

"But why?"

"Most begin farming with their fathers as soon as they are able or are apprenticed by age thirteen or so, or sent out to service, in the case of girls. For many, Sunday is their only day free to learn."

Abigail glanced at Miss Chapman. "And your sister teaches as well?"

"Yes, she is excellent with the younger children especially."

"Has there always been school here?"

"No, it's something we've started recently."

A young man raised his hand, and William excused himself to answer his question.

Leah came over and greeted her. "Hello, Miss Foster."

"Miss Chapman, it is very good of you and your brother to teach these children."

She shrugged off the praise. "I enjoy it."

"I suppose their parents contribute something—or is the schooling free?"

Leah shook her head. "I understand some schools charge a penny or twopence a week to help defray the cost of books and slates, but William insists we charge nothing. He buys what we need out of his own modest income."

"I'm sure if others knew of the work you're doing here, they would be happy to help."

"You're probably right. But William is proud and hates to ask for anything."

William returned and clearly overheard his sister's last few words. "You give me too much credit. I *have* asked for donations of books and supplies and have received a few, though many people don't believe in educating the poor. Some say it's futile, or even dangerous—rendering them insolent to their superiors."

"I take it you disagree?" Abigail asked.

He nodded. "I think every person deserves to understand enough of basic mathematics to take care of his expenses and know when he's being overcharged. To be able to read the newspaper and keep abreast of what is going on in the world. To know how to write a letter to a loved one. And to read the greatest love letter of all—the God-breathed Scriptures."

111

He flushed. "Forgive me. I did not intend to preach another sermon today."

"That's all right," Abigail said. "I admire your passion. And your efforts."

He grinned. "I'll take your admiration. But I'd prefer your help."

Abigail felt her brows rise. "Me? How can I help?"

Leah said, "Good idea, Will. You could help me with the younger children, Miss Foster. Take Martha there. She's joined us only recently. Neither of her parents can read, so she's a bit behind the others."

"I have no idea how to teach . . ."

"Just listen to her read aloud, and when she struggles, help her sound out the words troubling her."

"Very well," Abigail agreed.

She sat with the little girl for half an hour and did as Leah suggested. She soon found herself transported back to her younger days, sitting with Louisa when she was four or five, helping her read a children's book.

The time passed quickly and pleasantly, and soon Mr. Chapman announced it was time to clear away for the day. Around her, books closed and children rose and began stacking slates.

"All right, time for a closing hymn," Leah said.

The children gathered, and Leah named the hymn, "'Lord, Accept Our Feeble Song.' Ready?"

The children nodded and opened their little robin mouths and began to sing.

> "Lord, accept our feeble song!
> Power and praise to Thee belong;
> We would all Thy grace record,
> Holy, holy, holy Lord!"

As they warbled out the melody, Abigail tried not to wince, thinking, *Feeble song, indeed!*

When they finished, Leah suggested, "Shall we sing another?"

This time Leah named a hymn Abigail was familiar with, and she joined in.

> "Glory, glory everlasting
> Be to Him who bore the cross,
> Who redeemed our souls by tasting
> Death, the death deserved by us!
> Spread His glory
> Who redeemed His people thus. . . ."

William turned to stare at her. "My goodness, Miss Foster. You have a lovely singing voice."

She felt her cheeks heat. She hadn't meant to sing above the others or to show off. "Thank you. Sorry. Go on."

Leah chuckled. "Don't apologize, Miss Foster. You have a gift. Perhaps you might lead the children in singing from now on?"

Abigail hesitated. "I don't wish to usurp anybody's role."

"Don't worry about that," Leah said. "The two of us have more than enough roles as it is, I assure you. You would be doing me a favor."

"You would be doing all of us a favor," William added. The approval shining in his eyes did strange things to Abigail's heart.

She smiled self-consciously. "Then it shall be my pleasure."

Recalling their mother's dinner invitation, William and Leah asked Abigail to walk home with them, and Abigail happily agreed. She enjoyed the simple Sabbath meal of cold meat, pie, and salads, and a lovely sponge for dessert. She also enjoyed talking with Leah, the camaraderie and sparring between siblings, Mac's grumpy sense of humor, and Mrs. Chapman's infectious laugh. She did not mind the admiration in William Chapman's eyes either.

After the meal, Leah played a few hymns on their old harpsichord, and the family all sang together. Abigail tried to imagine her own family doing something so simple and reverent, but she could not.

Before she left, Abigail invited Kitty to come home with her and amuse herself with the dolls' house again, assuming her parents didn't mind. The girl eagerly accepted. Her parents less so.

"I'm sure Miss Foster doesn't want you loitering about, messing up her room and disturbing her things," Mac said.

"I don't mind," Abigail assured him. "Besides, they aren't my things really. Seems a pity that no one should enjoy them. I would be happy for Kitty's company, if you can spare her."

"Very well, if you are certain," Kate said. "But don't overstay your welcome, Kitty. And be sure to return everything to its proper place before you leave."

"Yes, Mamma."

William remained behind to discuss some church matter with Mac, and Abigail was oddly disappointed not to have his escort home. But she smiled and thanked everyone for their hospitality, glad to have his younger sister's company at least.

When Abigail and Kitty reached the house, the two went upstairs together. There, Kitty pulled a small basket from her pocket and handed it to her.

She said sheepishly, "I borrowed this the last time I was here, to show Leah. I shouldn't have done so without asking, and I apologize."

Abigail pressed her hand warmly. "I forgive you. Thank you for telling me." She nodded toward the dolls' house with a smile. "Now, go on."

Kitty said, "You needn't stay with me, if there is something else you need to do."

"Not at all. As I told your mother, I will enjoy your company. This house is far too empty and far too quiet." *Except at night,* she thought.

"I think I shall write to my mother right here at my dressing table. Oh," Abigail recalled, "I found another doll in the back of my own wardrobe. I've added her to the drawer."

The girl went eagerly to the cabinet and knelt before it and was all but lost from view, save for flashes of movement through the dolls' house windows.

"I adore these miniature furnishings," Kitty said. "The tiny balls of knitting wool. These tiny plates and pots and baskets."

"I do too," Abigail agreed, sitting at the dressing table and uncorking her inkpot. "Especially the miniature books with real pages."

"Where? Oh, I see. Here in the drawing room. This fat black one is supposed to be a Bible, I think. But its pages are blank. . . . Look! Someone has written in it."

Abigail rose and walked over. "Where? I don't recall seeing any writing."

"Here in the last two pages. They were a bit stuck together—from the ink, perhaps."

Kitty held up the miniature black book, her thumb holding it open to the spot. Abigail gently took if from her and squinted at the tiny writing. Foolishly, she hoped for a secret message. A clue to the location of the treasure, if one existed, even as she silently chastised herself for being ridiculous. She was glad Kitty could not read her private thoughts. Abigail was supposed to be the wise older female. Instead she felt like a silly adolescent, excited at the prospect of a secret treasure map.

But no map or message met her gaze. At least not that she could instantly decipher. Not even full words: *Gen 4 Eat + ed. Num + 10.*

"Does it mean something, like a code?" Kitty asked. "Or is it just scribbles?"

"I don't know."

"*Gen* and *Num* could be Genesis and Numbers. Books of the Bible," Kitty said, looking at the book over her shoulder.

"You're right." Abigail smiled at the girl. "Spoken like a fine clergyman's sister."

Kitty peered closer. "Genesis 4 and Numbers 10 . . . ? But see that symbol? Is it a plus sign or a *t*?"

"A plus sign, I think."

"Numbers *plus* ten? Ten books later?"

"We're looking for a code to decipher, when it probably means nothing," Abigail said. "Perhaps some child decided to write in the blank pages to make it seem more like a real book, but was caught in the act and stopped before he or she finished."

Kitty frowned. "Odd words to write."

Abigail agreed. "I wonder why he or she wrote these particular words in the back. Even I know Genesis is in the beginning of the Bible, not here at the end."

"Maybe it's a secret message." Kitty's eyes shone. "About a hidden treasure . . . ?"

Abigail looked at her. "You've heard the rumors too?"

"Of course." The girl glanced around Abigail's bedchamber. "Have you a Bible?"

"No," Abigail admitted, somewhat sheepishly. She had her lovely leather edition of the New Testament and Psalms and a prayer book but rarely delved into the Old Testament.

"Have you seen the Pembrooke family Bible somewhere?" Kitty asked. "Maybe there's a clue tucked inside at these pages."

"Good idea."

A knock sounded at the open door. Abigail looked over in surprise. William Chapman's profile came into view, though he averted his eyes, not looking directly into her bedchamber. In case she was *dishabille*?

"Kitty? Papa asked me to stop by and remind you not to stay too late. You are minding Mrs. Wilson's twins tonight."

Ignoring this, Kitty said, "William will know." She called to him, "William, does Genesis 4 and Numbers plus 10 mean anything to you?"

Abigail went to the door and opened it all the way, giving the man a welcoming smile. "I'm afraid we've stumbled upon a little mystery. Just a game, no doubt."

"I let myself in. I hope you don't mind," he said. "But the door was open, and as I know the servants have the day off . . ."

"William, what is Genesis 4 about?" Kitty called again.

He pursed his lips in surprise and then recollection. "Cain and Abel and their descendants, I believe. Why?"

116

She thrust the tiny book in his face, and he gently took it from her and held it at a better angle to read.

His eyes narrowed in thought. "Genesis 4. Eat plus e.d. Eated . . . Ate? Perhaps Genesis 4:8?"

"Oh! I had not thought of that. You're so clever, William," Kitty enthused.

Abigail privately agreed.

"Numbers plus ten . . ." he continued. "Ten books later? That would be . . ." He murmured to himself through the books. "Second Chronicles. Or perhaps it means to add ten to the chapter or verse? Four plus ten, meaning Numbers fourteen? Or eight plus ten equals eighteen?"

"Which is it?" Kitty asked.

"I haven't the foggiest. Have you a Bible handy, Miss Foster?"

"Not the Old Testament, I'm afraid."

"Then I'm glad for an opportunity to spur your interest in cracking open that volume."

"Even for a game—and no doubt a wild-goose chase in the bargain?"

He said gently, "One might open the book idly, but one never knows what treasures one might find."

She snapped her head up.

His blue eyes twinkled. "Though I'm guessing that's not the type of treasure you had in mind."

Abigail said, "Come. If you are both so interested, let us go down to the library. No doubt there's a Bible there. Perhaps even the family Bible."

Together they went downstairs and looked through the library—its desk and shelves—but found no family Bible. *Too bad,* Abigail thought. She would have liked to look inside and seen the births, marriages, and deaths recorded in the front leaves of the Pembrooke family Bible.

Mr. Chapman offered to run across the drive to the parsonage and retrieve his own Bible. He returned a few minutes later with a well-worn copy.

He opened the volume and flipped through the first thin pages. "Here we are. Let's see if I remembered correctly. Genesis 4:8. 'And Cain talked with Abel his brother: and it came to pass, when they were in the field, that Cain rose up against Abel his brother, and slew him.'"

Kitty frowned. "Perhaps that isn't the right verse."

"Perhaps it is . . ." he murmured.

Abigail wondered what he meant.

"And what about Numbers?" Kitty asked.

Mr. Chapman flipped past the rest of Genesis, Exodus, and Leviticus. He skimmed through Numbers 18 but apparently nothing caught his eye. Then he turned to Numbers 14. "Verse eight is about the land of milk and honey. . . ." he murmured. He slid his finger to verse eighteen, and read it aloud, "'The Lord is longsuffering, and of great mercy, forgiving iniquity and transgression, and by no means clearing the guilty, visiting the iniquity of the fathers upon the children unto the third and fourth generation.'"

"I like the first part of that verse but not the second," Kitty said.

"Does God really do that?" Abigail asked. "Visit the iniquities of the father upon his children for generations to come? That doesn't seem fair."

Mr. Chapman took her question seriously. "I don't believe children are guilty of their parents' wrongdoing. But we have all seen people who suffer because of their parents' neglect or abusive behavior, or other wrongdoing. And children often follow in their parents' footsteps." He shrugged. "Like it or not, sin has consequences. Which is why God lovingly warns us against it. Thankfully, He is merciful and ready to forgive if we ask Him. But that doesn't erase natural consequences of our actions. Cause and effect."

Abigail thought of her own father. He might forgive her—and hopefully, someday, Uncle Vincent as well—but that didn't erase the consequences he and the entire family would suffer. Oh, how she wished she could correct the mistake before it affected her sister and herself, not to mention their children and children's children.

What kind of inheritance could her father, could any of them, leave for future generations now?

Kitty frowned. "Another depressing verse. And I can't see that it's any sort of clue about a secret room or treasure."

"I'm afraid you're right," Abigail said, sharing a sad smile with the girl. "I'm sorry our discovery didn't turn out to be more amusing."

"This may not be a clue about a secret room," William agreed, "but that doesn't mean it isn't a message."

Abigail felt foreboding prickle through her. "Or a warning."

That night, Abigail lay in bed as she often did with drawing pencil and sketch pad in hand. She sketched idly, this and that. Plus signs and numbers giving way to letters of the alphabet. She began sketching the letter E—Eliza's brooch. She hesitated, turning the pad on its side, and suddenly remembered where she had seen a pin very like it. Had Duncan taken it from the jewelry box on Mrs. Pembrooke's dressing table to give to his lover? Her stomach cramped at the thought. The footsteps in the night, the candle lamp on its side, Duncan not wanting her in his room . . . It all rushed back through her mind, and with it the distasteful conclusion that Duncan had stolen the brooch. She hoped she was wrong. She would check the jewelry box, and if the brooch was missing . . . well, she would talk to Mac. He would know what to do.

In the morning, she returned to the mistress's bedchamber and opened the jewelry box, expecting the worst. Instead, there lay the brooch—not an M or W as she'd originally thought, but an ornate E, exactly like the one she'd seen Eliza wearing. Apparently the design was more common than she'd thought. Guilt and self-recrimination made her feel nauseated. She had misjudged Duncan and would endeavor to be kinder to him in future.

Later that day, Abigail received two letters. The first, a terse reply in Mr. Arbeau's neat hand.

Miss Foster,

I am in receipt of your letter but cannot satisfy your request. I have been instructed to not divulge the name of my client until he or she directs me to do so. I have contacted my client to communicate your wishes, but the request has been denied for now. My client neither confirms nor denies knowledge of the letters you mention. I do not intend to begin a guessing game with you, Miss Foster. But assuming this is your first and last guess, I can tell you that I have no client by the name of Miss Pembrooke.

> *I remain,*
> *Henri Arbeau*

The second letter was another missive in that now-familiar feminine hand. A newspaper clipping had been enclosed in the outer letter. She first read the handwritten note, addressed to her personally.

Miss Foster,

If anyone named Pembrooke comes to the house and asks for entry or shelter, I beg you refuse his request—despite his surname and likely protestations of his rights and even assertion that he is the owner of the place. For my sake and for your own well-being, as well as your family's, resolutely send him on his way. If he demands to know on whose authority you refuse him, you may refer him to the solicitor who let the house to you. He is paid well to deal with such difficulties.

This advice differed somewhat from what Mac had asked of her, but it held a similar edge of warning. After this note, a space had been left blank, followed by another single line.

In case you have not yet learnt this history of your newly acquired home, I thought I would send the enclosed to you.

Abigail picked up the clipping from a newspaper. In faded ink, someone had handwritten in the corner: *4 May 1798.*

Gentleman Killed in Queen Square

Robert Pembrooke, Esquire, of Pembrooke Park, Easton, Berkshire, was mortally wounded at his London townhouse Friday last. Violent entry and a missing purse suggest the work of thieves. Mr. Pembrooke suffered a fatal stabbing wound and was found dead by a maidservant the next morning. Officials also searching for Mr. Pembrooke's valet, a Walter Kelly, who has not been seen since the eve of the incident and is wanted for questioning.

Stabbed? Good heavens. Mac had mentioned nothing about a stabbing. The report made Abigail feel queasy. She could not help but imagine her reaction had thieves broken in to their London home and stabbed her father when he caught them in the act. How awful. Robert Pembrooke had been everything a gentleman should be, if Mac Chapman's account was not overly biased. What a tragic waste of life.

According to the newspaper, officials had wanted to question the valet. Had they suspected him of foul play? Mrs. Hayes had rattled on about "Walter's" fall at Pembrooke Park. Clearly, the report of his death had not reached London quickly, if ever.

Had the valet fled the scene of his crime? But then, why return to Pembrooke Park? Or had he returned to report the news of his master's death, only to somehow fall to his own death?

Again Abigail wondered why Miss Pembrooke—in spite of Mr. Arbeau's denial, Abigail still believed it could only be her—was writing to her, sending her information from the past and warnings

121

for the future. Good heavens. If Clive Pembrooke had not bothered to come knocking in eighteen years, he surely wouldn't do so now out of the blue, during the very first month she happened to live there. That would be too much a coincidence to be believed. Unless . . . Might the house being opened and occupied be the very trigger to raise the sleeping threat from unconcerned slumber at long last?

Where had that thought come from? Abigail shook her head at the fanciful notion. Very unlike her usual pragmatic nature. It was time to organize the larder, or sort her belongings, or . . . something.

Chapter 9

The day of Andrew Morgan's welcome home party arrived, and Abigail found herself looking forward to it more than she had looked forward to anything in a long time. It was to be her first social event with her new neighbors, other than the homey meals she had shared with the Chapmans. She planned to wear a pretty evening gown and ask Polly to help her dress her hair a little more elegantly than the quick, serviceable coil she usually preferred.

Andrew Morgan was an amusing, handsome man and would no doubt be a charming host. But Abigail especially looked forward to spending the evening with William Chapman. And she looked forward to seeing Leah in a different setting as well—dressed formally and the object of Mr. Morgan's attentions, if she didn't miss her guess. She was quite certain Mr. Morgan admired Miss Chapman. How wonderful if the two fell in love and were married. She would like to see Leah Chapman happy, and believed it was her family's fond wish for her as well.

True to her word, Mrs. Morgan had included Charles Foster in her invitation, but Abigail's father had yet to return.

Midmorning she received a note from him, apologizing but saying he had been detained in London even longer than he'd originally expected—called in again by the lawyers and Uncle Vincent in the dreaded bankruptcy proceedings. *Poor Papa* . . . Abigail sighed upon reading the words and the unwritten frustration between them. *And poor Uncle Vincent.*

She sent Duncan over to Hunts Hall with a note to Mrs. Morgan, modifying her earlier response, expressing her father's regrets but reiterating her anticipation of the evening.

William Chapman had told Abigail that he and Leah would stop by in their gig at six and the three of them would drive to Hunts Hall together.

Abigail began getting ready hours early. Polly and Duncan carried up pail after pail of hot water so she could have a real bath in a tub in her room, instead of the sponge or hip baths she usually made do with to avoid causing them extra work. She bathed and washed her hair, Polly coming in to help her rinse it with a reserved jug of clean warm water.

Later the maid helped her cinch long stays over her shift, before helping her into her gown. The dress Abigail had chosen for the evening was not as formal as a ball gown but was one of her finer evening dresses: gauzy white muslin with narrow blue stripes, a scalloped flounced hem, and crossover bodice. Polly curled her hair and pinned the curls high atop her head, with several braids looped like garlands at the back. Abigail missed the family jewels, which would have looked so well with the dress and its V neckline, but she made do with a single string of blue glass beads.

"You look beautiful, miss," Polly breathed.

"Thank you, Polly. If I do, the credit goes to you."

Abigail pulled on long gloves, then tucked a handkerchief into a reticule, stringing the small bag over her wrist. She carried a bright woven cashmere shawl for the ride home, should the evening grow cold, and made her way downstairs five minutes before the appointed time.

It felt strange to wait alone for callers—and to be attending a social event without family present. She hoped her father would not disapprove of her going alone. She didn't think he would and wondered again how soon he would finish his business and be able to join her.

She glanced out the hall windows, and there came the Chapmans' old grey harnessed to their gig. As Morgan's land agent, Mac had the use of a fine bay, leaving the rest of his family to share their old carriage horse. The small open carriage would be snug with the three of them, but Leah had assured Abigail that the entire family regularly traveled in it, though two had to sit on the back gate and Mac rode alongside.

Leaning forward to better view the gig, Abigail frowned. William Chapman sat at the reins, as she'd anticipated, but no one sat beside him. Abigail let the drapery fall as her thoughts raced and her stomach sank. Was Leah ill? Had William come to tell her they would not be going after all?

Duncan crossed the drive with unusual speed to hold the reins as Mr. Chapman hopped nimbly down. Was it her imagination, or did Duncan appear disappointed as well to see only Mr. Chapman in the gig? Abigail had mentioned to him in passing that both were expected, to emphasize the propriety of the arrangements.

Outside the two men exchanged a few words, and then William strode toward the door. She should have waited for one of the servants to open it for her, but she was too anxious to know what had gone amiss. She opened it on his first knock, and he seemed slightly taken aback.

"What's happened?" Abigail asked quickly. "Where is Leah?"

For a moment he stared at her, his gaze roving over her face, her hair, her gown. Slowly he removed his hat. "You look beautiful, Miss Foster."

"Thank you." She ducked her head, allowing herself a moment to relish the rare compliment, then asked again, "Is Leah all right?"

His face twisted. "I'm afraid Leah will not be joining us after all. She claims she feels too ill to go."

"Oh no. What is the matter?"

"My guess is a bad case of nerves and illogical fear. She honestly feels poorly, though whether brought on by anxiety or any real malady, I cannot say for certain. But she begs that you and I go on without her so as not to disappoint Mr. Morgan altogether."

"He will be disappointed by her absence no matter what."

"Yes. And I realize you, um, may not be comfortable going with only me."

Abigail hesitated, aware of Duncan watching them from the drive and of Molly hovering in the hall behind her.

Abigail drew her shoulders back and said in a pleasant, audible voice, "I am so sorry your sister will not be able to join us after all. But it is perfectly proper to ride in an open carriage to attend a party of respectable people." She lowered her voice, struck with another thought. "But I am thinking only of myself. What about you? If you prefer not to attend the dinner with me alone, I will understand."

"Miss Foster, I have been looking forward to this evening all week, and not because of the Morgans or the meal in store for us there. And certainly not to enjoy the company of my sister, dear though she is."

Abigail's cheeks warmed at his implied compliment. His striking blue eyes looked directly into hers, and the silence stretched between them.

She looked away first. "Well, if it won't pose a problem for you . . ."

"It may cause a bit of talk, I can't deny. But I am willing to brave it if you are."

"Then I should still like to go, yes. For Mr. Morgan's sake."

He raised his auburn eyebrows. "Only for Mr. Morgan's sake?"

Again she ducked her head.

"You look even prettier when you blush, Miss Foster."

She refused to meet his playful gaze and instead walked past him. "Shall we go?"

Mr. Chapman easily passed her with his long stride and reached the gig ahead of her, offering his hand. She flicked a glance into his handsome face, laid her white glove in his dark one, and allowed him to hand her up into the carriage. Then he walked around to his side, climbed in with graceful ease, and accepted the reins from Duncan.

Abigail smiled down at the manservant. "Lock up, will you please, Duncan? We are going to dinner at Hunts Hall, and I am not sure how late I shall be."

"Very good, miss."

Mr. Chapman called, "Walk on," and turned the horse through the gate. They crossed the bridge and followed the narrow, tree-lined road leading to Easton, then turned onto the Caldwell Road. The sun hung low in the western horizon, shining golden through the trees. They passed picturesque thatched cottages and well-tended farms divided by stone walls and blooming hedgerows. Birds called and in the distance a dog barked.

"What a lovely evening," Abigail said to break the silence.

She felt his gaze on her profile. "Lovely indeed."

They turned from the road through an iron gate and onto a long curved drive. At its end lay a squat square manor house, not as large as Pembrooke Park but elegant, with shaped hedges and formal gardens flanking its façade.

Ahead of them, a fine black barouche driven by a dignified coachman dropped off its occupant, hidden from their view, and drove around to the rear of the house. *August company,* Abigail thought, reminding herself not to be intimidated. Or at least not to show it.

As the Chapman gig reached the circular drive, a footman in livery and powdered wig exited the house and ceremoniously strode forward, extending a hand to help Abigail down. A groom appeared on the other side to take the horse and carriage to the stable around back.

As they walked to the front door, Mr. Chapman said quietly, "I'm sorry I can't deliver you in a fine barouche."

"Don't be. It doesn't matter to me."

"Nervous?" he asked, offering her his arm.

"Yes," she admitted. "You?"

"Not in the least. I likely would have been, had Leah been here.

Nervous for her. But you, Miss Foster, can handle yourself in any situation, I think."

She raised her brows. "We shall see about that."

William liked the feel of Miss Foster's hand on his arm. Her presence, he thought, would be sweet enough to compensate for the lukewarm reception he anticipated from Mrs. Morgan. Nor did he look forward to feeling like an outsider among the other guests, most of whom were from a higher social sphere. He was used to such snubs from his years at Oxford, but that didn't mean he had learned to enjoy being looked down upon for his humble birth.

Mr. and Mrs. Morgan stood inside the vestibule, receiving guests. Three women stood nearby, talking in low tones to one another.

Mrs. Morgan welcomed him civilly, if coolly. "Ah, Mr. Chapman. Welcome."

At the sound of his name, one of the three women whirled, mouth parted in surprise and, if he was not mistaken, alarm. Did she know he was a clergyman and dread his presence? Assume he would spoil their fun? Some people thought so, he knew.

The woman was handsome and dark haired, perhaps thirty or a little older. Her companions were a matronly looking woman in her forties and a young woman of about twenty—a mother and daughter, perhaps.

William pulled his gaze from the stranger's startled face and said to his hostess, "And this is Miss Foster."

"Yes, we met at church. A pity your father is unable to join us."

"Yes," Miss Foster said. "Thank you for understanding."

Mrs. Morgan turned to the three women. "Ladies, if you will allow me, I shall make informal introductions."

The women turned.

"Mr. Chapman is our curate and was at school with Andrew," Mrs. Morgan began. "And Miss Foster is new to the area. But you know how Andrew is, all goodness. He invited her to join us."

"Very neighborly, I'm sure," the youngest woman said.

Mrs. Morgan gestured first toward the handsome dark-haired

woman. "My late brother's wife, Mrs. Webb. And beside her, my dear old friend, Mrs. Padgett, and her lovely daughter, Miss Padgett, who have come all the way from Winchester to be with us tonight."

"To welcome dear Andrew home, we would have traveled farther yet," Miss Padgett said.

"You are very kind." Mrs. Morgan beamed, then turned to Abigail. "Miss Foster, you are from London, I understand?"

"Yes, born and bred."

Mr. Morgan spoke up. "Miss Foster is living alone for all intents and purposes in Pembrooke Park, abandoned these eighteen years. Quite a singular young woman to attempt it."

"And . . . your family is . . . ?" Miss Padgett let the question dangle.

"My father was here with me until recently, when matters of business necessitated his return to Town. He plans to return any day, and my mother and sister will be joining us at the end of the season."

Miss Padgett and her mother nodded and listened to Miss Foster politely, but William noticed the third woman, Mrs. Morgan's sister-in-law, kept glancing his way. The woman did not wear mourning so was not a recent widow. Did he make her so uncomfortable? He hoped he had not the opposite effect on her. She was too old for him, and he was there with Miss Foster. . . . No, surely he was mistaken. He turned and met her gaze directly.

A challenging glint shone in her grey-blue eyes. "Mr. Chapman, was it?"

"Yes."

"Forgive me for staring. You . . . remind me of someone."

"Have we met before, Mrs. Webb?"

She hesitated, lips parted. "I . . . don't think so." She turned to Miss Foster and held out her hand. "And a pleasure to meet you, Miss Foster. How are you getting on here? Missing London?"

It was a relief when the woman's keen gaze shifted to his companion.

"Actually, I miss London far less than I imagined I would," Miss Foster replied. "Although I miss my family, of course."

Mrs. Webb smiled thinly. "And how do you find living in the formidable Pembrooke Park?"

"Oh, it's quite something. A beautiful old house."

"But surely, after being uninhabited for so long . . . ?"

"It was difficult at first, I own. A great deal of dust and the like. But we've an excellent staff and have slowly put the place to rights."

"I am glad to hear it. No evidence of break-ins or damage?"

"Nothing beyond the usual decay one might expect. Mr. Chapman's father has taken it upon himself to guard the place, to keep out would-be thieves and vandals. Even repaired the roof himself, in his spare time."

"Did he indeed?" Mrs. Webb's thin brows rose, clearly impressed.

Hearing this, Mrs. Morgan said, "Well, he was once the Pembrookes' steward, after all, and old ways die hard."

Mrs. Webb ignored her. "That was excessively good of your father, Mr. Chapman."

Miss Foster glanced at him shyly. "Yes, it was."

She did not, William noticed with relief, recount how Mac had met them at gunpoint.

"Foster . . ." Mrs. Morgan echoed thoughtfully. "Your father wasn't mixed up in that awful bank failure business, I trust?" Her nose wrinkled in distaste.

Miss Foster's lip parted to reply, but she hesitated. "I . . ."

Mrs. Webb interrupted, "No, the names were something else, I recall. Austen, Gray, and Vincent, I believe. I thought of investing in their first bank a few years ago—such charming men and so certain of their success. But in the end, Mr. Webb talked me out of it."

Mrs. Morgan nodded. "Sounds like Nicholas. He had a good head for business and always made excellent decisions."

"Except in his choice of spouse, I think you mean, sister dear?" Mrs. Webb said archly, leaving everyone listening to understand Mrs. Morgan had not approved of her brother's choice of wife.

The attention had been deflected from Miss Foster, but William did not miss her averted gaze and distracted manner. There was something to the bank story, he guessed. He felt grateful to Andrew's aunt for diverting the conversation.

"Has Mr. Webb been gone long?" William asked kindly. He did not recall hearing anything about the man's death, which was understandable as the Webbs did not live in the area.

"Two years," she replied. "Hence you see me out of my widow's weeds. Never cared for black."

"Nor I," William said wryly, since clergymen stereotypically wore black, though he preferred not to.

Humor sparked in the woman's eyes, and she chuckled appreciatively.

"I don't see anything funny." Mrs. Morgan sniffed.

Mrs. Webb said, "Olive, do be a dear and allow me to sit by Mr. Chapman and Miss Foster. I think I shall enjoy their company."

"But . . . you are one of our honored guests, sister. I planned for you to sit on Mr. Morgan's right."

"Oh, I can talk to him tomorrow. Humor me."

Mrs. Morgan sighed. "Very well."

Andrew, who had been cornered by several men clustered around the decanters, broke away from the group and strode over beaming. "Will, good to see you. And Miss Foster, thank you for coming." He looked around. "But where is Miss Chapman?"

William made her apologies.

Andrew's smile fell. "I am very sorry to hear it. I had been looking forward to seeing her again. Er, seeing all of you, of course. You will tell her she was missed, won't you, ol' boy?"

"I shall."

"It's no use trying to sit by either Mr. Chapman or Miss Foster," Mrs. Webb teased. "For I have claimed them as my dinner companions."

Andrew smiled at the woman. "I knew you were an excellent judge of character, Aunt Webb."

"Yes, of course. Do tell Miss Chapman we hope she feels better," Mrs. Morgan interjected. Then she abruptly turned to Miss Foster and asked, "And how old is *your* sister, Miss Foster?"

"Nineteen."

"Ah yes, the perfect age to enjoy the season. Miss Padgett had a very successful season last year. Did you not, my dear? Yes, you see, Miss Padgett is not yet twenty. So young and full of life. I was married at eighteen, you know. It is so much better when the bride is young. Don't you agree, sister?"

Mrs. Webb shrugged. "I was very young when I married Nicholas, but we were not blessed with children even so."

"I already had three children by the time I was Miss Foster's age. What about you, Mrs. Padgett?"

Mrs. Padgett demurred, blushing and protesting that her hostess would not trick her into owning her age.

Meanwhile Mrs. Webb sidled closer to William and whispered, "What is my sister-in-law going on about? Does Andrew admire an older woman I don't know of?"

William sighed. "Andrew did invite my sister to come tonight, but that doesn't necessarily indicate a special regard."

"Ah. And how old is your sister?"

"Eight and twenty."

One dark brow rose. "So that is what we are calling *old* these days, is it? Then I am quite ancient, for I am even older than that. No doubt your sister was wise to stay home and avoid all this. Though I don't like to think of anyone cowering before my sister-in-law. Not if Andrew truly admires her."

"Again, I do not presume to guess where his affections lie."

"Yes, yes, Mr. Chapman." She patted his arm. "You are all discretion, never fear."

The butler announced that dinner was served, and people lined up according to precedence, with Mrs. Webb breaking social ranks to wait to enter the dining room with her chosen companions. Andrew, William saw, was nudged to lead in Miss Padgett. William offered an arm to Mrs. Webb, who accepted with a conspiratorial wink. Then he offered his other arm to Miss Foster.

The guests made their way into the dining room lit with candelabras and decorated with centerpieces of fruits and flowers. Footmen in livery and powdered wigs stood at attention, waiting to lay second, third, and fourth courses to a table already crowded with silver serving dishes, domed platters, and a massive soup tureen.

William held a chair for Mrs. Webb, but a footman reached Miss Foster's chair before he could do so. They sat down, and William counted himself fortunate to be seated between two lovely, intelligent women who initiated meaningful conversation and, more importantly, appreciated his sense of humor.

Abigail enjoyed Mr. Chapman's and Mrs. Webb's company as much as she enjoyed the meal: a first course of spring soup and crimped salmon, followed by duck with orange sauce and peas, braised tongue, beetroot and cucumber salad, and strawberry tartlets. Dishes were passed and savored for more than an hour. Around her, Abigail heard snatches of other conversations in progress, most of it vague pleasantries—the weather, betrothals from earlier in the season, upcoming shoots, races, and house parties.

Mrs. Morgan, a third of the way down the table, leaned forward suddenly and addressed her. "And why are you not in London, enjoying the season with your sister, Miss Foster?"

Mr. Chapman, she noticed, glanced over and watched her carefully, awaiting her response.

She said easily, "I have had my season. Two, actually. It is Louisa's turn."

"Did you enjoy your seasons?"

She shrugged. "Well enough, I suppose."

"But no offers of marriage came of it?"

"Um . . ." Abigail paused awkwardly. "Evidently not."

"Mamma!" Andrew Morgan gently chided. "Don't interrogate our guests. Besides, you are all supposed to be fawning over me and asking about my time abroad and all my adventures."

"Had you any adventures?" Mrs. Webb asked gamely.

"Give me another glass of this excellent claret and I shall tell you tales to make your ears burn."

"Hear, hear," Mrs. Webb said, lifting her glass.

"Andrew . . ." his mother warned.

"Oh, let the boy talk, my dear," Mr. Morgan senior urged. "It is why we are here after all."

And Andrew happily obliged.

Abigail silently thanked the man for coming to her rescue.

Later, as dinner was winding down and conversation quieted to small duets and trios around the long table, Abigail finally began to relax.

Mrs. Webb turned to William and asked, "I hope you don't think I am interrogating *you*, Mr. Chapman. But I would like to hear about your family. They all . . . live nearby . . . ?"

"Yes. My mother and father live not far from Pembrooke Park. Father is Mr. Morgan's land agent now, so that may explain why your sister-in-law takes exception to her son's choice of guests."

"Ah," she murmured noncommittally.

"I have two sisters, Leah and Kitty," William continued. "And a brother, Jacob."

"And, are they all ginger haired like you?"

"Ginger? I wouldn't go that far . . ."

He sounded almost affronted, Abigail thought, biting back a grin.

"My hair isn't as red as my father's, or my brother's for that matter," he explained. "And the girls have light brown hair, like our mother."

"I see. And they are all in good health?"

"Yes. Thank God."

"I am glad to hear it."

"And your family, Mrs. Webb?" Abigail asked. "Have you brothers or sisters?"

"I always wanted a sister," she said. "Here both of you have sisters, but I never did."

"I have one to spare if you'd like," William teased.

She smiled. "I doubt your parents would approve of that."

"Where do you live, Mrs. Webb?" Abigail added, "If you don't mind my asking. Not too far from your relatives here, I hope?"

"I have lived in several places, what with Mr. Webb being with the East India Company for many years. So no, not close to Easton, I'm afraid. In fact, I have not been here in years."

"How good of you to come for Andrew's homecoming, then."

"I was happy to come. He is a dear boy, and my husband was quite fond of him."

She looked closely at Abigail. "I do hope things have been . . . peaceful . . . since you've moved in to Pembrooke Park? No trouble?"

"Oh yes. For the most part. Very peaceful."

"For the most part? What does that mean, I wonder?"

"Oh, you know how old houses are. They creak and groan and make all sorts of odd noises. I understand the village children claim the place is haunted. But I've yet to see any evidence of that."

"I am relieved to hear it. Nothing . . . unsettling . . . since you've been there? No one where they ought not be?"

Abigail thought of the footsteps in the dust, the mislaid candle lamp, and the figure in the cloak. "I have seen no ghosts, I assure you, Mrs. Webb. And all I've heard is an old house complaining of its years and neglect, nothing more." To herself she added, *I hope.*

Candlelight glinted in Mrs. Webb's blue-grey eyes. "It is not the ghosts you need worry about, Miss Foster, but human beings that are very much alive."

Later, Abigail and Mr. Chapman rode home in the gig. Abigail was very aware of being alone with a man—a man she found increasingly attractive. Though she wondered if she would have found him quite so attractive had Gilbert not disappointed her.

It was late, but the moon shone brightly, and she could see Mr. Chapman's profile quite clearly. His straight nose, his firm, fair cheek. The waves of auburn hair falling over his ear, and his long, sculpted side-whiskers.

Perhaps sensing her scrutiny, he glanced over at her. "Did you enjoy yourself?" he asked.

"I did. And you?"

"Yes. More than I dared hope."

She wasn't certain what he meant but wished he would keep his eyes on the road so she could study him unobserved.

He turned the horse back toward Easton. As they passed through the sleepy hamlet, he slowed the horse to a walking pace. Candles flickered in the public house and a few other windows, but otherwise the street was quiet, shops closed, people abed for the night.

Leaving the hamlet, he clicked the horse to a trot, but the wheels hit a deep rut. The gig lurched and she swayed, knocking into his arm. Instinctively, he slid the reins into one hand and threw his other around her shoulders to steady her. "All right?"

She swallowed, self-conscious in his embrace. Self-conscious about how much she liked the warm security of his arm around her, her side pressed firmly to his. "Ye-yes. Fine."

He removed his arm and she shivered, whether from his nearness or the night air, she wasn't certain.

"You're cold," he observed. He halted the horse right there on the road and tied off the reins. He dug under the seat and pulled forth a folded wool blanket.

"I'm fine, really," she insisted. "I have my shawl."

"You're not fine. You're shivering. You females and your thin muslins. It's a wonder you don't all freeze to death."

He draped the blanket around her and settled it on her shoulders, his hands lingering. "Better?"

"Yes, except now I feel guilty that you are freezing."

"Then sit close to me and I shan't notice anything else."

Her gaze flew to his—saw his crooked grin, the playful sparkle in his eye. Sitting close as they were, their faces were very near. His breath was warm and smelled of cinnamon. Or perhaps that was his cologne. Whatever it was, it was spicy and masculine and made her want to lean nearer yet.

The horse stamped his hoof impatiently, no doubt eager to return to his stall and feed bucket.

She did not purposely move closer to him, but as the rock and sway of the carriage brought them nearer together, their shoulders brushing and occasionally their knees, she did not pull away, nor attempt to keep a proper distance between them. She did not want him to freeze, after all, she told herself, knowing all the while it was schoolgirl logic Louisa might have used to justify flirting with a man, but at the moment, not caring. It was dark, and they were alone, and dash it, it was cold. She liked the man, and she trusted him enough to know he would not take advantage of any of those factors. At least, not inappropriate advantage.

When they reached Pembrooke Park, Mr. Chapman tied off the reins and alighted from the gig. Coming around, he reached up, but instead of offering one hand to her, he lifted both. She hesitated, meeting his gaze with brows raised in question.

In a low voice, he said, "May I?"

His gloved hands hovered near her waist. In reality, she could have managed the step down with only a hand to assist her, but she pressed her lips together and silently nodded.

He grasped her waist and gently lifted, lowering her easily to the ground. For a moment longer, his hands remained, and he murmured, "You do have a tiny waist."

His hands felt large, strong, and sure. She swallowed nervously. Uncomfortable standing there so close to him, yet in no hurry to step away.

Behind him, the front door opened, and he released her. Glancing over, she saw Duncan standing in the doorway, candle lamp in hand.

With a rueful smile, Mr. Chapman offered his arm. Abigail placed her gloved hand on his sleeve and he tucked it into the crook of his elbow. Together they walked to the house.

"You two were out late," Duncan observed, his eyes narrowed. In suspicion, or disapproval?

"The dinner party was quite a long affair," Mr. Chapman said, coming to her defense.

Abigail added, "I didn't realize we would be back quite so late. Thank you for waiting up."

"I am surprised a clergyman thinks it wise to be out so late.

And without a chaperone yet. I seem to recall someone giving me a setdown for keeping a lady out after dark once upon a time."

Insolent man, Abigail thought, torn between offense and curiosity. *Who did he mean?*

"That situation was entirely different, as you will recall," Mr. Chapman replied. "The lady in question was out without her parents' consent."

Duncan rebutted, "As is Miss Foster, I believe."

Mr. Chapman met the man's challenging glare. "Your concern for your mistress is touching, Duncan. Take care your respect equals that concern."

Aware of the mounting tension between the men, visible in their clenched jaws and taut postures, Abigail extracted herself from Mr. Chapman's arm and said gently, "It is late, and I had better go in. Thank you again for the lovely evening, Mr. Chapman. And do give your sister my best."

Chapter 10

In the morning, Abigail lay snug in bed for a time, thinking back to the dinner party the night before, and the carriage ride home with Mr. Chapman. *Mr. William Chapman . . .* She liked his name.

She had *not* liked Duncan's reception when they'd arrived home. His sneering disapproval had spoiled an otherwise lovely evening. Had she done wrong, in spending so much time alone in the curate's company? She hoped not.

She recalled a few other moments that had been less than idyllic as well. Mrs. Morgan asking her in front of all of those people if her seasons had resulted in any offers of marriage. And later, Mrs. Webb's comment, *"It is not the ghosts you need worry about, but human beings that are very much alive."* Abigail wondered if she referred to treasure hunters in general or some specific human.

She rose, wrapped her shawl around herself, and wandered over to her mother's bedchamber. She stood at the window, looking toward the church. The grey day seemed as ambivalent as she—not sunny, but not raining. A fine mist hung in the air like a gauzy grey curtain. The window glass was foggy, and what lay beyond was as difficult to see as her future.

She tried to hold on to the happiness she had felt in the carriage the night before, but the quiet, lonely house drew it from her—her family so far away, Gilbert even farther . . .

Something caught her eye. A figure beyond the low churchyard wall. Abigail wiped a circle in the foggy glass and peered closer. Was it Eliza Smith again? Whoever it was wore a dark blue cape and hat with a heavy veil over her face. Her head bowed.

Perhaps it wasn't Eliza. Perhaps it was a widow come to visit her recently deceased husband. Or a mother grieving her child. She would ask Mr. Chapman if a family in the parish had suffered a recent loss.

Whatever the case, the sight of the lone figure in the misty grey churchyard moved Abigail with pity.

Several days later, two letters arrived for Abigail—the first was from her mother.

Dear Abigail,

 Your father is sorry the bankruptcy business has kept him in London for so long—far longer than he anticipated. We trust you are managing fine on your own, as usual. But do let us know if you are unhappy or need anything. I must say, it is a balm having your father here with us at this time. Things are not progressing quite as well as when last I wrote, and his company is a comfort.

 Unfortunately, the details of the bank incident have become public and have begun to overshadow Louisa's season—for otherwise I have no doubt she would be an absolute triumph. As it is, she has been overlooked by a few highly placed parties who would no doubt be clamoring for her attention if not for the banking scandal. A few gentlemen have continued to call in spite of these circumstances, which are of course quite beyond poor Louisa's control. Their par-

ents, however, do not share their enthusiasm. Regardless of these few setbacks and the occasional cut direct or spiteful comment, Louisa seems blithely and blessedly unaware and remains in good spirits.

Gilbert Scott continues to impress wherever he goes. It is a comfort to know that his regard has not been affected by the news of our change in circumstances.

Abigail's heart plummeted, thoughts of William Chapman fading. Gilbert . . . how she missed him. And would go on missing him apparently. She sighed and set the letter aside.

Hoping for something diverting, she opened the second letter, another old page torn from a journal.

The secret room. Apparently its location has been lost over generations and renovations. Does it even still exist? Did it ever? My father certainly thinks so. Why his sudden determination to find it now, when he lived in this very house as a boy? Has he some reason to believe something valuable has recently been hidden there?

The servants swear ignorance. The steward scoffs at the idea of hidden treasure. But that does not dissuade my father. He searches. He taps. He pokes. He pulls books from floor-to-ceiling bookcases. He looks behind portraits and up flues. He swears and curses and keeps looking. Occasionally in his frustration, he drinks himself into a stupor, and for a few days or a week he gives it up. But then another bill comes, or he sees a blood horse he wishes to buy, and he begins his frantic searching all over again.

A few days ago, he unearthed stacks of house plans and pored over them for hours. He hid them from the servants and even my brothers—not wanting to give anyone ideas. Not trusting anyone.

But he didn't hide them from me. I don't think he believes a mere girl capable of finding anything he cannot.

He doesn't see me as a threat. In fact, I think he barely sees me at all.

So I waited until he left the house and looked at those drawings myself. I admit I can make no sense of them. Cannot decipher which solid or dashed lines mean original vs. new walls vs. doors or windows. And in truth, I have no idea which of the plans has even been carried out. For the drawers of the library map table hold more house plans than actual maps, it seems to me.

But one thing did catch my eye. A detail in those plans that does not jibe with something I have seen in the house itself. Or am I not thinking of the actual house at all, but rather its scale model? I think I will compare the dolls' house to the plans tomorrow. . . .

Abigail felt a thrill of anticipation skitter up the back of her neck. Perhaps she could see something in the house plans the writer had missed. It might be worth a try. At any rate, she would certainly find the search interesting.

She went down to the library, folded back the window shutters, and stepped to the large map desk near the center of the room. She pulled out the deep, shallow drawers in order, starting at the top left and working her way down. There were old maps of the world, the West Indies, Europe, England, London, Berkshire, the parish, and the estate grounds.

Finally she found a sheaf of old drawings—building plans—yellowed with age. Were they the latest? Had the plans been implemented, or had they been passed over in favor of some other architect's vision? She spread them atop the map table and flipped through them quickly, looking for dates. She found an old one marked with roman numerals from the 1600s. It showed a central manorial hall with side wings for stabling, a gate, and a porter's lodge, which no longer existed. In fact someone had written *Destroyed* over it. By fire, most likely.

She flipped through several more pages until she found a plan that looked more recent. She saw no date, but the block handwriting seemed more modern and the ink less faded than the others. In this plan, a new addition had been built in the rear courtyard of the house, adding a drawing room below and a bedchamber above. That plan or at least one very like it had been carried out. The bedchamber above the drawing room was the newer one she planned to give Louisa. There were a few other details she was less sure of. If only Gilbert were there to help her understand everything she was looking at.

She retrieved a notebook and drawing pencil, donned bonnet, spencer, and gloves, and went outside on the temperate May afternoon. She slowly walked along the front of the house, surveying its exterior, noting the oriel windows, the gabled roof, and chimney stacks. She started toward the side of the house but paused at the sound of trotting horse hooves.

She turned and watched as a well-dressed gentleman on a dappled grey horse rode across the bridge. Andrew Morgan. He raised a hand in greeting and nudged his horse across the drive in her direction.

"Hello, Miss Foster."

"Mr. Morgan. Nice to see you again."

"I am out today issuing more invitations. Do you think I shall have better luck this time?"

With Leah Chapman, she guessed he meant. "I don't know, but one can always hope."

"Precisely. That is exactly what I am doing. How is Miss Chapman, by the way? Have you seen her?"

"I have. And she seems quite . . . recovered."

"Excellent. I am just on my way over to pay a call. In the flush of success from her little dinner party, Mother has decided to outdo herself by hosting a masquerade ball at Hunts Hall, just as we used to do back home. You are invited, of course. I do hope you will join us."

"Thank you. When is it to be?"

"The tenth of June. She is planning to invite friends from Town as well." Parroting his mother, he said with exaggerated hauteur, "'It is to be Easton's social event of the year.'"

"Of the decade, by the sound of it," Abigail amended.

"I shall tell her you said so. It will give her something to crow about to all her friends."

Abigail grinned.

"Good day, Miss Foster." Mr. Morgan tipped his hat.

"Good day, Mr. Morgan."

Before Abigail could continue her study of the exterior, a carriage and horses rumbled over the bridge. *Goodness.* Today was her day for receiving callers, apparently. She waited near the door while the yellow post chaise crunched across the drive and halted in front of the house.

A groom hopped down, opened the door, and let down the step. Her father alighted—he had returned at long last! Abigail felt unaccustomed tears prick her eyes. She had not realized how lonely she had been until that moment. She blinked the tears away, put on a smile, and walked forward to greet him.

"Hello, Papa. Welcome back."

She hesitated, not sure she should expect an embrace considering the rift between them, especially when he had spent the last several weeks dealing with tedious bankruptcy proceedings she might have prevented.

He gave her a weary smile and kissed her cheek. "Abigail. Good to see you looking so well. I have been worried about you, here all alone."

Her heart squeezed. "I am well, Papa, as you see."

"You weren't too lonely without us?"

"I . . . no, I managed just fine. Though I am of course glad you're here now."

"Well. Good. Good."

"Come inside, Papa. I shall call for tea."

"I confess I could drink a whole pot and eat half a loaf after that journey."

"That I can manage as well." She took his arm, and together

they walked inside, Pembrooke Park immediately feeling more like home.

Her study of the house and building plans would wait.

William sat sipping tea with his mother and sister in their cottage when Andrew Morgan stopped by to invite him and Leah to a ball. His sister received his friend's invitation with cool reserve, saying only that she would think about it. William had not pressed her at the time, not wishing to embarrass her in front of his friend. Though he didn't miss their mother's look of concern.

Once Andrew left, Kate Chapman said gently, "You might have at least thanked Mr. Morgan for the invitation."

"But I don't wish to go," Leah said.

Their mother's face clouded. "My dear, you've had so little entertainment in your life, enjoyed such limited society."

"By design," Leah said, then added quickly, "and by preference."

"Whose preference?" William asked. "Yours or Papa's?"

"William . . ." His mother frowned.

"I mean no disrespect, Mamma," he said. "But Leah is not a little girl any longer. I don't know why Papa insists on sheltering her so."

His father entered the house at that moment, pulling off his hat. He paused in the doorway, looking from one guilty face to the next. "What's all this, then?"

"Mac," his mother began, choosing each word carefully, "Mr. Morgan called to invite Leah . . . and William . . . to attend a ball at Hunts Hall. Isn't that nice? Wouldn't it be nice for our Leah, who's never had the opportunity to attend anything so grand?"

"I don't want to go, Papa," Leah said quickly. "It's all right."

"But, Leah," his mother insisted, "you ought to go to a ball. Every girl should, at least once in her life."

His father dropped his hat on the sideboard. "She doesn't want to go, Kate. Why push her?"

"*Why* don't you want to go, Leah?" William asked. "What are you afraid of?"

His sister did not deny the charge. She ducked her head, twisting her hands before her.

"Leave your sister alone, Will. You don't understand—that's all."

"Nor have I ever understood why you are so overprotective."

His father's eyes flashed. "That's right. You don't understand. So keep out of it."

"Mac . . ." Kate breathed.

William, too, was taken aback by his father's sharp reprimand. He prayed for wisdom, took a deep breath, and tried again. "The Morgans are a perfectly respectable family."

"That may be," his father allowed, "but we don't have any idea who else might be attending this *soiree* of theirs." He spit out the word as if it were burnt gristle.

"I am sure they are inviting other respectable people. What are you worried about?"

"It's all right," Leah repeated. "I haven't a proper gown anyway, and would no doubt make a fool of myself."

"But you love to dance, Leah," William insisted. "And so rarely have opportunity, beyond our little family Christmas parties. You learnt at school, I remember. And forced me to master every dance you knew."

"That was a long time ago."

"Perhaps Miss Foster might give us a refresher course. She no doubt knows the newer dances. And I'm sure Andrew Morgan would be happy to assist." He attempted a teasing grin, but Leah did not return it.

He added, "And if we embarrass ourselves by turning left when we are supposed to turn right, we shall have our masks on, remember, so no one shall know who we are."

"Masks?" their father asked.

"Yes, it's to be a masquerade ball."

"Is it?" Their father considered, chewing his lip. "And you would be there with her all the while?"

"I would," William assured him. "I would make certain no man made inappropriate advances to Leah, if that is what you are worried about."

Leah reddened, protesting, "I hardly think we need worry about that—at my age."

Their father looked at Leah. "Perhaps they are right, my dear. Perhaps it is time you enjoyed yourself. Started living."

She threw up her hands. "And what do you call what I've been doing?"

"Waiting." He flicked a look at William and said no more.

Leah sighed and excused herself, saying she would consider what her family had said.

After they taught Sunday school the following Sabbath, Abigail led the children in two hymns, then helped Leah pick up supplies and tidy the church.

Adding another slate to the stack in her arms, Abigail asked quietly, "So, are you going to the masquerade ball?"

"I don't know. I told my family I would think about it. But I am not familiar with the new dances and haven't a proper costume, so . . ." She allowed her words to trail off on a shrug.

"The invitation simply read, 'Masks required.' So I think we may wear traditional ball gowns and masks. You are welcome to one of my gowns. And I would be happy to teach you the popular dances, though I'm no dancing master."

"William suggested you might be willing to do so. But I couldn't ask that of you."

"You are not asking; I am offering. And I have several ball gowns. Not this year's style, but you might find one to suit you. We are not so different in size. If not, I shan't be offended."

"I am sure they're lovely, but—"

"Please. Come over and at least look. All right?"

"Go to Pembrooke Park . . . ?"

"It isn't haunted, I promise. And my father is back, so we shan't be alone in the house. Or I could bring a few gowns over to your house, if you prefer."

"No, it isn't right for me to ask that of you." Leah lifted her chin. "I shall come." She bit her lip. "May I bring someone from my family along?"

"Of course. Bring Kitty. I've been meaning to ask her over again in any case."

"Very well. I shall."

***

They had agreed to a time for the following afternoon. When the hour neared, Abigail began listening for the door, and when she heard the bell, hurried eagerly from her room. Descending the stairs, she glanced down into the hall and saw Duncan opening the door to their visitors, the Miss Chapmans. Even from that distance, Abigail could see his posture tense.

For a moment, he stood there not saying a word. Not ushering them inside.

Leah, she noticed, dipped her head and murmured an awkward hello.

Kitty showed no such reticence. "We're here to see Miss Foster," she announced. "We've been invited."

Abigail crossed the hall. "That's right. You are very welcome. I've been expecting you."

At this, Duncan turned stiffly and stalked away. She watched him go, then turned a questioning look toward Leah, but she merely shrugged with an apologetic little smile.

One of these days, she would ask about Duncan's history with the Chapmans. But not today, when Leah had finally agreed to her first visit.

"Come in, come in," Abigail urged.

Kitty beamed and walked in eagerly, but Leah hovered on the threshold, glancing warily around the hall and up to its soaring ceiling. Mr. Foster came out of the library for a moment to greet their guests before retreating back to his books and newspapers once more.

Abigail asked Miss Chapman, "Do you want to tour the house first, or proceed directly to the gowns?"

Leah's gaze strayed from one formal portrait to the next. "So much to see . . ."

"Have you been in the house before?" Abigail asked.

"Years ago. With my father."

"Ah. Back when he worked here."

She nodded vaguely. "How strange to walk through that front door. After all these years. . . ."

"I can imagine," Abigail agreed.

Kitty grabbed her sister's arm. "Come on, Leah. Let's go upstairs."

Leah resisted the younger girl's tug, her wide-eyed gaze following the stairway up to the first landing.

Abigail wondered why she was so nervous. Was it more than the rumors? Did she have some bad experience with one of the former occupants? Had one of the Pembrooke brothers she'd heard about been cruel to the neighbor girl—the steward's daughter?

Giving up, Leah allowed her sister to pull her toward the stairs. Leah looked ruefully over her shoulder at Abigail. "Sorry. Perhaps I ought to have come alone."

"That's all right. I can guess where she's headed."

They ascended the stairs, Leah's head swiveling back and forth, taking in the framed portraits, tapestries, and intricately carved panels. Abigail followed, oddly proud of the house and its ability to awe, though she was only a tenant.

At the top of the stairs, Leah paused before a glass display table filled with framed miniature portraits and silhouettes, but again Kitty tugged her along. Abigail knew the girl's goal—the dolls' house.

As they approached her bedchamber, Leah hesitated again, staring at the door.

"Come on, Leah. I want you to see the dolls' house," Kitty insisted.

"It's all right," Abigail assured Leah.

Leah formed an unconvincing smile and allowed Kitty to lead her into the room, Abigail trailing behind.

Kitty went at once to the dolls' house on its stand and knelt before it. Leah followed more slowly, turning in a slow circle to take in the canopied bed, the window seat, the wardrobe. She reached out a hand and touched the bed-curtains. Then the smooth oak surface of the dressing table.

"It's lovely, isn't it?" Abigail asked gently.

"Yes, it is," Leah breathed. "You have a charming room."

"It isn't mine," Abigail said with a shrug. "But I am glad I have the use of it for a while."

"So am I."

Leah gave her a genuine smile, and Abigail's heart warmed. Maybe they'd become good friends yet.

"Come and see," Kitty urged, and Leah went over to stand at her sister's shoulder. "Isn't it wonderful?"

"It is indeed."

"Have you ever seen anything like it?"

"Not in ages, no."

Abigail wondered if Leah had ever played with the daughter of the house. They'd been neighbors, after all.

Abigail turned to open the trunk she'd asked Duncan to bring in earlier. But for several minutes, Leah remained where she was, her gaze fastened on her little sister so enthralled with the dolls' house.

Abigail returned to Leah's side, watching as Kitty moved a small doll up the stairs and laid her on a canopied bed. Abigail glanced at Leah's profile, expecting to see an indulgent smile there. Instead, she was surprised to see tears in the woman's eyes.

Leah must have sensed her gaze. She glanced over and self-consciously wiped at her eyes. "I'm fine. It's just . . . good to see her so happy."

Abigail awkwardly reached out and squeezed Leah's hand. "She is more than welcome to come here and play any time she likes."

Leah blinked away the tears, then looked at Abigail with a distracted smile. "You are very kind. She would enjoy that, obviously."

"Come, let's look at the gowns. I was never a diamond of the first water, I'm afraid. I hope you aren't disappointed."

"I'm sure I won't be."

Abigail removed a protective layer of tissue and began lifting gowns from the trunk and laying them on her bed. She smoothed her hand over an elegant off-white muslin with an embroidered bodice and sheer lace over-sleeves. Its full skirt had a slightly shorter hem to allow for freedom of movement in dancing.

"I was thinking this one might look well with your coloring. But you are welcome to any that suit your fancy."

"It's lovely," Leah breathed.

"Would you like to try it on? See how it fits you? We have time to make a few alterations if needed."

A girlish smile dimpled Leah's cheeks. "Very well. If you'll help me."

Abigail happily did so, unfastening the back of Leah's day dress and then helping her on with the ball gown and lacing up the back.

Leah looked down at her neckline, pressing a self-conscious hand to her décolletage. "It's a little low, isn't it? I feel as though all is on display."

"Not at all. It's the fashion for evening wear. Though we could always tuck a little lace, if you prefer."

Abigail turned Leah toward the long cheval looking glass in the corner. "It's very becoming on you."

Leah looked at herself, unable to suppress the smile that sprung to her face.

"You're right—the dress is beautiful."

"*You're* beautiful, Leah," Kitty said in breathless awe, her attention lured away from the dolls' house at last. "You look like a duchess."

"I feel like one in this," she allowed, holding out the skirt and swaying side to side.

Abigail smiled. "Then you'll wear it?"

"But it's yours."

"I've had my joy of it. It is your turn. I hope you don't mind that I've worn it before you."

"Not at all. I haven't a mask, but I am sure I can fashion one. . . ."

Abigail dug once more in the trunk. "I have several from masquerades I attended in past seasons." She held up three. "If you'd like to wear one of them."

Leah selected the largest of them. "Perfect. Thank you. But what shall you wear?"

"I think this one." She held up a small oriental mask ornamented with glass beads. "And this dress."

Abigail set aside the mask and lifted a ball gown of white-on-white striped muslin with a low square neckline, a high belt of green, and matching green ribbon trim on its short, puffed sleeves. "What do you think?"

"It's lovely. When did you last wear it?"

Abigail thought. "At the Albrights' May ball." She had danced with Gilbert that night, she recalled, with a wistful little sigh. "And here I thought my dancing days were over."

"Yours, Miss Foster? Then what about mine? I am several years older than you are."

Abigail cocked her head to the side and regarded her new friend. "Oh, I think your dancing days are just beginning."

Later, as they left Abigail's room, gown folded over Leah's arm, Kitty pointed across the gallery. "We think that was Mr. Pembrooke's room." She gestured to the right. "And that was his wife's."

Leah's eyes lingered on the closed doorways. She looked over at Abigail. "Would you mind terribly if I peeked in?"

"Not at all. Go ahead."

Abigail followed as the Miss Chapmans crossed the gallery. Leah slowly opened the door and entered the mistress's bedroom—the room they assumed had been occupied by Mrs. Pembrooke—and the Mrs. Pembrooke before that.

Hands behind her back, Abigail stepped inside and glanced

around the room once more. "My mother shall have this room, when she arrives."

"Yes," Leah said quietly. "It is perfect for the lady of the house."

Leah ran a hand over the original bedclothes, now aired and cleaned. Then she touched the recently repaired lace cover on the dressing table. She fingered the vanity set—perfume bottles, hand mirror, and hairbrushes, murmuring, "I cannot believe all of this is still here. . . ."

"I know. I can't believe they took so little with them when they left."

Leah turned, her gaze arrested by the portrait over the mantelpiece. The handsome gentleman in formal attire.

"Your brother believes that is Robert Pembrooke," Abigail said. "I gather he has seen another portrait of the man. Though we haven't asked your father to confirm that."

Leah nodded. "William is right."

"You met him?" Abigail asked.

"I did, yes. Though it was a long time ago."

"The other portrait is missing," Kitty said.

Leah dragged her eyes from the image to look at her sister. "Hm?"

"The portrait of the missus, to match this one. Come and see . . ."

Leah shook her head. "No, Kitty. That's Mr. Foster's room now."

"Oh, he won't mind," Abigail assured her.

Kitty led the way along the galley and into the master bedroom. She pushed open the door and stepped inside, gesturing with a sweep of her arm. "See?"

Leah looked around at the masculine bedclothes, the heavy mahogany furniture, the desk and leather-padded chair near the window. She walked slowly over, ran her fingers over the blotter on the desk, and rested her hand on the arm of the chair. Finally, she turned, glancing up with interest over the mantelpiece.

"You can tell that was hung later," Kitty insisted. "It should be a larger portrait, like the one in the other bedchamber. And I shall never believe that is Robert Pembrooke's wife."

"No," Leah agreed. "I suppose it's only natural that the new family wanted to hang their own portraits. In fact, I am rather surprised the portrait of Robert Pembrooke still hangs in the lady's bedchamber."

"I wonder where they put the one of Robert's wife," Abigail mused.

"Are you simply guessing there was such a portrait, or has someone said so?" Leah asked.

Abigail shrugged, not wanting to mention the letter. "Guessing, I suppose."

"It's a mystery," Kitty pronounced.

Leah slowly shook her head. "Not so mysterious, Kitty, surely. Someone new moves in and doesn't want someone else's wife or ancestor staring down at them in their beds? Doesn't sound like a mystery to me."

Kitty flicked a hand toward the portrait. "Who'd want that old biddy staring down at them instead?"

"Kitty . . ." Leah gently admonished. "That isn't kind."

"Mac said she might have been Robert Pembrooke's old nurse," Abigail commented. "Do you recognize her?"

Leah shook her head. "I have never seen her, that I recall."

Abigail considered the portrait. "You have to admit she is a stern-looking woman of considerable years," she said diplomatically. "And all that black crepe . . ."

"And those eyes . . ." Kitty shuddered.

"All right, you two—that's enough," Leah said. "You shall give yourself nightmares." Leah gave one last glance at the portrait, and admitted, "And I might not be far behind."

The gowns for the masked ball settled upon, Abigail's thoughts moved next to the dancing. She spoke to William Chapman about the brush-up class he had suggested, and he in turn paid a call on Andrew Morgan, who eagerly agreed to join them. The dance practice was arranged for Saturday. Mrs. Chapman offered to accompany them on the Pembrooke Park pianoforte. Abigail invited her father to join them, but he declined.

At the appointed hour, Abigail and Leah entered the salon together.

Inside, Mr. Chapman and Mr. Morgan rose as one. Mr. Chapman watched his sister's face carefully, Abigail noticed, while Mr. Morgan bowed, looking confident and eager.

"Shall we begin?" Abigail suggested. "As there are only four of us, perhaps the Foursome Reel?"

Mrs. Chapman, already seated at the pianoforte, struck a few experimental notes. The old instrument was out of tune but would suffice.

The gentlemen stepped toward the center of the room, while Leah hovered near her mother.

Abigail and Mr. Morgan demonstrated the opening steps, while the Chapmans watched. Then, so that each couple had the benefit of an experienced partner, Abigail suggested Mr. Morgan dance with Miss Chapman, while she danced with Leah's brother.

Leah reluctantly crossed the room to join them. Together, they walked through the dance the first time, then again up to tempo. Mr. Morgan, Abigail saw, gently whispered or gestured to Leah, or turned her in the right direction when she needed a reminder. Soon both William and Leah had mastered the steps and patterns.

Abigail realized this "class" was a good reminder for her as well, as she had not danced in nearly a year. "All right, Mrs. Chapman, I think we're ready for music."

Mrs. Chapman nodded, and Abigail said to the others, "I will call out the steps the first time through to remind you. Watch Mr. Morgan if you forget what to do."

Mrs. Chapman launched into the jaunty introductory bars. Then Abigail said, "Ready, and . . . set to your partner."

Leah and Mr. Morgan began the swishing side-to-side step, which Leah performed with lithe grace, looking more like a young debutante than a woman nearing thirty. Andrew Morgan danced with effortless skill, his eyes lingering on her appreciatively.

Leah glanced up and, finding Mr. Morgan looking at her so closely, ducked her head. But not before Abigail saw the blushing smile on her pretty face.

Would a man like Andrew Morgan—eldest son and heir of Hunts Hall—take a respectable interest in a steward's daughter? Abigail hoped so. She prayed Andrew Morgan's intentions were honorable—and extended well beyond fondness for a friend's sister.

Mr. Chapman, meanwhile, danced quite competently beside her, step for step, their hands and sides occasionally brushing, as they moved through the dance. Abigail tentatively met his gaze, as etiquette dictated. In return, he smiled warmly down at her. When the dance called for the joining of hands, his long fingers enveloped hers, and Abigail felt their warmth spread through her.

Abigail realized she had missed dancing, especially with an attentive, handsome partner like William Chapman. She'd forgotten the pleasure of whirling hand in hand, or skipping down a line of friendly faces, and returning smiles of men and women alike. Of good company, good cheer, and good music. Perhaps she was not quite ready to put herself on the shelf after all.

Once more she glanced at Leah, who seemed to be enjoying herself as well. She wanted to say to her new friend, *"See? You are here in Pembrooke Park, and nothing bad has happened."* But she made do with catching Leah's eye and sharing a smile.

William Chapman was enjoying the dance lesson more than he'd imagined he would. He could barely keep his eyes from Miss Foster, noticing the graceful sway of her slender figure in a becoming gown, the pink flush of happy exertion in her cheeks, the dark curls bouncing at her temples.

He enjoyed the feel of her smaller hands in his as they turned around each another, her lovely profile several inches below his. Her skin shone smooth and fair, her dark brows well-defined arches above her lovely brown eyes. She looked up at him and smiled into his face. His chest tightened, and he returned the gesture, though a little unsteadily.

Standing so near her, he smelled rose water and springtime in her hair, and longed to kiss her cheek right then and there. Knowing his mother was in the same room helped him overcome the urge.

He reminded himself that this young woman was a member of his congregation, his flock. But at that moment, he wished she were far more.

They went on to learn two newer country dances and another reel, then finished with a review of the customary last dance of many a ball, the Boulanger. When the final tune ended, everyone clapped for his mother.

She beamed at them. "Well done, one and all." She glanced at the long-case clock and rose. "Good heavens, I had better get home and check on dinner or it shall be eggs and cold kippers." She smiled good-naturedly and gathered her shawl.

"Thank you so much for playing for us," Miss Foster said. "I for one enjoyed every minute of it."

William and Morgan were quick to agree. Even Leah nodded shyly.

Miss Foster continued, "May I suggest one more class before the ball?"

Everyone assented, and they picked another day and time.

William left a short while later, relieved to know the skills he'd learned during his years at Oxford had not evaporated in the intervening months. He was also relieved to see Leah looking more relaxed and enjoying herself. He was not quite sure how he felt about his friend's obvious interest in his sister, and again prayed Leah wouldn't end up being hurt.

Chapter 11

William glanced from the vestry into the nave, and his heart sank. Empty. Was no one coming? Would he be forced to read the annual prayers in honor of the King's birthday to vacant pews? The ill monarch was still a popular figure—far more so than his son, the prince regent—though the regency and the weather had cast a pall over the day.

William could usually count on his family to attend prayers during the week, if no one else, but his mother and sister were spending the day with their grandmother, who had taken a fall. And his father had been called out early that morning to help a tenant repair a fence before all of his livestock escaped. In the absence of his parish clerk, William went into the entry porch and rang the bell himself, then returned to the vestry.

Resigned to the lonely task, William donned a white surplice, determined to do his duty—flock or not.

He reentered the unoccupied church and stepped to the reader's desk with a sigh.

The outer door banged open, and a figure scuttled in beneath a dripping umbrella, slipping on the slick threshold. He glimpsed wet half boots and damp skirt hems. The umbrella lowered, revealing its bearer's face.

William's heart rose. *Miss Foster.*

He felt comingled relief and embarrassment to have her witness his failure to draw a crowd.

She looked about her, uncertainty etched on her brow. "Did I mistake the time?"

"No. I was just about to begin."

Shaking the rain from her umbrella, she said, "I am sorry I'm late. I thought if I waited, the rain might lessen. But quite the opposite, I'm afraid. No doubt that's what has kept the others at home."

How kind of her. "Thank you for braving the weather, Miss Foster."

She shrugged, uncomfortable under his praise. "Easy for me. I live the closest. Save for you." She hesitated. "My father . . . isn't much of a churchgoer, I am afraid. I hope you aren't offended."

"Not at all. Won't you be seated?"

"Oh yes, of course. Forgive me, I'm holding you up." She left her wet umbrella and walked forward, her heels echoing across the nave.

She straightened her bonnet and took her customary seat. She looked charming with coils of dark hair made springy by the dampness framing her glistening face.

He cleared his throat and began, "Today we meet to honor our venerated sovereign, King George the Third. And to pray for divine healing and protection in his fragile state of health."

He looked down at the official prayer he was meant to read but hesitated. He glanced up once more.

Miss Foster sat there, hands clasped in her lap in the posture of dutiful listener.

He admitted, "I feel silly standing here, pretending to talk to a crowd."

Lips parted, she glanced to the side as though to verify he was talking to her. "You . . . don't look silly."

He stepped from behind the desk and walked toward her. "Would you mind if we made this less formal, since it is only the two of us?"

"Not at all."

He placed a hand on the low door of the enclosed box. "May I?"

"Of course," she said, but he did not miss the convulsion of her long white throat as she swallowed.

William sat beside her, several feet of space between them on the pew.

"Shall we pray?"

She nodded and solemnly closed her eyes. For a moment he sat there, taking advantage of her closed eyes and proximity to look at her, allowing his gaze to linger on the fan of long, dark lashes against her fair cheek, her sweet upturned nose, and delicate pink lips. Then he cleared his throat and shut his own eyes—not that he felt closed eyes were required to commune with his creator, but he knew he needed to block out this particular feminine distraction.

"Almighty God, we pray for King George, as you have instructed us to pray for the leaders you have placed in authority over us. We ask that you, Great Physician, touch his body and his mind and restore him to health. We pray for his son, the prince regent, who rules in his stead, and ask you to guide him. Oh, that he would seek to walk in your ways.

"Father, we are grateful that you are our perfect eternal King, sovereign forever, and that you love us and forgive us and adopt us as son and daughter. We are in reality unworthy peasants, but you see us as prince and princess, children of the King, through the sacrifice of your Son, Jesus, our savior and deliverer, and it is in His name we pray. Amen."

"Amen," she echoed.

They sat there a few moments in silence, William looking straight ahead, knowing he should move away but not wishing to.

She asked quietly, "Is that what you'd planned to say?"

He shrugged. "I prayed what was in my heart. If you would prefer I read the formal prayer, I will happily oblige. . . ."

"That's not necessary. I was only curious. I like that you are less formal in your prayers and sermons. Less practiced."

"Less practiced," he repeated with a quick grin. "Now you sound like the parishioners who admonish me to practice more to make up for the deficiencies of my delivery."

He felt her gaze on his profile and wondered what she saw.

She said, "I can hardly conceive of a more difficult profession. People can be nearly impossible to please, but you have to be polite and react with Christian forbearance and pretend to care about each and every grievance."

"I hope I do more than *pretend* to care."

"Yes, I think you do. I see that you care about your parishioners. In word and deed. You have my sincere admiration—you and your sister both."

He looked at her, taken aback by her praise. His heart warmed, and he sat taller against the hard wooden pew. She gazed at the altar, with no coy or flirtatious looks or apparent awareness of the deep compliment she had paid him, nor her effect on him.

The candle on the reader's desk guttered and swayed in the draughty nave. The rain tapped against the roof, and in the distance, thunder rumbled. His stomach grumbled in reply, and William felt his neck heat in mild embarrassment. He braved a sideways glance at her.

She grinned. "Hungry?"

"Very."

It was on the tip of his tongue to invite her into the parsonage for something to eat, only a few feet beyond the vestry door. But he knew he should not. Not just the two of them alone in his rooms.

As if reading his mind, she said, "Would you like to come over to the manor and join me for tea? Do you think that would be all right, since my father is there?" She added, "I suppose you have to be very careful."

Very careful indeed, he thought. *The eyes of God—and Mrs. Peterman—are everywhere.*

"I have another idea," he said. "We were to have cider today after the service, in honor of the occasion. Why don't I fetch us two glasses?"

"If you like."

He rose. "I'll be right back." Making haste into the vestry, he replaced white gown with coat and hat and dashed across the rain-slashed path to the parsonage. He returned a few minutes later with a basket.

She met him in the vestry. "You're dripping wet!"

"Not too bad." He handed her the basket and shed his long coat and hat.

"You might have borrowed my umbrella."

"*Now* you offer," he teased. He pulled a chair from the corner of the room toward the small desk and chair against the office wall. He wished for the hundredth time the old place had heating—a simple hearth or even a stove.

He poured two glasses of cider and prised up the lid from a tin of biscuits his mother had brought over the day before.

He handed Miss Foster a glass and lifted his own. "Will you drink King George's health with me?"

"I shall indeed." She lifted her glass, and they both sipped.

He offered her the tin.

She eyed the biscuits in surprise. "Don't tell me you made these."

"What do you take me for—useful?" he quipped. "No, Mamma is the baker in the family."

Miss Foster took a bite. "And very accomplished she is."

But William's mind was not on cider or biscuits. He found his gaze lingering on Miss Foster's beguiling mouth and lovely white teeth as she nibbled dainty bites of ginger biscuit. He swallowed.

In the small room, she sat very near, their knees only inches apart, and he could smell something flowery and feminine—perfume or floral soap. He noticed a crumb on her lower lip, and watched in fascination as her pink tongue licked it away. He felt a stab of longing and took a deep, shaky breath. *Steady on, Parson. Steady on.*

"Miss Foster," he said, his voice low and not perfectly even. "I am very glad you came."

"To church?" she asked.

"To Pembrooke."

She smiled. "So am I."

The damp weather persisted. From the morning-room window, Abigail looked out across the drive toward the church, remembering fondly her time there with Mr. Chapman. She had seen him again during the second dance class, which Abigail thought went even better than the first. She had been so pleased to see Leah looking relaxed—and enjoying Mr. Morgan's company.

From beyond the rain-spotted glass, movement caught her eye. It was the woman in the dark blue cape and veiled hat again, walking into the churchyard, something bright yellow in her hands. Was it Eliza Smith? She had seen a small veiled hat on a peg in Mrs. Hayes's cottage, though it hadn't been a full, heavy veil like this one. And there was something about the woman's posture that suggested wealth and breeding.

Molly came in with fresh coffee and the newspaper.

"Molly, do you know who that is . . . in the churchyard?"

The lower housemaid walked over to stand beside her at the window. "No, miss. Don't recall seeing a woman in a veil like that round here before."

Abigail thanked the girl. She sat back down, took a sip of coffee, and read the headlines, but she soon found her attention returning to the churchyard. She went to the hall cupboard, pulled on a hooded mantle and gloves, and stepped outside. But by the time she crossed the drive, the woman was gone.

Abigail entered the churchyard anyway, and walked to the spot where she thought the woman had stood—if she was not mistaken, also very near the place Eliza Smith had stood not so long ago. She saw no fresh graves, no temporary crosses or sparse grass yet to grow in. By appearances this plot of graves had lain undisturbed for decades. She looked closer at the trio of headstones and read the names: *Robert Pembrooke, Elizabeth Pembrooke*, and *Eleanor Pembrooke, Beloved Daughter*, surrounded by many other Pembrookes of generations past. She supposed it wasn't so surprising that the grave of the well-liked lord of the manor should receive visits from not one but two women in as many weeks. Though this time flowers—a bouquet of yellow daffodils—had been left on Eleanor Pembrooke's grave rather than Robert's.

She looked at the death dates. Robert Pembrooke died twenty years ago, as Mr. Chapman had said. Killed in London, she now knew from the newspaper clipping. His wife and daughter had died only a few days apart the year before. Typhus, Mac had said. Poor Mr. Pembrooke, to lose his wife and child at the same time like that. How sad. His final year could not have been a happy one. And then to die so violently himself. . . .

She stood there a moment longer, missing her own mother and sister, and then returned to the house. Her father would be coming down to breakfast soon and she wanted to be there to greet him.

Another letter arrived three days later, and when Abigail read its first line, hair rose on the back of her neck, and she experienced that prickly sensation one sometimes feels when being watched. She looked at the date—the letter had been sent the day after she had visited the churchyard. How eerie and fascinating that she should receive this particular journal page after so recently visiting those particular graves.

> *I visited their graves today. Robert Pembrooke. Elizabeth Pembrooke. Eleanor Pembrooke. As well as my grandparents and great-grandparents. But I felt little connection to them. Only guilt. I don't feel I have any right to claim kinship with these people, nor any right to live in their house.*
>
> *I put flowers on Eleanor Pembrooke's grave. After all, it is her bedchamber I occupy. Her canopied bed I sleep in. Her dolls' house I amuse myself with. She and her mother died in an epidemic that swept the parish last year. Although she was younger than I, I wish I had known her.*
>
> *Father was keen to see the birth and death dates for his*

*brother's wife and offspring, so he looked for the family Bible
but could not find it. He then went and spoke to the rector,
asking to see the parish records. He says familial feeling drives
him. A longing for communion and closure. But I know better. He wanted to see the proof with his own eyes that his
brother's family are all dead. He found the proof he was
looking for, but I wished he had not.*

*I admit I sometimes wonder who put Robert Pembrooke
in his grave. They say some nameless thief killed him. But
as I listen to my father rant and hear the scurrilous things
he says about his brother, I have to wonder if the thief has
a name after all. A name I know all too well.*

Heart pounding, Abigail read the final paragraph again. Did
it imply what she thought it did? Then she remembered Mac's
warning about Clive Pembrooke.

Perhaps it meant exactly that.

William called on ailing Mr. Ford. Afterward, he thought he
might stop by and see Mrs. Hayes. He had not visited the woman
in some time but knew his father often did so. He glanced up at
the ominous sky, hoping the rain would hold off a little longer.

As he approached the house, he was surprised to see his father
dropping an armload of chopped firewood near the door with a
hollow clunk.

"Papa. I could have done that. Or Jacob."

"I don't mind."

"I was just going to call in. How is she?"

"About the same, physically. Though her mind is slipping." His
father wiped a handkerchief over his brow and said, "You know,
Will, I think it best if you leave the visiting to me."

"Oh, why?"

Mac shrugged. "We're old friends, she and I. Worked together at

Pembrooke Park. Unless . . ." He glanced at the house and lowered his voice, asking, "Or is it Eliza you were hoping to see?"

"Not especially, no."

Eliza was a pleasant, pretty woman, whom William had known since childhood. In fact, one of his earliest memories was playing hide-and-seek with her belowstairs in Pembrooke Park. He might once have considered courting her—before Rebekah had turned his head and broken his heart. Before Miss Foster . . .

"Good." His father continued, "You don't want to encourage a girl like Eliza, or give others the impression you are courting her."

"What do you mean, 'a girl like Eliza,'" William asked. "An orphan?"

"No, that's not what I mean." Mac grimaced. "Never mind. I would simply prefer to call on her and her aunt myself. All right?"

There was more going on than his father wanted to tell him, William realized, but he decided not to push the matter.

"Very well, Papa. I shall leave you to it."

On his way home, a heavy rain began to fall. William put up his umbrella and braced himself for a damp walk. A short while later, he drew up short at the sight of Abigail Foster standing huddled beneath a mulberry tree on the edge of the Millers' farm.

"Miss Foster?" He diverted from the road, stepping over a puddle to reach her. As he neared, he noticed the rain had curled the hair around her face into spirals. She looked both miserable and charming. His eyes were drawn to her lips, stained dark red. The sight of those unusually red lips, in such contrast with her fair skin, captivated him. He found himself staring at her mouth. Wishing he might kiss her.

Instead he asked, "Are you all right?"

She nodded. "I went out for a walk and wasn't paying attention to the sky. This tree doesn't offer much protection, I fear, but some."

"But it does offer refreshment, I see."

"Oh. Yes." She ducked her head and tucked stained fingers behind her back. "I did eat a few mulberries. Well, more than a few. I'm wet and cold but at least not hungry." She glanced down at

a stained hand. "I didn't want to spoil my gloves. This will come
out, won't it?"

"Eventually."

"I must look ridiculous."

"On the contrary. You look charming. I confess I've never eaten
mulberries. But on you they look delicious." Good heavens, had he
just said that aloud? He felt his ears heat. Just what he needed—to
draw more attention to his prominent ears.

He collected himself. "Would you care to share my umbrella,
Miss Foster? I hate to see you catch your death. We have a ball
tonight, remember."

"Thank you." She took a step nearer, and he positioned his
umbrella over the both of them.

"And what are you doing out in the rain?" she asked.

"Calling on Mr. Ford. Recovering from an apoplexy, poor soul."

"I am sorry to hear it."

"It appears he'll be all right in time. Thank God."

"Do you pay calls in all weather?"

"When the need arises, yes, my trusty umbrella and I venture
bravely forth." He smiled, hoping to make light of the comment,
not wishing to boast.

"You are very kind, Mr. Chapman. Very good."

"Kind, perhaps, but only God is truly good. I am all too aware
of my failings to allow you to saint me just yet."

A gust of wind blew the rain at a sharp angle, down Miss Foster's neck. She shivered.

"Here." He repositioned the umbrella directly over her head.

"But now you are getting wet," she protested. "Stand closer,"
she insisted, and he was only too happy to comply.

He should have simply given her his umbrella, or walked her
directly home. But he was enjoying her company too much to do
the practical thing. The rain fell around them like a curtain, blur-
ring out the landscape around them.

"It's like we're all alone in the world," she said. "Under a little
canopy of our own."

"Yes," he agreed, his eyes again lingering on those berry-stained lips.

"I like the rain, actually," she said, looking across the pasture. "The way it makes the colors of the leaves and flowers more vibrant. The way it smells. The way it makes you feel thoughtful and yet more alive . . ."

"My goodness, Miss Foster. That is quite poetic. And here you call yourself a practical creature."

"I am. Usually."

"Well then, I am glad I'm here to share this rare moment with you." He held her gaze a moment, then said, "Do you know, I have always thought of mulberries as bird feed."

"You've really never eaten them?"

He shook his head.

"Then you must try one." She reached out and plucked another from the tree.

"Oh no." He held up his last pair of good gloves in defense.

"Allow me. My hands are already stained."

Who could resist such an offer? He allowed her to feed him a berry, enjoying the intimate act of her delicate fingers near his lips, placing a berry in his mouth.

"Well?" she asked in eager anticipation.

He chewed, concentrating as though very serious. "Difficult to tell. A bit sour, and crunchy. Consistency of a grub."

"That's the seeds. But it shouldn't be sour. I must have given you one that wasn't quite ripe." She searched until she found a deep purple berry. "Here, try this one. It will be delicious, I promise."

He ate the berry. Then, unable to resist, he captured her upraised hand in his, bringing her purple fingers to his lips for a slow, lingering kiss.

She sucked in a little gasp of surprise, but not, he thought, displeasure.

"You're perfectly right," he said. "Delicious."

Her voice thick, she whispered, "Would you like more?"

He looked into her wide brown eyes, innocent yet unknowingly alluring. His gaze dropped to her red lips. Oh yes, he wanted more. And knew her lips would be far more to his liking than even her fingertips had been. Instead he cleared his throat. "I never knew mulberries could be quite so tempting. But for now, you and the birds are welcome to them."

He noticed her shiver again. "Here, take my coat. . . ."

"No, I couldn't."

He handed her the umbrella. "Hold this for me a moment." He shrugged out of his long greatcoat, the cold air biting his bones even through his fitted wool coat. He whipped it around her and settled it over her, enjoying the excuse to allow his hands to linger on her shoulders.

"I don't want to drag it on the ground," she said plaintively, glancing down at her ankles. Being several inches shorter than he, it grazed her hem but remained above the damp ground.

"It's fine," he assured her.

"But we can't have you catching cold. I have been here long enough to see how many people depend on you. I would never forgive myself if I caused you to fall ill."

A small price to pay for one of your smiles, he thought.

Seeing the admiration shining in her deep brown eyes, satisfaction thrummed through him. His hand reached out of its own accord and stroked her cheek. "You had better take care or your words will quite go to my head and there will be no living with me after that." *Living with me?* Where had that come from?

She chuckled awkwardly, ducking her head, but he noticed pink tinge her complexion.

"Only teasing, Miss Foster."

"Yes. I have come to realize how much you enjoy teasing me."

"It is quite bad of me, I know." He swallowed. "But if we stay huddled out here alone much longer, I shall be tempted to do much more than tease you."

She flashed a look up at him from beneath her lashes. What did he see there? Alarm, fear . . . hope?

He cleared his throat. "Come, Miss Foster. The rain has let up a little. Allow me to walk you home before I lose my head." *Or my heart.*

Again, that nervous little chuckle. "I cannot imagine the respectable clergyman doing anything improper."

"Your confidence is misplaced, Miss Foster. I daresay you are safe with me, yes. But though I may be a clergyman, I am still a man. And you, as I hope you know, are a very attractive young woman."

She blushed and averted her gaze.

He grinned. "I shall never see a mulberry again without thinking of you." He angled away and offered her his arm. "Come."

With a wobbly smile, she put her arm through his, allowing him to escort her home.

When she returned, Molly greeted her at the door. Abigail wondered briefly where Duncan was.

"Miss Foster. There you are. There's a caller come. Your father asks that you join them in the drawing room as soon as may be."

It reminded Abigail of a similar summons when Mr. Arbeau had first come to them in London. Had he returned?

"Who is it?"

Eyes wide and expectant, the girl lowered her voice and said, "A Mr. Pembrooke, miss."

Abigail started and felt her pulse race as though a ghost had been announced or a man come back from the dead. *Foolish girl,* she chastised herself. Not Robert Pembrooke. Hopefully not his long lost brother either, but some other more distant relation.

She met the housemaid's curious gaze as evenly as she could. "Mr. Pembrooke?" she repeated, needing to confirm the name.

The girl nodded almost frantically.

"Very well. Thank you, Molly." She thought again of Mac's warning, and the letter writer's plea that she send away anyone named Pembrooke. But he had arrived while she was out. Was it too late?

Molly helped her remove her wet things and brought a cloth for her hands and face. Then Abigail stepped to the hall mirror and tidied her hair.

The drawing room door opened, and her father came out, flushed and harried looking.

"Abigail! There you are. Thank heavens." He closed the door behind himself. "You won't believe it. A Mr. Pembrooke is here. I fear he may be the rightful owner of the place and has come to tell us he wants his house back."

Abigail's heart pounded. *Oh no* . . . Had he really come to ask them to leave when they had barely settled in? After all the work to ready the place—was someone else to enjoy the fruit of their labors? But if he was the owner, whose estate funds had paid for the renovations and servants, who were they to complain? Would they have to begin their house search all over again? It would be a rude awakening indeed to have to move into some small cottage or townhouse after living in magnificent Pembrooke Park.

Abigail whispered, "Has he said that's why he's come?"

"No, he hasn't stated his business, and I haven't asked him, truth be told. Didn't give him the chance to speak. I seated him, ordered tea, asked the housemaid to look for you, and then excused myself to see if you'd been found. I left him with the tea tray, no doubt set with his own china!"

"Calm yourself, Papa. We were offered this house, remember. Asked to agree to stay for a twelvemonth at least. Perhaps this isn't Mr. Arbeau's client at all. Which Mr. Pembrooke is it?"

"Said his name was Miles, I believe."

The name meant nothing to her. At least it was not Clive Pembrooke—the brother Mac had warned her about.

"All right. Well, let's not keep him waiting any longer or he will think us very rude indeed."

"Right." Her father opened the door and ushered her inside.

The gentleman seated at the tea table rose when she entered. He looked to be about thirty years old. He was of average height and impeccably dressed with brown hair swept over his forehead and sharply defined side-whiskers coming forward to a point, which emphasized his cheekbones. His eyes were dark and framed by long lashes. He was handsome, if a bit dandyish, with a quizzing glass hanging by a ribbon from his waistcoat, and a walking stick near at hand.

"Mr. Pembrooke, may I introduce my daughter, Miss Foster."

"Charmed, Miss Foster, charmed." He bowed with gentlemanly address.

Abigail curtsied. "A pleasure to meet you, Mr. Pembrooke. Please, be seated."

He pulled out the chair beside him. "You will join us for tea, I hope."

"Thank you." Abigail sat in the proffered seat, Mr. Pembrooke reclaimed his seat next to hers, and her father sat across from them.

She asked, "Shall I pour?"

"If you would." Mr. Pembrooke nodded. "Ladies always seem to do so with such impeccable grace."

"Now that you have set such a high standard, Mr. Pembrooke, I shall no doubt spill it all over myself."

"I doubt that. But if you do, it shall be our secret." He smiled at her, revealing a narrow space between his front teeth. His smile lent his face a boyish quality she found disarming.

She finished pouring, handed round the plate of shortbread, and began, "You are the first Pembrooke we have had the pleasure of receiving. Is it you we have to thank for the opportunity to let this fine old house?"

"Not I, no. I have only recently returned from overseas."

"Oh . . . I see," Abigail faltered. "Then, may I ask your connection to the family? My father is keen on genealogy, but I confess, I am not as familiar with my father's Pembrooke relations."

"Are we related? Delightful!" He beamed at her. "I am so pleased to hear the old place has family living in it again. About time, I'd say."

She exchanged a quick glance with her father and felt her anxiety release a bit, like air from a balloon.

Mr. Pembrooke sipped his tea, pinky finger lifted, then set down his cup in its saucer with impeccable manners. "Forgive me. You asked about my family. My parents were Clive and Hester Pembrooke. My father was born and raised here. And later, we lived here for a time when I was a boy. I haven't been back since."

Then why are you back now? Abigail wanted to ask, but instead she gently inquired, "And where, if I may ask, are your parents living now?"

"In the ever after, Miss Foster. In the ever after. At least my mother, God rest her soul. She left us last year."

"I am sorry."

"Yes, as was I. Especially as I had been out of the country for so long. The war and all, you understand." He looked about him once more. "Thought I'd like to see the old place again, now I've returned. I hope you don't mind."

"Not at all. You are welcome, of course." Abigail considered her next question, then asked tentatively, "I am surprised Mr. Arbeau didn't write to let us know to expect you."

"Mr. Arbeau? Who's that?" he asked, his expression open and politely curious.

"Oh. I . . . assumed you would know him. Sorry. He's the solicitor who arranged for us to let Pembrooke Park on behalf of its owner. I thought—"

"Owner?" he asked, looking mildly concerned.

"Ah. Well, he didn't say *owner* specifically, now I think of it. Rather the executor of the estate, I believe he said."

"Ah, yes." He raised his chin. "That would be Harry. Well good. About time, as I said. None of us has ever wanted to live here. But it would be a pity to let the place fall to ruin."

"I agree." Abigail felt the remaining anxiety seep away. Easygoing, friendly Miles Pembrooke had put them at their ease. She supposed Harry was his brother but didn't ask. She decided she had pried quite enough for their first meeting.

"You say you have been out of the country, Mr. Pembrooke," her father said, crossing his legs. "May I ask where?"

"Indeed you may. Gibraltar. Have you ever been?"

"No. But I have heard of it."

"It's twice as beautiful as they say, and twice as dangerous."

Mr. Pembrooke went on to entertain them for a quarter of an hour with tales of his time in Gibraltar.

When he finished, her father said, "You must join us for dinner, Mr. Pembrooke. How long are you planning to visit the area?"

"I haven't decided."

"Well then. You must stay here with us."

Miles Pembrooke held up his hand. "No, now, I didn't come to beg an invitation. I only wanted to see the old place again."

"Well, it's too late to start a journey now. You must at least stay the night. I insist. The servants have recently finished readying the guest room. Is that not so, Abigail?"

Abigail hesitated. Again the letter writer's admonition flashed through her mind: *"If anyone named Pembrooke comes to the house . . . send him on his way."* Yet she found herself liking the man, and though she was not sure how she felt about him staying in the house with them, she found herself unable to politely decline. The estate was likely still in his family. Might even be his one day. She rose. "Yes. If you will give us a few minutes, I will see that all is in order."

"That is very kind. Excessively kind, I must say. But I don't want to inconvenience you."

"No trouble at all," her father said. "You are family, after all."

Miles Pembrooke offered his charming, boyish smile. "We are indeed. Happy thought. Well then, I accept. And gratefully."

Abigail thought of the masquerade ball that evening. She couldn't very well extend an invitation to this man. It wasn't her place to do so. How awkward. "I am afraid, Mr. Pembrooke, that I have a prior engagement tonight. I hate to be rude and desert you, but—"

"Don't give it another thought, Miss Foster. You go and enjoy yourself. I shall be perfectly fine here on my own. I may poke about just a bit—see my old room, that sort of thing—if you don't mind."

"Of course not. Make yourself at home," Abigail said, hoping she would not come to regret those words.

Her father spoke up, "I was not planning to attend anyway, Mr. Pembr—"

The man interrupted pleasantly. "Miles, please."

"Very well . . . Miles."

She noticed her father did not offer the use of his Christian name in return, but then again, he was quite a bit older than his guest.

Her father continued, "I was included in the invitation, but as I have never even met the family, I declined. I was in London on business when Abigail made their acquaintance. The Morgan family—perhaps you know them?"

"I'm afraid I have not had that pleasure, that I recall."

"They are new to the area," Abigail explained. "Mr. Morgan inherited Hunts Hall from his cousin."

"I do recall the name Hunt, yes."

Her father said, "You and I shall dine together then, Miles. If that suits you."

"Very well, sir. I look forward to it. And I shall look forward to improving my acquaintance with your lovely daughter as well. Perhaps tomorrow?"

Abigail smiled. "Tomorrow it is, Mr. Pembrooke. Do let us know if there is anything you need while you're here."

"I shall. Thank you. You are generosity itself, and I am ever in your debt." He bowed.

Abigail excused herself to inform Mrs. Walsh of their guest and to ask Polly to put fresh bedclothes on the guest bed and carry up hot water. But even as she did so, she couldn't help but wonder if inviting Miles to stay would land them all in hot water.

Chapter 12

With the upper housemaid's help, Abigail dressed for the ball. She tied silk stockings over her knees and stepped into shift and underslip. Polly cinched long bone stays over her shift, and helped her on with the white gown, doing up the lacing and the tiny decorative pearl buttons at the back of the bodice. The maid curled her hair with hot irons, pinning up the majority with soft height, but leaving bouncy ringlets on either side of her face. She pinned tiny white roses amid the curls, to match her shimmering muslin gown.

While Polly made the final touches to her hair, Abigail powdered her nose and brushed just a hint of blush on her cheeks and lips. Then she touched dainty dabs of rose water to her neck and wrists. Finally she pulled on long white leather gloves, and Polly helped her tie them with ribbons above her elbows.

"You'll be the prettiest girl there," Polly assured her.

"I doubt that, but you are kind to say so." Abigail gave her reflection in the glass a final look. She did look pretty, she admitted to herself. And without Louisa in attendance, she felt she just might hold her own with the likes of Miss Padgett from Winchester.

Taking her reticule, mask, and a colorful India shawl with her,

Abigail went downstairs and was surprised but pleased to see her father waiting in the hall.

He rose from the sofa, his eyes widening. "You look beautiful, my dear."

The endearment sounded a bit stilted, stiff from lack of use since their falling-out, but she was happy to hear it nonetheless.

"Thank you, Papa."

Perhaps this was a taste of the favor Louisa was accustomed to receiving—people ready to forgive her anything because of her beauty. It felt strange. Good and somehow deflating at once. Was she only to be treated well when she put such efforts into her appearance? She felt weary at the thought.

"Mr. Pembrooke will be down for dinner shortly, no doubt, but I wanted to be here to see you off."

He helped her settle her shawl around her and gave her shoulders a quick squeeze. "Have a good time, Abigail. Mr. Morgan is sending his carriage?"

"Yes. For the Chapmans as well. It should be here any time."

"Very thoughtful of Mr. Morgan. Is there something I should know? Shall I expect a call from him sometime soon?" His eyes twinkled.

Confusion flared, followed quickly by comprehension. "Oh. No, Papa! Mr. Morgan doesn't admire *me*. Not in that way. He may admire Miss Chapman, I think, though his kindness extends to me as well, as her friend."

Frown lines creased his brow. "But you are a lady, Abigail. A gentleman's daughter. I don't know that I like you being reduced to the same level as Mac Chapman's daughter. . . ."

"Father, don't say that. Miss Chapman is everything good and ladylike."

"Well." He drew back his shoulders. "Don't hide in her shadow, Abigail. Our circumstances may be reduced, but you are a Foster—kin to the Pembrookes. Remember that, and do us proud."

Her father's snobbish vanity made Abigail uneasy. Who were they to view themselves above others? It was on the tip of her tongue to tell him that some people in the area had tied the name Foster to the banking scandal, knowing it would knock him down a peg or two. But looking at him now, in the fading evening sunlight slicing through the hall windows, her father suddenly looked older than his fifty years. Perhaps he had been knocked down enough already.

The rumble of carriage wheels and the jingle of harnesses announced the arrival of the Morgans' coach-and-four.

Her father opened the door and she bid him good evening. Outside, a liveried groom hopped down off the rear board to open the coach door and let down the step. Mr. Chapman and Leah were already inside.

Leah said, "You look beautiful, Miss Foster."

"Yes, she does," Mr. Chapman agreed, eyes shining.

"So do you," Abigail said, admiring Leah's curled hair and glowing complexion, the dress so becoming on her.

"Which of us?" William joked.

"The both of you."

He grinned. "Forgive me, Miss Foster. I did not mean to beg a compliment."

"Yes you did. And why not?" she teased. "It's a pleasure to see you formally attired—and not in black forms or surplice."

"You think this is formal?" Mr. Chapman said. "You've never seen me in my university gown—then you would be truly impressed." He winked at her.

Mr. Chapman did indeed look handsome in his dark frock coat, striped waistcoat and elegant cravat, breeches and white stockings outlining muscular calves. The man obviously did more with his time than compose sermons.

Noticing Leah's nervous expression, Abigail reached over and squeezed her hand. "Are you all right?"

"I shall be," she replied, with a brave smile.

They arrived at a Hunts Hall awash in light—torches lined the drive and candle lamps glowed in every window.

"Time for our masks," Abigail reminded them, pulling forth her own. "Though we probably won't need to wear them all night."

"I don't mind," Leah said, tying on hers.

William followed suit, his mask a thin strip of black silk with cut-out eyeholes.

The groom helped Abigail and Leah down, and William escorted them to the door. Inside, liveried footmen took their wraps. Since it was a masked ball, no butler called out the names of those arriving, which would of course render the masks futile.

In truth, masks did not disguise everyone's identity. Abigail knew she would recognize Andrew Morgan with his curly dark hair and athletic build, mask or not. And there was no disguising William Chapman's deep red hair. And the black mask framed his telltale blue eyes to great advantage.

Leah, however, in a gown so much more elegant than her usual plain dress, and with her hair curled and arranged so beautifully atop her head, looked far different than her usual self. And with the large mask she'd chosen to wear, extending from forehead to mouth, she was nearly unrecognizable.

Andrew, however, no doubt identifying William, lost no time in coming over to greet them.

"Who are these mystery women?" he teased. "And how does such an ordinary ginger-haired fellow come to have two such enchanting ladies on his arm? It isn't fair." He gazed at Leah warmly. "Do me the honor of taking my arm, miss, whoever you may be." He playfully offered his arm, and Leah took it with a faint smile, though Abigail did not miss the nervous tremor of her hands as she did so, nor her eyes darting around the room from behind her mask.

"Will she be all right, do you think?" Abigail whispered after Andrew led Leah away.

"I hope so," Mr. Chapman said. But he looked worried as well.

He and Abigail strolled slowly around the anteroom for a few minutes, Mr. Chapman greeting the people he recognized and performing introductions.

From inside the ballroom, musicians struck up a minuet.

"I don't care for the minuet, Miss F . . . fair lady. But if you have your heart set on it, I will of course dance it with you."

"I don't mind sitting it out."

"Then may I have the honor of the next set?"

"You may indeed."

He bowed. "I am off to pay my respects to Mr. and Mrs. Morgan. If I can find them. But I shall be back to claim you."

She nodded and walked slowly into the ballroom, taking in the modest number of dancers opening the ball. Were Mr. and Mrs. Morgan among them? She thought not. But there was Andrew Morgan dancing the old-fashioned, formal minuet with a lady *not* Leah Chapman. Had he abandoned her already? Apparently, his mother had insisted he open the ball with a different young lady. Miss Padgett, she guessed, taking in the woman's blond ringlets, low-cut heavily flounced gown, and tiny mask, no wider than a pair of spectacles.

Abigail looked this way and that for Leah but did not see her in the ballroom. So she returned to the anterooms—card room, vestibules, and then dining room, where servants were busy setting up an overflowing buffet table for the midnight supper.

She asked a footman where the ladies' lounge was located and found Leah inside, staring at her masked reflection in a cheval looking glass. Seeing Abigail, she quickly touched a hand to her coiffure.

"Just checking my hair," she said. But again Abigail noticed her hand tremble.

Abigail stepped nearer. "What's wrong?" she asked quietly.

Leah shook her head. "It's nothing really. Mrs. Morgan has every right to ask her son to open the ball with the lady of her choosing. Who wasn't, of course, me."

Abigail pressed her hand. "Come, let's join the others," she urged. "No doubt Andrew will want to dance with you as soon as his duty allows."

Leah forced a smile. "You go on. I'll be there in two minutes, I promise."

"Very well. But if you're not, I shall come back and drag you out." Abigail winked, pressed Leah's hand once more, and left the lounge.

Crossing the hall, she was about to return to the ballroom, when a man's profile caught her attention. She froze, heart pounding.

"Gilbert . . . ?" she called. She would recognize him anywhere, ill-fitting mask or no.

He turned to face her, eyes widening behind his mask. "Abby! I had no idea you knew the Morgans."

"Nor I you."

He walked nearer. Though not a tall man, he still cut an impressive figure in his evening coat, waistcoat, and cravat. He said, "I only recently met Mr. Morgan in Town. He hired my employer to design an expansion for Hunts Hall and invited us down for several days. A bit of a house party."

"I see. I was glad to hear you had returned from Italy safely."

"Thank you, yes. It was an excellent experience, but I'm glad to be back in England."

His eyes lingered on her face, masked though it was. "And I must say I am relieved to see you looking so well. I feared the move would be difficult for you."

"It has been a great deal of work, but I've enjoyed it. It's a wonderful old house. You should come by and see it while you're here. In fact I was thinking of you only last week, wishing you were here to help me decipher some old house plans I'd found." She suddenly realized how forward she might sound. "Forgive me, I'm prattling on. I'm sure you shall be much too busy. . . ."

"I would enjoy seeing your new home, Abby," he quickly assured her. "In fact, I wouldn't miss it. Susan would never forgive me if I came all this way without seeing our old neighbors."

"Susan . . ." The memory of his sister and her old friend squeezed her heart. "How is she?"

"Excellent, last I saw her. And your father? He is in good health, I trust?"

"He is—and will be glad to see you."

Gilbert reached out and gently lifted her mask from her eyes to her hairline, his touch sending nerves and warmth through her. Again his gaze roved her face—her eyes, her mouth, her hair. "I can't get over how well you look." He smiled. "I've missed you, Abby."

She lowered her gaze from his admiring one. "Thank you," she murmured, and an awkward silence followed. She forced herself to ask casually, "And how was Louisa when you saw her last?"

It was his turn to look away self-consciously. "Oh . . . well. She seemed in good spirits at the Albrights' ball. You and I danced at that a few years ago, you may recall."

"I do," she managed in a choked little voice.

He continued, "Louisa was sorry, but all her dances were spoken for save the final Boulanger by the time I arrived. She was greatly in demand and generally admired by the gentlemen, if not their mammas. But she seemed happy enough to see me. Full of apologies for not writing more often. You had all been quite busy with selling the house and the move and all, I understand."

"Ah . . ." Abigail murmured noncommittally, for in truth Louisa had done very little. She said gently, "Louisa is young and has had her head turned by all the attention. I'm sure when the fanfare has faded and the invitations dwindle, she'll come back down to earth and remember her . . . friends."

He slowly shook his head. "I hope she does come back down to earth, as you say. And the sooner the better, for her sake. But I . . . But never mind that. I am so glad to see you. I—"

Mr. Chapman appeared. "There you are, Miss Foster. I've come to claim you for our dance."

He looked from her to Gilbert and hesitated. "But if you are . . . otherwise engaged . . ."

"Mr. Chapman, allow me to introduce an old friend from London, Mr. Scott. Mr. Scott, this is Mr. Chapman, our parson and neighbor."

"How do you do, Mr. Chapman?"

"Well, I thank you." The two men shook hands. "A pleasure to meet any friend of the Fosters." Mr. Chapman sent Abigail a raised-brow look of question.

Abigail said, "I had no idea Mr. Scott would be here tonight."

"A pleasant surprise, I hope," Gilbert put in.

"Of course."

Mr. Chapman smiled. "Well, if you wish to visit with your old friend, I shall release you from your obligation and leave the two of you to talk."

"Not at all, Mr. Chapman," Abigail assured him. "I am looking forward to our dance. If you will excuse us, Gilbert?"

Gilbert bowed. "Of course. Perhaps I may have the pleasure of a later dance?"

"If you like."

Mr. Chapman offered his arm, but she noticed a subtle stiffness in his bearing.

He looked down at her in concern and asked quietly, "Are you all right?"

"I . . . think so. It was quite a shock seeing him here."

"Is he the architect who disappointed you in favor of your sister?"

She pressed her eyes closed. "I wish now I'd never mentioned it."

He laid his free hand over hers. "Any man who would let you go for another woman isn't worthy of you, Miss Foster."

"You have never met my sister." *And I wish you never would,* she added wistfully to herself.

He pursed his lip. "When I came upon the two of you, I was certain I saw admiration in his eyes. Nearly challenged him to a duel on the spot."

She managed a grin. "What you saw was fond affection between two old friends. That's all."

He looked at her, eyes wide in compassion. "You are not very convincing. Are you sure you wish to dance?"

"Yes. Quite sure."

"Shall I make passionate love to you to make him jealous?"

Abigail felt her cheeks heat, and Mr. Chapman stopped in his tracks, stricken. "Forgive me, Miss Foster. What a cavalier thing to say. Have I shocked you terribly?"

"A bit, yes. Not very parson-like of you, I will say. I admit the notion is not without appeal, but I shouldn't like to use you in such a manner."

"I promise you, Miss Foster, it would take very little acting ability on my part."

She looked up at him and saw the sincerity shining in his blue eyes, and her heart squeezed. "Thank you, Mr. Chapman. You are very kind to restore my fragile feminine ego."

"My pleasure."

The musicians finished their introduction, and around them couples filled in, ladies and gentlemen facing one another in long columns. Across the ballroom, Abigail saw that Gilbert had been partnered with Miss Adah Morgan, Andrew's younger sister. She forced her attention back to William. Unfortunately, he had noticed the direction of her gaze, but he smiled gamely and took her hand in his as the dance began.

Together they danced their way up the line. As they waited their turn at the top of the dance, Abigail noticed a striking woman in a fine black ball gown looking their way. No mask marred her pretty face, and she appeared remarkably attractive for a woman in mourning. She was a very young widow, perhaps Abigail's own age or even younger.

"Who is that woman in black?" Abigail asked her partner.

"Hm?" William turned to look and stumbled.

"She is staring at us." Abigail added, "As I have never met her, I assume she is looking at you."

"That is Rebek—er, Mrs. Garwood."

Her eyes flashed to his as he fumbled the words. She saw the sparkle leave his eyes, replaced by stoic acceptance.

"Andrew's elder sister. Recently married, and even more recently widowed."

"So young," Abigail breathed.

"Yes. Completely unexpected. I did not realize she would be attending. In mourning as she is."

"I see," Abigail murmured. And with another glance at him, thought, *Oh yes, I do see. . . .*

When their dance ended, Mr. Chapman excused himself and went to ask his sister for the next, dutiful brother that he was. His kindness warmed Abigail's heart. Abigail went to the punch table and accepted a glass from a footman, then found a place along the wall to catch her breath.

A woman joined her in the out-of-the-way corner. Her gaze flickered over Abigail's hair and mask. "Miss Foster, I presume?"

Abigail turned to the thirtyish woman in a peacock-blue ball gown. She wore no mask, and Abigail easily recognized her thin dark brows, blue-green eyes, and sharp nose. "Yes. It is good to see you again, Mrs. Webb."

The woman nodded. "My sister-in-law is in quite a pique, I can tell you, over so few of her guests embracing the spirit of the masquerade."

"And where is *your* mask?" Abigail asked.

Mrs. Webb arched one thin brow. "Oh, disguise of every sort is my abhorrence,"

Abigail grinned. "Ah! That is from *Pride and Prejudice*. Mr. Darcy says it to Elizabeth Bennet."

Again the woman nodded. "I am impressed, but not surprised. I had already pegged you as a kindred spirit." She lifted a hand. "Look about you. Most of the guests have already removed their masks. Except that woman dancing with your Mr. Chapman. Who is she? Do you know?"

Abigail turned and saw William Chapman dancing a reel with Leah, still masked.

"That is Leah Chapman, his sister."

"Ah, the dastardly 'older woman' Mrs. Morgan wants Andrew to pass over for young Miss Padgett?"

"Yes. Unfortunately."

The woman's keen eyes fastened on hers. "Are you well acquainted with Miss Chapman?"

"Fairly well, though she is a rather private person. Even so, I can say unequivocally that she is a genteel, accomplished woman of good character."

"Yes, yes. But has she anything more interesting to recommend her? Is she good company, able to laugh at herself, or a witty conversationalist? Has she any intelligence in her pretty head?"

"Yes, definitely. All of the above," Abigail replied. "And she has read *Pride and Prejudice* three times, *Sense and Sensibility* twice, and *Mansfield Park* only once."

The woman's eyes glinted with wry humor. "That is in her favor, indeed. I can tell you are an excellent judge of character, Miss Foster, and I shall put in a good word for her with the Morgans, based on your high opinion."

"I would be happy to introduce her, if you like, and you may decide for yourself."

"Perhaps another time. But first, tell me. Does your high regard extend to her brother? Are the two of you . . . ?" She let the question dangle, but her arched brow and her meaning were clear.

Abigail's cheeks heated. "Oh, I . . . No. We have only recently met."

"But you admire him," she suggested, eyes alight.

"Well, yes, I suppose I do. But . . . that is, we are not . . . courting."

"Pity." Mrs. Webb turned to look at Mr. Chapman once more. "I would like to see him happy, since my sister-in-law disappointed his hopes once before."

"Oh? How so?"

"I overheard her talking to one of her cronies. Congratulating herself on putting a stop to a courtship between Mr. Chapman and her daughter Rebekah a few years ago. Olive was very pleased with herself when Rebekah married rich Mr. Garwood instead. And now that he is gone, she fears the lowly curate will try once again to woo the wealthy widow. Her words, mind, not mine."

Abigail suddenly felt queasy. "And would Mrs. Garwood welcome his attentions?"

"I don't claim a close acquaintance with my elder niece, living distantly as we do. I gather her previous regard for Mr. Chapman was genuine, but she is only recently widowed, so . . ." She shrugged. "Time will tell."

"Yes," Abigail murmured. "I suppose it will."

Mrs. Webb sent her a sidelong glance. "So, how goes life at Pembrooke Park since I saw you last?"

"Very well. My father has rejoined me from London. I confess I feel more at ease with him there. And we have a houseguest."

"Oh?"

"He just turned up today, without warning. Used to live there, I gather."

Her eyes widened. "Good heavens. Who is it?"

"Miles Pembrooke—son of the previous occupant."

"Miles . . . Pembrooke?" She blinked. "I am surprised."

"As were we. We feared he'd come to reclaim the house for himself and cut short our lease."

Mrs. Webb looked into her empty glass. "I thought everyone in that family was long gone from the area."

"So did I. But he's recently returned from abroad and says he just wanted to see the old place again. Father invited him to stay."

Her brows rose again. "Did he indeed? That is . . . unexpectedly gracious of your father, isn't it? To invite a stranger to stay? With an unmarried daughter under the same roof?"

Abigail shrugged. "He is family, after all. Though granted, we are only distantly related."

"It does not . . . worry you?"

Abigail inhaled thoughtfully. "I confess the timing does give me pause. That he should happen to return just after we've opened up the house again—when it had been shut up for so long. But he seems harmless. Quite polite and charming, really."

"Be careful, Miss Foster. Appearances can be deceiving."

Abigail turned to look at the woman, surprised at her somber tone.

Gilbert approached and bowed. "Miss Foster. It is time for our dance, I believe."

Abigail dragged her gaze from Mrs. Webb's concerned face to Gilbert's smiling one.

"Oh, yes." She lifted a hand and began introductions. "Mr. Scott, have you met Mrs. Webb, Andrew Morgan's aunt?"

"I have not had that pleasure. How do you do, ma'am?"

"Very well. Thank you," Mrs. Webb drew herself up, cool distance returning to her expression. "You two enjoy your dance."

Gilbert and Abigail joined the line of couples as the woman at the top of the set called for a country dance.

"Are you enjoying yourself, Abby?" he asked.

"I am. And you?"

"I hope you weren't sorry to see me here."

"Surprised, yes, but not sorry."

"Good. You seem to have made many friends here already."

"I have been fortunate in that, yes."

"Mr. Chapman seems quite taken with you."

Abigail looked away from Gilbert's inquisitive gaze. "I don't know about that."

"Oh, come. Even a thick-skulled male like me could instantly see he admires you. I would be jealous, if . . . I had any right to be."

"You, jealous?" Abigail forced a laugh. "Don't talk foolishness. I've never seen you jealous in my life. Let's talk of something else. I notice you have been quite in demand tonight."

"Only because there are many ladies in want of partners and Mrs. Morgan is determined to remedy that."

"I don't know. . . . She is very exacting, and if she singled you out for the honor of dancing with her young daughter, you must have done something to earn her regard."

"It's not *her* regard I'm concerned about." He looked at her earnestly. "Are we all right, Abby, you and I? Susan boxed my ears after my going-away party. Charged me with being insensitive and selfish. You are very important to me, and I hope we are still . . . friends?"

"Of course we are, Gilbert. Now hush and let's dance."

After he danced with his sister, William offered to fetch her some punch, but when he returned with two glasses to where he'd left Leah minutes before, he could not find her. Looking all around the ballroom without success, he then went out to the hall. He finally found her in a quiet corner of the vestibule, still wearing her mask.

"Leah, what are you doing back here? Come in with the others."

She shook her head. "I need a few minutes alone. So many people staring. Whether because they are trying to figure out who I am, or because they cannot figure out why Leah Chapman has been invited, I don't know. But . . . I should never have come."

"Leah, you are too sensitive. You imagine stares and criticism, when there are only looks of curiosity or admiration for a beautiful woman. A moment later everyone has returned to his or her own thoughts—his empty glass, or unpaid bills, or gout . . . Not you, my dear, I promise."

She tried to chuckle, but it fell flat. "Did you see how Mrs. Morgan greeted me? She could not have expressed her disapproval any more clearly without saying the words aloud. Why did Andrew invite us? Why expose us to such mortification?"

William took her hand. "I don't think Andrew puts as much stock in birth and rank as others do. I am sure he had no intention of hurting you. He merely wished to spend time in your company."

Leah nodded and then looked at him with empathetic eyes. "Forgive me, William. Here I am feeling sorry for myself, while you . . ." She winced. "Is it difficult seeing Rebekah again?"

"Not too bad." He pulled a face, not wanting to talk about the painful past. "Now. Let's go kick up our heels and show the world how resilient we Chapmans are."

Leah managed a wobbly grin, then stilled, staring across the hall through the open door beyond. "That woman. I know her, don't I?"

William turned to look. He saw Mrs. Webb conversing with Andrew's father, neither of them wearing masks. "That is one of Andrew's aunts. We met her at his welcome home dinner. But I'm surprised you would know her, as you weren't there."

His sister stared at the woman, frowning in concentration. "I'm not certain I do. But there's something . . . familiar about her."

"Shall we go over and meet her?"

Leah adamantly shook her head. "No."

"You could take off your mask now, you know," William said gently. "Nearly everyone else has by now."

"That's all right. I'm more comfortable this way. And we won't be staying much longer, will we? Shall I see if Miss Foster is ready to leave? After this dance with her old friend?"

After their dance, Gilbert escorted Abigail to the side of the room and excused himself to speak to Mr. Morgan senior, his host.

Leah approached surreptitiously and whispered, "Miss Foster, will you be ready to leave soon?"

Abigail looked at her in surprise and concern. "If you like. Why? What's the matter?"

"Nothing, I—"

"Miss Chapman, there you are," Andrew Morgan called, striding over to join them. "Tell me I am not too late to claim a dance. I have been dreadfully occupied with host duties all evening but am free at last. Please say you will dance with me?"

"But . . ." Leah hesitated, looking at Abigail for help. "I think we are leaving. Are we not, Miss Foster?"

Seeing Mr. Morgan's crestfallen expression, Abigail hurried to say, "That's all right. I can wait another set if you are engaged. In fact I shall enjoy watching you dance and seeing the fruits of our little lessons at Pembrooke Park."

Gilbert returned to her side. "No sitting out for you, Miss Abby. If no other man has been wise enough to snap you up, then I insist you dance again with me."

Abigail glanced quickly around the room and saw William Chapman speaking gravely to Andrew's widowed sister. At that moment, Mrs. Morgan appeared with young Miss Padgett in tow and presented her to Mr. Chapman as a potential dance partner. She then took her daughter's arm and led her away.

Abigail returned her gaze to Gilbert. "All right," she agreed.

Mr. Morgan clapped Gilbert on the back. "Good man, Scott. Knew I liked you."

"Oranges and Lemons" was called, a square-set dance for four couples. Gilbert offered Abigail his arm and led her onto the floor. Around the ballroom, couples grouped together. Abigail and Gilbert found themselves with Andrew Morgan and Leah, William Chapman with Miss Padgett, and a fourth couple they did not know.

The music began. Gilbert reached out and took Abigail's hand, and around the square the other couples joined inside hands as well. She liked the feel of her gloved hand in his, his familiar smile, the comfortable way he held her gaze without awkwardness. As they danced and laughed with the others, she felt a thread of their old camaraderie vibrate to life, tighten, and pull. She had missed it. Missed *him*.

The couples stepped forward and back twice, then released hands. Each honored his partner, then turned to honor his corner. The men joined hands and circled around before bowing to their partners, then their corners once more. Then the ladies followed suit.

"Lovely partner, Mr. Chapman," Abigail said when the dance brought them together.

He nodded. "I agree." He held her hand a little longer than the dance required and looked into her eyes. "Though not as pretty as my first."

The pattern was then repeated in the opposite direction. When Gilbert reclaimed Abigail's hand at last, he said, "I'd forgot what a good dancer you are."

She caught Mr. Chapman's eye across the square. "I've had quite a bit of practice lately."

Gilbert smiled. "It shows."

Abigail now and again glanced at Andrew Morgan and Leah as they danced. The man couldn't take his eyes off her, masked or not. Leah, for her part, tried in vain to suppress the smile on her pretty face. It was the happiest Abigail had ever seen her.

Before they parted for the night, Gilbert asked Abigail to name a time for him to call the following day. They settled on two o'clock, though Abigail said she would be at her leisure all afternoon.

He bowed over her hand, then looked up at her, eyes sparkling. Abigail's heart squeezed to see such warmth and fondness in Gilbert's eyes. It had been too long.

Don't be a simpleton. He is just being friendly. She reminded herself that she was the only person Gilbert really knew there, so of course he would seek her out. They were comfortable with each other. They had history. Their families were old friends. She told herself all this with her practical sensible mind, but her foolish heart still beat a little too hard.

While they waited for the Morgans' coach-and-four to be brought around, William stood companionably with Miss Foster. His sister stood a few yards away, talking to Andrew. They had already bid him and his parents farewell, but Andrew had insisted on escorting Leah out, clearly reluctant to let her go.

He felt Miss Foster's gaze on his profile. She asked quietly, "Was it awkward for you? With Andrew's sister there?"

He looked at her in surprise.

"I hope you don't mind. But Mrs. Webb mentioned you once courted her."

"Ah." He lifted his chin in understanding. "Actually, it was not as bad as I would have guessed. I confess having you there with me was quite a balm."

She looked up at him sharply.

Concern filling him, he said, "Forgive me. I don't mean to presume anything about our . . . friendship. But even if you think me an absolute dunderhead, the fact that Rebekah Garwood saw me enjoying myself with a beautiful woman eased the sting. Not to mention nipping in the bud any supposition that I hope to wrangle another chance with her, now that she is widowed."

Miss Foster pressed her lips together, then asked, "You don't wish another chance with her?"

He looked at her, surprised at her boldness. He inhaled and looked up at the night sky as he considered the question. Then he met her gaze and said quietly, "Not anymore."

William watched her face. Did she believe him? Was she relieved?

He hesitated to ask the same question of her. He had seen her with Mr. Scott. Seen the way the young man looked at her, his proprietary air as he escorted her across the room. The easy familiarity in which he held her hand and smiled into her face as they danced and laughed together.

The sight had filled William with an uncomfortably sickly feeling he recognized as jealousy—stronger even than what he had felt when Rebekah broke things off with him in favor of Mr. Garwood. He didn't like it—knew it to be an unworthy emotion. But heaven help him, he felt it all the same.

The carriage arrived, and the groom opened the door for them, giving a hand up to both Miss Foster and Leah. Then William climbed in after them and, after vacillating for a second, sat beside his sister. Andrew stood at the window and gave them all a final farewell.

William glanced at Leah, saw the contented smile there, and hoped it would remain, even as he doubted it.

As the coach rumbled away, something William saw outside the window drew him upright. There, through the throng of waiting carriages and horses, passed a figure in a full-length green cloak, like those worn by naval officers on deck during storms. Why would anyone wear a deep hood on such a fine night, unless he meant to conceal his identity? Was it the same person he and Miss Foster had seen crossing the bridge near Pembrooke Park?

William's pulse rate accelerated. He glanced in concern at his sister, fearing she would see the figure as well, but was relieved to see her gazing idly out the opposite window, a dreamy smile still hovering on her lips. He would not be the one to send it flying by drawing her attention to a sight that would surely frighten her. So he said nothing.

Perhaps he was wrong. It had been a masquerade ball, after all. Perhaps the cloak was part of some man's costume. He hoped that's all it was. Even so, he would have to tell his father. Just in case.

Chapter 13

*E*ven though Abigail was tired from being up late the night before, she resisted the urge to sleep in, rising only an hour past her usual time. She summoned Polly by a pull of the bell cord, when the kind young woman no doubt intended to let her sleep, not even tiptoeing inside to turn back the shutters. Abigail went to the washstand, resigned to the notion of washing her face in last night's cold water, but was surprised and pleased to find it warm. Polly had snuck in without waking her. The housemaid was certainly skilled. Thoughtful in the bargain.

While she waited, Abigail washed for the day and began brushing out her hair, extra full and curly from the night before. She thought back to Polly's eager questions when she had helped her undress after the ball. Her maid had wanted every detail, and Abigail did her best to supply them, assuring her she had enjoyed herself and that everyone had admired her hair. Polly had beamed.

The housemaid entered a few minutes later. "You're up early, miss. Thought you'd sleep till noon after all the doings last night."

"We have a guest, so I thought it best to rise and be hospitable."

"He and your father are already eating breakfast, so no hurry. Mrs. Walsh is in a tizzy, having a gen-u-ine Pembrooke to cook for, and Duncan is in a foul mood at having another to tote and carry for, as you can imagine."

"Yes, I can well imagine." In fact, her father was the only person Duncan didn't seem to mind serving. He served him cheerfully, and in turn her father thought highly of him.

"How's that blister this mornin'?" Polly asked.

Abigail regarded her little toe. She had danced quite a bit last night—more than she had in a year's time—and her dancing slippers had rubbed a tender spot.

"Oh, it's fine."

"The price you pay for bein' the belle of the ball."

A small price, indeed, and well worth the minor discomfort, Abigail thought. She had enjoyed being sought after as a dancing partner. A new experience.

Polly stepped to her closet. "Your buff day dress and cap today, miss?"

"Em, no," Abigail said. "I was thinking of my blue walking dress."

The maid turned in surprise. "Going out again?"

"I am expecting a caller this afternoon."

"Oh? One of the gentlemen you danced with last night, paying a call? How romantic! I'll do your hair up nice again."

"It is only an old friend of mine from London."

"A gentleman friend?" Polly's eyes glinted mischievously.

"Don't go seeing romance where there is only friendship," Abigail said to the maid, silently reminding herself to heed her own advice.

When Abigail went down to breakfast twenty minutes later, she found her father and Mr. Pembrooke seated in the dining room lingering over coffee, tea, and conversation.

Her father saw her first. "Good morning, Abigail."

Miles Pembrooke rose abruptly. "Good morning, Miss Foster. A pleasure to see you again."

She dipped her head. "Good morning, Mr. Pembrooke. I hope you slept well?"

"For the most part, yes. Except for the ghosts I heard rumbling about all night."

Abigail drew up short. "Ghosts?"

He smiled playfully. "Only in my mind, I assure you. No need to be alarmed. Being here has stirred many memories."

She helped herself to tea and toast from the sideboard, and then took a chair across from his.

He sipped his tea, eyeing her with amusement over his cup brim. "Don't tell me I frightened you, Miss Foster. You do not strike me as the sort of female to believe in ghosts or gothic tales."

"I . . . don't. But this old place makes many noises that might be mistaken for nighttime visitors of some sort. I do hope you were able to sleep, considering."

"The first night in a new bed is always a struggle. I'm sure I shall sleep better tonight."

Abigail shot a quick look at her father.

Miles apprehended her surprise and said, "Your kind father has invited me to stay on longer. I hope you don't mind."

"Oh, I . . . Of course not," Abigail faltered, but she felt suspicion trickle through her mind and pinch her stomach.

She nibbled her toast and collected her thoughts. "Have you . . . specific plans while you are here? Former acquaintances you wish to visit?"

At that moment, Molly knocked softly on the open door and entered, bobbing a curtsy. "Begging your pardon, miss, sir. But a messenger from Hunts Hall delivered this for Mr. Pembrooke. He's outside, awaitin' his answer."

"For me?" Miles asked in surprise. He accepted the folded note and read it. His dark eyebrows rose. "I've been invited to call at Hunts Hall at my earliest convenience."

He looked up at Abigail. "You must have mentioned me to your hosts."

"I don't recall mentioning you to the Morgans, though I may have done. I hope that doesn't pose a problem?"

"Not at all."

Abigail said, "I did not realize you were acquainted with the Morgans."

"Neither did I." He smiled and rose to leave. "If you will excuse me, I shall let my horse remain in the stable and go directly with the messenger. That way I can pay my respects without delay."

Surprised, Abigail watched him go. Her surprise increased when she noticed him limp and use his walking stick for support—the implement not merely a dandy's affectation as she'd originally assumed.

Her father followed her gaze, then said, "War wound, he told me."

"Ah."

"Did you have a good time last night?"

"I did, Papa. Thank you. And you'll never guess who was there. . . . " At the raising of his eyebrows, she supplied, "Gilbert Scott."

His mouth momentarily slackened. "You don't say."

Abigail explained Gilbert's connection to the Morgan family through his new employer.

Her father nodded in understanding, then said, "I hope you invited him to call on us while he's here."

"I did. He seemed eager to see you again, and the house as well."

"Emphasis on the latter, no doubt, and who could blame him? I'm surprised we haven't had more people showing up, asking to tour the place."

Abigail managed a weak grin and nodded her agreement, thinking of Miles Pembrooke. Strangers showing up for tours was not what worried her.

Abigail situated herself in the drawing room ten minutes before two o'clock. She had forewarned Mrs. Walsh she would likely be asking for a tea tray. She didn't wish to appear as though she'd been eagerly awaiting Gilbert's visit, but she knew better than to request any baked goods without giving Mrs. Walsh proper notice.

Arranging her skirts around her, she picked up a book, a biography of architect Christopher Wren, but found it difficult to concentrate.

Her palms were damp. She felt jumpy and nervous, quite unlike her normal reserve.

Stop being foolish, she told herself. This was Gilbert, plain old next-door Gilbert, whom she'd known through his awkward, pudgy days, his blemish days, his voice-changing days. Whom she'd played with and argued with and studied with and . . . loved. She began to perspire anew.

Two o'clock came and went. Two thirty. Three. Abigail's heart deflated, and her stomach sank. She'd been nervous for nothing. Worn a pretty dress and had Polly arrange her hair . . . for nothing.

Her father came in. "No sign of Gilbert?"

Abigail shook her head, astonished to find tears stinging her eyes. She sternly blinked them dry and said as casually as she could, "Apparently I misunderstood him. Or the Morgans had other plans for him today."

"That's it, no doubt. I'm sure he'll be by when he can. I'll be in the library. Do let me know when he comes."

Abigail nodded and resolutely turned a page in her book.

A few minutes later, Molly popped her head in and looked curiously about the room, probably sent by Mrs. Walsh to discover how long to keep the water hot.

"Apparently we shall not be needing tea after all," Abigail said, rising. "Please apologize to Mrs. Walsh for me and let her know my father and I will happily eat whatever she has prepared for our dinner tonight."

"Very good, miss."

Abigail left the drawing room, feeling restless. Should she change her clothes? No, she decided. She was wearing a walking dress, so she would walk. Gathering bonnet and gloves, she went outside and walked back to the gardens. She stopped in the old potting shed and found shears and a basket, planning to cut flowers. Instead she began pulling weeds from a border of lilies. She had asked Duncan to do so, but he had yet to get to it. Perhaps it was time to ask Mac to recommend a gardener or at least a youth who could help with outside chores. Next she yanked a clump of grass from the flower bed. The exertion felt good. She released a bit of frustration with every weed she yanked from the ground. If only she could root out her worries and disappointments as easily.

Weary at last, she returned the gardening tools to the shed and made her way back to the house. As she rounded the front, Gilbert appeared, crossing the drive on foot, hands extended in supplication.

"Abby. Forgive me. I know I'm late. Mr. Morgan gathered all the men for a shooting tournament, and I didn't feel I could refuse, being a guest there and with my employer no less. The contest lasted far longer than I anticipated. But I remembered you said you were at your leisure today, so I decided to come over late. Have I been presumptuous?"

"You know you are welcome, Gilbert. Papa will be happy to see you."

"But are you?"

"Of course I am."

He smiled into her eyes, and for a moment she felt herself falling into them, but then she drew herself up. "So, who won the tournament?"

"A young sir somebody. I forget. But then Mr. Morgan summoned his land agent, and he easily bested our champion."

"Mac Chapman?"

"Yes, that was his name."

"I am surprised Mr. Morgan brought Mac into the contest."

"Wanted to give the proud young buck a setdown, I gather. Either that or he is awfully proud of his agent."

"He used to be steward here," Abigail said. "I am fairly well acquainted with him. He's our curate's father."

"Ah. The red-haired chap. I should have guessed." He smiled playfully. "The local competition."

Abigail realized they were no longer talking about a shooting competition. Was Gilbert flirting with her?

An annoying tendril of hair kept blowing across her face. She brushed it away with a swipe of her glove.

Gilbert smiled indulgently, reached out, and stroked her cheek.

She stilled, inhaling a long breath.

He held up his buff glove to show her the smudge of soil there. "How did you manage to smear dirt on your face, fair lady?"

"Oh . . . I was pottering about in the garden." She ducked her head, self-consciously wiping the spot again. She glanced up at him tentatively. "All right?"

"More than all right. Perfect."

Her cheeks heated. She was not accustomed to Gilbert paying her compliments. No doubt a skill he'd learned in Italy. Weren't Italian men notorious for flirting with every female they encountered? It didn't mean anything.

She gestured toward the house. "So, what do you think?"

"Beautiful."

Something in his voice caused her to turn her head. His eyes remained on her face.

She'd had enough. "I'm talking about the house, Bertie, as well you know." She referred to him by an old nickname, hoping to dissolve the unfamiliar tension between them.

Gilbert dragged his eyes from her, up toward the house, taking in its gables, arches, and elaborate oriel windows.

He released a low whistle. "You live here?"

She nodded. "It's something, isn't it."

They slowly walked around the house. After they turned the corner, Gilbert paused and pointed up. "Looks like a water tower. Do the upper floors have running water?"

"No. Only the kitchen belowstairs."

"Hm. The main hall is clearly fifteenth century. But that shaft looks like a later addition to me."

"To accommodate a servants' staircase, perhaps?"

"Bit narrow for that." He squinted upward. "But if it was a water tower, evidently it has fallen out of use. Cheaper and easier to have servants haul water than to maintain the system, apparently."

They walked around the back of the house.

"Another later addition," Gilbert noted, gesturing toward the two-story structure occupying part of the rear courtyard.

"Yes. That's the drawing room on the ground level, and a lovely bedchamber and dressing room above."

"Your bedchamber?" he asked.

She shook her head. "I thought Louisa would like it."

He said nothing, but his gaze lingered on its windows.

From the side of the house, her father came striding toward them, hand extended, smile creasing his thin, handsome face. "Gilbert! How good to see you here, my boy."

"Mr. Foster. A pleasure to see you again, sir."

The two shook hands.

"I saw you from the windows," her father said. "I hope you don't mind, but I was eager to greet you."

"Not at all, sir."

"We were just coming in to find you," Abigail said, hoping that the servants had not already eaten all the cake.

In the spacious, sunny drawing room a few minutes later, the three visited together over tea and slices of cake, her father asking Gilbert questions about his family and his new position. Then he asked, "How long can you stay?"

Gilbert glanced up at the clock on the mantelpiece. "I should return in time to dress for dinner."

That didn't give them much time. Abigail smiled at Gilbert. "Before you go, may I show you those house plans I mentioned?"

Gilbert met her gaze with a knowing look and rose. "Very well."

He bid her father farewell, and he and Abigail excused themselves.

As they crossed the hall, Abigail asked, "May I tell you something in confidence?"

His eyes roved hers. "Of course."

She led the way into the library and stepped to the map table. Behind her she heard the door latch click and turned in surprise. Gilbert had shut the door, and now walked toward her, a small smile on his face.

Abigail licked dry lips and looked away. She retrieved the old plans from their drawer and spread them atop the map table, her hands slightly unsteady.

"You really wanted to show me house plans?" he asked, his voice tinged with surprise.

She shot him a questioning look. "Yes. . . ." Realization dawned, followed by embarrassment. "Did you think it a ruse to get you alone? My goodness, Gilbert. You were in Italy too long."

He sighed playfully. "Can't blame a man for hoping . . ."

She turned away sharply, but he touched her arm, his voice apologetic. "Abby . . ."

She gentled her voice and faced him. "You should know that Mamma has written to me. She mentioned that you have called on Louisa since your return."

"Ah. . . ." He finally had the decency to look sheepish.

She inhaled and turned back to the plans. "Yes, I really wanted your opinion on these plans. You see, there are rumors of a secret room somewhere in Pembrooke Park, and if it exists, I want to find it."

"A secret room?" he echoed, brows rising.

"Yes. Supposedly it hides a treasure of some sort, though the former steward assures me those rumors are nonsense. Still, I would like to find the room."

"Have you anything to go on beyond the rumors?"

"A little. I've received a few letters from someone who used to live here. She mentioned studying the plans for clues." Abigail decided not to mention the dolls' house to Gilbert when he already looked skeptical.

"And did this former resident find the room?"

"She hasn't said. Yet."

He gave her a doubtful glance.

"Just look at them, Gilbert, and tell me what you see."

"Very well." He sighed. Offended, or disappointed?

He began a casual survey, then frowned and bent his head closer to the drawings.

"May I have more light?"

"Certainly." She went and drew back the drapes all the way and opened the shutters.

Gilbert pored over the drawings. "These are a series of renovation plans. Do you happen to have the original plans?"

"I don't know about original. But these are older. Before the west wing was added."

She spread another set beside the others.

He compared the two. "Yes, see? At some point, the tower was added in the corner there. Probably mid-1700s, when many modernized their ancestral homes by adding water closets. A cistern on the roof collected rainwater, which then ran down through a series of pipes drawn by levers below. Then at a later date, another wing was added in front of the tower."

He looked up at her, eyes alight with interest of a different sort now. "Perhaps it is time you gave me the tour of the house."

Satisfaction. This was the inquisitive Gilbert she knew.

Together they walked from the library into the main hall. There, he pointed up. "This is the original hall, open several stories high to allow the smoke of open fires to dissipate in the days before chimneys. You can see that staircase is a later addition, as well as the gallery above it."

They walked through the morning room and into the dining room. Gilbert glanced around, then stepped to the corner of the room and pressed his hand against a panel of wooden wainscoting. The panel slid open.

Abigail's heart lurched and she hurried forward. "Did you find it?"

"I found the hoist from the kitchen belowstairs."

"Oh. I hadn't noticed that before." Embarrassment singed her ears.

"No doubt the servants raise trays with this pulley, and lay breakfast on the sideboard before you raise your pretty head from the pillow."

Hearing Gilbert mention her pillow felt strangely intimate. *Silly female,* she remonstrated herself. Had she not hit Gilbert with her pillow on several occasions when they were children?

He walked to the other side of the dining room, to a narrow door beside a recessed china cupboard. "Having looked at the older plans, I would have imagined the servants' stairs on this side of the room." He opened the narrow door, but it led only to a linen cupboard.

"What's above this room?"

Abigail thought. "My bedchamber." She hesitated. "Would you like to see upstairs as well?"

"If you don't mind showing me."

"Of course not." Abigail led the way up the hall staircase, around the gallery railing, past the door to Louisa's room. She supposed she should offer to show him, but she did not. She saw how he had looked up at the windows, and she had no wish to help him imagine Louisa in her bedchamber, or anywhere else for that matter.

"Is there a housemaid's closet on this floor?" he asked.

"Not that I know of."

They proceeded to her bedchamber. She opened the door and looked inside, making sure she had left no item of feminine apparel in plain view. She saw the room with new eyes—with Gilbert beside her, the flowery pink bed-curtains and dolls' house suddenly seemed too little-girlish.

He hesitated on the threshold. "May I?"

"Of course," she whispered, feeling self-conscious about having a man in her bedchamber—even if the man was her childhood friend. Abigail remained in the doorway. Polly walked past with an armload of linens, her eyebrows rising nearly to her hairline to see a man disappear into her mistress's bedchamber. Abigail gave her a closed-lip smile and said quietly, "It's all right."

Gilbert walked slowly around the room, pausing to look at the dolls' house. "Someone went to a lot of trouble. My employer built a scale model of his London house for his daughter. It was quite the undertaking."

He paused again at the door to her closet. "May I?"

"If you like."

He opened it and knocked on the wooden panels, pulling and pushing on the various shelves and gown drawers within. Then he opened her oak wardrobe cupboard beside it and pushed and prodded there as well. "No false back or moving panels."

"No. I couldn't find one either."

"And the dining room is below us?"

"Yes."

"So the kitchen hoist is on this wall downstairs."

"Right."

In the end, he shook his head and said, "In my professional opinion, I would say your 'secret room' was this closet. At some point, it might have served as a housemaid's closet or water closet, but the pipes have been removed. Perhaps the door was not as it is now, but a hidden panel like the one used to conceal the hoist below it."

"Ah . . ." Abigail swallowed her disappointment. "I should have known there was a logical explanation for the rumors." She sighed.

He gave her an indulgent grin and tweaked her chin. "Not too disappointed, I hope."

"No." She braved a smile. "There is an attic as well, with a storeroom and a few servants' bedchambers, if you would like to see them, but . . ."

"What time is it?" He glanced around for a clock and not finding one pulled out his pocket watch and consulted the face.

"I had better head back or I shall be late for dinner, and Mrs. Morgan will scowl at me."

"Horrors," Abigail teased.

He patted his pocket and said, "Before I forget, Susan sent a name you asked for. She says she'll write a proper letter soon, once their next edition is printed." He extracted a slip of paper from his pocketbook and handed it to her. "A writer for her magazine, I think she said?"

"Mm-hm." Abigail read the name but didn't recognize it: *E. P. Brooks.* "Thank her for me."

Together they walked companionably back downstairs and to the front door.

"Thank you for coming," she said.

"Better late than never, I hope."

"Yes, definitely. I hope you enjoy the rest of your stay at Hunts Hall."

"I don't know how much of my time shall be my own, but if I find myself free, may I call again?"

"Of course. You are always welcome."

"Thank you, Abby." He reached out and gently grasped her fingers. Bending low, he pressed a slow kiss to the back of her hand for the first time in her memory.

The spot remained warm and sensitive long after Gilbert had crossed the bridge and disappeared from her view.

For nearly an hour after Gilbert departed, Abigail walked around the house and about her tasks in a contented daze, thinking she would give up her search. If Gilbert was right, there was no secret room, beyond perhaps her own closet. But the notion left her unsatisfied. Perhaps Gilbert was wrong. For all his education and experience and travel, he didn't know everything.

Illogical or not, she put on her bonnet and clean gloves and went back outside. Again she walked slowly around the house, looking up at the rooflines, the windows, and the tower Gilbert had pointed out, perhaps eight feet square. Something caught her eye in the tower, some twenty feet or more above her. There were no windows in that narrow wall. But . . . what was that? It appeared as if the stones of a roughly rectangular section were lighter than those around it. As if there had been a window there decades ago but it had been filled in.

Perhaps if the tower had begun as a servants' staircase and then been converted to a water tower or water closets, windows would have been unwanted. Might that explain it?

"What are we looking at?"

Abigail started and whirled about, surprised to see William

Chapman standing there, hands behind his back, staring up at the house as she'd been doing.

"Mr. Chapman. You startled me."

"Forgive me. I didn't intend to."

She pointed out the area above. "Do you see that section of lighter stone—at about the second level?"

He squinted up at it. "Yes. It looks as if there used to be a window."

"That's what I thought."

"No big mystery," he said with an easy shrug. "Many people have bricked over or otherwise covered unnecessary windows, to avoid exorbitant glass taxes."

That was logical. She felt foolish not to have thought of it herself. Likely some thrifty owner or steward of generations past had ordered some of the windows to be filled in to save money. Had he covered other windows as well? It didn't make sense to brick over merely one window for tax reasons. She stared up higher, trying in vain to see evidence of another filled-in window on the level above. She did not see one at the ground level either.

A gig came rumbling up the drive. Abigail glanced over and saw Miles Pembrooke seated beside the coachman, returning from Hunts Hall. When the gig halted, Miles gingerly climbed down, one leg buckling a bit before he righted himself. He waved to thank the driver and turned toward the door. Seeing them standing there at the side of the house, he lifted his hat and hobbled toward them, leaning on his stick.

"That's Miles Pembrooke," she said. "Do you know him?"

Beside her William stiffened but said nothing.

"Hello, Miss Foster," Miles called out as he neared. "Don't you look a picture in that bonnet."

"Thank you, Mr. Pembrooke. Did you enjoy your visit to Hunts Hall?"

"It was most . . . enlightening." Miles glanced with interest at William. When Mr. Chapman said nothing, Miles looked back expectantly at her.

"Forgive me," Abigail said. "I thought perhaps you two knew each another. Miles Pembrooke, may I introduce William Chapman."

"Will Chapman . . ." Miles echoed. He offered his hand, but William continued to stare at the man's face, as if he didn't notice. "I can't believe it," Miles said, shaking his head in wonder. "You were but a wee ginger-haired scamp last I saw you. Perhaps, what, four or five? Darting about the place like a redbird. Of course I was only a lad myself."

"What brings you here, Mr. Pembrooke?" William asked, his voice uncharacteristically stern and clipped.

Miles hesitated, then took a step nearer Abigail. "I wanted to see the house again. And my good friends and distant relatives the Fosters have been kind enough to invite me to stay. Haven't you, Miss Foster?" He beamed at her.

She felt self-conscious and illogically guilty under Mr. Chapman's disapproving gaze. "Yes, Father is very kind," she murmured.

"I saw *your* father today, Mr. Chapman," Miles said. "Though only from a distance. Shot a cork off a bottle at fifty yards. How well I remember Mac. He frightened the wits out of me when I was a boy. Though not nearly as much as—" Miles broke off. "He is in good health, I trust?"

"Yes."

"Do greet him for me."

"I shall certainly tell him you're here."

Arms crossed, William glanced at her and then looked at Miles, as if expecting the man to excuse himself and take his leave.

But Miles held his ground. He looked from Mr. Chapman to Abigail, as though trying to sort them out. Finally he said, "Miss Foster, you have not been here that long, I gather, so you have only recently become acquainted with our former steward and his family. Is that right?"

"Yes. They are excellent neighbors. And perhaps you are not aware, but Mr. Chapman here is our curate."

"Will Chapman? A clergyman? Inconceivable." His dark eyes glinted with humor. "You *can't* be old enough."

"I am indeed. I am nearly five and twenty, and recently ordained."

"Astounding. Well. Good for you."

Still neither man made a move to leave. Miles glanced up at the exterior of the house. "And what have you two found so interesting out here?"

Mr. Chapman looked at her, waiting for her to answer. But for some reason, she was hesitant to point out the stoned-in window to Miles Pembrooke.

In her stead, Mr. Chapman reluctantly began, "Miss Foster just noticed that—"

"That the clematis are climbing the wall in such profusion this year," she interrupted. "Had you noticed? I adore flowering vines on old houses."

Both men blinked at her.

Miles politely agreed, "Very charming, yes."

Abigail hesitated. She didn't want to mention the secret room, but thinking Miles might be able to tell her something about the tower, she said tentatively, "We were discussing past renovations to the house, Mr. Pembrooke. Do you know anything about it?"

He pursed his lip and shrugged. "You may ask me anything, Miss Foster. I am yours to command. But remember I lived here as a boy between the ages of ten and twelve, not an age to notice things like walls and climbing vines."

"You're right. Never mind. Shall we go in? I imagine Father is already dressing for dinner. Will you join us, Mr. Chapman? You would be most welcome."

With another uneasy glance at Miles Pembrooke, Mr. Chapman said, "Thank you, Miss Foster. I should enjoy that. But perhaps another time?"

"Very well."

"And now I shall bid you both good day." He made a brief bow toward Abigail, and then turned and walked away, not in the direction of the church and parsonage, but rather in the direction of his parents' home.

Miles watched him go. "Hard to believe Will Chapman is so grown. Almost makes me feel old."

Abigail followed the direction of his gaze on William's retreating back. Then she felt Mr. Pembrooke's focus swivel to her.

She glanced over, saw another glint of humor in his brown eyes. "That was your cue to assure me I am not at all old, Miss Foster."

Abigail complied. "You are not old, Mr. Pembrooke. I'd guess you are only, what, thirty?"

He pressed a hand to his heart. "You cut me deeply, miss," he said, with melodramatic flair. "I shan't be thirty for two whole months yet."

"Then I beg your forgiveness," she said, matching his mock serious tone.

"And I shall forgive you . . . on two conditions."

"Oh?"

"Tell me how handsome I am and agree to sing for me after dinner."

"Mr. Pembrooke!" she mildly protested.

He ducked his head and playfully pouted. "You don't think me handsome?"

"Yes, you are handsome, as you well know. In fact you would be more so if you did not beg compliments."

"Touché, madam. And you will sing for me? I hear you have a lovely voice."

"Who told you that?" She doubted either William or Leah would have offered the information to this relative stranger.

"Some lads I met along the way. They asked me who I was and where I lived. When I told them I was a guest at Pembrooke Park, they said, 'That's where the lady who sings like the angels lives.'"

"The boys exaggerated, I assure you."

"Allow me to be the judge of that." He offered his arm. "Shall we?"

William found his father cleaning his guns after the recent shooting tournament.

"Papa, have you heard the news? Miles Pembrooke has returned. He's staying in the manor as a guest of the Fosters."

His father's whole body stiffened, and his eyes narrowed. "The devil he is."

"It's true. I just met him. In fact, he said he saw you today out at Hunts Hall, but from a distance, while you were shooting."

"Did he indeed? Good thing I didn't see him. Though I doubt I'd recognize him after all these years."

"Dark hair. Dresses like a dandy. He walks with a limp now, and carries a stick."

"A stick? But he can't be more than, what, thirty?"

"Something like that. An injury of some sort, apparently."

"Does Leah know?"

"Not from me. I came to you first."

"Good. Don't say anything yet. First we need to know why he's here and where he's been all these years. Where is the rest of his family?"

"He said he is only here to see the house again. But I did not demand to know his intentions or the whereabouts of his family upon our first meeting."

"You should have."

"Then perhaps you ought to pay a call yourself."

Mac rose. "I shall indeed."

William grasped his father's arm. "I know you have reason to despise Clive Pembrooke. But remember this is not that man himself but his son—who was only a boy when it all happened."

"I know. But I also know that the apple doesn't fall far from the tree."

After dinner, Miles and Abigail adjourned to the drawing room. Her father said he would join them after he smoked his pipe alone, as he always did, since his family had never liked the smell. A short while later, Molly brought in coffee. As she set down the tray, she leaned near to Abigail and whispered that Mac Chapman was waiting in the hall.

The news surprised Abigail, but she said, "Ask him to join us."

A minute later, Mac appeared at the drawing room door. He'd removed his hat but still wore his Carrick coat. He said, "I wish to speak with Mr. Pembrooke, if you don't mind."

"I . . ." She looked toward Miles in concern. "Do *you* mind?"

"Of . . . course not," Miles said, then asked Mac, "May Miss Foster stay?"

"You may not want her to hear our conversation."

"Miss Foster may hear anything I say to you. I would like her to stay."

"If you wish."

Abigail resumed her seat, torn between wishing she might have been excused this scene and curiosity to hear more.

Mac remained standing. "Why are you here, Mr. Pembrooke?"

The man's confrontational stance and glinting eyes reminded Abigail of her first sight of Mac Chapman, gun in hand, ready to shoot any intruder to protect his beloved Pembrooke Park.

Miles appeared slightly nervous, but anyone targeted by that green-eyed glare would be.

"I . . . I wished to see Pembrooke Park again. That's all."

"Why do I doubt that?"

"I have no idea." Mr. Pembrooke's brow furrowed. "Mr. Chapman, I don't know what I have done to so vex you, but I—"

"Do you not? You were only a boy at the time, but you're a man now. Surely you heard the rumor about your father and Robert Pembrooke's death."

"Yes. And I am sorry to say the rumor is likely true."

Mac's eyes flashed. "You mean he admitted he killed his own brother?"

Miles raised a hand. "I never heard him admit it, no, but I am ashamed to say I can believe it of him."

Abigail thought of the Genesis verse referenced in the miniature book. *"Cain rose up against Abel his brother, and slew him."*

Mac clenched his jaw. "And where is he now? Did he send you here to check up on the old place and . . . the lot of us?"

"Heavens no. I have not seen Father since we left Pembrooke Park eighteen years ago."

"We thought you all left together."

Miles shook his head. "My mother, brother, sister, and I left together. Father was . . . delayed."

"Is he still alive?"

"I . . . don't know. As I said, we have not laid eyes on him these many years. My mother believed him dead, but there is a part of me that fears he might still be alive."

"Fears?" Abigail asked.

Miles looked at her. "You did not know my father, Miss Foster, or you would not ask such a question."

"True enough," Mac agreed. "And the rest of your family?"

"My brother died not long after we left here, and my mother died last year. There is only my sister and me now."

Abigail interjected, "But you said Harry was the executor of the estate. I assumed you meant your brother. But how can that be if he is dead?"

Miles turned to stare at her. "Oh! No, Harri is my sister. Short for Harriet."

"Oh . . ." Abigail said, feeling foolish. But then she realized it was the first time she had heard the given name of the executor, the person who had likely been sending her the journal pages— Harriet Pembrooke.

Mac asked, "And how long will you be staying?"

"I have not yet decided. Mr. Foster has been kind enough to invite me to stay on as long as I like."

"Has he indeed?" Mac pierced Abigail with an accusing look, then returned his focus to Miles. "Do you intend to take over Pembrooke Park?"

"Me? Good heavens, no. Besides, there is some question of ownership."

"A problem with the will?" Mac ventured.

"You'd have to ask my sister, but I believe the will is clear. Pembrooke Park was to go to Robert Pembrooke's oldest child. It isn't entailed away to the male line, as you may know."

Mac nodded. "Aye, I know."

"Since his family have all died, my father would have been next in line. As he is missing, the lawyers have it tied up in probate, and Harri refuses to pursue the matter. She doesn't want the place, but nor is she keen on seeing it come to me for some reason. Which is fine by me, as I have no interest in living here again—beyond a visit, of course." He smiled broadly at Abigail. "And a very pleasant visit it is."

"Why not?" Mac asked, clearly skeptical.

"Bad memories here for us, as you might guess. Though being here with such charming hosts has soothed some of the bad memories, I own. Yes, I could quite get used to living in such fine quarters, with such pleasant company." Again he smiled at her, his eyes shining with possessive warmth that sent a prickle of unease through Abigail's stomach.

"I would'na advise it," Mac said.

"Oh? And why not?" As much challenge glinted in Miles's eyes as in Mac's.

"You'd best be on your way. And leave these good people in peace."

"Peace?" Miles looked at her and asked pleasantly, "Am I disrupting your peace, Miss Foster?" He pressed a beseeching hand to his chest. "Pray, do tell me if I am, and I shall leave forthwith."

Mac's eyes narrowed. "I'll be watching you."

Miles smiled. "I am flattered, Mac, by your attention."

Her father came in and drew up short at finding Mac Chapman there. "Oh, I didn't realize . . ."

"I was just leaving." Mac stepped to the door, then turned back. "I trust your houseguest will very soon follow my example."

After the conversation between Mac and Miles, something niggled at Abigail, some little detail that lingered on the murky edges

214

of her memory. Why did Miles's sister allow the will to languish in probate? And why warn *her* to turn away anyone named Pembrooke? Did Harriet Pembrooke want the "hidden treasure" for herself? The second verse marked in the miniature book—the one from Numbers—flitted through her mind: *"Visiting the iniquity of the fathers upon the children unto the third and fourth generation."* Was that somehow related?

After Polly helped her into her nightclothes, Abigail sat on the edge of her bed and pulled out the bundle of letters and journal pages. As she reread the last one she'd received, one line jumped out at her: *A detail in those plans that does not jibe with something I have seen in the house itself. Or am I not thinking of the actual house at all, but rather its scale model?*

That was the detail she'd been forgetting. Had Abigail overlooked a clue about the secret room in the dolls' house itself? She crossed the room and regarded the model of Pembrooke Park.

There were the master's and mistress's bedchambers with their matching fireplaces, except for the missing miniature portrait, just as in the house itself. Two smaller bedchambers lay beside each large bedroom, instead of behind them across the gallery as they were in reality. But surely this was a simple contrivance for practicality, to make all the rooms of the dolls' house accessible from one side.

Abigail knelt in front of the dolls' house until her knees ached, opening tiny doors, and searching the drawer beneath by candlelight. Nothing. She noticed a black streak painted up the kitchen wall above the open hearth. A very realistic effect. But otherwise she saw nothing she hadn't noticed before. Suddenly she glimpsed her reflection in the looking glass and stilled.

What was she doing? She was a woman of three and twenty, not a little girl. And a practical woman at that—not some dreamer or desperate gambler. She rose stiffly and returned to her bed. She closed her eyes and listened but heard nothing. The house was unusually quiet. No winnowing voices. No trespassing footsteps. When was the last time she had heard any? Apparently Duncan, or whomever it was, had long ago given up the search.

It was time for her to do so as well.

She blew out her candle and pulled up the bedclothes. As of tomorrow, she would lay aside her search for treasure and find a more useful way to spend her time. She had been foolish to entertain the notion. To hope.

Would Gilbert expect the woman he wed to bring a hefty dowry into the marriage? He was just starting out in his career, likely many years away from financial success. Even a poor clergyman like William Chapman no doubt hoped for a wealthy wife, or at least one with some sort of dowry. She sighed. It couldn't be helped. She had no dowry, and the majority of her father's wealth was gone. And no mythical treasure was going to appear to replace it.

The next afternoon, another letter arrived. Abigail had begun to fear she had received her last word from that source. She opened it right there in the hall and read the journal page eagerly.

> *How strange it feels to benefit from the misfortune of others. To live in the house of relatives I have never met and now, never shall. My father says I am being ridiculous.*
>
> *"This is your grandparents' house—the house I grew up in. I have every right to be here, and so do you."*
>
> *If this is my grandparents' house, why have I never been here before? Why no Easter visits, Christmas dinners, or leisurely summer holidays?*
>
> *Apparently there was a falling out between him and his parents when he was young, and he'd had to join the navy to earn his own way in life—as he often told us, part bitter, part proud. But now he seems determined to act the part of a landed gentleman, ordering fine suits and fast horses. He wants so badly to win the admiration of our neighbors, and is growing increasingly angry as he realizes that taking over his brother's house has not brought him the respect he sees as his due.*

I once had an aunt who died of typhus. I once had a cousin who died as well. A girl like me, who liked pretty frocks and played with the dolls' house in my room—her room.

Aunt and Uncle Pembrooke. Eleanor. I feel I am coming to know them at least a little, through what they left behind. Beautiful clothes, well cared for. Beautiful gardens, well appreciated. Beautiful pianoforte—well used.

They were reverent or at least religious. There is a family Bible hidden away, and a well-worn prayer book in the family box in the estate church, though we attend but rarely.

The girl was loved. Cherished even, if the carefully stored baby clothes mean what I think they mean. Indulged, if the dolls' house was hers and not our grandmother's collection.

And the girl knew, I believe, where the secret room was. Discovered it, and kept it to herself. As I have.

Aha! Abigail thought in triumph. The writer had found the secret room. Unless she had some reason to prevaricate, to lead Abigail on a wild-goose chase for her own personal amusement. And why would that be? Unless . . . Was she hoping Abigail would do the work—find the treasure for her? But if she already knew where the room was, why would she give a stranger clues to its whereabouts?

Gilbert would say that the room the writer had found was likely now the closet in her bedchamber. However, Gilbert might have missed something. After all, he had not read the journal pages. Perhaps she ought to have shown them to him. But she prized them as her personal secret to savor. . . .

Abigail went down to the library, determined to look at the plans again.

Chapter 14

Over the next few days, Abigail endeavored to study the plans and search the house at every opportunity, but her search was hindered by the presence of a houseguest. Miles Pembrooke took an active interest in her concerns and movements and often asked to accompany her whenever she went for a walk or even to sit in the library, saying he would simply keep her company while she read or wrote letters or whatever she was about.

She felt she couldn't—or shouldn't—study the plans with Miles looking over her shoulder. So she made great headway in the novel she was reading entitled *Persuasion*. She would be able to give it to Leah in a few days' time at this rate.

One afternoon, the post arrived as she prepared for what she hoped would be a solitary walk. Her heart lifted to see another letter in that now-familiar hand, but Miles came upon her before she could open it, and she quickly slipped it beneath a letter from her father's solicitor.

His eyes glinted knowingly. He must have seen her less-than-deft attempt at concealment.

"A letter?" he asked. "From whom, pray tell?"

"I . . ." Abigail hesitated. She believed the letter writer was Miles's own sister. Likely he could look at the writing and confirm whether that was true, and the mystery would be solved. Why then did her spirit catch at the thought of showing it to him?

Abigail lifted her chin. "Forgive me, Mr. Pembrooke. But I hardly think it your concern."

"Ah! A love letter, is it? I am all devastation."

"No, it is not a love letter."

"Then what has you looking so flushed and secretive?"

"Your persistence, sir!" she protested.

"From Mr. Scott, perhaps? Or the good parson?"

"Neither. And that is my last word on the subject. However, if you'd like the new *Quarterly Review*, I am sure my father would not mind your reading that to your heart's content."

He reached out and stroked a thumb across her chin, smiling indulgently. "You are charming when you're vexed, Miss Foster. Has anyone ever told you that?"

"No."

"Ah. That honor is mine at least. If not first in your esteem, at least I am first in something."

Deciding to forgo her walk, Abigail excused herself, took the letter upstairs, and carefully latched the door of her bedchamber before opening it.

The letter began with two lines in bold print:

I hear you have a houseguest by the name of Pembrooke.
Why did you not heed my warning?

This was followed by a long letter written in that familiar script. It was not a page from a young girl's journal, as most of the others had been, but instead appeared to have been written recently.

We had been living in Pembrooke Park for more than a year when I first saw her. She stood in the rose garden, staring up at the house with haunted eyes. I stood at my bedchamber window, contemplating the grey sky, wondering whether or not to bother going out for a ride or if I would end up soaked.

Riding was the only diversion I enjoyed, beyond reading novels. I had no friends. Not one. We had not been in Easton long before I realized our neighbors despised us. It was almost as if they feared us. Why, I wondered, when they don't even know us? It seemed devilish unfair to me.

No one allowed their daughters to accept my invitations. Nor their sons to spend time with my brothers. The boys at least had each other. But I had no one. Maybe that is why I noticed her. A girl, perhaps a few years younger than myself, standing close to the house and partially hidden behind the rose arbor. I wondered if she was bent on mischief or simply afraid to be seen. Did she think we would run her off, not realizing I, at least, would welcome her warmly, so rare was a visitor to Pembrooke Park?

I thought I had seen most of the village girls at least from a distance, at church or on market days. But I had not seen her before. She had golden hair peeking out from her bonnet and wore a stylish spencer over her frock. She didn't look poor, but neither was she a girl "equal to my station," as mother referred to it. That was how she tried to console me—telling me it was just as well no girls my age called, for she wouldn't want me to spend too much time in the company of uneducated rustics, not when I was well on my way to becoming an accomplished young lady. I confess I snorted a bit at that. A year earlier, we'd been living in a pair of shabby rooms in Portsmouth and wearing castoff clothing. Of course that was before Father had received his prize money and helped himself to the contents of his brother's safe.

The first time I saw the girl with haunted eyes, I did nothing. When I noticed her a few days later, I raised my hand, hoping she would see me. But she didn't. So I opened the window, thinking I would call out a greeting, but the sound of the latch startled her, and she bolted like a wild hare fleeing a fox.

When the girl didn't return for several days, I went in search of her. Eventually I found her in a hideaway she had made between the potting shed and walled garden, quite out of view of the house. To a casual observer—or a boy—the arrangement of planks, bricks, colorful glass jars, and a pallet covered with a cast-off petticoat might look like an odd collection of rubbish. But I saw it for what it was. A playhouse.

Not wanting her to flee again, I decided not to risk a direct approach. Instead I returned later in the evening to leave flowers in one of those glass jars along with a note assuring her I meant no harm and asking if I might play with her the next day. I signed it, *Your Secret Friend.*

I was afraid she would leave as soon as she discovered the note and knew someone had been in her hiding place. Instead, when I walked over the next afternoon, she stood there and watched me approach, looking solemn and older than her years.

"Why do you want to play with me?" she asked.

I decided to be honest with her. "Because no one else will."

"And will you promise not to tell anyone?"

I nodded. "I promise. It shall be our secret."

"Very well." She tilted her head in thought. "You may call me Lizzie," she said. "And I shall call you . . . ?"

"Jane," I supplied, giving her my middle name. Afraid she would refuse to associate with me if she knew who I really was.

And that was the beginning of our secret, mismatched friendship. We met nearly every afternoon when the weather was fine, for most of that summer. We performed the little plays I had written, and played house, creating families and situations and lives more appealing or interesting than my own—likely than her own as well.

I didn't ask about her family, because I didn't want to invite similar questions in return. I didn't want to talk or even think about my real family. Especially my father. I wanted to escape for an hour or two into the company of this new friend. And into a world of make-believe.

221

Before long, I figured out who her family was, and heard her real name. And I assume she learnt mine. But we never spoke of it. It was as if to do so would break the spell and end our private world, the sanction of our friendship.

But all too soon it ended anyway. My little brother saw us together, and she was afraid word would get back to her family. She left me a note behind a loose brick in the garden wall. Ending our friendship as I had begun it. Fitting, I remember thinking later. At the time, I thought only how unfair life was.

Abigail felt a heavy sense of sadness as she finished the letter. She wondered where the girls were now, and if they ever saw each other again. If Harriet Pembrooke, or "Jane," had ever made another friend. And what of Lizzie, the village girl? Was she married, with a little girl of her own playing house somewhere nearby? Or was she alone?

Wherever the girls were, Abigail hoped they were happy. But somehow, after reading this account, she doubted it. Again she wondered if she should show Miles the letters. Why was she so hesitant to do so? Perhaps she could at least ask Miles about his sister.

She went and found him in the library, perusing the fashion prints in a copy of the magazine Susan and Edward Lloyd published.

"May I join you?"

"Of course!" he said, beaming. "Look at this well-dressed couple in their new fashions for spring. That could be you and me—we are easily as handsome. And what about this promenade dress and tall hat? I think it would suit you."

She glanced at it with feigned interest. "I never cared for ostrich plumes. But that bicorn hat would look well on you," she added, earning herself a smile.

She sat down with her novel, and he returned to his magazine. The ticking of the long-case clock had never sounded so loud.

After a few minutes pretending to read, she said casually, "Miles, may I ask about your sister?"

"What about her?" he said, eyes still on the page.

"Where does she live, for starters?"

He looked up at her. "She splits her time between Bristol and London, I believe. When she's not traveling about."

Abigail thought of the Bristol postmark on the letters she received. "How does she fare? Are you two in contact?"

He shrugged. "Not really. I've only seen her twice since I returned to England."

Seeing his discomfort, she changed the subject. "I was surprised when you told Mac your brother had died. I don't think anyone here knew that. I suppose no one thought to send word back to the parish."

Miles nodded vaguely. "We only lived here for two years after all."

Abigail swallowed, and then said tentatively, "May I ask how he died?"

"You may well ask. You may ask how . . . and why. I know I did for years. Still do."

She waited for him to explain, the clock ticking loudly again. But he did not. He sat there, wiping at some invisible spot of dirt on his breeches.

Abigail said gently, "I spoke with old Mrs. Hayes, who used to be the housekeeper here. She's blind now, poor old dear. She told me she found blood in the hall after your family left."

"Blood?" Miles echoed. "What a thought!" He tucked his chin. "I say, Miss Foster, you read too many gothic novels. My dear brother was alive when we left here. And is now buried in a churchyard in Bristol, near my mother's family."

"And . . . your father?"

"I honestly don't know. We never saw him again. And I hope we never shall." He rose abruptly. "Now, if you will excuse me, I am weary and would like to rest before dinner."

"Of course. I am sorry to have upset you. I shouldn't have pried."

He paused beside her chair and reached down his hand. Uncertain of his intention, she tentatively raised her own. He took it in his and pressed it warmly.

"You do not upset me, Miss Foster," he whispered with a sad smile. "You are a balm to my soul."

Standing in the nave of the church the next afternoon, Abigail handed William another taper as he replaced the spent ones in the chandelier.

"May I tell you something?" she began.

He shifted his weight on the ladder. "Of course."

"I haven't told anyone yet, though I'm not sure why. It's been going on for some time."

He looked down at her, a wary light in his eyes. "What has?"

"I have been receiving letters."

"Letters?" he asked carefully. "From a gentleman?"

"No. At least I don't think so. They're anonymous."

"A secret admirer?"

"Of course not. From someone who used to live here."

He stiffened. "From Mr. Pembrooke?"

"No. From his sister, Harriet, I think. About the years she lived here."

"Why would she not sign them?"

"I don't know. But some of what she writes does not reflect well on her father, so perhaps anonymity gives her the courage to divulge her secrets."

"What sort of secrets?"

"Apparently she was afraid of her father. She also writes about her friendship with another girl from the village."

"Oh, who?"

"Someone called Lizzie."

"Lizzie is a common name. No surname?"

Abigail shook her head. "And Harriet didn't give her real name for fear the girl wouldn't associate with her. I gather the Pembrookes were ostracized while they were here."

"Yes, they were."

"I wonder where the girls are now," Abigail continued. "They would be about thirty, give or take a few years, if I've done my sums correctly. Do you know any Lizzies that age?"

William paused to consider. "Mrs. Matthews's given name is Elizabeth. She is in her early thirties—the woman with the five boys?"

"Ah, yes."

"And Mrs. Hayes's niece is named Eliza. I don't think I've ever heard anyone call her Lizzie, but it's possible. . . . Though she is only in her midtwenties.

Abigail thought of Eliza, taking care of her aunt, who once worked and lived in Pembrooke Park. She *had* seen Eliza writing something, and standing near Pembrooke graves in the churchyard. . . .

William climbed down the ladder, adding, "I could ask Leah— she might remember if there were any other girls by that name."

"Thank you. Or I could ask her myself next time I see her. Was Leah acquainted with Harriet Pembrooke?"

"I don't think so. She was away at school for a year when they lived here."

"Still, it wouldn't hurt to ask."

William slanted her a telling glance. "I forget you don't know my sister all that well yet. She doesn't like to talk about herself. Or the past. Or the Pembrookes."

Abigail nodded, recalling Leah's reticence to enter Pembrooke Park, and again wondered if she'd had a bad experience there. Or if one of the Pembrookes had mistreated her. She couldn't imagine charming Miles doing so. He'd only been a boy at the time. And Harriet had been so desperate for a friend.

The older brother? Or Clive Pembrooke himself? Abigail felt a little shiver pass over her. She prayed she was wrong.

Chapter 15

The next day Gilbert sent over a note, letting Abigail know he was returning to London. He had not visited her again. Could he have not at least come and said good-bye? Drawing her shoulders back, she went and gave her father the news with feigned nonchalance.

Abigail left her father and Miles playing a game of backgammon and took herself out of doors. She walked to the garden and began pulling weeds again, to clear her mind, to think, and to avoid Miles for a while. Natty Mr. Pembrooke would not be offering to help her in this chore, she knew.

The day was sunny and mild, and her only company was the occasional bee and a pair of warblers flitting about a wild service tree, its white blooms garlanding the garden wall.

Sometime later, Kitty Chapman appeared and joined in the task without being asked.

Abigail paused to smile at the girl. "Thank you, Kitty. I would be happy to pay you something for your trouble."

"That's all right. I needed to get out of the house for a while anyway. Will and Papa were arguing about something."

"Oh? I'm sorry to hear it."

The girl shrugged, then brightened. "But I wouldn't say no to some flowers, if you wouldn't mind."

"Of course not. Help yourself."

They pulled weeds for a time, then Abigail walked over to the potting shed for shears. She hesitated, looking at the quiet corner between the potting shed and the walled garden with a pinch of sadness, thinking of the time the two secret friends had spent there. For a moment she closed her eyes and imagined them, could almost hear their young voices, reading lines from some play. She breathed deep, and found the air smelled deliciously of thyme and honeysuckle. She opened her eyes and was surprised to find two butterflies had alighted on her rose-colored sleeve—a garden white and an orange-tipped butterfly. So different, yet so alike. The sight stilled her for some reason. Then the two fluttered away in opposite directions.

Abigail rejoined Kitty in the garden and handed her the shears. She watched as the girl began selecting oxeye daisies, yellow irises, lilies, and wild roses.

"Who will you give the flowers to, Kitty?"

"My grandmother. She has come to stay with us."

"Has she?"

The girl nodded, adding some greenery to her clutch of blooms. "She's had another fall, and Mamma frets so. Grandmamma says she'll be up and about in no time and wants to return to her own house as soon as may be, but . . . well, we'll have to see."

"It's kind of you to bring her flowers."

"I thought they might cheer her. We only have the three bedrooms, and I share with Leah. So we put her in Jacob's room and set up a little bed for him in the back porch. William's offered to have him in the parsonage, but Papa wants him at home. I thought the flowers would help decorate my brother's room. And hopefully overcome the smell of his foul stockings." Kitty grinned and winked. The expression reminded Abigail of William's wry smiles and mischievous winks.

Abigail said, "I hate the thought of all of you being cramped when we have so much room, but I don't suppose your father would allow you or Jacob to stay at Pembrooke Park while your grandmother is recuperating?"

Kitty shook her head, an impish glint in her eye. "You suppose correctly."

They finished their work, then Kitty said, "Come to the house, Miss Foster. Grandmamma would love to meet you."

"And I her. But . . . what about the argument?"

"Oh, it's sure to have blown over by now." Kitty shielded her eyes. "In fact, there goes Will now."

Abigail glanced over her shoulder and saw Mr. Chapman leaving the grove and striding toward the parsonage. She was surprised he did not stop to say hello, but perhaps he had not seen them there in the garden.

"See?" Kitty grinned at her. "Coast is clear."

But first Abigail asked Kitty to follow her into the house and belowstairs, where they found a simple glass vase for the flowers and asked Mrs. Walsh for something to take as a welcome gift. When they explained who it was for, Mrs. Walsh's reserve fell away and she bustled about, gathering a bottle of jugged hare and a small plum pudding to take to Mrs. Reynolds, apparently an old friend of hers.

Armed with gifts, Abigail walked back to the Chapman cottage with Kitty. She met Mrs. Reynolds ensconced in the small bed-chamber, bound leg raised on a cushion. The pleasant-looking old woman, in face very similar to Kate Chapman, accepted the flowers and gifts with smiling gratitude. Abigail talked with her for several minutes before wishing her a speedy recovery and excusing herself.

Leah was waiting for her outside and seemed happy to see her. "Can you stay and talk for a few minutes?" she invited, offering her a glass of lemonade.

"I would like that. Thank you."

The two women sat on a bench in the little garden in front of the house, since it was a beautiful day, and because the house was quite crowded at the moment. They talked about everyday things for a few minutes—Leah's grandmother coming to stay, the upcoming Sunday school lessons, and the glorious weather.

Then Abigail said tentatively, "We have an unexpected house-guest as well. Have you heard?"

"Yes. Papa told me."

Abigail hesitated. "Kitty mentioned your father and brother had a row earlier. I hope that's not what they argued about?"

"No. Not . . . directly." Leah avoided her eyes and asked, "How is it going with him there?"

"Fine, I suppose," Abigail said. "Miles is quite charming, really. Though I do wonder how long he plans to stay."

She noticed Leah begin to fidget, her grip tightening on her glass.

"But let's not talk about that," Abigail said quickly. "I haven't seen you in several days. Tell me what has been happening since I saw you last. Any word from Andrew Morgan?"

Leah's pretty face fell, and Abigail knew she had wandered from one sore topic to another.

Leah looked off in the distance and said flatly, "I don't think I will be seeing Mr. Morgan again."

"Why do you say that? I am certain he admires you."

Leah nodded slightly. "Admiration is one thing. But he is too honorable to do anything about it. I overheard his mother, you see, chastising him for even inviting me to the ball. Apparently, William has sufficient respectability as a clergyman and former schoolmate of Andrew's. But his parents cannot overlook the fact that my mother had been in service. And my father, as their agent and a former steward, is little higher."

"But certainly Andrew will persuade them."

She shook her head. "I am older than you, Miss Foster, and a little wiser in the ways of the world, so don't be offended if I disagree. When a woman marries a man she also marries his family, for better or for worse. And that is how it should be. I shouldn't want a man who would have to extricate himself from his family in order to be my husband, nor a man who would alienate himself from my family in order to please his. And his parents clearly want him to marry someone else. You saw Miss Padgett—young and wealthy. It is not as though I ever stood a chance, objections to my parentage or not."

Abigail reached over and pressed her hand, feeling a painful twinge of empathy. For a moment the two sat in companionable silence.

Then Leah added, "The Morgans are new to the parish, you see. They only visited the area a few times before inheriting Hunts Hall. They don't know . . . can't be expected to understand . . ."

When her words trailed off, Abigail prompted, "To understand what?"

"How . . . well respected Mac Chapman is, and—"

At that moment, Kitty ran out of the house, waving a piece of paper over her head like a flag. "Jacob has a love letter. Jacob has a love letter. . . ."

Jacob came barreling after her, long arms pumping. "Give that back! It's mine!"

Leah sent Abigail a wry glance. "And how very genteel my family truly is."

On Sunday morning, Abigail glanced at her father, intently slicing his sausages, then looked across the breakfast table at Miles.

"Mr. Pembrooke," she began, "I . . . don't suppose you'd want to go to church with us?"

Miles opened his mouth. Closed it again. And then smiled at her fondly. "Thank you for inviting me, Miss Foster, however equivocally done."

"I did not mean to—"

He held up a hand to forestall her protests. "I understand. And don't worry—I am not offended. I did not plan to go in any case. I could not stand to face him."

Her father spoke up. "To face Mac Chapman, do you mean? Come, Miles. I hope you don't mind, but Abigail mentioned the rumors about your father all those years ago. Stuff and nonsense the lot of it, I imagine. But you cannot let a few small-minded busybodies keep you from living your life and going where you will." He laid down his knife and fork with a clank.

"You are kind, Mr. Foster. But I don't stay home to avoid Mac or any one particular person. I meant that I dare not face God." He added in apparent good humor, "It is His house, after all. And I am definitely not an invited guest, if you know what I mean. I don't belong there."

"Of course you do." Abigail's heart twisted to see the wounded vulnerability on the man's face, beneath his humorous façade. "Church is for everyone," she said. "And so is God. Did Jesus himself not eat with sinners and tax collectors?"

"You flatter me, Miss Foster."

"I don't mean that you—"

"Heavens, you are fun to tease." He patted her arm. "No, no. I appreciate your thoughtfulness and shall consider what you say. But for now I will stay here. I will not interrupt the worship of all those good souls, and you can't pretend my attendance wouldn't do so. It is not as though I could sneak into the place, what with a mere two dozen parishioners?"

"Give or take," Abigail allowed.

"There, you see. But I shall wait here for you. And . . . if you thought to include me in your prayers, I should not mind."

"I shall indeed," Abigail earnestly assured him.

After Sunday school that day, Abigail took Leah's arm, planning to walk her home and hoping for a private chat on the way. She began, "If you are determined not to see Andrew Morgan, then I should like you to meet Miles. I know you don't like strangers, but he isn't—not really. He is a distant relative of my father's and your former neighbor. And yes, he is a Pembrooke, but he's very agreeable—and quite handsome."

Leah protested, "Miss Foster, I don't—"

Abigail looked up and paused, surprised to see the very man in question on the path. "There he is now. Come, let me introduce you."

She tugged, but Leah froze like a statue, her arm as yielding as a stout branch.

Seeing them, Miles Pembrooke smiled and walked over, his limp less noticeable. Perhaps he made more effort to conceal it when meeting new people, or at least when meeting pretty ladies.

"We were just talking about you," Abigail said and turned to Leah. "Miss Leah Chapman, may I introduce Mr. Miles Pembrooke."

Abigail watched Miles for his reaction. Saw his eyes widen slightly and his expression soften as his gaze roved Leah's gentle features, her large pretty eyes and honey-brown hair. His head tilted to one side as he regarded her in apparent admiration and . . . something else—curiosity, or perhaps recognition.

He bowed low to her. "Miss Chapman, what a pleasure."

Leah stared at him. Dipped a stiff curtsy without removing her gaze from his face. Dare Abigail hope she was as taken by his handsome face and polite address as he obviously was with her beauty?

"Mr. . . . Pembrooke?" Leah echoed in a high, pinched voice.

"Yes. Miles," he clarified, tilting his head to the other side. "I believe we have met before, Miss Chapman. When we were children. I don't flatter myself you would recall."

"Did we?" Leah asked almost timidly.

"Soon after you came home from school, I believe it was. Of course that was years ago. I no doubt made a nuisance of myself, mischievous boy that I was. At least, my sister always thought so."

"Ah. Yes. Perhaps. Well. As you say, it was a long time ago." Leah tried to extract her arm from Abigail's, but Abigail held fast.

Leah swallowed and asked, "So . . . what are you doing here now, Mr. Pembrooke?"

"I wished to see my old home again—that's all."

"And where is the rest of your family?"

"My mother died last year, God rest her soul. My brother died not long after we left here."

"I am—" it seemed as if the word stuck in Leah Chapman's usually polite mouth—"sorry to hear it."

"Are you? Or are you glad there are a few less Pembrookes in the world?" Miles's grin did not reach his eyes.

Leah's mouth slackened. "Of course I am not glad—"

"We are the last of a dying breed, you know," Miles continued amiably. "My brother died young. My sister has had no children. And I have not been blessed with a spouse to shower with love as I have long wished for. And you, Miss Chapman? Dare I hope you are not yet attached?"

She paled. "I am not attached, nor have I plans to become so, especially . . ." She let her words trail away.

Hurt shone in his round eyes. "Especially to a man like me?"

"That's not what I meant. But no, I could never become attached to a Pembrooke. No offense."

He looked at her with a sad smile but said nothing.

Leah cleared her throat and asked, "Your sister is in good health?"

"Yes. Last I saw her."

"And will you be staying long in the area?"

"I have not yet decided."

Abigail spoke up, "How interesting that you two knew each other as children. Has Miss Chapman changed a great deal in your estimation, Mr. Pembrooke?"

Miles smiled. "Well, you must remember I was only a boy of eleven or twelve at the time, and not really noticing girls. But I will say Miss Chapman has grown uncommonly pretty."

Leah looked away, disconcerted by his admiring gaze.

William Chapman approached, hesitated at seeing the three of them talking together, then strode forward, face thunderous.

"Leah! What are you doing? Come with me. Now."

Leah blinked up at her brother. "William?"

"Come." He took her arm and turned cold eyes on Abigail. "Excuse us, Miss Foster."

"Mr. Chapman, what is it? What have I done?"

He turned on Miles sharply. "Stay away from my sister, Mr. Pembrooke. Do you understand me?"

Miles's mouth drooped open. He looked at Abigail, and she met his stunned, hurt expression with one of her own.

Abigail stayed Miles with a quick hand to his sleeve, then hurried after William and Leah.

She caught up with them outside their cottage. "Mr. Chapman, wait."

He urged Leah inside, then whirled on Abigail. "What were you thinking? To introduce him to my sister? If my father had come upon them instead of me . . . I shudder to think what might have happened."

"But why? I don't understand."

"That's right. You don't. And it would be better for all involved if you stayed out of matters that don't concern you."

Tears stung her eyes. Never had she imagined William Chapman speaking to her in such a cutting tone. Or imagined seeing such anger in eyes that had previously regarded her with warm friendliness—even, she thought, admiration. But that look was now soundly replaced with disillusionment and betrayal. Did he feel betrayed on his friend Andrew's behalf? Or was he so prejudiced against Miles? Even if the old rumors about Clive Pembrooke were true, it shocked her that he would blame the son for his father's wrongdoing. Especially when Miles had been so young at the time. But perhaps he was not as compassionate as she'd believed him to be.

Even so, thoughts of losing his admiration and Leah's friendship were like twin knives thrust into her heart. Tears filled her eyes. She turned away to hide them and returned to Pembrooke Park alone.

Miles was waiting for her in the hall. "My dear Miss Foster, are you quite all right? You look very ill indeed. I do hope Mr. Chapman has not overly upset you."

"And I hope his rudeness has not offended you. I am quite at a loss to explain it. Usually he is perfectly amiable and polite. I have never seen him treat anyone so unkindly."

Miles studied her face, his expression measuring and disappointed. "Oh dear. Apparently you admire the man a great deal. I am sorry to have caused strife between you." He certainly appeared sorry. But she somehow doubted he would lose any sleep over it.

He added, "I had hoped the old prejudices would have faded after all this time. Against me and my sister, at any rate. I am the first, you see, to dip my toe back into this pond, to make known my presence. Harri is very reluctant to do so. She remembers all too well how people shunned us when we lived here. As I said, I don't really blame anybody for those days. My father being the sort of man he was. But now? After all this time? I do not look forward to telling Harri she was right not to trumpet her presence."

After Miss Foster turned away in retreat, William closed and latched the cottage door and turned to face Leah.

Expression pained, she asked, "Do you think that was wise?"

"Wise?" he echoed. "I find you in tête-à-tête with Miles Pembrooke, and you ask me if *my* actions were wise?"

"Hardly a tête-à-tête. Miss Foster was there as well, you remember. You *should* remember, having hurt her feelings in such a callous manner."

He blinked away the image of Miss Foster's wide, pained eyes. "But why were you even talking to him, considering . . . everything?"

"I was constrained by politeness. Miss Foster introduced us."

He looked heavenward, jaw clenched and biting back an oath.

"Why do you look so fierce? Remember she is not acquainted with our family history, as you have recently become. You were quite harsh with her. With them both."

He shook his head, his emotions still in a tangle. "I didn't think. Only reacted. My only thought was to protect you. To remove you from harm's way."

"Did you really think he would have harmed me—then and

there? Do you not see that by your very noticeable overreaction you have brought me to the notice of Mr. Pembrooke, rendering my own attempts to appear civil and unaffected void? Have we now not raised questions in his mind? Made him think twice about my history with his family?"

"I hope not." He pressed his eyes closed and sent up a prayer for mercy.

"I know this is hard for you," Leah said. "I have had years— almost my whole life—to get used to the idea. To learn to hide my feelings." She laid a hand on his arm. "I do understand, William. And I hope Miss Foster will as well. Eventually."

Chapter 16

For the next few days, the entire Chapman family seemed to make a point of avoiding Abigail, and Pembrooke Park in general. Not even Kitty stopped by, and there was no invitation to dinner after the midweek prayer service for their rector, Mr. Morris, who had come down with a worrisome fever. During the service, William and Mac avoided meeting her eye, and Leah departed as soon as the service concluded without staying to chat. Abigail began to fear that she had lost Leah's fledgling friendship and her brother's admiration forever.

Abigail tossed and turned in her bed well past eleven that night but was unable to fall asleep. She rose and paced her room, then quietly crossed the gallery into her mother's empty room. From its windows facing the churchyard she could see the parsonage. A light shone in the window.

Mr. Chapman was up late. Could he not sleep either? *Oh, God, help me heal the rift between us.*

Knowing she would not sleep unless she did something, Abigail decided to take a risk. She returned to her room, pulled on stockings and shoes, and slipped a dressing gown and shawl over her nightdress. Taking a candle lamp with her, she tiptoed back into the gallery. Seeing no light under her father's door, she decided not to disturb him and crept quietly down the stairs.

The servants had likely been asleep for some time. Even so, she tiptoed across the hall, quietly unbolted the door, and let herself outside, closing the door as silently as she could. The night air shivered through her muslin nightdress, and she wrapped the shawl more tightly around herself as she hurried along the verge, avoiding the gravel of the drive. She entered the moonlit churchyard, not allowing her gaze to linger on the gravestones or the swaying willow branches bowing in grief over the dead.

She shivered again, only partly from the cold.

Reaching the parsonage, she paused to collect herself. Her heart beat hard, more than the slight exertion of the walk justified. She took a deep breath and knocked softly. Then again.

A moment later, she heard faint footsteps within, the latch clicking, and the door opening. There stood William Chapman. Dressed in trousers and shirtsleeves, his shirt open at the neck, his hair tousled, his eyes weary, then widening in surprise as he recognized his late-night caller.

"Mr. Chapman, forgive me for showing up on your doorstep at such an hour. I saw your light, so I hoped I wouldn't wake you."

"No, I was not asleep." He gestured vaguely toward the desk inside, where a candle lamp burned and a Bible lay open, paper and quill nearby.

"I couldn't sleep," she said. "I feel terrible. I never meant to upset Leah, or you. I did not think it through. Or realize how strongly you felt about the Pembrookes. Won't you forgive me?"

"Miss Foster . . ." He paused, opening the door wider. "Here, step inside out of the cold for a moment."

She hoped she would not get him into trouble—or ruin her own reputation in the bargain. But she was too cold, and too upset, to worry about propriety at the moment.

He did not invite her any farther than the entryway, she noticed, and left the door ajar behind her. Again he gestured toward the desk. "I was writing you a letter. For it is I who should apologize to you. For a moment I thought I'd fallen asleep mid-letter and dreamt you on my doorstep."

She shook her head. "I should never have stuck my nose in. What was I thinking to introduce Mr. Pembrooke to your sister? Me—playing matchmaker! As though I have any experience in courtship."

"True. I don't recommend a future in matchmaking for you—or for anyone, for that matter. Even so, I should not have spoken so harshly to you. I overreacted, and I apologize."

"I have heard the rumors about Clive Pembrooke, of course," she said gently. "I know people believe he may have killed Robert Pembrooke. And I know how highly your father esteemed that gentleman. Had Mac reacted so vehemently, I would not have been shocked. But—"

"But that I, a clergyman, would hold the sins of the father against his son?"

Again, the Numbers verse ran through her mind. "Yes. After all, his family did nothing to yours."

"I am afraid it is not quite that simple, Miss Foster."

"If Miles did something—either as a boy or since his return, I am certain he would be happy to try and make amends."

"It is not within his power to do so."

"I don't . . . understand."

William ran a weary hand over his face. "I know you don't. And again, I'm sorry. There is more to the story, but it isn't my story to tell. Just believe me when I tell you, we have reason to dislike and distrust our former neighbors. No good can come from trying to foster a relationship between Miles Pembrooke and my sister."

She shook her head. "I shall never try that again. Be assured of that. I have learnt my lesson. I only hope Leah will forgive me in time. And you will too."

"I have already done so. And I hope you will forgive me."

"Of course I do."

A grin quirked his lips. "And here I've been sitting an hour, trying to compose an apology that was accepted in five minutes."

She managed a wobbly smile.

Then, remembering something, she said, "I know you offered to ask Leah about anyone named Lizzie she might know, but never mind that now. I—"

He said, "Actually, I think it would be best to leave Leah out of these sorts of questions, Miss Foster. All right?" A hint of defensiveness crept into his voice again, and Abigail regretted mentioning it.

"Very well."

He looked suddenly over her shoulder, eyes narrowing. "What's that?"

"Where?" She turned to see what had caught his eye.

"That light in the window."

She looked, and there in an upper window, light from a single candle bobbed past. Her breath caught. "That's my mother's room. But it's unoccupied at present."

Who was in there? The candle was partially shielded, not reflecting on its bearer, perhaps by design.

"It's probably Duncan. Or one of the maids," she supposed aloud.

"At this hour?" He frowned. "Did you happen to lock the front door when you left?"

"No. I didn't think to. I didn't plan to be gone more than a few minutes."

William Chapman's jaw clenched. "Perhaps I should go rouse my father. . . ."

"Your father and his gun? I don't think that necessary. Or wise. Perhaps it's my father wandering about for some reason."

"Looking for you?"

"I wouldn't think so." The thought pinched her with guilt. She hoped not. She didn't want to worry him, but nor did she want him to learn she'd left the house at night to speak to a man.

"Let's go see who it is." William grabbed his coat from its peg and shrugged it on. I don't want you entering the house alone. Just in case a prowler has let himself in."

240

He grasped her hand and led her across the lawn, taking the verge as she had done earlier to avoid the gravel drive, and then stepped lightly across the paving stones to the front door. He opened it with care, listened, then stepped in first, keeping her shielded behind his body. The main level was dark and quiet.

"Come on," he whispered, leading her across the hall and up the main stairs. She liked the feel of his larger warm hand engulfing hers. Her heart pounded a bit too hard from his proximity, and the sense of danger in the air.

"This way," she whispered at the top of the stairs, gesturing toward her mother's bedchamber. She felt rather brazen, holding his hand, but did not let go.

The door to her mother's room stood ajar. Had she left it open when she'd looked from its window?

"Shh," she urged. They paused where they were, listening. A faint tap-tapping reached them from within. Again, he stepped in front of her, shielding her and slowly pushing open the door wide enough to enter.

In a dim arc of candlelight, Miles Pembrooke stood, candle in one hand, tapping against the wall with his stick, ear pressed close to the wood. Listening for the sound of an empty chamber behind the paneling?

"Looking for something?" William asked, his quiet voice cracking like a cannon in the dark room. Miles jumped, and Abigail squeezed William's hand a bit too hard.

For a moment Miles froze, like a thief caught. Then he relaxed and a smile eased across his face.

"You two frightened the wits out of me."

Abigail asked, "What are you doing in my mother's room, Mr. Pembrooke?"

"I think you mean *my* mother's room, Miss Foster. Or at least it was. I was looking for, ah, some memento. I'd hoped perhaps something of hers had been left here."

"This late at night?"

"Yes, I found myself awake and missing her. And you, Miss Foster?

I am surprised to see you up and about and keeping company with our good parson so late at night."

Abigail glanced at William, then away, releasing his hand at last. No explanation presented itself.

"Miss Foster need not explain herself to you, Mr. Pembrooke," William said. "But I judge it safe to say that a memento wasn't all you were looking for. The treasure, I take it?"

"Well, yes, if you must know. I've been thinking about my father's obsession with a treasure hidden somewhere in the house. All stuff and nonsense no doubt."

"No doubt."

Abigail said, "In future, Mr. Pembrooke, if there is something you wish to see in the house, or if you want to visit your mother's former room, you need only ask. That is, until my own mother arrives, of course."

"Of course."

"Surely Mr. Pembrooke doesn't intend to stay that long," William said, sending the man a challenging look. "Do you?"

"Ah. Well, I have no definite plans. Though I admit I have been looking forward to making the acquaintance of the rest of Miss Foster's family. We are related, after all."

"Only very distantly," Mr. Chapman said, smile forced.

"Well, closer than you will ever be."

"Is that so?"

"Yes."

For a moment the two men stood, eyes locked, shoulders squared, jaws clenched.

Abigail hurried to diffuse the tension, saying, "All right, gentlemen. It is late, and I think it time we all called a truce and returned to our bedchambers. All right?"

"Very well," Miles said, shuffling to the door, his limp less noticeable than usual.

They followed him out into the gallery.

William Chapman waited until the door to the guest room had closed behind Miles, before he turned to Abigail once more. "Are you sure you'll be all right? I hate the thought of him here in the house with you."

"Mr. Pembrooke is harmless, I assure you. A thief I might believe, but not a murderer. Besides, my father's room is just there."

"Even so, promise me you will lock your bedchamber door tonight and every night."

In the darkness she could not clearly see his eyes, but his voice rumbled in solemn concern.

"Very well. I shall."

Now that Mr. Chapman had forgiven her, she thought she would sleep soundly at last. But perhaps a locked door would be a good idea as well.

The next day, Abigail paid a call at the Chapman cottage, hoping to make things right with Leah as well. Leah herself came to the door, and Abigail braced herself to be rebuffed.

"I've come to apologize, Miss Chapman," she began. "I hope you will forgive me. If I had known there was such enmity between you and Mr. Pembrooke, I would not have made the introduction. I never intended to upset you."

Leah sighed. "I know you meant no harm, Miss Foster. Come, let's take a walk, shall we?"

The two walked through the grove together. Abigail did not risk, however, trying to take her arm.

Abigail said, "I didn't realize you were even acquainted with Mr. Pembrooke."

Leah shrugged. "I was away at school when Clive Pembrooke moved his family into Pembrooke Park. But they were still here when I returned—though they remained only about a year longer."

"Did you meet Miles then?"

"Not that I remember. He was only a boy. And my father wouldn't let us have anything to do with the Pembrooke family. He mistrusted—even detested—Clive Pembrooke, and that distrust extended to his wife and children as well. I was forbidden to set foot on the grounds, even though our property was adjacent to the estate."

"Surely you saw each other at church or around the village?"

She shrugged again. "The Pembrookes didn't often attend church. And when they did, they had their box in front—entered after we were all seated and left before the rest of us. By the time I returned from my year at school, everyone in the village was either afraid of them or hated them. I didn't care about the parents, I supposed they deserved it. And the Pembrooke boys had each other and didn't seem to notice."

"And the girl?" Abigail prompted. "You must have met her."

She resolutely shook her head. "I never officially met Harriet Pembrooke. But I saw her from a distance. And that was enough to make me feel sorry for her. I often wonder where she is now, and if she is happy."

Yes, Abigail thought. *So do I.*

"When they left," Leah continued, "everyone was relieved. Now Miles Pembrooke's return has raised the old fears once more." She sighed and looked pensively off into the distance.

Abigail took a deep breath and asked gently, "Did one of the Pembrookes do something to hurt you in some way?"

Leah glanced at her with troubled eyes, then looked away. "Me? How could they hurt me . . . ?"

Abigail bit her lip. "I don't know. But again, I am sorry."

"I know you are. And I forgive you." Leah managed a smile and took her arm. "Now, let's finish our walk."

When she returned to the manor, Abigail walked into the servery, hoping for a cup of tea, and stopped midstride, taken aback to see Duncan and Molly standing shoulder to shoulder, heads together.

"What is going on here?" she asked, her tone sharper than she'd intended.

Molly straightened and whirled, face suffusing with color. "I . . . Sorry, miss. We were only talking for a minute. Honest."

Duncan slowly raised his head, sending her a lopsided grin. "I was showing Molly a most interesting book." He lifted a thin, well-worn volume in his hands.

The girl's eyes begged for understanding. "That's right, miss. That's all."

"Thank you, Molly. Go about your work, please," Abigail said.

The maid bowed her head and hurried from the room.

When they were alone, Duncan said, "It's an old copy of *Steele's Navy Lists*. You might find it interesting as well. It's most telling about your houseguest—a man who passes off his limp as a war wound to gain sympathy from females."

Abigail frowned. "Mr. Pembrooke is *not* pretending to have a limp, I assure you."

"Pretending, exaggerating, I don't judge. It worked, didn't it? He looks harmless—the poor injured war hero—and is invited in to stay like some wounded pup." He shook his head. "Probably murder us all in our beds."

"Duncan. I don't appreciate your attitude, or your gossip."

"Ain't gossip, miss. I know you don't think much of me, but you have to give me credit. I did my research. He's right here on page 72. Served on the *Red Phoenix*. Do you know anything about the *Phoenix*, miss?"

She shook her head.

His eyes glinted. "One of the only ships to escape the war with barely a scratch."

Abigail's stomach soured. "Perhaps he was injured in a land skirmish then, or during training."

"Whatever helps you sleep at night, miss." Duncan's voice dripped with sarcasm. "Far be it from me to discredit a *war hero*."

Later that afternoon, Abigail received the new edition of the Lloyds' magazine in the post and took it into the morning room to read while she drank her tea. The magazine held news articles, fashion prints, poetry, and short stories. She read the magazine mostly out of loyalty to Susan Lloyd, and because it made her feel closer to her friend to recognize her "voice" in an editorial, or piece of society news, although most of the articles were written by others.

Abigail flipped past the fashion prints and skimmed the table of contents.

One author's name caught her eye. Condensed as the type was, she at first misread the name as Pembrooke, but then looked closer: *E. P. Brooks.*

Ah! The local author . . .

She turned to the gothic story, entitled "Death at Dreadmoore Manor." She skimmed through the introduction of a young woman, the daughter of an earl, kidnapped after his murder and raised as a lowly housemaid by plotting relatives. Unprotected, the poor young woman was left to her own defenses when an evil rake came calling. Would someone discover her true identity and rescue her in time?

The story reminded Abigail of Cinderella stories she'd heard, and a French opera, *Cendrillon*, she'd seen in London. The young heroine of the story was selfless and unbelievably good-natured in the face of hardship. The preening, mustachioed villain with a maniacal laugh came across as nearly comical instead of terrifying, as the author no doubt intended. Although she was no expert, Abigail thought the writing quite good, despite its flaws.

Again, she regarded the author's name, E. P. Brooks—or rather, her pseudonym—as Susan had told her most female writers submitted under a *nom de plume.*

She thought again of Eliza's ink-stained fingers and the periodicals she had seen in her kitchen. Could it be . . . ?

Abigail decided to pay another call on Mrs. Hayes and Eliza. The older woman was napping in a sitting-room chair when she arrived, but Eliza invited Abigail into the kitchen to wait while she put the kettle on. "She'll rouse herself when the tea kettle whistles."

Abigail casually wandered around the kitchen while Eliza set the tea tray. With a jolt of recognition, she saw the latest edition of the Lloyds' magazine on the table, and ventured, "I read this as well."

Eliza glanced over. "Do you? I thought I was the only one in the county who subscribed."

"No." Abigail added tentatively, "In fact, the editor is a friend of mine." She watched the woman's reaction.

Eliza's hands momentarily stilled over the sugar bowl. Then she said, "Oh? How interesting."

"Yes, she finds it very interesting work. Do you . . . enjoy the magazine?"

"I do, yes, when I find the time."

Abigail was disappointed Eliza didn't take the opening she'd offered but decided not to press her. Perhaps she was mistaken in the matter.

Eliza picked up the tray. "Come, Miss Foster. Let's join Auntie and have a nice visit."

Abigail followed the woman into the sitting room.

The old housekeeper looked up eagerly at their entrance. "Another visitor? Has Master Miles called again?"

"No, Auntie, it's Miss Foster."

"Oh . . . too bad." The woman's expression fell, and she turned her attention to the tea.

Eliza explained, "Mr. Pembrooke called here a few days ago."

"Did he?" Abigail asked, taken aback.

"Indeed he did," Mrs. Hayes said over her teacup. "And how well he has turned out. So charming and well spoken. Twice the gentleman his father ever was. But you didn't hear me say a word against the man." She turned sightless eyes toward the door, as though Clive Pembrooke himself might be hovering nearby.

Eliza held up the plate. "Here, Auntie, have a biscuit."

She took one, adding, "And so attentive to Eliza."

"He was only being polite," Eliza insisted, pouring another cup.

Mrs. Hayes shook her head. "I may be blind, but even I could see he was interested in you."

Eliza sent Abigail a pained look, silently shaking her head to signal her disagreement.

Abigail took her hint and changed the subject. Lifting her teacup, she began tentatively. "You mentioned your aunt raised you, Miss Smith. May I ask about your parents, if that is not too painful a question?"

"Painful, no, though perhaps a bit uncomfortable for delicate ears."

Abigail tipped her head back in surprise. "Oh? How so?"

"My mother was housemaid at Pembrooke Park until she came to be with child."

"Oh." Abigail swallowed, the hot tea scalding her throat and her eyes watering. "I . . . see . . ."

Eliza looked at Mrs. Hayes. "And we don't talk about my father—do we, Auntie?"

"Your father was a good man," Mrs. Hayes insisted. "He let her stay on at Pembrooke Park far longer than many a master would have."

Abigail stared. *Good heavens.* Was she insinuating Robert Pembrooke was Eliza's father? Or even . . . Mac? Is that why he visited so often? Helped around the house? No, it couldn't be. She reminded herself that Mrs. Hayes wasn't in her right mind.

The former housekeeper took a noisy sip, then turned in her general direction. "You do know that Robert Pembrooke had more than one daughter, don't you, Miss Foster?"

No, that was one rumor she hadn't heard.

"Auntie . . ." Eliza warned, with a worried glance at Abigail. "We are not to talk about that."

Mrs. Hayes sipped again, then set down her cup with a clank. "Miss Foster living in Pembrooke Park. It isn't right! Not when another young woman deserves it so much more. E for Eliza. E for Eleanor . . ."

Did Eliza fancy herself a Pembrooke? The astounding question was on Abigail's lips, but she swallowed it down with hot tea and bile.

Eliza gave Abigail a tight smile. "You mustn't listen to her, Miss Foster. Lord knows, I don't most days."

Abigail forced a smile in return. "Your mother died when you were very young?"

"Yes. I was only five."

"I'm sorry."

Eliza shrugged. "I don't remember her very well. Or my father for that matter. Though Auntie tells me he passed on his way with words to me."

Abigail thought again of the local writer's pseudonym: E. P. Brooks. A play on E. Pembrooke, perhaps? Maybe neither aunt nor niece were quite sound of mind.

Suddenly eager to quit the place, Abigail thanked the women for tea and took her leave, feeling queasy from the bitter cup and uncomfortable conversation.

When she neared the bridge on her walk home, a black barouche rumbled past, forcing Abigail to step to the far edge of the road. She had seen the equipage before, she thought, but she couldn't remember where. Heavy draperies hung on the windows, obscuring her view of the occupant.

Continuing on her way, Abigail became aware of an acrid odor. She sniffed and walked on. Was someone burning brush? Crossing the bridge, she looked ahead to the estate. A crow shrieked and flew away, drawing her attention skyward as she followed its flight. Her heart thudded. A roiling column of grey and black smoke spiraled upward . . . from the church? No, behind it. The parsonage!

For a moment Abigail remained frozen, mind whirling. *William.* She looked this way and that and saw no one to call to. Then she hitched up her skirts and ran—through the gate and around the church to the parsonage.

Flames shot from the rear window. Abigail pushed through the door and looked inside. There was William, trying to beat out the flames leaping up the window curtains.

Seeing her, he yelled, "Ring the bell!"

Why hadn't she thought of that? She ran back through the churchyard, jumping over abandoned gardening tools and a watering can, and hurried into the porch. Hands quaking, she reached for the rope spooled on spokes high on the wall away from youngsters' reach, and nearly too high for her as well. Rising on tiptoe, she managed to uncoil the rope. She gave it several jarring pulls, the *clang, clang, clang* lacking the usual solemnity of a service toll. Then she ran back to the parsonage, pausing to snatch up the watering can and carry it with her. Not that one pail of water would do much good against the growing flames, but it was all she could think to do.

Duncan called from Pembrooke's front door, "What is it?"

"Fire!" she yelled back, pointing toward the billowing smoke.

Duncan gaped upward, then disappeared back into the house. She hoped he had some idea of how to help. Reentering the parsonage, she saw daggers of flame leap from the curtain onto William Chapman's shoulder and arm.

"William! You're on fire!" she shouted.

The roar of the fire had grown, and he didn't appear to hear her. Stepping forward, she sloshed the contents of the watering can onto his shoulder, missing the mark, and getting half of it on his neck and the back of his head. Still, it extinguished the flame.

He whirled at last, stunned.

"Your arm was on fire," she said. "What else can I do?"

"Gather everyone you can and start a fire brigade. And pray."

She blinked. She had no experience with one and not much with the other. But she hurried outside to do his bidding.

With relief she saw Mac—stern, competent Mac—barking orders and forming a line down to the river, which was thankfully quite close, encircling most of the estate as it did. Duncan, Molly, Polly, Jacob, Leah, Mrs. Chapman, and even Kitty ran over from the direction of the cottage, stables, and perhaps the potting shed with various pails and cans. Other people ran over the bridge from the direction of nearby Easton and began filling in the line. She recognized several of the older boys from Sunday school among them, as well as Mr. Peterman, Mr. Wilson, and Mr. Matthews, and several other parishioners she knew by face if not by name.

Her eyes stung from the smoke and the awful beauty of seeing a close-knit community sweating, straining, and working together like the loyal family they were.

Abigail joined the line.

Half an hour later, they'd managed to put out the fire. By then, the greater portion of the rear wall and two interior rooms were all but destroyed.

"Kitchen fire, was it?" someone asked.

Another quipped, "That's what happens when you give a bachelor his own kitchen."

"Never leave a cooking fire unattended." Mrs. Peterman wagged her finger at William. "If you had a wife, she would have known better."

Her husband added, "Don't worry, Parson—we'll help you patch 'er up."

Patch? Abigail thought incredulously. It would take far more than a patch to repair the damage.

William said little, neither confirming nor denying their theories. He stood, hands on hips, staring at the ruined parsonage, jaw tense and soot-streaked, his red hair marled with black.

The villagers began to drift home, Mrs. Chapman and Leah thanking everyone for their help as though hosts at a party. Or a funeral.

When only Abigail and his father stood beside him, William said, "This was no kitchen fire."

Mac asked, "No? What do you think, then, Will. A spark from the stove?"

"In my bed?" William snapped. "I think not."

"In your bed? I thought it started in the kitchen."

William shook his head, mouth pursed, his eyes measuring, thinking. . . .

"Did a candle lamp fall or something?"

"No, Papa."

"Are you saying you don't think it was an accident?"

"Keep your voice down, but yes. Someone started that fire."

"You can't know that."

"If you mean can I prove it? No. But I know it. In here." He pressed a hand to his chest.

"But who would do such a thing?" Mac asked. "And why?"

Abigail spoke up, "I don't know if I should mention it or not, but I saw a black barouche drive past when I walked up the lane and spied the fire."

"Whose barouche?"

"I don't know, but there can't be many vehicles that fine around here."

William shook his head. "I don't think we need to look any farther than Pembrooke Park for a suspect."

"Duncan, do you mean?" Abigail asked, having witnessed the manservant's clear dislike of the Chapmans.

Again he shook his head.

Abigail blinked. "You don't mean *Miles*? I can't believe he would do such a thing."

"He was clearly angry with me last night, and perhaps jealous in the bargain."

Mac's eyes narrowed. "What happened last night?"

"I'll tell you later, Papa." He looked at her. "Where is Mr. Pembrooke now?"

As if summoned by their conversation, Charles Foster came jogging over, Miles Pembrooke hobbling behind with his stick.

"Molly just came and found us," her father said. "Is everyone all right?"

"Did you not hear the bell, Papa? Or see the smoke?"

"We were playing chess in the drawing room—it's at the back of the house, so we didn't see anything. We did hear bells but assumed it was some special service we didn't know about."

William and his father exchanged a look. Was he chagrined to have suspected Miles unfairly? Or did he suspect him still?

"Good heavens, Mr. Chapman," Miles said, pulling a face. "Your shoulder looks horrendous."

"Hm?" William craned his neck to look at it.

Mac frowned down at the angry patch of charred shirt and skin, which looked as if some wild cat had clawed William's shoulder. Perhaps the shock and his focus on putting out the fire had masked the pain, for it seemed as if William—as if all of them—were only now becoming aware of the injury. He swayed slightly.

"Sit, lad. Here," his father said, guiding him to one of the kitchen chairs they'd dragged out to salvage from the flames.

He sat heavily down.

"I'll ride for the surgeon," Miles offered, surprising everyone. "Those burns should be seen to."

"Mr. Pembrooke, I don't—"

"Don't worry. I can't run with this leg, but you've never seen anyone saddle a horse faster." He turned and began hobbling toward the stable. "Mr. Brown still surgeon here?"

"Aye," Mac called after him. "Same green house."

True to his word, Miles Pembrooke was seen galloping over the bridge on his horse a short time later.

After he had gone, Charles Foster looked at William and said kindly, "Come, son. Let's get you into the manor. "You can't stay here. Not with all the smoke. The surgeon can see you there."

Soon William found himself lying on a velvet sofa in the Pembrooke Park morning room. How strange it felt to be there, his parents and the Fosters gathered around him. A clean sheet covered the fine old velvet—the housekeeper had seen to it—and considering his sooty state, William took no offense.

Mr. Brown had come, tended his burns in private, and laid an ear to his chest to listen to his heart and lungs. Then he'd asked the others to join them.

"I'll be back tomorrow to check on the bandages and reapply salve," he'd announced. "I recommend plenty of rest and liquids for a few days. And clean air—stay clear of the parsonage."

"But I need to board up the broken windows, at least, and cover the hole in the wall."

"Now, lad, don't you worry about that," his father said. "Leave it to me."

"That's right. Listen to your pa," Mr. Brown admonished him. "Don't try to return yet. Not with all that soot and smoke in the air. Bad for the breathing." He looked at Mac. "Keep him from overexerting himself for a few days at least."

"If I have to tie him down."

Kate Chapman added, "We'll nurse him at home, Mr. Brown."

"But there isn't room," William said. "Not with Grandmamma staying with us now."

"My wife's mother has recently moved in with us while she recovers from a fall," Mac explained. "But we'll make do."

William shook his head. "I don't want to put anyone from their beds."

Mr. Foster spoke up. "Your son must stay here with us, Mac. We have so many spare rooms. You and your family may come and go as you please—and Mr. Brown, of course—until your son is quite recovered and the parsonage repaired."

"We could'na do that, Mr. Foster. But thank you for your offer."

"Why on earth not? Come, Mac, it would be our pleasure. The least we can do for our parson and neighbor."

"It is a very kind offer, but—"

"You may have your pick of the empty rooms upstairs. Or we might fit out this room, if you prefer, so he doesn't have to negotiate the stairs."

"I am not an invalid," William objected. "But even so, I must say the notion appeals to me. For one, if I might have this room here at the front of the house, I could keep an eye on the parsonage. If the fire was the work of vandals, I would be on hand to see their return."

He glanced at Miss Foster to gauge her reaction and then addressed her father. "I sincerely appreciate the offer, Mr. Foster. And hopefully after a few days, the worst of the smoke will have cleared and I will be able to make sufficient repairs to return."

"That seems a bit optimistic, Will," Mac said. "I think the damage is worse than you realize."

Mr. Foster said, "You are welcome to stay as long as need be. We don't mind at all. Do we, my dear?"

Miss Foster's face remained impassive, her hands folded primly before her. "Not at all, Papa."

Abigail walked out of the room with her father, leaving Mr. Chapman to rest, while Mac went to gather necessities for his son.

When they were out of earshot, she said, "That was very kind of you, Papa."

He said, "You know, I quite liked doing it. I must say I was surprised by the surge of . . . em, patronage I felt. I suppose this is what it must feel like to be of the manor born, to experience a paternal fondness for one's tenants and neighbors. A compulsion toward condescension and benevolence. Yes, I could quite get used to being lord of Pembrooke Park."

His words stirred warnings in Abigail. "Be careful not to grow too accustomed to it, Papa. Remember what Mr. Arbeau said. You have not inherited the place. You are merely its tenant."

"For now, yes. But once the tangle of the will is figured out . . . who knows?"

"Miles Pembrooke knows, I would imagine. Or his sister perhaps."

He sighed. "I suppose you're right. Still, I could see myself here. Doing . . . this. Forever."

She touched his arm. "We shall enjoy it while we can, Papa. But try not to become too attached to the place, all right? I would hate to see you disappointed again."

He patted her hand. "That's my Abigail. Always the practical one."

Her brave smile faltered. "Yes. That's me." She added, "I don't mean to steal your joy, Papa, and I quite agree with you—you would make an excellent *lord of the manor,* as you say. In fact, I was quite proud of you just now when you offered Mr. Chapman a place to stay."

He sent her a sidelong glance. "Yes, I thought you might like that."

She looked up at him in surprise, relieved to see no censure in his expression but rather an understanding light in his eyes. She tried to act nonchalant, as if she had no idea what he meant, but she could not quite stifle a small grin.

The grin faded, however, when she thought of Miles Pembrooke. He would not be happy to learn he was no longer their only houseguest.

Chapter 17

*A*nd so, feeling eager and self-conscious, Abigail oversaw the arrangements to settle William Chapman in Pembrooke Park's morning room—an informal parlor with large windows where a family might spend time together reading, playing games, or doing needlework.

Mac returned to the parsonage and brought back a valise of William's least smoky clothes. His mother and sisters took the rest home to be cleaned. While they were gone, Abigail and the servants fitted up the sofa with proper bedding, and brought down a small bedstead from the attic for Mac, who was determined to stay with his son for at least that first night to make sure he fared well, had everything he needed, and didn't trouble the Fosters inordinately.

This answered the question in Abigail's mind of who would help William dress and bathe, since his burned arm was wrapped and not terribly useful. With Mac there, she would not yet have to ask much more of Duncan, who would not be eager to serve Mr. Chapman.

Mrs. Walsh, however, was only too eager to have a Chapman under the same roof to cook for and immediately went about preparing a selection of healthful soups and jellies, as though William were ill and not simply injured. She refused Kate Chapman's offer to send over food, saying, "I would enjoy nothing better than cooking for our curate. You'll not rob me of that pleasure, I trust?"

Mrs. Walsh brought the tray up herself that evening, making a fuss over William. He thanked her warmly, but said, "Only for tonight, mind. I shan't let you spoil me for long. I'm not really an invalid, Mrs. Walsh, though I do appreciate all the trouble you are taking over me."

"Aye, and what else would I do?" She winked and told him she wouldn't be satisfied until he had eaten every bowl clean.

She offered to bring a tray for Mac as well. He politely but firmly refused. "I shall go home to Kate's table. Don't want her getting jealous," he teased lightly, "or our cook, for that matter." But a wary glint in his eye made Abigail wonder if he had other reasons for not wanting to dine in Pembrooke Park.

Abigail ate in the dining room as usual that evening, with her father and Mr. Pembrooke. When her father mentioned William Chapman was in residence, Miles surprised her by reacting with apparent approbation.

"You are all goodness, Mr. Foster," he said. "I declare. I am quite proud to be related to you. First you invite me to stay and then our poor injured curate. Your generosity knows no bounds."

"Well, I wouldn't go that far," Mr. Foster said with a wry twist to his lips, but his eyes shone at his guest's praise.

Miles looked at her with a knowing grin. "And wise to put him on the ground level, sir, away from the family bedchambers. A clergyman cannot be too careful—one's reputation is not to be trifled with."

Was that a barb directed at her? Abigail wondered. Her father had shown no such scruple about keeping Miles Pembrooke away from the family bedchambers. But then again, he considered him family and therefore harmless.

Abigail hoped he was right.

After dinner, Abigail gathered her courage, reminding herself it was perfectly acceptable for a hostess to check on her injured houseguest. The morning room door stood ajar, which made her feel more comfortable in approaching and knocking softly on the jamb.

"Come," Mr. Chapman called in reply.

She pushed wide the door but remained in the threshold. William lay on the sofa, cocooned in bedclothes, his wrapped arm propped on a cushion. Hands, face, and hair scrubbed clean.

"Just checking to see if you have everything you need."

"I do. Thank you."

She glanced about the room. "Where is your father? I thought he was staying with you tonight?"

"He is. But he insisted on going to Mr. Brown's for laudanum. He should be back shortly."

She winced in empathy. "Is the pain very bad?"

"I've felt better," he allowed.

"I . . . should leave you. If there is nothing I can do."

"Stay and talk to me until he returns. Won't be long. I could use a pleasant distraction."

"Of course—if you like." Leaving the door open behind her, she crossed the room and sat in an armchair facing the sofa.

Closer now, she noticed the tension in his jaw and mouth, as if gritting his teeth against the pain.

He asked, "How is Mr. Pembrooke taking the news?"

"Actually, he congratulated my father on his largesse."

He chuckled. "I am sorry if I accused him unjustly. And I do hope you are . . . comfortable with my being here."

"I don't know if that is the word I would use, but I definitely approve of my father's decision to ask you to stay."

"Hmm," he murmured thoughtfully, watching her with a measuring look.

For a few moments they sat in companionable silence.

Knowing he wished her to distract him, she said, "It was kind of Miles to go for the surgeon today."

"I agree. Though perhaps shortsighted."

"Oh? How so?"

"Mr. Brown told me something interesting about Mr. Pembrooke while he was tending my wounds. Granted, I was distracted by the pain, but I am fairly certain I heard correctly. Did not Miles say his limp was the result of an old war wound?"

"He mentioned that, yes. Though he might have been jesting to brush it off lightly."

"Or to avoid uncomfortable questions, perhaps."

She frowned, remembering Duncan's doubts on the subject. "Why? What did Mr. Brown tell you?"

"He said he recalled Miles as a lad, when he lived here with his family. He was called in to set his leg—broken, apparently, during a fall down the stairs."

"No . . ." Abigail breathed, her heart twisting at the thought of a young boy falling down those many stairs.

William nodded. "He also intimated that the family did not immediately call him. And by the time they did, he was unable to set the leg as well as he would have liked. Mr. Brown said he suggested they take the boy to the hospital in Bath, but as far as he knows, they never went. He said it disappointed him, seeing Miles limp after all these years, and wished he'd been able to do more for him."

Abigail bit her lip as she considered, then asked, "Don't tell anyone else, all right? I'd like to talk to him myself."

"I won't." He reached across the distance and pressed her hand. "You have a compassionate heart, Abigail Foster."

Or a foolish heart, she thought but did not say so.

Abigail left Mr. Chapman and joined Miles in the drawing room for coffee. She found him staring out the window at the twilight sky, idly rolling the handle of a spoon between his fingers. As usual her father had remained in the dining room to smoke after dinner.

She sat across from him and began, "I understand Mr. Brown was called in to treat you here when you were a boy."

260

Miles lowered his eyes, his long lashes fanning over his cheek. "Ah . . ." he murmured. He smiled a sad little smile and continued to roll the spoon in his hand. "And I suppose he told you I broke my leg in an accident?"

"Yes. A fall down the stairs. Though perhaps you reinjured it in battle . . . ?"

She waited, watching the curtain of thoughts and emotions shifting across his golden-brown eyes.

He looked at her, then away again. "I did fall, yes. Clumsy Miles. But with so many injured in the war, I find it easier to call it an old war wound. Better to be one of the honorable veterans, injured in a noble cause, than a cripple since boyhood, an object of pity or scorn."

Abigail's heart ached for him, and she wished she had kept her mouth shut.

He shrugged. "It was not a complete fabrication. I did serve in the navy. An attempt to follow in my father's footsteps. To make up for all the other ways I had disappointed him. I bound my leg and hid my limp as best I could. It worked, for a time. I wasn't the strongest sailor, but I was clever, and worked my way up. But in the end, I hadn't the stomach for fighting. My father always told me I was too soft. And he was right." His mouth twisted. "So far."

"I understand, Miles," Abigail said. "And I don't blame you."

He met her gaze. "And will you forgive me for not being completely honest with you?"

"Yes."

He reached out and tapped a finger beneath her chin. "What a dear creature you are, fair cousin. If only everyone were half as understanding as you."

Later that evening, laudanum administered and pain beginning to ease, William and his father sat companionably in the Pembrooke morning room.

Mac looked around him at the fine furnishings and old portraits on the paneled walls. "How strange to be here," he murmured, "to have one of my children sleeping in Pembrooke Park. Never would I have believed it."

William looked at his father's pensive profile and said, "But I am not the first of your children to sleep here, am I?"

Mac looked away without answering.

William asked gently, "Were you ever going to tell me . . . if Miles Pembrooke hadn't returned and forced your hand?"

His father shrugged. "You were so young when it happened. One doesn't entrust important secrets like that to a four-year-old. Later, when the thing seemed to have been largely forgotten, it seemed risky to bring it out again, to open old wounds. Leah seemed to want to forget, to pretend it never happened. I suppose it made it easier to live day to day. And I certainly thought it the wisest, safest course, not to talk about it."

William regarded the older man. Wondering what else he didn't know about his family. About the past. "So many things I want to ask you . . ." he began, then winced his eyes shut, trying in vain to focus his laudanum-dulled thoughts. "Were you here that night?"

"Aye. That I was." Mac slowly shook his head, his gaze straying to the door and the hall beyond.

"Show me where it happened," William urged, pushing aside the bedclothes.

"No," his father protested. "Not after the day you've had. Stay in bed."

"I don't feel too bad, not with the laudanum taking effect." William swung his legs over the side of the sofa and made to stand.

His father stepped quickly to his side and took his arm to steady him. "Oh, very well. But just for a moment."

They went out into the hall. Mac's gaze swung around the soaring room and trailed its way up the grand staircase. "There." With his free hand, he pointed to the front door, then up the stairs. "The valet, Walter Kelly, rushed in with the news that Robert Pembrooke was dead. Murdered. And not long after, Walter himself died right there." He pointed to the bottom of the stairs.

"An accident—a fall—as we've always been told?" William asked. "Or was he pushed?"

Mac grimaced. "He and Clive Pembrooke argued at the top of the stairs. I believe Clive struck him a mortal blow, perhaps with the butt of his gun or some other object, then pushed him down the stairs to make it appear an accident."

"You didn't actually see it happen?" William asked.

Mac shook his head. "No. But I heard it."

William watched him, unsettled by the eerie glint in his father's eyes. Then he looked around the open two-story hall for possible places of concealment. Seeing only a hall cupboard, he asked, "Where were you?"

For a moment, Mac didn't answer, his expression distant in memory. Then he whispered, "In the secret room."

Abigail was about to blow out her bedside candle when she heard someone pounding on the front door below. She tied on her dressing gown over her nightdress and left her room, pushing her long hair back over her shoulder. Who would be calling at this late hour? She hoped Mr. Chapman was all right.

She descended the stairs and reached the hall in time to see Mac standing at the open front door, talking in a low voice to an adolescent male caller. Mac nodded and shut the door.

Concerned, Abigail asked, "Is everything all right?"

He turned, wearing a grimace. "Nothing to alarm you, Miss Foster. It's only that Mr. Morgan's favorite hound has gone missing. Like a second son to the man he is. And as I am his land agent . . ."

Abigail shook her head. "Don't tell me you've been asked to go out and find the man's dog . . . at this hour?"

"I'm afraid so. William is sound asleep or I wouldn't go. I think he'll sleep through the night, especially after the hefty dose of laudanum Dr. Brown sent over. Still I hate to leave him, should he waken . . ."

"I will ask my father to look in on him. Or Duncan."

"Thank you, Miss Foster. Don't disturb your father, but if Duncan will check on him, I think it will be all right to leave for an hour or two." He retrieved his overcoat from the hall cupboard.

Abigail hesitated. "I'm curious, Mac. Why did you hire Duncan? No offense, but he clearly isn't fond of working here. If he didn't treat my father so well, I likely would have dismissed him before now."

Mac bit his lip, then said, "I was afraid of that. It's a bitter pill to find himself a house servant. He'd hoped for more. Please be patient with him, lass."

Abigail studied his earnest face. "Very well."

"Thank you." He picked up his hat and turned to the door. "Well, I'm off. Hopefully, the dog will have shown up at Hunts Hall by now."

"I agree. But don't worry, we shall look after William until you return."

"Much obliged, Miss Foster."

Abigail went belowstairs to talk to Duncan but discovered his room empty. Where was he at this hour? Out drinking at the public house? Meeting Eliza?

Drawn by Abigail's knocking, Mrs. Walsh peeped out of her own room across the passage, her hair in paper wrappers. Abigail asked if she knew where Duncan was, but the housekeeper said she thought he'd gone to bed and was surprised to learn his room was empty.

Abigail borrowed paper and ink from Mrs. Walsh and left a note for Duncan, asking him to check on Mr. Chapman when he returned, and to take him fresh water in the morning. The note would also serve to let the man know she was aware of—and not pleased with—his late-night absence.

She sighed, resigned to go upstairs and ask her father to look in on William. Remembering Miles's comment about reputations, she doubted it would be proper for her to do so. Crossing the hall, she

paused outside the morning room door, to assure herself William
Chapman slept on, undisturbed. If so, she would let her father sleep
awhile longer. Perhaps Duncan would return soon and she wouldn't
have to wake her father. His "lord of the manor" condescension
might not extend to middle-of-the-night visits to his houseguest's
sickbed.

She pressed her ear to the closed door, but a groan broke the
silence she'd hoped for. Her heart banged against her ribs, and her
stomach plummeted. All thoughts of propriety fled.

She inched open the door and peered in. Mac had left a candle
lamp glowing on a side table, which illuminated William's form on
the makeshift bed. Seeing he was dressed in nightshirt and covered
by bedclothes, she opened the door wider and tiptoed inside. Again
she heard a pitiful groan.

She cautiously approached. His eyes were closed, but his face
was bunched up in a grimace of pain, or anxiety.

"Noooo," he moaned. "Leah . . ."

She was startled to hear him calling for his sister. He must be
having a nightmare.

Abigail bent near. "Mr. Chapman?" she whispered. "William?"
When he didn't respond, she gently touched his arm. "You're all
right. Just a dream."

She had heard laudanum could give people horrid nightmares,
sometimes even hallucinations. She hoped the surgeon hadn't pre-
scribed too great a dose.

"You're all right," she repeated, gently shaking his arm.

Slowly, groggily, he opened his eyes. He looked at her with a
bleary gaze.

"You were having a nightmare," she said quietly, kneeling on the
footstool. "I only came in to wake you. Are you all right?"

"Leah?" He looked past her, toward the door.

"She is at home in bed. Sound asleep, no doubt. You are here in
Pembrooke Park—do you remember?"

"Leah was here too," he murmured. His expression tightened
in alarm. "Hiding in the secret room. He was coming for her."

Leah, in the secret room? Abigail thought. *Someone coming for her?* What a dream for him to have.

"Only a nightmare," she repeated.

"Was it? It seemed so real." He sighed. "What a relief."

His expression relaxed, and he took a slow, deep breath.

"Are you all right now?" she asked. "Are you in pain?"

He lifted one corner of his mouth in a lopsided grin. "The pain is a distant thing—off shore. I feel . . . good." His gaze roamed her face. "Abigail Foster is at my bedside . . ." His eyes twinkled. "How can I not feel good? In fact, I feel very . . . warm."

His hand found hers, and he entwined his long fingers around her shorter ones. "Like . . . warm jelly that hasn't set. My bones are soft. Your skin is soft. So soft . . ." He looked down at her pale wrist as though it were an awe-inspiring sight, and ran a thumb over it.

It sent a thrill of pleasure up her arm.

She supposed she now knew how William Chapman would behave were he ever foxed. And considering he stayed away from liquor, this was likely as close as he would ever come. She hoped he wouldn't feel the worse for it when the laudanum wore off. She wondered if he would even remember this conversation in the morning.

His voice thick, he said, "I've never seen you with your hair down." He reached out and captured the end of a dark curl and caressed it between his thumb and fingers.

She bowed her head, embarrassed and self-conscious, yet at the same time supremely aware of her femininity, her long dark hair falling on either side of her face and over her shoulders like a veil.

"Sorry. I had already dressed for bed."

"Don't be sorry. It's beautiful. You're beautiful."

"Thank you," she whispered, unable to meet his earnest gaze.

He continued to hold her hand, and she continued to let him. His eyes took on that dazed quality once more. He said languidly, "Abigail Foster in my bedchamber at night. I must be dreaming . . ."

He lifted her hand to his lips and pressed a slow kiss to one fingertip after another. "Mulberries . . ." he murmured. "I find I like them after all."

He gave her a roguish grin.

"You are feeling very pleased with yourself," she observed.

"Of course I am. You are with me, so I am on top of the world . . . yet strangely numb to the world at the same time."

She gently extracted her hand from his. "I think you are quite well enough for me to leave you. In fact, far too well for me to stay." She rose.

His head snapped toward the door, and his brows furrowed. "Who's that?"

Startled, she turned toward the door she had left open, but saw nothing. "Where?"

"Who's there?" he called.

"I don't see anyone. Probably only a trick of the shadows." *And the laudanum,* she added to herself.

He shook his head. "I saw someone—someone in a hooded cloak."

Abigail walked to the door, her heart beating a little too hard, first from William's touch and now this scare. If anyone was there, it was likely only Duncan, coming to heed her summons at last. Or perhaps her father. Or even Miles Pembrooke. She hoped not the latter. He would certainly not like finding her in William Chapman's bedchamber, sickroom or not.

But she saw no one in the hall, even though the moonlight leaking in through the windows left plenty of shadows and dark corners.

She returned to his bedside. "I didn't see anyone."

But William had already nodded back to sleep.

Had there been someone there? Abigail wondered. Someone in a hooded cloak? A shiver snaked up her neck at the thought.

Sometime later, Abigail jerked awake to find Mac bent over her, gently shaking her shoulder.

"Hm?" She had fallen asleep in the armchair. Her gaze flew to William. "Is he all right?" Relieved, she saw him sleeping peacefully.

Mac said, "I'm here now. Go to bed, Miss Foster."

She rose, her neck stiff from sleeping in an awkward position. Massaging it, she murmured, "Find the dog?"

"Eventually. In the last place I looked, of course. Snake Ravine. Still don't know what he was doing down there." Mac sighed and unbuttoned his Carrick coat.

Her cue to depart. "Well. Good night," she whispered, stepping to the door.

"Thanks for sitting with him," he said. "You didn't have to, you know."

"I didn't mind."

"I thought you were going to ask Duncan . . . ?"

"I couldn't find him. He was out, apparently."

"Out? Out where?"

"I don't know. But I shall ask him in the morning. It's late. Get some sleep."

He ran a weary hand over his face. "I'm halfway there already."

The following morning, when Polly came in to help her dress, Abigail asked her, "Do you happen to know if Duncan saw my note?"

"Aye, miss. He saw it."

Something in the maid's tone of voice told Abigail that Duncan had been none too pleased about it either.

When Abigail went downstairs for breakfast, she first diverted to the morning room. She knocked, assuming William would be fully dressed by then, thanks to Duncan's begrudging help, if not Mac's.

She expected Mac to answer the door, but instead she heard a muffled "Come in" from inside and tentatively inched open the door.

William Chapman sat on a stool near the desk-turned-washstand, breathing hard and catching his breath. He was dressed—

thankfully—in trousers and shirt, one arm in his coat sleeve, struggling to wriggle his injured arm into the other.

"Where is your father?" she asked.

"He left just after Duncan came in with water. Went home to change—he had an early meeting at Hunts Hall. I suppose he assumed Duncan would help me."

"So did I. I asked him to do so."

Mr. Chapman gave up his struggle. "He did bring water and helped me shave, but he has many other duties, so I assured him I could finish dressing on my own."

She gave him a wry look. "As I see." *Yes,* she thought. No doubt Duncan enumerated his many *pressing* duties with long-suffering martyrdom.

"I don't blame him," William said. "To tell you the truth, I was surprised he did that much. He isn't exactly fond of me, remember."

"So I've noticed. Are you ever going to tell me why?"

"Let's just say he once admired Leah, but Father and I discouraged his interest."

"Ah. Then I am surprised your father recommended him for the position here."

"Oh, Papa isn't the type to hold a grudge."

Abigail gave him a pointed look, and William quickly recanted.

"You're right, he *is* the type. But in this case, Duncan's wrongdoing was of the sort men understand. Pursuing a beautiful woman beyond his reach."

His eyes flashed with pain or longing. She hoped he was not thinking of Andrew Morgan's sister again.

"I see." She turned away, toward the small bed, neatly made. "Your poor father. It looks as though he barely slept. Did he tell you he was summoned to go out and find Mr. Morgan's hound after you fell asleep?"

"No, he didn't mention it."

"Yes, I spoke to him before he left." Abigail explained, "I looked in on you in his absence, since I couldn't find Duncan anywhere." She tilted her head to one side in thought. "Perhaps it's a good thing I did."

"Did you?" He winced in thought. "I had the strangest dreams last night. . . ."

"Yes, I know you did," she drawled.

He looked up at her, mildly alarmed. "Oh dear."

Abigail stepped forward. "Here, let me help you." She pulled the frock coat around him and helped him angle his arm into the sleeve, gently tugging the lining over the bandages.

"Thank you." He asked, "Did I . . . talk in my sleep? I sometimes do, Jacob tells me."

"I'm not sure how much was sleep and how much was the effect of the laudanum."

"That bad, eh? Not sure I want to ask what I said."

She playfully narrowed her eyes. "It wasn't so much what you said, as what you *did*."

His eyes widened, then sparked with humor. "You are enjoying teasing me, I see. Or perhaps *tormenting* is the better word." He added, "I do hope I didn't embarrass myself, or you."

"Nothing to worry about. Shall I help you tie your cravat? I've often helped my father."

"If you like. I'm not sure I can manage with only one good arm, but I can do without or wait for my father, if you prefer."

"I don't mind, if you don't." She lifted the long swath of linen cloth from the back of the chair and circled it around his neck once, then again, pulling it snug, but not too tight.

"Do you plan to strangle me?"

"Probably not." She grinned and began tying a simple barrel knot. With him seated, and her standing near his knees, his head reached her about shoulder level. She felt self-conscious performing the little domestic chore, yet the light of admiration shining in his eyes boosted her confidence.

He smiled up at her and said, "You know, as sorry as I am that the parsonage was burned, I cannot be truly sorry that I have ended up here, in your company. Something good from the bad, I suppose. God excels at that."

His words, his nearness, made her feel strangely warm, and her stomach tingled. As she straightened the cravat around his neck, her fingertips brushed his chin. The same fingertips he had kissed last night. She wondered what he would do if she leaned down and planted a kiss on his freshly shaven cheek, or if she dared, his lips. Her heart beat a little faster at the thought. And what would *she* do if he pulled her onto his lap, wrapped his good arm around her, and soundly kissed her? Would she slap his face? Reprove him there and then, or send her father in to do so? She doubted she would do any of those things. Not when a part of her wished he would do just that.

Feeling nervous, she changed the subject. "Do you remember your nightmare last night? You groaned in your sleep. I had to wake you."

He squinted in concentration. "I don't think so."

"You called for Leah. You were clearly frightened for her."

Eyes distant in recollection, he murmured, "Oh yes . . ."

"You said something about her hiding in the secret room and that someone was coming for her."

He stilled, then his mouth formed an O. "Did I?"

She nodded, watching his face.

He chuckled rather lamely. "That is a strange thing to dream . . . or to say."

"Is it?" she asked.

For a moment their gazes met and held. He opened his mouth as if to reply, but at that moment, footsteps sounded behind them.

She stepped back abruptly and said a bit too brightly, "There. That should do it."

She looked guiltily over her shoulder. Her stomach sank.

Miles stood there, eyes alight. "Who is hiding in the secret room?"

Abigail said quickly, "Mr. Chapman had a nightmare. That's all it was."

"A nightmare?" Miles echoed, shaking his head. "Sounds like a dream come true to me."

The following day, William left behind his invalid status and joined the Fosters in the dining room for the evening meal. *This ought to be interesting,* he thought. And perhaps a test of his forbearance as well as his tact, what with Miles Pembrooke seated across from him and Duncan serving at table, along with two housemaids. He hoped the maids would keep the resentful man from spitting in his soup. Or worse.

Pushing such thoughts from his mind, William asked Mr. Foster questions about his boyhood. While he was at it, he asked what Miss Foster had been like as a young girl, and her father obliged with tales of how, by the age of six, she had started organizing the nursery and arranging her pinafores by days of the week, and keeping the rest of the family in line.

Miss Foster ducked her head, a becoming blush on her cheeks. "Papa . . ." she gently protested.

But William could tell she enjoyed the fondness and pride in her father's eyes and in his tone of voice. Who wouldn't?

He found his gaze drawn across the table to Miles Pembrooke. Had *his* father ever praised or fondly teased him? Somehow he doubted the man had ever known a father's love or approval. William's heart twisted at the thought, and he determined to make more of an effort with him.

He asked Miles about his travels and politely avoided the sore subject of his family. Miles obliged with tales of his time in Gibraltar, all of them determinedly ignoring Duncan's snort heard from the servery.

Then William decided he would attempt to pique Miles's interest in God—the true source of unconditional love every human heart longed for—by first encouraging him to attend church.

"You ought to join us on Sunday, Mr. Pembrooke," William said. "My sermon is about your favorite topic."

"My favorite topic?" Miles raised his eyebrows. "Oh my, what could it be? Miss Foster, perhaps?" He tsked. "I don't think your parishioners would approve."

"No."

"Then what are you suggesting is my favorite topic?"

William met the man's challenging gaze with a warm smile. "Treasure."

Chapter 18

O
n Sunday William dressed in his black forms, his newest bandage less bulky than the first and his arm more mobile now that the pain, without the aid of laudanum, had dulled somewhat. His father came to Pembrooke Park, wearing his customary black coat and grey waistcoat, which he thought befitted his position as parish clerk. Mac had returned to his own bed after the first two nights, once assured that William was doing well on his own.

"Ready?" his father asked.

"I think so, yes."

"Don't worry, lad. Folks won't expect much of you this morning. They'll understand you've been in no fit state for writing sermons."

"Some believe that to be my perpetual state," William quipped.

"Well. Can't please everyone."

"Don't I know it." He grinned at his father. "I would likely hear more complaints were most people not in awe of my fierce Scots father."

Mac grinned. "If only Mrs. Peterman were of that same persuasion."

When the church bells rang, people crowded into the boxes and pews, more than had attended in some time. William was surprised to see Miles Pembrooke in church, sitting with Miss Foster and her father, and his spirit quickened at the sight of him. At the opportunity. Around the nave, people stared at Miles and spoke in whispers and hushed grumbles and supposition.

Mac called the service to order, perhaps more sharply than usual, and everyone quieted.

Standing near a communion table swathed in white linen, William prayed the Lord's Prayer and then continued on to the Collect and readings. He said, "And now let us proclaim our faith together. . . ."

Everyone stood to say aloud the Nicene Creed, words shared with fellow believers across the centuries and around the world. "I believe in one God the Father Almighty, Maker of heaven and earth, and of all things visible and invisible: and in one Lord Jesus Christ, the only-begotten Son of God . . ."

When it came time for William to give a personal greeting and announcements before his sermon, he slowly looked around the nave, smiling at one and all.

"It is good to see so many in attendance this morning, though I know curiosity to view the damage done to the parsonage—and to the parson—may have drawn more of you than my fine oratory skills."

A few quiet chuckles rumbled across the nave. Mrs. Peterman, however, sat ramrod straight, her mouth its usual stern line.

"Whatever the case, you are all welcome and I am glad to see you." He glanced at Miles Pembrooke as he said it. "And again, my deepest thanks to those of you who came to help. My mother invites you all to our house after the service for tea or cider and her famous biscuits as a small token of our gratitude."

This announcement was met with murmurs of approval.

When the crowd had quieted, William said, "It is good to draw together as a community after such an event. When problems strike, it is also a good time to draw close to God personally, to take stock of your own heart, your own life." He looked again at Miles. "With this in mind, I am going to deviate from the planned text for the morning and hope you will indulge me."

Mrs. Peterman, he saw, rolled her eyes.

William sent up a silent prayer, asking God to help him choose his words wisely and well. He began, "What would you do if your house burned to the ground? Perhaps it has. Which of us can forget the Wilsons' fire of five years ago? So much loss. What if *you* were to lose all your worldly possessions because of fire, or theft, or financial tragedy?"

Mr. Foster, he noticed, shifted uncomfortably.

"Are your dearest possessions fireproof? Your valuables safe forever? Do you spend your time in the constant quest of attaining more?"

His father read from the sixth chapter of Matthew. "'Lay not up for yourselves treasures upon earth, where moth and rust doth corrupt, and where thieves break through and steal.'"

William looked out at the congregation. "And, I might add, where fire destroys."

Again his gaze snagged on Miles Pembrooke. William hoped he was not using his sermon as a chance to bludgeon the man indirectly. For Mr. Pembrooke was a treasure seeker, whether or not he'd had anything to do with the fire. *Lord, guard my mind and tongue.*

"Some of us go through life spending a great deal of effort accumulating possessions or wealth, saving for a rainy day or an uncertain future. And if our means are modest, we spend our energies thinking about where our next meal will come from.

"Don't misunderstand me. Those of you who are husbands and fathers are right to think ahead, and take care of your families. And I commend you for it. But there is a difference between providing for our families and laying up treasures. Longing after riches. Or searching for some mythical treasure "out there" somewhere to try and make ourselves happy. But we all know that earthly treasure will never satisfy the deepest longings of our souls, don't we? I can hear Mr. Matthews say, 'No, Parson, but it sure would help feed my five strapping sons.'"

A few chuckled, including the blacksmith himself.

William continued, "And yes, adequate means make life easier. Or so I hear." He grinned at that. "Though often *need* draws us close to God like plenty never can."

At this point, William hesitated. Should he? Dare he confront the issue directly? Taking a deep breath, he plunged ahead. "Throughout history, stories and myths have included the lure of treasure—whether chests of pirate gold or the goose that laid the golden egg. And local lore whispers about hidden treasure much nearer at hand."

Miss Foster blinked up at him. Mr. Pembrooke's eyes shone with amused irritation. Around the nave, people exchanged uneasy glances.

"Can you imagine the waste of a life spent searching for a treasure that doesn't exist? Or of hiding a treasure, only to have thieves break in and steal it? Or to finally unearth the long-sought treasure, only to find it rusted and destroyed? Worthless?"

Miles Pembrooke frowned.

"Where are you investing your time, attention, love, and talents?" William asked. "In earthly matters or eternal ones? Where do your affections lie? What does your heart seek above all else?"

He nodded to his father, who read, "'But lay up for yourselves treasures in heaven, where neither moth nor rust doth corrupt, and where thieves do not break through nor steal: For where your treasure is, there will your heart be also.'"

When he finished, William said, "When I discovered the parsonage was in flames—my bed, my belongings, my books—of course I tried to put out the fire. And because the parsonage belongs not only to me but to the entire parish, I perhaps tried even harder than I would have done, were it mine alone. But I can honestly say, that my thoughts during those tense moments were not for my belongings. I was thinking of those dearest to me. Of the safety of those helping me. Of what it would do to my family were I injured or killed. And the loss to all of you, should the fire spread to the church itself.

"No, I am not happy that my favorite green coat was burned

or my university gown ruined. You shall grow tired of seeing me in my black forms, no doubt." Again he smiled. "But I am not devastated. The parsonage does not hold my real treasure. My faith, my soul, my greatest treasure lies not within four walls, or my purse, nor any possession. My hope is in God alone." Again he let his gaze travel slowly over his parishioners. "And I pray the same for each of you."

Abigail released a long breath and unclenched her hands, relieved the uncomfortable sermon had ended. Mr. Chapman turned next to the offertory, and Mac collected the alms for the poor. Holy Communion followed, but Miles, she noticed, did not go forward to receive the bread and wine. Did he see himself as unworthy? Weren't they all?

When the service concluded, people didn't linger as long as usual, eager to walk over to the Chapmans' to be first in line for tea, cider, and biscuits.

"You two go ahead," Miles said. "I'm going back to the house. I've caused enough stir for one day, I think. My work here is done." He winked. "And on the Sabbath no less."

Her father said, "You know, my dear, I am not sure I am eager for a community-wide chat just now either."

"Then no need," Abigail said. "We'll all go home. We may have to wait for our dinner, however, for I wouldn't dream of asking Mrs. Walsh and the others to forgo the pleasure."

Mr. Morgan senior stopped to talk to her father, so Miles and Abigail waited on the edges of the exiting crowd. Several people, she noticed, stopped to thank Mr. Chapman for the sermon, warmly shaking his hand. She was happy for him. True to form, Mrs. Peterman stopped to give her opinion as well, and from the look on her face, it was not favorable. *Poor William.*

Miles said, "I think our friend Mr. Chapman has missed his calling. He ought to have been one of Wesley's itinerant preachers. You don't suppose that sermon was directed at anyone in particular—do you, Miss Foster?"

She noticed the twinkle in his eye, and said, "Perhaps. But I think it had something to say to all of us."

"Not you, Miss Foster. Surely you have not been tempted after treasure?"

She sent a guarded glance toward her father, and seeing him still engrossed in conversation, quietly admitted, "It has crossed my mind."

His brows rose. "Delightful! Nothing like a little healthy competition."

She shrugged. "No point for me to search, really. The treasure wouldn't be mine to claim. I would no doubt have to surrender anything I found to the estate."

"Ah. Then you don't know about the reward?"

She looked at him, not believing they were having this conversation right after Mr. Chapman's sermon.

Miles explained, "My father was so convinced there was a significant treasure, possibly an entire room full of treasure, that he put up a portion of his own prize money and offered it as a reward, hoping some reluctant servant would suddenly recall the location of the supposed treasure. The reward has never been retracted; it is still held in trust by the solicitor, ready to be claimed."

Abigail took it in. If true, it put a different perspective on things. There might be hope for the Foster finances—and her dowry—yet.

He leaned near and whispered a sum. The reward was sizeable. It would not replace all the money her father had lost, but it would allow her to make some recompense. And yes, she could replace her dowry. Not enough to draw fortune hunters, but if a man already held her in high regard, might a tidy sum sweeten her charms and win over any reluctant parents?

Leaning on his stick and staring at the house across the drive, Miles Pembrooke murmured on a sigh, "Sometimes I can't believe I am really back here. . . ."

Realizing the man had grown weary standing there, Abigail

said, "Come, Mr. Pembrooke. You and I can head back. Father will catch up when he's ready."

Miles drew himself up. "Whatever you like, dear cousin." He offered his arm, and thinking he might need the support more than she did, she linked her arm with his.

As they slowly made their way to the house, Miles began, "The treasure and the reward would be enough for me. If I find it, you are welcome to keep the house, as far as I am concerned. Truth be told, I would probably only sell it if it were mine. But if I came into a fortune, it would be within my largesse to allow you to remain in the house at such ridiculously generous terms."

He squeezed her arm and sent her a sidelong glance. "Don't misunderstand me. Harriet explained why she chose to funnel the income from the estate back into its coffers—paying for the servants and repairs and upkeep—so you wouldn't have to. She assures me it was a sound investment, that otherwise the house would have continued to disintegrate past the point of redemption, becoming worthless to either inherit or to sell."

They let themselves in and retired to the drawing room to wait for her father and their dinner. Settling into a cushioned armchair, Miles smiled at her as she straightened her skirts on the chair next to his.

"So you see, I am quite happy to let you remain here, Miss Foster. Perhaps I might visit now and again. Or perhaps you would like to come with me when I leave . . . ?" He watched her with an expectant lift of his brow.

"Mr. Pembrooke!"

"I realize I am older than you are, but I am young at heart. You cannot deny it."

"No, I certainly cannot."

"And you are old for your age."

Abigail huffed in offense.

He laid a cool hand on her shoulder. "Now, now. I don't mean you look old. Of course not. You look charming, as you well know. But I do think you are an old soul. At the very least, mature for your age."

"I cannot deny it has always been said of me."

"There, you see? We are perfect for each other."

He was teasing her, surely. Or was he? Abigail slowly shook her head, regarding the man with amusement, begrudging fondness, and . . . distrust.

William returned to Pembrooke Park after a long day of sermon-making, too much tea, and too much talking, followed by a Sunday school full of children who'd eaten too many sweets. All he wanted was to lie down and sleep. For all his belief in the Scriptures and God's command to rest on the Sabbath, for William, Sunday was the most tiring day of the week.

Miss Foster and her father had not come to his parents' house after church, but neither had Miles Pembrooke, so he wouldn't complain. Instead, he had enjoyed a long talk with his friend Andrew Morgan, who insisted he looked worn out and needed a holiday—as if he'd ever have the time to indulge that whim. Still, it had been pleasant to contemplate.

He pulled off his cravat and slumped onto the sofa in the morning room. He'd barely closed his eyes when Kitty stopped by, ostensibly to visit him, but he guessed she hoped to visit Miss Foster and the dolls' house as well. After looking around his temporary bedchamber, she said, "Dick Peabody and Tommy Matthews got into fisticuffs after Sunday school today."

"Did they?" he asked in concern. "Why?"

"Dick said you were picking on Mr. Pembrooke in your sermon. That you two are sworn enemies. But Tommy scoffed at him and said he didn't know anything. He said you and Mr. Pembrooke are friends."

"Did he?" That was more surprising than the fight. "Based on what, pray?"

"Said you and he play chess together. Things like that."

"Chess? Mr. Pembrooke and I have never played chess."

Kitty's face puckered. "That's odd. Tommy said he saw Mr. Pembrooke knocking on your door, carrying a box. And when he asked Mr. Pembrooke what was in the box, he said it was a chess set, that he'd come to see if you were ready for a rematch. Something like that at any rate."

William frowned in thought. "I must not have been at home, for Mr. Pembrooke has never been inside the parsonage." *Or has he?* There it was—the suspicion was back.

He asked, "When was this? Do you know?"

Kitty shrugged. "Tommy didn't say. He's about the place quite a lot with that fishing pole of his. Could have been any day."

But William guessed he knew very well which day it had been. Then he remembered that Miles and Mr. Foster had played chess that day, so Miles might have been in earnest. *God forgive me,* he thought, ashamed of his uncharitable thoughts. Perhaps Miles had come to the parsonage seeking him out as an opponent in a friendly game. But somehow he didn't believe chess was the rematch the man had in mind. Although if Miles had been occupied with Mr. Foster for quite some time, how could he have set the fire? William hoped his dislike and distrust of the man wasn't coloring his judgment.

What had really been in that box?

William rubbed his hand over his eyes. He needed a break from Pembrooke Park and its inhabitants—both those he disliked and the one he liked too much for his own good. He decided then that he would take Andrew up on his offer to be his guest in London for a few days.

On Monday, Abigail went down to the lamp room herself, irritated that Duncan had yet to replace the faulty lamp in the first-floor passage as she had repeatedly asked him to do. Striding down the dim corridor belowstairs, she saw the lamp room door slightly ajar and heard scraping and the ting of brass on brass within. Good, Duncan was getting to the trimming at last.

She pushed open the door, the manservant's name already on her lips. "Duncan . . . ?"

Miles turned from the rear counter, his expression quickly transforming from sheepish to wide-eyed innocence.

"Oh . . . Mr. Pembrooke!" Abigail exclaimed. "I didn't expect to find you here."

He smiled. "I imagine not. Sorry to startle you. I am not Duncan, but I am your servant, madam, to command." He gave her a pert little bow, then wiped his sooty hands on a cloth. "At the moment I even look the part. If there is something you need help with, you need only ask."

"Oh, I . . . Thank you. I was only looking for a lamp."

"As was I. I was thinking of going up into the attic and wanted a nice stout lamp to light my way."

Her expression must have communicated surprise as well as disapproval.

He pressed a hand to his heart. "My dear Miss Foster, I was under the impression from several things you and your excellent father have said, that I was free to look about as I pleased while here. To 'make myself at home,' as it were—temporarily, of course. But if I have erred, you need only tell me and I shall keep to my room from now on."

"No, of course you need not keep to your room, Mr. Pembrooke."

He said, "Perhaps you would come up to the attic with me, Miss Foster. Unless . . . Are you afraid of ghosts? Perhaps you might tremble in fear and I shall be there to offer a steadying arm?" He grinned.

"I am not afraid of ghosts, Mr. Pembrooke."

"Pity. So inconvenient when ladies are brave and practical. Robs us poor gents of our chance to rescue you from billowing draperies and figures shrouded in bedsheets." He repositioned his stick. "Then perhaps you might lend me your courage, Miss Foster. I shall *have* to act brave with you there to see me."

"Why the attic?" she asked.

"When we were children, my siblings and I often played up there. Especially on rainy days, when we were trapped indoors. We acted out little pantomimes and played hide-and-seek. In my memory, it is a huge looming space with piles of valises, bandboxes, and trunks of every size and description. But my memory is no doubt colored by being young and small at the time. Perhaps I shall be disappointed."

"You don't need me to chaperone you, Mr. Pembrooke."

"I would enjoy your company, truly. And it's Miles, remember?"

She cocked her head to one side. "Tell me, Miles. Have you some reason to think the mythical treasure might be hidden in the attic?"

"Not especially, no."

"I am curious. If you didn't find it when you lived here for two years, why do you think you will find it now?"

"But I was only a boy then and lacked the proper motivation. Besides, I might ask the same of you, Miss Foster. If you have looked these several weeks before my arrival without success, why do you hesitate to admit that I might be of assistance? Surely my history with the house offers some advantages? You are clever—I can see that—but I have history on my side. What say you, why do we not work together? Join forces as it were? Would we not make excellent partners?"

"I don't know about that. . . ."

"I'll tell you what. If we are successful, I will keep the treasure and you may have the reward. Is that not fair? For Pembrooke Park and its treasures will never come to you or your father. Surely you know that?"

Abigail wondered if Miles had the right to any valuables found in the house either. Might he take what he found unlawfully if she "condoned" his search?

She said, "It is my understanding that the courts are still debating the rightful heir, due to your father's disappearance. What if you find the treasure but they rule in someone else's favor? Will you promise not to abscond with whatever valuables we might find?"

"Yes. I agree," he said, a little too quickly to reassure Abigail.

He added, "Though one might ask, then, what is in it for me?" He looked toward the ceiling in thought and then snapped his fingers. "Tell you what. If we find a treasure and it belongs to someone else, then I will share the reward with you."

She considered this. "Equally?"

"Of course. Then . . . have we a bargain?" He held out his hand, like a businessman might, but Abigail hesitated. What would it hurt? Fifty percent of nothing was still nothing and was likely all they'd ever see for their efforts. But if they were successful . . . ?

She was tempted to agree, but a catch in her spirit stopped her. For all the logic of his proposal, why did she feel to agree would be making a bargain with the devil?

"You know what, Mr. Pembrooke. Maybe this isn't a good idea after all."

He raised a brow, eyes glinting in challenge. "Feeling greedy, Miss Foster?"

"Not at all. Feeling foolish for even considering entering into an agreement with a man I barely know over a treasure that most likely doesn't even exist."

He dropped his hand. "Practical Miss Foster. You do steal a man's fun." He sighed dramatically. "And here I thought we were going to be good friends."

On Tuesday another letter arrived, but this one bore no postal markings and had been delivered by hand. Kitty Chapman brought it to her, saying a woman in the churchyard had asked her to give it to Miss Foster.

"Did this woman wear a veil?" Abigail asked.

"Yes! How did you know?"

She is near, then, Abigail thought. Did this confirm that the veiled woman in the churchyard was Harriet Pembrooke? She unfolded the old journal page and read it there in the hall.

I finally found it. The secret room. It was there all along, so close. And just in time. His rages are growing worse. And during the worst of them, I slip inside to hide and wait for the storm to pass. But now I'm wracked with guilt. I should have let my brothers in on the secret. But I did not, selfish creature that I am. And now he's hurt. And it's my fault, at least in part. I should have protected him. I can still hear my father's growl and my brother's sickening cry. The clunk and tumble down the stairs. My mother's scream.

I thought my heart would burst when I saw him, a tangle of limbs on the marble floor. One leg bent at such an unnatural angle.

Papa refused to send for the surgeon until we all agreed to say it was only an accident. My brother moaned all night until I thought I would go mad hearing it. The following day, in desperation, Mamma agreed and asked us all to lie, which she hated to do. Hated him, for asking it of her. Finally he sent for the surgeon, and the man came, astounded at the damage. He asked when and how it had happened.

Papa looked at Mamma and challenged, "Yes, how did it happen, my dear?"

"He fell down the stairs," she gritted out, pale and sullen. "A terrible accident."

Mr. Brown asked, "Why did you not send for me immediately?"

This time Mamma refused to answer and stared defiantly at her husband.

"Oh," he said casually, "we weren't sure the injury was serious enough to require a surgeon's attention."

Mr. Brown looked from the twisted leg to my father as though he were a madman. And perhaps he is.

The surgeon set the leg as best he could, but suggested my father take his son to a hospital. Papa wouldn't hear of it. I think he's afraid of what we might do in his absence. Or that none of us would be here when he returned.

Abigail's stomach lurched. She thought of what the surgeon had recently told Mr. Chapman, his own similar account of the "accident." Poor Miles. Had his father really pushed him?

Miles came hobbling across the hall, dressed in riding clothes and leaning heavily on his stick. Her heart twisted anew to think how it had become injured in the first place.

"Miles, may I ask about your . . . ?" She hesitated. Dare she ask about his father?

"About what, Miss Foster? You may ask me anything."

Her courage failed her. "About your sister, Harriet?"

He pursed his lip. "There isn't much more I can tell you. As I said, I have only seen her twice in the last dozen years. I left the country when quite young, remember, and she moved elsewhere, both of us eager to leave the past behind."

"Did she ever marry?"

Miles hesitated. "She wouldn't want me talking about her private affairs, Miss Foster. You must forgive me. Even though she and I are not close, I am duty bound to be loyal to her as her brother."

"Of course."

"But I will say she has been unlucky in love . . . and leave it at that."

"I am sorry to hear it."

"I have not been lucky in love either, in the past. But I hope my fortunes are changing in that regard?"

Was that a statement or a question? Abigail wondered uncomfortably. "I hope so, for your sake."

Abigail thought again of the veiled woman. "Does your sister ever visit this area?"

Again he hesitated. "I . . . think so, yes. But not often. Again, I don't keep track of her comings and goings."

"I suppose she has had to inspect the place over the years—as executor, I mean?"

He shrugged. "I think she has left most of that to her solicitor."

Abigail nodded vaguely, and Miles continued across the hall.

She wondered again what drew the woman to the churchyard—and to write her letters, if indeed they were one and the same person.

"Miles," she called after him, then waited until he had turned before asking, "You didn't fall down the stairs, did you?"

He smiled easily. "Oh, but I did. I told you."

"I mean . . . it wasn't an accident, was it. You were pushed."

His smile fell. He looked at her, nostrils flared, fist clenched on the handle of his stick. But his voice when he spoke was incongruously gentle. "Who . . . told you that?"

Abigail swallowed, not wanting to reveal her source. She said quietly, "You were not the only person your father pushed."

"Ha." A cracked little laugh escaped him. "Only the youngest."

She felt tears sting her eyes. "I am sorry, Miles. Truly."

His mouth, his entire face, twisted in displeasure. "I don't want your pity, Miss Foster. That is the last thing I wanted you to feel for me."

The next day, Abigail sat in the window seat in her bedchamber, looking idly out over the back lawn and gardens beyond. She was bored and lonely. William Chapman had gone off to London for a few days with Andrew Morgan, and the house, the neighborhood, seemed empty without him.

Suddenly she saw something through the window, and her heart banged against her ribs. She bolted up and pressed her nose nearer the glass. There was the veiled woman again. What was she doing in the garden, behind the potting shed? As if sensing she was being watched, the woman began walking away.

Abigail's nerves tingled to life. This was her chance to test her theory of the woman's identity. She rushed around, finding her slippers, tripping in her haste on the woven carpet and nearly falling. She dashed out into the corridor and toward the stairway. Duncan came carrying two huge cans of water up the stairs—her father must have requested a bath—so she had to wait at the top of the stairs. When the manservant and his heavy load finally passed by, she skimmed down the stairs and across the hall, hoping the woman had not already disappeared.

She eagerly threw open the front door, and it banged loudly against the wall.

In the drive, two women stood in conversation. The veiled woman and . . . Leah Chapman?

Both whirled at the sound. The veiled woman turned away and stalked toward the barouche waiting just outside the gate.

Abigail jogged across the drive, but Leah grasped her arm and hissed, "Abigail, don't."

The woman called something to the coachman—Abigail heard only her last word, "Quickly!"—and then let herself inside without waiting for help. The coachman cracked his whip and urged his horses to "Get up."

"Who was that?" Abigail asked.

Leah appeared shaken. "I'm not sure. I saw her as I was leaving the churchyard." She shivered. "I found it eerie, talking to that woman, her face covered in that heavy veil."

Abigail watched the barouche pull away and rumble over the bridge. If she ran fast enough, she might be able to overtake it before the horses picked up speed, but what would she do then? Leap up on the footboard and demand admission? She was no highwayman. "You didn't recognize her?"

Leah shrugged. "I don't think so . . . I could only see her eyes, and her mouth when she spoke. But it was her voice that struck me. Strange and yet familiar all at once. She asked me who put flowers on Robert Pembrooke's grave."

"What did you tell her?"

"I . . . didn't. I wasn't sure I should. Eliza Smith leaves them now and again."

"Yes . . ." Abigail remembered seeing her near his grave that day. "Do you know, I think Eliza believes Robert Pembrooke might have been her father."

Leah frowned. "She told you that?"

"Not directly, but her aunt hinted at it. Eliza as well."

Leah winced. "Papa told me Mrs. Hayes has become confused in her old age, and talks about a connection that doesn't exist. He thought Eliza knew better than to listen, but apparently not." She sighed. "Leave it with me, Miss Foster. I'll speak to Papa. He'll know what to do."

"And the veiled woman . . . Any idea who she might be?"

Leah shook her head. "She reminded me of someone, but no, I could not place her."

But Abigail had a definite idea of who she might be.

After talking with Leah a few minutes longer, Abigail returned to the house. On an impractical impulse, she decided to write an anonymous letter of her own. Going into the library, she sat at the desk, pulled forth a small sheet of note paper, and paused to think.

She dipped a quill in ink and, remembering Harriet Pembrooke had not used her real name, wrote:

Dear Jane,
I would like to talk to you. Will you meet me here in person?

Abigail did not sign it.

Nor did she suggest a specific meeting time. She left the note behind the loose brick in the garden wall, not knowing when, or if, it would be found.

Chapter 19

The following week, Abigail again sat in the library, large drawing pad and pencil in hand, architecture books spread around her, as well as the renovation plans of Pembrooke Park for inspiration.

"Good day, Miss Foster."

Startled, Abigail looked up. There stood William. She hadn't heard him enter. "Mr. Chapman, you're back!" She quickly rose to her feet. "How was your time away?"

"London made for a nice change of pace for a few days, but I am glad to be home."

"Me too. That is, uh . . . Mr. Morris's sermon was twice as long as yours."

He grinned, then glanced over her shoulder. "What is it you're working on?"

She quickly turned over the drawing pad. "Oh. Nothing. Just sketching."

"Looked like a building of some sort—what I saw of it. Glad to see you haven't given up your interest in architecture."

She smiled vaguely.

"Is it a plan for a house?" he asked. "Or . . . ?"

"Yes. That's it. Just playing around." She cleared her throat and asked, "How did the repairs progress in your absence?"

"Well enough, I suppose, though Papa thinks the entire front wall should be torn out and replaced. The old window is warped anyway and does little against a fierce wind, and it leaks whenever the rain comes from the south. His opinion is that we ought to take advantage of the damage to do some other repairs as well."

"I agree with him," Abigail said eagerly. "How would you feel about an entry porch or small conservatory to shield the sitting room from the worst of the weather whenever the front door is opened? Or you might even add a study, with an extra bedchamber above. . . ."

He raised a quizzical brow. "Is that what you've been drawing? The parsonage?"

She ducked her head, hoping to hide her blush. "I was only playing around, as I said."

He held out his hand. "Let me see."

"No, it's nowhere near ready for anyone to see. Merely rough sketches for my amusement."

He looked at her with a fond smile overtaking his face. "I am touched by your interest, Miss Foster. And if it were my personal home, I would trust your judgment implicitly and eagerly discuss your every idea. But as it is, I would have to get the rector's approval, who in turn would likely have to get the approval of the estate executor or trustees. I doubt they'd approve or finance any more than rudimentary repairs."

He tilted his head and looked at her, eyes warm as they lingered on her face. "I must say, I quite like the idea of adding rooms to the parsonage. If I had someone to share it with me."

Abigail felt her cheeks heat, pleasure and embarrassment warring within her. She found she could not hold his intense gaze.

He stepped nearer. "Miss Foster . . . Abigail . . . May I call you Abigail?"

"I . . ."

"Abby!" her father called, rushing into the library, waving an open letter in the air. He drew up short at seeing William. "Oh, sorry, Mr. Chapman. I did not know you were here."

"That's all right, sir," William said, stepping back.

"We were just discussing repairs to the parsonage," Abigail said. "What is it?"

"A letter from your mother. She and Louisa will be joining us early next week. Is that not good news?"

Louisa is coming already? Abigail's stomach sank. She said, "But that is sooner than we expected. Is everything all right?"

"Yes, yes. But I gather they are weary of the constant rounds of balls and callers. And your mother may have hinted that too much of dear Aunt Bess can be tiring as well." He grinned.

Abigail nodded. "She is a dear, but yes, I can imagine it must be difficult to be a houseguest for so long. . . ." She looked at William. "I don't refer to you, of course, Mr. Chapman. You have only been here a short while."

"And I shan't be in your way much longer."

"No hurry at all." She looked back at her father. "What day do they plan to arrive?"

"Monday, if they can hire a decent coach. If not, Tuesday."

Time to start sheilding her heart. She squared her shoulders. "Well, I have a great deal to prepare. Thank you for letting me know so promptly, Papa. Now, if you will excuse me, Mr. Chapman . . ."

"Of course." William's eyes narrowed in concern as he studied her face. "Are you . . . Is everything all right?"

"Of course." She smiled brightly but could not leave the room fast enough.

William felt restless. His first night sleeping in the parsonage again after his few days in London and his nights at Pembrooke Park. Living under the same roof as Miss Foster, he'd been ever aware of her movements. Where she might be at various times of the day, looking for her to come down the stairs in the morning, and anticipating shared meals with pleasure. Yes, he'd had to put up with Miles Pembrooke at those meals, but it had been worth it to be in her company.

Now he was back living on his own. The roof and walls temporarily patched. He felt the emptiness, the solitude of the place, as he never had before. He'd missed her in London and he missed her now. Which was ridiculous, he told himself, because she was right across the drive. Even so, he missed being near her.

He paced his small sitting room for a time and then, giving up, peeled off his coat, shirt, shoes, and stockings. He would go for a nighttime swim. He used to swim often in the river in summertime. But with people living in the manor, he'd been less willing to do so. Why not? It was late and still warm, and the moon was full. Mr. Brown had removed his restrictions on bathing during his last visit. His arm was healed and his shoulder well on its way to recovery.

He took a threadbare towel with him and quietly slipped from the parsonage. Pembrooke Park was quiet. No lights shone in the windows. He was safe from discovery.

He found his old spot where the bank gradually sloped to the water and waded in, then dove beneath the gently moving current. *Ahh . . .* The cool water felt good on his skin, on his shoulder, on his every part. Peace enveloped him. He was able to forget, for a little while, his troubles, his suspicions, and a certain female neighbor.

Abigail stopped in her tracks and stared. Was she hallucinating? There beneath a tree along the riverbank hovered a ghostly white figure. Heart lodged in her throat, Abigail could not scream. The pale figure did not look like a mortal man. No dark coat or boots marred the unbroken white of his being.

There is no such thing as ghosts, she told herself.

Even so, she stood there, unable to run, every muscle tense, waiting for the specter to fly at her, to pounce, to—

"Miss Foster . . . ?" a voice asked. It was not a ghostly voice but rather an earthly one she easily recognized. Relief was quickly replaced with . . . shocking awareness.

"Are you na—dressed?" she squeaked. The word *naked* refused to come.

"Uhhmm . . . not really, no. I didn't expect to encounter anyone. I am wearing breeches, never fear."

"Oh. Well. That's all right, then." A lame chuckle bubbled from her lips. As if those snug breeches, low on his hips and as pale as his skin, were all the clothing required for this season's well-dressed man.

He stepped out from under the tree, and moonlight shone on him more fully. She tried not to stare but couldn't help herself. She had no brothers. She had never seen a shirtless, half-naked man before. And she might never again, once Louisa arrived.

He slowly walked toward her, and her mouth went dry. His shoulders were broader than she would have guessed, even without the aid of a well-cut and padded frock coat. They curved in a smooth bulge of muscle above equally taut and strong-looking arms. His shoulders angled deeply to a narrower waist, his chest defined, his abdomen flat and masculine. She was glad the darkness hid her blush.

She had noticed his lean but defined legs before—fitted pantaloons regularly revealed all. But she had never seen the shape and contours of his upper body. He must help his father around the grounds, or row, or ride a great deal. Or perhaps he chopped great piles of wood and played ball with his friends for hours on end.

Moonlight glistened on his damp bare skin. She swallowed and dragged her gaze to his face. His wet hair hung in dark tendrils across his brow. He lifted his arms, and she realized he held a small towel in his hands. He rubbed it over his hair and face. Lifting his arms like that caused his biceps to swell, his chest to rise, his abdomen to elongate. So impossibly fair. Were all redheads so pale?

"Perhaps you could . . . em, wrap that towel around yourself."

He tilted his head to one side, amusement and moonlight

glimmered in his eyes. "I am afraid this towel is barely bigger than a facecloth. Sorry." He grinned, not looking sorry at all. "What brings you out at this hour, Miss Foster?"

"I couldn't sleep," she said, thinking, *And now I never shall. . . .*

"Nor could I." He raked a hand through his hair, and it remained sculpted off his forehead. He looked different with his hair waving back instead of falling forward. He had such a handsome face.

He stepped closer, and Abigail drew in a shallow breath, pulse quickening. Her flush moved from her face, down her neck.

"Do you often swim late at night?" she asked, to dispel the tension between them.

"When I was younger, yes. But it has been some time. I thought I ought to get in one last swim before more ladies move in and increase my chances of discovery. I promise you I had no intention of shocking maidenly sensibilities."

He looked at her. "Are you shocked?"

She pressed dry lips together and lied. "No."

"Well, thank goodness I wore breeches."

"Yes. Thank goodness. How is your shoulder?"

"Much better." He twisted his shoulder forward and craned his neck to look at it. "See?"

Her glance skittered over the scarred skin, to his chest and arms once again. He was standing so close now that she could have reached out and touched him.

"How does it look?" he asked, eyes on his wound.

"It looks . . . good," she murmured, eyes on the rest of him.

"That reminds me . . ." he began, looking back at her.

She guiltily snatched her gaze away from his torso, struggling to meet his eyes. Had he noticed her staring? Even her ears heated at the thought.

"It is because of your quick actions that my burns were not worse. I never thanked you properly for dousing me with water."

Nervously, she said, "Tell me you don't plan to douse me in return. . . ."

"A few years ago, I might have done just that. Or picked you up and pretended I was going to toss you in the river. But when I look at you now, those are not the first impulses that come to me."

"No?" she said breathlessly. "Well. Good."

"I wouldn't be so sure if I were you. . . ."

Her gaze flew to his. He was looking at her with such intensity, such warmth, that her heart ached to see it.

His hand touched hers, and she felt a jolt of surprise. Long fingers encircled her wrist like a pliable bracelet, tickling the delicate skin of her inner wrist with feathery pleasure. Then he bent his head as if in prayer and pressed a warm kiss to the back of her hand. "Thank you, Abigail Foster."

Her heart raced. Her knees felt soft and unsteady. He had kissed her hand before, but this time no laudanum influenced his actions.

Keeping hold of her hand, he lifted his head and studied her. Then, as if gauging her reaction, he slowly, slowly moved his face toward hers.

Her breathing came shallow and fast as he neared.

His breath tickled the hairs at her temple as he whispered, "I am in your debt forever."

She stood perfectly still, all of her focus on that spot where his mouth hovered. He pressed a kiss—warm, delicious—on her cheekbone, and she closed her eyes to savor it. When her eyelids fluttered open, he had moved slightly, his eyes on hers and then lowering to her mouth. She looked at his. What would it be like to be kissed on the mouth—by *that* mouth? Kissed by a man? She nibbled her lower lip at the thought.

He stared, riveted. Then he drew in a long shaky breath and took a half step back. She breathed deeply as well and returned her gaze to his injured shoulder. Safe territory.

Her hand reached out, following her gaze. William watched her movements, eyes uncertain.

She touched his shoulder lightly. "Does that hurt?"

Voice thick, he murmured, "Not . . . exactly."

"I am so glad it's going to heal."

She retracted her hand, but he captured it in his, holding it to his heart.

He held her gaze and whispered, "Yes. I believe it will."

Abigail returned to the house in a warm, weak-kneed daze. But in the morning, in the light of day, without the magic of moonlight and water and a half-naked man, her better judgment returned. What had she been thinking? How was touching William Chapman—allowing him to touch her, to take her hand and kiss her cheek—going to help her? She was supposed to be shielding her heart, preparing for disappointment.

She groaned, sighed, and determined to do better.

Chapter 20

*M*iles left to visit his sister for a few days. And, Abigail guessed, to give the Fosters time to settle in as a family without a guest to worry about. Abigail thought it kind of him to do so but didn't doubt he would soon return.

On Monday, she stood beside her father as the hired post chaise rattled up the drive. The postilion expertly reined in the horses and brought the coach to a smooth halt before the manor. Abigail fidgeted, unaccountably nervous. Her father stood beside her, hands behind his back and rocking on his heels in anticipation, standing with pride before *his* manor house, awaiting their impressed reactions. She hoped he would not be disappointed.

The groom opened the door, let down the step, and held up a hand to assist first her mother, then Louisa. Both ladies were dressed in the height of fashion in smart new carriage dresses and matching bonnets. Even the lady's maid, the last to descend, was smartly dressed. Abigail suddenly felt shabby in her printed muslin day dress.

"My dears!" Mamma held wide her arms and walked toward them.

Her father broke his pose long enough to step from the arched doorway to kiss his wife's upturned cheek. Then she turned a sweet smile Abigail's way and enfolded her in a warm embrace. Instantly, Abigail repented of every resentful thought she'd ever had about her mother favoring Louisa. In fact she felt tears prick her eyes. She hadn't realized until that moment just how much she had missed her mother these last few months.

Louisa walked forward more slowly, and Abigail was reminded anew of how beautiful she was. Her sister's dark hair was similar to hers, but her eyes were blue compared to Abigail's ordinary brown ones. Her cheeks were rounder, her lips and bosom fuller.

Louisa tipped her head back to take in the stately façade of the house. "It's certainly big enough," she said.

"It is, isn't it." Her father beamed proudly. "And just wait until you see the rooms, and all the grand furniture. And how Abigail and I have been longing to hear you play the fine old pianoforte."

Louisa accepted her father's kiss, and then turned to her. "Abby. I am happy to see you. I've missed you."

"Have you? I'm surprised you've had time to miss me."

"True. But on Sundays, or rainy days when we were trapped indoors with Aunt Bess, then I definitely missed you. What a whirlwind it's been." Louisa took her arm, and together they followed their parents toward the house.

"I can only imagine," Abigail said. "But you enjoyed yourself, I gather—from Mamma's letters?"

"Oh yes. It was glorious. A huge success."

She did not, however, mention an offer of marriage, thought by many to be the crowning achievement of a truly successful season, but Abigail didn't ask. There would be plenty of time to hear all the details—and boasting—later.

Their father smiled over his shoulder at them. "No dawdling, girls. The staff are eager to meet you."

"I'm surprised you didn't have them all lined up outside to greet us, Papa," Louisa said.

His smile dimmed fractionally. "We wanted to greet you ourselves first. And have a moment alone as a family. But they have been busy preparing for your arrival."

"Do curtail your expectations a little," Abigail added nervously. "It is a very old house after all and was neglected for many years."

"But Abigail and the servants have worked hard to put it to rights," her father insisted. "Come in and see." He held the door, ushering them inside.

Both Mother and Louisa looked up in pleasure at the soaring great hall with its grand staircase, the chandeliers and many formal portraits. Father led them through the ground-floor rooms with many sweepings of arm and barely contained smiles, his chest puffed out with pride, as though he had designed and built the place himself—or as if he really were lord of the manor.

Abigail, on the other hand, suddenly noticed minor flaws she'd missed when she'd walked through these rooms alone. They now leapt out at her in high relief. The loopy threads of a cobweb hanging from the candelabra in the dining room, and another in the corner of the crown molding. The shabby upholstery of the sofa in the drawing room. The dingy windows and musty smell of old books and dry leather in the library. Why had she or the maids not noticed these things before?

Molly, likely the appointed sentry, alerted Mrs. Walsh, and when the Fosters returned to the hall, the servants had assembled—Mrs. Walsh in austere black dress, the housemaids and kitchen maid in their best frocks and aprons, while Duncan wore a black coat and a crisp neckcloth, his hair for once combed smooth.

Introductions made, Mr. Foster led the way upstairs, leaving the unloading of trunks, bandboxes, and valises to the care of the lady's maid and Pembrooke Park staff.

Louisa asked in a loud whisper, "Those can't be all of the servants? Not for a place this size?"

"Yes," Abigail answered in lower tones. "Though now you're here, we shall have Marcel as well."

"But we had more servants in London, and our house there wasn't nearly as large."

"Yes, well, we are making do. And you will too."

As they walked along the upper gallery her father said, "Abigail has selected a room for each of you, so I shall let her do the honors."

She hoped they would approve her choices. "Mamma, this is the mistress's bedchamber, the match to Father's room on the opposite side of the stairway. Your dressing room is through there. . . ."

Her mother entered and gazed appreciatively around the room— the fresh flowers on the polished side table and lace-covered dressing table, the sunlight spilling through the oriel window onto the floral bed-curtains and brightly woven plush carpet. "It's lovely, Abigail. Thank you."

Then Abigail briefly showed them the guest room where Miles had been staying, and explained he would return in a few days. They already knew about their guest through Abigail's and Mr. Foster's letters and were eager to meet him. Louisa especially.

Then Abigail led the way into the room she'd chosen for Louisa. "I thought you would like this room, Louisa. It's in the newer part of the house, over the drawing room, with a lovely view of the rear courtyard and ponds beyond."

Louisa glanced about the room and out its windows.

"I believe it's one of the largest bedchambers," her father added helpfully.

"Bigger than yours, Abby?" Louisa asked, one brow high.

"Yes. I chose one of the older, smaller bedchambers."

"Why?"

"I like it. It was clearly the former daughter's room, and still contains her old books and dolls' house. Come, I'll show you."

She led the way back through the central gallery to her own room. She certainly hoped Louisa wouldn't ask to switch. For she definitely saw it as *her* room now.

As they entered, Mrs. Foster enthused, "Look at this baby house! It's lovely and very like Pembrooke Park, is it not?"

"Yes," Abigail agreed. She eyed her sister surreptitiously as she surveyed the small four-poster bed and girlish furnishings and draperies.

If she expected any thanks for selecting this room and giving

Louisa the far larger and brighter one, she would have been disappointed. Louisa said little, seeming to take the best room as her due. And in this instance, Abigail was only too glad of it, relieved by her sister's vague smile and faint attempt at praising the window seat and garden view.

"Well," Abigail said, "shall we go down for tea? You are both no doubt tired and hungry after your journey."

Everyone agreed. As they went downstairs, Abigail was surprised to see William Chapman stepping out of the morning room, books in hand. *Oh no. Not already . . .*

He turned and hesitated at seeing them. "Forgive the intrusion, but I realized I'd left two books behind."

"No intrusion at all," Mr. Foster said with a smile. "You are just in time to be the first to meet my wife and younger daughter." He turned to them. "My dear Mrs. Foster, may I introduce Mr. William Chapman, our curate."

Mrs. Foster dipped her head. "How do you do, Mr. Chapman."

William bowed. "A pleasure to meet you, Mrs. Foster. I think I speak for the entire parish when I say you are very welcome here. We have all looked forward to meeting you."

"You are very kind. Thank you." Mother stepped aside, revealing Louisa, who'd come down the stairs behind her. "And this is our younger daughter, Miss Louisa Foster."

Louisa dipped a dainty curtsy and smiled sweetly up at the man.

Abigail held her breath, every muscle tight, and forced herself to look at William, to watch his expression like a person watching two carriages about to collide.

His broad mouth, the lips so often quirked in irony, drooped as if dumbfounded. His eyes widened, his brows rose high. He darted a glance toward Abigail and her parents, blinked, and then faltered, "Miss . . . Louisa. How . . . good to meet you. At last."

Abigail's heart sank. Her stomach twisted until she felt she might be sick there and then.

Louisa's smile widened, and her eyes twinkled knowingly, on familiar territory with a stunned-speechless admirer.

"Have we met before, Mr. Chapman?" she asked.

"I . . . no. I have not had that pleasure."

"Ah. You look vaguely familiar, so I thought . . . but my mistake."

Abigail pressed her eyes closed and whispered a silent prayer for composure. And that the man would leave quickly.

Instead her father said, "We were just about to have tea, Mr. Chapman. Would you care to join us?"

He hesitated, clearly conflicted. "I . . . thank you, but no. I am afraid pressing parish business calls. Perhaps another time?"

"Of course."

Relieved, Abigail said, "Yes, I'm sure you are very busy. Don't let us keep you."

He looked at her, verses of confusion and apology passing behind his blue eyes. Though perhaps she was only imagining it, and he was simply smitten and perhaps embarrassed at his reaction. And perhaps already regretting the warm words and caresses he'd bestowed on the pretty girl's older, plainer sister.

Chapter 21

*H*ow was it that with her mother and sister in residence,
the house felt emptier than before? And Abigail felt
lonelier as well, what with William and Miles gone,
and having to share her father with two others. He kept busy showing his wife and younger daughter the grounds and village, listening
to Louisa play the pianoforte and to his wife's endless accounts of
invitations received, gentlemen they'd met, balls and concerts and
routs they'd attended.

Abigail had planned to wait at least a week before checking the
note she'd left behind the loose brick in the garden wall. But two
days after her mother and sister's arrival, restless and needing a
reprieve from all the talk of London, she could resist no longer
and walked out to take a look. She strolled, hoping to appear at
her leisure, taking a turn around the grounds and not bent on
any specific purpose. She told herself she was foolish to feel self-
conscious, as though watchful eyes followed her movements. But
even so, the hairs at the back of her neck prickled. *Just the cool
breeze,* she told herself. *No one knows or cares what I'm doing.*

She rounded the potting shed, feigning interest in a blooming
vine. She ought to have brought a basket and shears to aid her
ruse. Next time she would. She looked at the pallets and planks

and bricks, but all seemed as she had left it. She checked behind the loose brick. Her letter was still there. Giving up, she returned to the house, steeling herself for more Mozart and more tales of Louisa's conquests.

Abigail went back out to the garden the next day, and the next, but her letter remained. Miles returned and was at his charming best, flattering both Louisa and their mother in equal turns, and easily winning their affections. Even now the three of them were ensconced in Mamma's bedchamber, rehashing the season, and laughing together over some of the dreadful new fashions in the new edition of *The Lady's Monthly Museum* Miles had given them.

Dressed in spencer, bonnet, and gloves, Abigail decided to head out for a walk alone. But as she strolled along the drive, she saw Gilbert Scott crossing the bridge on foot.

Heart lifting, she raised a hand in greeting. "Gilbert!"

"Abby!" He returned her wave with a smile and hurried through the gate and across the drive to join her.

She said, "I didn't know you had returned."

"I've come down for a few days to oversee the construction at Hunts Hall. The workmen will begin digging the foundation the day after tomorrow. My design, my drawings, and I get to see them implemented right before my eyes. This won't be like in school, winning awards for conceptual drawings. Something I designed will actually be built and stand forever. Or at least, for many years—if I've done my job right."

"It is very exciting. I am so happy for you, Gilbert."

"Isn't this what we always talked about when we were children? Dreamed of?"

She nodded, and their gazes caught and held in a long, fond look.

He grasped her hand. "Come and watch us break ground, Abby. I want you to be there. Mrs. Morgan has even planned a picnic."

Pleasure warmed Abigail's heart. She dipped her head to hide her flush of pleasure. "I would love to be there. But before I accept I should tell you that—"

"Gilbert!"

He turned his head, and Abigail followed suit. There in the open window of her mother's bedchamber stood Louisa, waving vigorously, her wide smile evident even from a distance.

". . . that Louisa is here," Abigail finished with a lame little laugh. Did he know? Is that why he'd come?

"So I see," Gilbert murmured, his expression difficult to discern. If he was delighted, he hid it well. "I didn't realize she and your mother were coming so soon. I thought they intended to remain in London through the end of the month."

"So did we. Apparently their plans changed. Or Aunt Bess grew tiresome."

"Ah." He nodded his understanding, having met their aunt on a few occasions.

Abigail said gently, "So I will understand perfectly if you wish to invite Louisa instead. I won't mind."

He grimaced. "You know Louisa has never shown any interest in architecture."

Did he sincerely prefer her company—in this instance, at least— or was he simply too polite to retract his invitation?

"True," Abigail allowed. "But she has shown interest in a certain architect."

He ducked his head, chuckling awkwardly. "Touché."

Louisa bounded out through the front door, and they both turned toward her. Abigail said to him in a private aside, "Shall I leave you?"

"No, stay. Please."

Louisa reached them, smile still in place. "Good day to you, Mr. Scott," she said, in mock formality. "What a happy coincidence to see you here." Her eyes twinkled gaily, as though he'd paid her a great compliment, or as though there was a secret between them.

Abigail hoped Gilbert hadn't prevaricated when he'd feigned surprise in discovering Louisa in residence.

"No coincidence about it," he said. "My firm is handling a project nearby. I am here to oversee the work."

"All the way out here?" Her eyebrows rose, and a playful grin lit her face. "What are you building—a hen house? A stable?"

"Very funny. No, a new wing to an ancestral home by the name of Hunts Hall."

"Hunts Hall?" Louisa echoed, her teasing smile fading. "I have heard of it. . . ."

"Yes, I imagine you have," Gilbert said dryly. "It's where Andrew Morgan and his family live."

Abigail felt compelled to add, "Gilbert has just invited me to watch the workmen break ground. But if you would like to join us . . ."

"I'm sure Louisa won't wish to miss an opportunity to see Andrew Morgan. And the home to which he will someday be heir."

Louisa lifted her chin. "You are quite wrong. I have no interest in seeing the place or the man." She effected a casual smile and added, "But you two go ahead."

Leah Chapman came through the gate on her way toward the church, a basket of flowers in her hands. Abigail waved her over and introduced her.

Louisa warmly thanked Miss Chapman for the welcome gifts she had sent over for her and Mamma, while Leah brushed off her praise and shifted credit to her mother. When she excused herself to continue on to the church with flowers for the altar, Louisa asked if she might accompany her. She probably hoped for a chance to see William Chapman again, Abigail realized, feeling queasy at the thought.

When the two had walked off together, Abigail returned her attention to Gilbert. "Can you stay and visit?" she asked. "My parents will wish to see you."

"And I them. I would say that's why I'm here, but the truth is, I came to see you."

Abigail gave him a searching look. Was this more of his Italy-inspired flattery, or was he sincere?

His eyes held hers earnestly. "Abby, look. I did call on Louisa once or twice when I first returned to London. She's a beautiful girl—I don't deny it. But beyond that, she is . . . Well, she is not you, Abby. You are beautiful inside and out. Louisa is young and doesn't know who she is or what she wants. I had already decided not to call on her again before I saw you at Hunts Hall. And now that I have seen you again, I know that I was right not to."

Abigail felt her heart warm, and her stomach tingled as if she'd swallowed a caterpillar. Her practical mind whispered, *But what about Louisa? And what about William Chapman?* How torn she might have felt had she not seen the look on Mr. Chapman's face when he laid eyes on her beautiful sister.

Later that evening, Leah Chapman sought out Abigail's company, asking her to take a turn with her and talk. It was a lovely, mild summer evening. Frogs chirped along the riverbank and a dove called in the distance. The smell of roses perfumed the warm air. They walked across the bridge and down the tree-lined lane, arm in arm.

Leah began, "So tell me, Miss Foster. Gilbert Scott—is there something between you? I saw you dance together at the ball, and now he's back. I saw how he looks at you."

Abigail waved away the thought as though it were a hovering bee, afraid to let it land and sting her. "He's here to build on to Hunts Hall, not merely to see me. Gilbert and I are old friends. We grew up next door to each another."

"Only friends?"

Rare irritation prickled through Abigail. "Forgive me, Miss Chapman. But I am surprised you wish me to share all of my history with you when you have shared so little with me. You have been secretive about Duncan and your past and your fears and almost everything, and yet you expect me to share my most personal stories in embarrassing detail?"

"You're right, Miss Foster. Please forgive me." Miss Chapman turned away, but Abigail caught her arm.

"Don't go. I only meant . . . if I am going to divulge all my secrets, could you not tell me just one of yours?" Abigail grinned, hoping to lighten the moment.

"My secrets are mine, yes, but they affect my entire family. My father would be upset if he knew I'd been talking about the past."

Leah must have some awful secrets, Abigail thought, or a tendency to be overly dramatic.

She said, "I want you to know you can trust me, Leah. So I will go first." Abigail sighed. "Yes, I have long hoped Gilbert and I would marry someday. I admired him and saw his potential long before he won awards at school or obtained a good position with a noted architect. And I thought he saw something of worth in me. I know I'm not especially beautiful, but in Gilbert's eyes I saw genuine admiration and affection. My own London seasons were not successful, partly because I'm no great beauty, but I suppose the truth was I didn't try very hard because I preferred Gilbert to any man I met."

She took a deep breath, and continued, "I don't think I was alone in my feelings. We never spoke of marriage directly, but we spoke of the future and of each other in it. We even . . . You will think me very foolish, but over the years Gilbert and I sketched many houses, sparring over which design, which style was best. We even designed what we called our ideal home." Abigail felt her neck heat, but continued, "We debated the size and layout of rooms, and how to make the guest chamber commodious and yet not so comfortable that our families would be tempted to stay *too* long."

Leah chuckled.

"We discussed how many bedchambers we would need for our children," Abigail went on, her face heating again. "You see, even when Gilbert was an awkward adolescent, even when I thought he was proud and hardheaded because he failed to see the superiority of my ideas, even then I admired him. Long before he turned anybody else's head he had turned mine, and I thought the feeling mutual."

Again she sighed. "But before he left for Italy last year, he told me he didn't think we ought to shackle ourselves with promises. *Shackle.* That's the word he used."

Leah winced, then said, "Perhaps he thought it wouldn't be

fair to you to enter into an official engagement before he left the country. In case he should become ill or . . . something."

Abigail nodded. "He said something along those lines to me, and I wanted to believe him. But later that same evening, I came upon him and my sister in a private tête-à-tête. She gave him something— a lock of her hair I found out later—and he accepted it."

"That doesn't necessarily mean anything," Leah said as they turned and headed back through the wood. "You don't know that he asked her for the lock of hair or wore it in a ring."

"That's true."

"Then perhaps he was simply too polite to refuse it."

"That's what I tried to tell myself. But if you had seen how he looked at her . . ." Abigail shook her head. "Before then, I thought he still saw her as a pesky little sister. That he was blind to the fact that she had grown more and more beautiful with each passing year. But finally even Gilbert couldn't keep his eyes off of her."

Leah pressed her hand. "Miss Foster, I am very sorry."

Abigail continued, "But that isn't the worst of it. When Gilbert returned to London, suddenly fashionable and invited to some of the same routs and balls Louisa attended, he apparently sought her out. Mamma mentioned it to me in her letters, that he had turned Louisa's head. Even called on her several times."

"Ohhh . . ." Leah had no rebuttal for that one, Abigail noticed.

Abigail shook her head again. "But now I don't know what to think. Today he told me he was here to see me, specifically. That he had decided not to call on Louisa again. He certainly *seems* interested in me. But I wonder if he is only angry with her."

"Why would he be angry?"

"Louisa met several gentlemen during the season—men of wealth and connection. My mother has certainly encouraged her to consider her options and not to settle too quickly on any one man. Gilbert has felt the sting of this. I gather Louisa views him as her if-all-else-fails plan, if a better match does not materialize."

"Surely you don't think he's only interested in you because your sister snubbed him—not with your long history."

"I hope not. But I know Louisa is far more beautiful and charming. Men always think so. Even—" She bit back the words *"Even your brother is not immune."* It was too painful to say it aloud, especially to his sister. Instead she said, "Even so, I had always been content in the knowledge that Gilbert Scott admired me."

"Poor William," Leah murmured.

Abigail sent her a quick glance. Leah did not know that William was following in Gilbert's footsteps, already dazzled by the beautiful Louisa.

"And now"—Abigail drew herself up—"enough about me. Your turn."

"Very well," Leah said. "There isn't much to tell about Duncan, but I will tell you about someone far more important from my past." She gathered her thoughts and began. "When I returned from a year away at school, I found a place I liked to go on the very edge of the Pembrooke property. A place in the garden, behind the potting shed. Hidden by trees on one side, and the garden wall on the other." She gestured into the clearing ahead. "Come, I'll show you."

Ah . . . Abigail thought, realization dawning.

Together they walked past the old gamekeeper's lodge and onto the nearby grounds. They paused behind the potting shed and surveyed the jumble of pallets and planks.

"In those days, there were also a few sticks of cast-off furniture, even an old mirror," Leah said. "A mother cat had a litter of kittens beneath a lean-to I built of old boards, and throughout that summer I tamed them one by one. I came here every afternoon when the weather was fine and Mamma didn't need me at home. I played here for hours. One day this was a house, the next a ship sailing the high seas with me at the helm and the kittens as my crew. I played church and school and house and pirate. It was diverting for a lonely, imaginative girl.

"But one day," Leah went on, "when I came to what I considered *my* play area, I was surprised to find that someone had left fresh flowers in my favorite green jar. I knew little William had not done so, and feared one of the Pembrooke boys had found my hiding place. But the flowers were neatly cut and arranged. I looked around and noticed a few other changes as well. Someone had fashioned a table out of a plank and two large blocks. And set the flowers upon them. It had to be another girl. I was irritated and yet secretly hopeful. I had become accustomed to the company of girls when I'd been away at school, and I longed for a friend.

"Then I found a letter left for me, signed by *Your secret friend*, asking to play with me here. Suddenly I felt self-conscious to play where I had played without second thought only the day before.

"The next day I came again . . . and so did she. She said I should call her Jane. I gather she assumed that I would have nothing to do with her if I knew she was indeed Harriet Pembrooke."

Abigail said, "But you told me you didn't know her—"

"No. I told you I'd never officially met Harriet Pembrooke, and I did not. But I spent many a fond hour with a girl named Jane. I never told her my real name either. For I did not want word to get back to Papa that I had spent time with Clive Pembrooke's daughter when he had forbidden me to do so."

"Do you think she knew who you really were?"

"Who I really was? No, I don't believe she did."

Abigail shook her head in secret wonder. She had found the village girl. Now, where was "Jane"?

Leah continued, "Later we began leaving secret notes to each other behind a loose brick in that wall there." She pointed to the spot. A curious light came on in Leah's eyes, and she walked toward the wall.

Abigail's stomach clenched in alarm. Her pulse began to pound. How would Leah react to finding Abigail's letter to "Jane" there? Would she be unhappy to learn Abigail already knew of her from another source, and feel betrayed?

Abigail blurted, "I don't think you ought . . . Let me first tell you, that I—"

Leah bent and pulled the brick from its place, revealing the hiding place of Abigail's letter.

But the letter was gone.

Leah replaced the brick. "It was silly to think . . . But still. For old times' sake."

Abigail released the breath she'd been holding. Her heart continued to beat fast, however, though now for a different reason.

Before they parted ways, Abigail said, "I am planning to watch the workmen break ground at Hunts Hall the day after tomorrow. Will you go with me?"

Leah gave her a shrewd look. "Trying to play matchmaker again, Abigail?"

"Guilty," Abigail apologized, but she was unable to stop the smile from widening across her face to hear Leah Chapman call her by her given name.

Chapter 22

The next day, Abigail returned alone to the hidden spot in the garden. All seemed undisturbed as before. But then she sucked in a breath. That glass bottle, sitting on a plank, held a single black-eyed Susan. Her heart began to pound, and she stepped to the garden wall. Hands damp within her gloves, she removed the brick, hoping to find a letter of reply. Instead, the space remained empty. Her heart fell. *Foolish girl.*

She heard a footstep and whirled. There stood the veiled woman at the corner of the potting shed. Abigail's pulse raced. Was this Harriet Pembrooke at last?

The woman reached up gloved hands and slowly lifted her veil, revealing not a stranger's face but the face of Mrs. Webb, Andrew Morgan's widowed aunt.

Abigail pressed a hand to her chest. "You startled me."

One thin eyebrow arched. "Not who you were expecting?"

"No."

The woman frowned. "Well, you are not who I was expecting either, so we're even on that score. Though it did cross my mind that you might have written the note. After all, I had sent you several unsigned letters, and turnabout is fair play."

Abigail sputtered, "You wrote the letters?"

"Yes. Who were you expecting . . . Jane?"

"I was expecting Harriet Pembrooke."

"And here I am, in the flesh." Mrs. Webb spread her hands, an ironic quirk to her thin lips. "I thought you, being the clever girl you are, would have figured that out long ago. And no doubt you can guess who I was expecting—or at least, hoping—to find here."

Abigail nodded. "I am sorry to disappoint you. I haven't told her about the letters you have written to me. Or this meeting. I wanted to meet you first myself." Confusion pinched Abigail's thoughts. "But I still don't understand. Someone would have mentioned if your maiden name had been Pembrooke."

Harriet glanced back toward the house and began, "When we left here, my mother thought it wisest not to use the Pembrooke name. She feared Father would pursue us to the ends of the earth. So she reverted to using her very common maiden name of Thomas, and I followed suit."

She gestured toward the walled garden. "Come. Let's take a turn."

The two women strolled through the relative privacy of the secluded garden, Abigail not really seeing any of the flowers they passed, her mind whirling with thoughts and questions.

Harriet continued, "When I was twenty, I married Nicholas Webb and was quite happy to leave all ties to Pembrooke buried in the past."

She regarded Abigail. "That is the unsung benefit of marriage, Miss Foster. It gives you a new name, a fresh start in life, a way to leave behind the person you once were."

"I hope your marriage gave you more than that."

Again that thin dark brow rose. "Do you mean love? No. But I didn't expect love. I did receive a new identity, however. People no longer know me as Harriet Pembrooke. No longer judge me by what I did or what my father did. That Harriet is gone. Thank God and thank Mr. Webb. No one sees me and thinks of that desperate, clutching, awkward girl. The daughter of a murderer. Except for Miles."

She shrugged. "And though Nicholas was much older than I, he was good to me. He gave me financial security, the means to leave Pembrooke Park behind forever. It was finished, or so I thought." She exhaled a heavy sigh. "You would think I would be happy with that."

"But you're not," Abigail said gently. It was not a question. The answer was clear on the woman's long pale face.

She shook her head. "Nicholas died and I felt lost, untethered. My identity shaken all over again. I began having nightmares of the old days. Of my years here. Guilt over what my father did . . ."

Again, she looked at the old house over her shoulder and shuddered. "I cannot find peace. I thought, if only I could somehow make restitution for my father's wrongdoing. Pay the price somehow—as he never did, at least as far as I know. Otherwise, I fear I shall be held accountable, pay for 'the sins of the father' because I've never confessed what I knew, because I kept his secret all these years. Oh, there were rumors. Suspicions. But they never amounted to more than that. We were all too afraid to say a word."

"So, he did . . . kill . . . Robert Pembrooke?" Abigail hesitated to say the words to his distraught daughter.

"Of course he did." Her eyes flashed. "Don't tell me you are surprised or I shall think I misplaced my trust in you. And my journal as well."

"I didn't wish to believe the rumors. To . . . presume."

"Why not? Everyone else did, and rightly so. And no matter what Miles might have told you, neither he nor I have any right to the estate. Not after that. I always thought—or at least wished—there might be a more deserving relative to give the place to.

"Once I found the family Bible, I thought perhaps that rumor had been true as well. But I failed to find any close relations of Robert Pembrooke, so I sought out more distant relatives—and found your father. I also wanted to see the house occupied for another reason.

I thought it would lessen the temptation for Miles. I know he told you he only wanted to see the old place again. He told me the same. I hoped rather than believed him sincere. Tell me honestly, has he been searching the house?"

"Yes."

Harriet winced. "It is as I feared. And the parsonage?"

Abigail stared. "The parsonage? What has he to do with that?" The air left her. "Oh . . ."

"I hope I am wrong," Harriet said grimly. She pulled a sealed letter from her reticule. "I was going to post this when I returned to Bristol, but I suppose there is no more need for anonymous letters. Still, you might as well read this one."

She held forth the letter, and Abigail reached for it. For a moment, both women held the sealed paper.

Abigail said, "May I ask . . . why did you begin writing to me in the first place?"

Harriet shrugged and said coolly, "Why does anyone write anything? To make known and to be known. It was time to open the door, to let all the dark secrets escape into the light at last." She turned and walked away.

Abigail called after her. "But what about the secret room? Won't you tell me where it is?"

Harriet turned back. "Now, what would be the joy of that? You're a clever girl. You'll find it so much more satisfying, dare I say *rewarding*, when you find it on your own."

Abigail thought about following after her to argue the matter, but curiosity about this latest—and perhaps last—letter kept her where she was. She unsealed it, unfolded it, and read.

> *Have you noticed the black stain up the kitchen wall in the dolls' house? Perhaps you thought it intentional, painted that way purposely by the builder, an effect for realism's sake. But no.*
>
> *I came into my bedchamber one afternoon to find smoke*

*hanging heavy in the air over the dolls' house. I shrieked, as
you can imagine, and ran to it, stunned to find a very real fire
burning in the miniature kitchen hearth. I knew right away
who'd done it and confronted him as soon as I'd put it out
with water from my washing stand. He said he only did it
to see if the chimney actually worked. But I knew better. He
did it to be cruel. To be like Father.*

*Mother took him to task over it, but in her presence he
denied it, blaming his brother. And she believed the favored
boy's weeping protestations of innocence. So Harold took
the blame, as usual, earning a wallop and an early bedtime
without supper. I shudder to think what would have befallen
him had Father been home. He was away in London at the
time. At some gentlemen's club that had accepted him as a
member based on the Pembrooke name. I don't know if he
would have laughed it off, or beat Harold. We could never
be sure how he would react.*

*Considering the light penalty, I abandoned the argument
when I realized Mother had made up her mind. But perhaps
I shouldn't have. Miles has learnt to get away with things, to
manipulate his way out of consequences for most of his life.
Only once did he experience our father's full wrath. And I
admit, I never did. He never once struck me. And I feel guilty
for that as well. To have suffered so little, when everyone else
in my family suffered so much.*

Shaking off a chill at the words, Abigail folded the letter and
left the garden. Did a boyish act of mischief—dangerous though
it was—mean Miles had anything to do with the parsonage fire?
Unlikely. Even so, Abigail thought she might stop by the parsonage
and talk to Mr. Chapman.

But as she rounded the corner of the manor house, she saw that
very man standing near Louisa in the churchyard, talking earnestly.
Heart sinking, Abigail halted on the drive, but her foot scuffed a
stone and sent it skittering across the gravel.

He looked up at the sound and stopped speaking midsentence, his fair face reddening. Abigail's stomach clenched, and she turned toward the house in retreat.

Suddenly, the thought of seeing Gilbert again seemed more appealing than ever.

William Chapman jogged after her. "Miss Foster? Did you need something?"

She paused at the door, feeling embarrassed and self-conscious. "I . . . no."

"Oh. I thought you might be coming over to speak to me."

"I . . ." She hesitated, her thoughts a muddled blur. "It's nothing. Never mind."

He touched her arm. "Tell me."

She decided not to betray Harriet's confidence about Miles. Instead she said, "I . . . only wished to ask what you would say to someone who said she wanted to redeem the wrongdoings of her family. To pay for the sins of her father?"

His brows furrowed in surprise, and he looked at her in sober concern. Did he think she was asking for herself?

Was she?

He inhaled deeply and looked up in thought. "I would say . . . while I agree it is good to make what restitution we can, we can never *pay* for the sins of others, let alone our own. That has already been done. God's Son has already paid the price for your sin, your father's, and mine, once and for all. If you will only ask him and trust him with your life, He will redeem the past, your future, and give you peace for today."

Abigail's heart ached at his words. If *she* longed for assurance that she was forgiven for her part in her father's fall, how much more must Harriet Pembrooke long for forgiveness and peace?

She looked at him in reluctant admiration. "You said that very well."

He shrugged. "Thank you. But remember no one is perfect. I have my own sins and mistakes to ask forgiveness for."

Louisa approached them with a brittle smile. "Mr. Chapman,

here are your gloves. You left them on the churchyard wall during our little . . . tête-à-tête."

Her sister's eyes glinted with what—flirtation, or irritation? Irritated at *her*, Abigail guessed, for interrupting their private talk.

Was the time Mr. Chapman spent with Louisa one of the mistakes he regretted? Abigail wondered. Or his time spent with *her*?

Since both Louisa and Leah declined to accompany her, Abigail planned to go to Hunts Hall on her own. She would have a long walk ahead of her, so she left the house early the next morning, glad the day had dawned warm and sunny. But she had barely crossed the drive when Mac Chapman clattered through the gate in his gig.

"Leah told me you were going out to the hall this morning."

"That's right."

"Hop on, if you like."

"Thank you."

He shrugged and said, "I was going anyway."

Maybe so, she thought, but she knew very well he would have ridden his horse and not bothered with the gig just for himself. She was touched but knew he didn't want her to make a fuss.

They rode in relative silence for several minutes, and then he asked one terse question: "Miles Pembrooke back?"

"Yes."

He set his jaw but said no more.

She asked, "What do you remember about him and his siblings?"

Mac sat silent for several moments, staring straight ahead. She'd decided he was not going to reply, when he surprised her.

"The eldest boy, Harold, was hot-tempered and rash, like his father," Mac began. "Though he did what he could to protect his ma—I'll give him that. Miles was harder to judge. A real charmer, yet manipulative as well. Knew when to sulk and when to smile to get his way." He shook his head. "'Course, he was young and his character not fully developed. Perhaps he has improved since then. Or gone bad." He shrugged. "Wish I knew . . ."

"And the girl?"

He nodded thoughtfully. "Harriet." Mac chewed his lip as he considered how best to reply. "She was a quiet girl, and no doubt lonely. Difficult enough to be the daughter of the manor when all the others in the parish are daughters of farmers or shopkeepers. But folks round here took against the entire family. When Leah came home from school, I forbade her to have anything to do with the girl. You will think me harsh. But I knew very well no good could come from such a friendship, and plenty of harm."

Poor Harriet, Abigail thought. At least Leah had her family and a loving father.

She thought again about Eliza, but could not bring up the delicate subject of her father's identity with Mac. Hopefully Leah had remembered to do so.

As they rumbled up the drive to Hunts Hall, Abigail saw Harriet Webb in the distance, strolling with a parasol across the front lawn. Seeing her arrive with Mac, Mrs. Webb turned abruptly and walked in the opposite direction. To avoid her . . . or Mac?

When Mac had gone off with the men, Abigail sought her out alone.

"Good morning, Mrs. Webb."

She inclined her head. "Miss Foster." She hesitated. "I thought you might bring Miss Chapman along."

"I invited her, but she declined."

"Ah."

"She did, however, confide in me a closely held secret. She led me out to the walled garden and told me about a secret friend she used to meet there."

Harriet's eyes sparked with tentative hope. "Did she indeed?"

"I think she would consider meeting you again. But I have not suggested it. She has already chastised me for trying to play matchmaker with gentlemen, so I doubt my attempt to reunite old friends would meet with better success."

Harriet nodded and asked, "And the letter I gave you?"

The sunny day suddenly seemed less fair. A ragged cloud passed over, marring the otherwise blue sky. "I read it, of course," Abigail said. "But I hope it doesn't mean what you seem to think it means."

"I hope so too."

Abigail looked across the roped-off building site and saw Gilbert shaking Mr. Morgan's hand and handing him a shovel to scoop the first token of earth. She waved to him, and he beamed across the distance at her. For a moment their gazes held, and much passed between them in that long look. Past disappointments. Dreams. Apologies. Hopes for the future.

Abigail said, "Let's not talk about the past any longer. New beginnings are always exciting, are they not? So full of promise."

"If you say so."

On the opposite side of the site, a group of onlookers cheered politely. Then the group drifted over to the blankets and makeshift plank tables covered with fine linens, where a picnic feast awaited them.

Harriet and Abigail remained where they were, isolated by the noise of the laborers—the clank of pickaxes, the sharp cut of shovels, and the jingling tack of mules, hauling away loads of dirt.

She felt Mrs. Webb's gaze on her profile and glanced over.

Disapproval tightened the woman's lips, and she said tartly, "That little hat of yours may look smart, but it offers very little protection from the sun. Here." She sidestepped closer and repositioned the lacy parasol over Abigail's head as well.

Her brusque concern reminded Abigail of Mac's cranky thoughtfulness and pierced her heart. Standing there shaded by Harriet's parasol, Abigail was momentarily transported back to the idyllic moments she had shared under William Chapman's umbrella. . . . She then recalled their more recent conversation.

She began, "I have been thinking about what you said about marriage. How it gave you a fresh start. That people no longer judged you by what your father did, because you had a new identity."

"Yes . . . ?" Harriet agreed warily.

"But you also admitted it wasn't enough. That you are still unhappy—guilty over the past . . . and frightened for the future."

"What of it?"

Abigail's heart burned within her. She had never spoken like this to anyone but felt compelled to do so now. "You long to redeem the wrongdoings of your family. But Mr. Chapman says we can never *pay* for the sins of others, let alone our own. That has already been done, once and for all."

How Abigail wished William were there. He would have said it so much better than she could.

"God is merciful and ready to forgive," she continued. "He gives us a new identity in Christ. *That* is the real second chance you long for."

Abigail shook her head. "I am sorry. I am saying this very poorly, I know. And I don't mean to give the impression I am a perfect Christian, for I am not. Far from it. But I see how unhappy you are. How much you long for peace. And that's the one treasure I know how to find." Steeling herself for rejection, she reached out and pressed the woman's hand.

Harriet Pembrooke blinked in surprise. For a moment she allowed Abigail to hold her hand, as stiff and cool as marble, and then she gently extracted it.

"Thank you, Miss Foster," she said flatly. "I know you mean well. I am not one for church myself, but I do know that some things are too big for religious niceties to overcome."

Abigail inwardly groaned. Oh, she *had* made a muddle of it! "I am not talking about religion," she insisted. "And there is nothing 'nice' about God's Son dying a cruel death to pay for our sins. I am talking about forgiveness and freedom. True new life, whether you ever enter a church building or not."

"Again, I thank you for your concern. And now, if you will excuse me."

Mrs. Webb lifted the parasol and turned and walked away, disappearing into the house—not even joining the rest of the party or partaking of the picnic. Guilt swamped Abigail, and she heaved a dejected sigh.

Andrew Morgan waved Abigail over to join them, and she obliged, though with a heavy heart. She felt terrible for spoiling the day for Harriet. She had done herself no favors either, for the few bites she nibbled were like wood shavings in her mouth, though she smiled encouragement to Gilbert whenever he looked her way.

When the party began to break up later, Abigail was surprised to find Mrs. Webb standing beside her once again. "Will you do me a favor and give this note to Miss Chapman for me?"

Abigail hesitated. "Whom shall I say it's from?"

"I sign it as Jane, but you may tell her who it's really from—though it may mean she won't accept my request to meet, especially if her father finds out. You are welcome to read it first and proceed as you think best."

With that, Harriet turned and retreated into the house once more.

Abigail tucked the letter into her pelisse pocket to read later, just as Mac came and asked her if she was ready to head home.

Entering the hall of Pembrooke Park a short while later, Abigail distractedly laid aside her hat and gloves and pulled out the folded, unsealed note. The outside was blank but inside it was addressed to Lizzie:

Dear "Lizzie,"

You may well be shocked to receive a letter from me after all these years, but I hope it is not an unhappy surprise.

I have thought of you so often, always hoping you were well and happy. I imagined you with children of your own, perhaps even playing in our secret place. Having now visited Easton on a few recent occasions, I must say I was disquieted to discover you were still unmarried and, if I may say so, looking ill at ease and even afraid of your own shadow. Or perhaps . . . of someone else's shadow?

When we met as girls, you likely knew my real name and where I lived. But I wanted to thank you for overlooking it

back then, when no one else would. Those hours we shared
between the potting shed and garden wall were the happiest
I spent in Pembrooke Park. Nay, they were the only happy
memories I have of those years.

I did not like seeing you looking troubled. Or to hear Mrs.
Morgan speak to you in such a horrid manner. You have a
good heart, and deserve better than that. If there is anything
I can ever do for you, please don't hesitate to let me know.
Miss Foster will know how to contact me.

Fondly,
"Jane"

Abigail called on Leah after dinner and asked to speak to her
alone. The two women sat outside on the garden bench in the
fading sunlight. Abigail handed her the letter and waited quietly
while she read it.

Leah looked up at her with tear-bright eyes. "Please don't tell
my parents. Especially Papa. He forbade me to have anything to
do with her."

"But certainly now, after all these years . . . What can it matter?"

"It can. It does. You'll have to take my word for it."

"Very well. Do you want to see her again?"

"I'm not sure. You have talked with her, I take it? What is she
like now?"

"You spoke with her as well. The woman in the veil?"

Leah's brows rose. "That was her? I thought her voice was familiar."

"You may have met her too. I know William has. She is Mrs.
Webb now, Andrew Morgan's aunt by marriage."

"That's who she was!" Leah stared off thoughtfully. "Andrew's
aunt . . . I only saw her from a distance. I told William she looked
familiar at the ball, but it never crossed my mind she could be my
Jane."

"Yes. She married Nicholas Webb when she was quite young.

By then, she and her mother had begun going by her mother's maiden name."

"Which explains why we never heard of a marriage with anyone of the Pembrooke family."

"Yes. She was eager to cut all ties to this place and to the Pembrooke name."

Leah's face dimmed. "How sad. To lose all ties to one's family. To her home. Her name . . ." Pain shone in her eyes.

"Harriet said she was glad to take a new name. It was like a second chance at life for her. A new beginning."

"Born again . . ." Leah murmured. Her gaze remained distant, and her thoughts seemed very far away.

Abigail sat quietly, not wanting to hurry Leah or pressure her. She felt comfortable in the companionable silence between them, glad their friendship seemed on better ground at last.

Finally, Leah said, "I will meet her. But only if you will go with me."

Chapter 23

Abigail's parents invited Gilbert to Pembrooke Park for dinner to celebrate his first major building project. They decided to limit the party to family and old friends: themselves, Miles, and Gilbert. But Louisa took it upon herself to invite William Chapman to join them.

She justified, "After all, he is our nearest neighbor and our parson and all alone in that forlorn, damaged parsonage just across the drive."

"Very neighborly gesture," their father said approvingly.

Their mother looked less convinced, perhaps concerned her pretty daughter might form an ill-advised attachment with a poor curate. Abigail had mixed feelings about him being there as well.

At the last minute, Miles bowed out—to even their numbers, he said. Father tried to convince him to stay. "Don't leave on that account. We don't care about that—not at an informal family dinner."

Miles thanked him but said he was going to again see his sister, who was visiting the area. Abigail wondered if Harriet would tell him about their meetings, but somehow she doubted it.

The dinner passed pleasantly, with much teasing and laughter and toasts to Gilbert's success, and to friends old and new.

After dinner, Mr. Foster lit his pipe and the others strolled toward the drawing room for coffee.

Gilbert said, "Abby, I've been thinking about those renovation plans you showed me. May I see them again?"

She looked at him quickly, and knew he had something else in mind. "Very well."

Abigail glanced over her shoulder as they walked away. Louisa barely seemed to notice their departure, but William hesitated at the door of the drawing room, watching them go with apparent resignation. Louisa linked her arm through his and led him into the room. No doubt she would soon put a smile on his melancholy face.

Inside the library, Abigail walked over to the map table and pulled out a random drawer. Even if he really had no interest in seeing the plans, they would provide an excuse if someone looked in the open library door and saw them alone together. The act also gave her nervous hands something to do.

Coming up behind her, he touched her arm. His voice was low and warm and somehow made her hands tremble all the more.

"Abby, dear girl, I . . . wanted to talk to you. I—"

"Which did you want to see?" she blurted, pulling out a set of plans without really seeing them.

"Abby, I don't really . . ." He hesitated beside her. "What's this?" Gilbert picked up a drawing that had lain beneath the plans. With a start she recognized the drawing he was looking at. Her ideas for the parsonage.

His brow furrowed. "Have you shown these to Mr. Chapman?"

"No . . . not really. He saw me working on them, but I told him they were not for anyone else's eyes."

Expression cautious, he asked slowly, "Why . . . are you drawing plans for Mr. Chapman's parsonage?"

"Because the old one was damaged, of course. And you know me. I couldn't resist the challenge."

He looked away as he considered, biting his lip. Then he turned to face her, and said soberly, "Do you know what *I* would think, if you drew a plan for my future house?"

So apparently he *had* forgotten the plans they had drawn together. To conceal the hurt, she jested, "That it was amateurish, no doubt." She self-consciously tried to tug the drawing from his grasp, but he held tight.

"No. I would think you wished to live there with me. That you were designing those four snug bedchambers—one to share with me, perhaps, and the other three for our future children. At least, I hope you are the sort of woman who looks forward to sharing a bedroom with her husband, instead of insisting upon having a room of her own."

Abigail felt herself flush, and mumbled, "I don't think he would jump to that conclusion."

He looked at her earnestly. "I even tried to find the house plans you and I drew up years ago, but I could not find them anywhere. I don't know if Mamma cleaned out my things while I was gone, or if I misplaced them, or—"

"I have them. Upstairs in my room."

He paused, expression brightening. "I should have known." He dropped the drawing and grasped her hand. "I don't want you to plan his house, Abby. I want you to share mine. I know I was a fool where you are concerned. And Louisa. A blind fool. Susan was right. But I am seeing clearly now, and what I see is the woman I want to share my life with."

She stared at him, her heart beating like a fluttering bird, unsure whether to nest or to fly away. "Gilbert, I . . ." Words failed her. Her mind swam, struggling to navigate foreign waters, the waves too high, the undertow strong.

He grasped her other hand as well and squeezed both. "You must see it, Abby. Our growing up side by side as we did. Our common interests. We have always understood each another and been the best of friends. It can't be for nothing. It must be for a reason."

Releasing her hands, he wrapped his arms around her, drawing her close. "I know we should wait for a while before I begin courting you—allow time to pass since my calls on Louisa. But tell me it is not too late for us. Tell me I have not spoiled things between us forever. . . ."

Abigail hesitated in his embrace. Torn between relaxing into the arms of a friend, throwing her arms around him like a long-lost lover, or pulling away.

Over Gilbert's shoulder, movement caught her eye. She glanced up and saw William Chapman stop abruptly in the library doorway. His dark expression sent her heart plummeting. Before she could react, he turned and left without a word.

With numb fatalism, William turned on his heel and stalked away. He'd been stunned to find Abigail in Mr. Scott's embrace. But why should he be surprised? He knew Scott was the man she'd loved for years. It had only been a matter of time. Any man would have to be a blind fool not to realize Abigail Foster's worth, her character, her heart, her beauty. And apparently Mr. Scott had at last done so, as William had feared he would.

He returned to the drawing room, heavy resignation descending over him. He suddenly felt exhausted, as though he'd not slept in days. What could he do? With Mr. Morris planning to do all in his power to assure the living of the parish went to his nephew when he retired or died, William might never be able to support a wife— not as long as he remained in Easton, near his family. At least, not a wife like Abigail Foster, who would expect—who *deserved*—a certain standard of living. There was no point in persisting and no point in staying.

He made his way to Mrs. Foster's side and quietly thanked her and excused himself early. He didn't want to be there if that embrace was soon to be followed by an engagement announcement. He wasn't ready to see Abigail walk into the room on Gilbert Scott's arm, her face aglow with love for another man. He was not comfortable in flirty Louisa's company either. Even the thought of Rebekah's renewed interest provided no comfort.

He would be happy for Abigail someday—he would, with God's help—but it wouldn't be today.

The look on William Chapman's face when he'd stood in the library doorway stayed with Abigail for the rest of the night. What had she seen in his expression? Disapproval of their indiscreet embrace? Disappointment? Resignation? How could she guess his feelings, when she struggled to understand her own?

Gilbert had asked if he might court her, but she'd put him off, telling him she'd have to think about it. How would William Chapman react if she agreed? And how would Gilbert react when she confessed she had no dowry? She hadn't been brave enough to tell him. Afraid he would withdraw his offer. Afraid he wouldn't . . .

Though her mind and heart were still unsettled the next day, she went with Leah as promised to see Harriet Webb. Leah had suggested her grandmother's cottage as a neutral and discreet meeting place, since it was currently unoccupied while the older woman recovered at the Chapmans'. And Abigail had sent a note with place and time to Mrs. Webb at Hunts Hall.

Half an hour ahead of schedule, Abigail walked with Leah to her grandmother's cottage and waited.

Nervous, Leah tidied the sitting room, and straightened a knitted blanket folded over the back of the sofa. Glancing around the small cottage, she said, "I'll never forget the first night I came here. Never liked the place since . . ."

"Really?" Abigail asked in surprise. "I think it's charming. And your grandmother seems so kind."

Leah sat down at last. "Oh, she is. She's a perfect dear. The only grandparent I've ever known, really." She grimaced. "I just . . . don't like her cottage."

Mrs. Webb appeared alone and on foot at the appointed hour. Abigail opened the door for her.

Leah rose stiffly and clasped her hands nervously over her stomach. "You wished to see me, Mrs. Webb?"

Harriet regarded her in surprise. "So formal. And how strange to hear my married name on your lips. Do you not remember me— your old friend of the potting shed?"

"Yes, I remember you . . . Jane."

A flash of a smile transformed Harriet's weary face, and for a moment she was young and beautiful again.

"That's better. Thank you, *Lizzie*." She smiled wryly. "You and I have gone by several names in our lives."

Leah's head snapped up, and she looked at Harriet warily. "What do you mean?"

Harriet pursed her lips. "Only that you have gone by Leah Chapman and Lizzie, and I have gone by even more names: Harriet Pembrooke, Jane, Miss Thomas, and Mrs. Webb."

Leah stared at the woman through narrowed eyes a few seconds longer, as though searching her expression for sincerity or hidden meaning.

"Why?" Harriet asked, brows high. "What did you think I meant?"

But Leah replied with a question of her own. "May I ask, Mrs. Webb, if you have sought me out of your own volition? Or is it at the behest of your father? And why now, after all these years?"

It was quite an onslaught of questions, Abigail thought, but she remained silent.

Harriet tilted her head to one side and studied Leah's face. She asked quietly, "I know your father resents mine, but what are *you* so afraid of?"

Leah lifted her chin. "You haven't answered my questions."

"I have not seen my father in eighteen years, Miss Chapman," Harriet said, reverting to formal names as Leah had done. "And I would certainly never act as his puppet in this, or anything else for that matter. We assume he is dead. I would even say we hope that is the case."

Leah asked, "*Why* do you assume he is dead?"

Harriet's eyes narrowed as Leah's had. "Why do you wish to know?"

"I want to know for certain that he is gone—that he will not return someday and . . ."

"And what?" Harriet prompted. "Yes, I believe he probably killed his brother as well as the valet to get his hands on Pembrooke Park. But even if he were still alive, what harm would he do *you?*"

Leah again answered the question with one of her own. "If your father went to such lengths to get Pembrooke Park, why abandon it so abruptly? And why would he stay away all these years?"

Harriet's eyes hardened. "That is why we believe he is likely dead, though no report of his death has ever reached us. Or perhaps he is alive but fears some evidence of his crimes exists and has fled the country to avoid hanging, never to return."

"If only we could be sure he was well and truly dead!" Leah's voice rose on a plaintive high note. Then she seemed to realize what she had said to the man's daughter and sheepishly ducked her head. "Forgive me. That was an unfeeling thing to say."

Both Abigail and Mrs. Webb stared at Leah's tortured expression. Why did she feel this so personally?

Leah swallowed and said, "I was sorry to hear that your mother and brother are gone."

"Yes. There is only Miles and me now. And you know *I* don't mean you any harm."

"And Miles?" Leah asked.

"Why would he?"

Leah feigned a casual shrug. "Do you not find it . . . suspicious, his coming here as he has, so soon after the house was opened and occupied again?"

"Yes, I do," Harriet allowed. "I worry about that as well, but only because I fear he will follow in our father's footsteps and carry on his mad pursuit of the supposed treasure. Why would you think Miles means you any harm? He barely remembered you from the old days, is that not right? In fact, he mentioned to me he had no idea why you found him so repugnant."

Leah looked away sheepishly once more. "I don't find his person repugnant. I am sorry if I gave that impression. But Papa and I did find his return suspicious and feared he might be here on his father's behalf."

"You give Miles too much credit. If Miles is here, it is because Miles wants to be here, because he believes there is something in it for him."

Abigail frowned. "Did he say as much when he came to see you last night?"

Harriet's thin eyebrows rose again. "Me? I have not seen Miles in a week or more."

Abigail felt her brow furrow. "Well, apparently his plans changed. In any case, he's told me quite emphatically that neither of you had any wish to claim Pembrooke Park or to live in it again."

Harriet nodded. "I don't think Miles wants to live there. But I do think he'd like to find whatever *treasure* he can, and take it with him if he could."

"But you know where the secret room is," Abigail said. "You found it—is that not right?"

"You know where it is?" Leah asked the woman in surprise.

Harriet nodded. "Yes."

"And Miles?"

Harriet shook her head. "I never told anyone. It was my own secret." She lifted one shoulder. "Though I was not the only person who knew about it. It seemed clear to me at the time I found it that someone else had been inside recently."

"What do you mean?" Leah asked.

"You have to remember that I found the room nearly twenty years ago, so I don't recall every detail. But when I first entered, I remember I didn't find thick dust and heavy cobwebs. The room was neat—a little storeroom or hiding place."

"What's inside?" Abigail asked.

Harriet flicked her a wry glance. "Don't tell me you share my brother's fascination?"

"Naturally I am curious."

"I remember shelves and a jumble of boxes. A small chair, and several portraits. One of a beautiful woman, I recall, though I cannot see her face in my mind's eye any longer. I do remember wondering if she was my Aunt Pembrooke who died."

The missing portrait . . . Abigail thought, then asked, "But no treasure?"

Harriet gave her a sardonic look. "I don't know that it would be wise to further fuel your interest, Miss Foster. I don't need two Mileses on my hands. Mostly papers, if I recall correctly. Boxes of old baby clothes and things. But I will say there were a few pieces of jewelry. Family heirlooms, I believe."

"Still there?" Leah breathed. "Like what?"

"I recall a necklace and earrings . . ." She squinted in memory. "Some other jewelry, though I forget what. In any event, I was careful to only enter the secret room when no one was about, so I would not give away its location. I didn't want my father, or even Mac Chapman, to—"

"You didn't want Mac Chapman to what?" That very man appeared in the doorway, scowling down at Harriet. His gaze flicked to Abigail, then to sheepish Leah, before returning to the former Miss Pembrooke.

"Harriet Pembrooke . . ." he breathed, his dark red eyebrows like lobster claws, drawn low.

For a moment, no one said a word, and the tension in the room thickened.

"You might have knocked, sir," Harriet rebuked.

"Why? What have you got to hide? Besides, 'tis my mother-in-law's house you're making yourself at home in. But your lot excels at that."

"Papa, stop," Leah said, rising. "I invited Mrs. Webb here."

"Mrs. Webb, is it?" His eyes shifted to Leah. "And why would you do that?"

"Because I wanted to ask her about her father."

"And what did she tell you?"

"She assumes he's dead but doesn't know. But she does know where the secret room is."

"Does she indeed?" Now his eyebrows rose like a redbird's wings. "Did you take anything from there?"

Harriet met his suspicious green glare with a cool blue gaze.

"Anything like, say, personal letters, or jewels, or the Pembrooke family Bible? No, I did not."

Abigail asked eagerly, "Won't you tell us where it is? Or show us?"

Harriet shook her head. "I already told you. You can find it on your own, Miss Foster—I know you can—and collect that reward for yourself."

Harriet sent Mac a knowing glance and wagged a finger. In a singsong voice, she urged, "No helping her, now."

Chapter 24

Motivated by Harriet's smug challenge, and her mention of the outstanding reward, Abigail went to the library to retrieve the old building plans again. As she flipped through them, something on the back of one drawing caught her eye. Someone had traced the tower section from the reverse side and sketched in something . . . a ladder? It looked like steep narrow stairs had been penciled in. Perhaps someone had proposed adding a staircase in the unused tower—a set of servants' stairs to reach the bedchambers directly. From the look of the quick sketch, it had only been an idea, likely never implemented.

She carried the plans up to her room and spread them on the floor, orienting the drawing with the room. Gilbert had concluded the water tower had been converted into a closet above and kitchen hoist below. She shook her head. The water tower would have been *near* her closet. But exactly? She wasn't convinced.

Once again she knelt before the dolls' house. Kitty had found a doll inside the small wardrobe. Might something else be hidden inside as well—something they had both missed? She opened one of the wardrobe's small doors. But with the fading daylight casting shadows it was difficult to see inside. She tried pulling the wardrobe out of the dolls' house, but it was anchored to the wall.

That gave her pause. She tried the bed and then the dressing chest, but those pieces moved easily. Had the wardrobe been purposely glued to the wall, or had it been placed there while the paint was still wet, creating a seal?

She glanced up at the full-size wardrobe against her bedchamber wall, then rose and peered behind it. It was difficult to see behind the tall cabinet, but in the crack of space she saw no obvious straps or anchoring bolts.

She stood back and considered the wall the wardrobe stood against. A four-foot section of wall between a tall window and the closet door, trimmed in oak like the wardrobe itself and covered in rosebud wallpaper. If the drawing was accurate, the water tower would have been on the other side of this very wall.

Stepping to the window, she opened it and stuck her head out—a wall of about eight feet jutted out at a ninety-degree angle. If it was a shaft used to collect rainwater in former days, it was unlikely there would be an access point from her room.

Was there something behind that wardrobe worth hiding? A young girl like Harriet could not have moved the wardrobe herself. Had she asked Mac for help? Or some servant long gone? Then left this clue, if clue it was, in the dolls' house? There was one way to find out.

Who could Abigail get to help *her* move the wardrobe?

Duncan? When she believed he may have been searching the house at night before Miles even arrived? No.

What about Miles, who had suggested they join forces? No. Harriet would never forgive her if she did anything to inflame his interest.

Gilbert was still in the area, overseeing the construction at Hunts Hall. He would be willing, though he would likely tease her for her overactive imagination, or perhaps even be offended to learn she questioned his opinion of the placement of the old water tower. Besides, she wasn't ready to give him her answer.

Her own father was not exactly a strapping man, but Mac Chapman was. What had Mrs. Webb meant when she'd told him, *"No helping her, now."* Even if the former steward knew where the secret room was, it didn't mean he would be eager to assist her.

Or . . . Jacob Chapman was only fifteen. But he was already nearly as tall as his brother and strong from helping William chop wood for the family. He and William together would certainly be able to move it. But would she need to confide in them the reason she wished it moved? And then be embarrassed if she was wrong?

Would she need to share the reward with whomever helped her find the "treasure"? She wouldn't mind sharing the reward with William Chapman, if it came to that. He could certainly use the money, and a more deserving man she could not imagine.

———————

She sought him out the next day and found him in the church, checking the water level in the baptismal font. "Mr. Chapman, might I ask you and Jacob to help me with something?"

He turned, auburn eyebrows lifting in surprise. "Of course." In his wary uncertainty, she thought she saw the question *"Why not ask Mr. Scott?"* flicker there. But she was likely flattering herself.

"I'm afraid it's not a very glamorous favor," she said. "I need two strong men to move something for me."

Another question flickered, and she answered his unspoken thought before he could voice it. "I hope you aren't offended. But I don't want to ask Duncan. I don't trust him—not fully."

"Very well. What is it?"

"Could you and your brother come by the manor this afternoon—whenever it's convenient for you? I'll tell you then."

He thought. "I have a christening shortly, but I could come this afternoon. I'll bring Jacob with me."

"Thank you. And I shall ask Mrs. Walsh to prepare a cake for your efforts."

He lifted one corner of his mouth in a grin. "Or *you* could make us a cake."

She shook her head, mirroring his grin. "Oh no, you wouldn't want that, I promise you."

The door opened, and Mrs. Garwood, Andrew Morgan's widowed sister, entered, child in arms. She hesitated at seeing Abigail there but greeted her politely. She shifted the child, apparently trying to open her reticule for the christening fee, and William quickly offered to hold the infant for her.

Seeing William comfortably and naturally hold that child in his arms caused Abigail physical pain. Here was the woman he once loved and her fatherless child . . . Would he offer to fulfill that role in the child's life? Would he marry Rebekah as he'd once wished to, and maybe still did?

Suddenly that seemed more probable than a union between him and Louisa. Despite her flirtation and his stammering admiration, her sister was unlikely to marry a poor curate. But Rebekah Garwood, a wealthy widow? The thought hurt to contemplate.

But why should it? she berated herself. *Gilbert wants to court me, as I've long hoped. What is wrong with me? Lord, tell me this is not a case of only wanting what I cannot have. I am not such a fool, surely.*

Before the men arrived that afternoon, Abigail moved the dressing table herself, lifting first two legs, then the other two atop a thin rag rug. This allowed her to slide the dressing table over the wooden floor with relative ease—and quiet. She placed it on the other side of the fireplace, freeing up a space for the Chapmans to move the wardrobe into. Did she need to reveal why she wanted it moved? She hated to lie, especially to a clergyman, but could she trust his adolescent brother with her secret—whether successful or mortified?

She wasn't sure.

At least she didn't have to tell her family. Papa had taken Louisa and Mamma out for a drive to see the progress of the new wing at

Hunts Hall as well as its grounds, but Abigail had begged off. And Miles had ridden away that morning and had yet to return. She wondered again where he'd gone the night he said he was going to visit his sister. But whatever his destination, with him absent, the timing seemed perfect.

Polly knocked and popped her head in. "Mr. Chapman and his brother and sister are here to see you."

"Oh? Which sister?" she asked.

"The younger girl—Kitty. I've showed them into the drawing room, miss."

"Thank you, Polly." Kitty coming along was a blessing in disguise. Otherwise, would the maid not have wondered why Abigail had invited two young men into her bedchamber? "And, Polly . . . ?" she called and waited until the maid turned back. "Don't be surprised if we all come up here for a while. No doubt Kitty will want to amuse herself with the dolls' house again, and Mr. Chapman and I can as easily discuss our business here and keep her company."

"Oh . . ." A furrow appeared between the girl's brow. "I see. As you like, miss. Shall I . . . ?"

"You go on and have a rest, Polly. Perhaps take some tea. I shall go down and greet the Chapmans myself."

"Very good, miss. Thank you."

When she had gone, Abigail checked her reflection in the mirror, then hurried downstairs to the drawing room.

William, standing at the window, turned when she entered. "Kitty heard where we were going and begged to come along," he explained. "I hope you don't mind."

"Not at all. I imagine Kitty is eager to see the dolls' house again. In fact, why do we not all go upstairs together."

"We needn't . . ." he began, then stopped. After studying her face for a moment, he said, "If you wish."

"I hope you didn't ask me here to play with a dolls' house, Miss Foster," red-haired Jacob said. "If the other chaps found out, I'd never hear the end of it."

"Don't worry, Jacob. I have something else in mind for you. But when you see what it is, you might wish for something as easy as rearranging dolls' furniture."

She led the way upstairs, feeling unaccountably nervous. Would they tell their father? Mac might be angry to learn she had disrupted rooms he saw as a sort of shrine to Robert Pembrooke and his family. Would they all laugh at her gullibility in believing tales of a secret room and treasure? *But it isn't just a story,* she reminded herself. *Harriet Pembrooke has been inside the secret room. And perhaps Mac has as well.*

She opened her bedchamber door for them, and Kitty eagerly entered first, pulling Jacob along by the sleeve behind her. "Come and see, Jacob. You'll be impressed. Even if you are a boy."

William hesitated just inside the doorway, his eyebrows arched question marks.

Abigail glanced back into the corridor to make sure they were alone, then said, "Please don't scoff. But I would like you and Jacob to move the wardrobe to that wall there."

He lifted a shrug, his lower lip puckering. "No problem. Doing a little . . . redecorating?" His eyes glinted with interest.

"Something like that," she replied vaguely.

He regarded the large piece of furniture, then looked back at her. "That is a two-man job. I see why you asked me to bring Jacob along."

Relieved he did not press her for reasons, she added quietly, "Do you think you can manage it?"

He looked at her in mock offense. "You injure my male pride, Miss Foster. We Chapmans are a strong lot."

"I know you are. That is why I asked you."

"Is it?"

She looked down, then up at him again. "Not the only reason. But may I tell you the rest later"—she leaned closer and lowered her voice—"when we are alone?"

Something sparked in his eyes at her intimate tone. He lowered his own voice and replied, "I shall look forward to it."

Perhaps he wasn't enamored with Louisa—or Rebekah Garwood—after all.

He crossed the room and gestured to his brother. "Jacob, Miss Foster would like us to move this wardrobe to that wall there. Doing a little rearranging. It's what females do. Come on, show off your muscles. . . ."

Abigail quietly closed the bedchamber door behind her.

But after they had moved the wardrobe, nothing about the exposed wall looked either suspicious or promising. A coating of grey dust clung to it where the wardrobe had stood, out of reach of the housemaid's duster. But otherwise, it looked like any other wall in the room. No inset door panel, no cutout opening, no "X marks the spot."

Disappointment sank deep. But she pasted on a false smile and thanked the Chapmans warmly. "I knew you two strong men were the very ones to ask. Now if you wouldn't mind not mentioning it? I wouldn't want anyone to think that I am making myself too much at home here or . . . anything else either."

William's eyes searched hers, but he didn't pry.

Jacob shrugged and said, "Where's this cake I was promised?"

"Jacob . . ." William gently reprimanded.

"No, no," Abigail soothed. "Jacob is quite right. I promised cake, and cake you shall have. Mrs. Walsh didn't allow me to help her bake it, but she did allow me to ice it. My first time, so be kind."

They returned to the drawing room, where tea and a somewhat streaky-looking iced cake were waiting. Fortunately, it tasted much better than it looked.

Jacob forked down large bites, as if sending pitchforks full of hay into a barn. Then he looked up at the long-case clock. "Is that the right time?"

"I believe so, yes."

"Will you excuse me?" He rose. "That is, if you don't need my help with anything else?"

"Of course. You're all through."

He turned to his brother. "I promised Fred and Colin I'd join them for a match at four." Jacob looked back at Abigail. "William was the best football player in the county before he went and became a parson."

William demurred, "I don't know about that."

"You were," Kitty insisted, then set down her fork as well. "May I go along?"

Jacob scowled. "Only if you promise not to go all moony over Colin. We all know you like him."

Kitty shrugged. "So?"

William nodded. "Very well, but behave yourselves. Jacob, look out for your sister. And be home by five."

Jacob grabbed his cap from the sideboard and let himself from the room. Kitty thanked Abigail politely and dashed after her brother. A moment later the large front door banged shut in the distance.

William set down his cup and saucer and looked at her expectantly.

Abigail sipped her tea and avoided his eyes.

"Well? You do trust me, I hope, Miss Foster?"

"I do, but . . . now I feel so foolish." She glanced toward the door and, seeing no one about, said, "I studied the old plans, and had reason to think the secret room might lie behind that wardrobe."

"I thought it might be something like that," he said gently. "I am sorry, Miss Foster. Life is full of disappointments sometimes." He looked as if he knew that fact from firsthand experience.

"Miss Foster, I—"

Suddenly Miles Pembrooke appeared in the open doorway, his eyes darting around the room. He looked expectantly from one to the other, his smile faltering somewhat on finding the two of them alone together. "Hello."

"Hello, Miles." Abigail smiled brightly, hoping to dispel the awkward moment. "You have just missed Kitty and Jacob Chapman. They left only moments ago. Do come in and join us for cake."

Miles set aside his hat and gloves and approached the tea table. "And where is the rest of your good family?"

"Gone for a drive. Father wanted to show Mamma and Louisa the progress at Hunts Hall and its grounds, which I have already seen."

"Ah. I see. What lucky timing then that Mr. Chapman should call when you were otherwise alone, and keep you company."

"Yes. And what have you been up to today, if I may ask?"

His eyes glinted. "I shall tell if you do."

Beside her William stiffened.

Choosing to ignore the implication of impropriety, Abigail prompted, "Have a good ride?"

"Yes, I went to pay another call on our former housekeeper."

Ah! Is that whom Miles had visited instead of his sister? Abigail said, "That must have been pleasant."

"Yes. It was very . . . interesting. Mrs. Hayes said it would be 'poetic justice' if I married my cousin." Miles gave her a sly smile. "I wonder what she meant, *cousin dear?*"

Or whom, Abigail mused, thinking of Eliza. Glancing at William, she saw his jaw clench and quickly said, "You mustn't take anything Mrs. Hayes says to heart, Mr. Pembrooke. I am afraid her mind isn't what it once was."

Miles nodded. "Ah. Well. Happens to the best of us."

William rose. "Thank you for tea and the delicious cake, Miss Foster. Lovely icing. Perhaps we might talk about this further another time?"

"Yes, of course."

"Talk about what, pray?" Miles asked. "Don't let me interrupt."

"Not at all, Mr. Pembrooke," William said. "I was just leaving."

At dinner that night, Abigail listened distractedly while her mother and sister told her everything they had seen and everyone they had met during their afternoon drive and tour of Hunts Hall. Afterward, Abigail took herself to bed early, while the rest of her family lingered over coffee in the drawing room. Polly helped her undress, and when she went to return Abigail's pelisse to the closet, suddenly drew up short at the sight of the relocated wardrobe.

"When did you go and do that?" she asked, brow puckered.

"This afternoon. Just wanted to try a different arrangement. The Chapman brothers helped me while Kitty played with the dolls' house. I'll move it back before we leave."

"Don't fret. You can move the furniture where you like. It's your house now—for the time being anyway. Come tomorrow, I shall give the floor and wall there a good cleaning. Likely hasn't seen the light of day—or a mop—in years."

"Thank you, Polly. But I can do it. I don't want to cause you more work."

"No bother. Now, anything else before I go?"

"No, thank you. That's all."

"You're turning in early tonight. Are you feeling all right?"

"Yes. Fine. A little tired is all."

Polly closed the shutters and turned to go. "See you in the morning, then, miss."

"Good night." After Polly had gone, Abigail lay in bed, listening to her retreating footfalls and staring across the room at the newly exposed wall. The very ordinary-looking wall.

Even as she told herself she was becoming worse than Miles and Duncan combined, she rose, lifted her bedside candle lamp, placed it on the nearby dressing table, and regarded the wall again.

She pressed her palm against the four-foot panel, then tapped it, the sound startlingly loud in the quiet room. How odd to feel self-conscious in her own bedchamber! Did it sound hollow? She tapped again, then tapped against another section of wall to compare. The two did sound different. But a difference in the structure of an interior versus exterior wall, or one with windows versus without, could account for it. She felt along the seams, coming away with dusty fingers. Then she lifted her candle lamp and held it nearer the wooden trim. Was that the narrowest slit—a simple seam where the wallpaper met the trim, or something else?

Her heart rate began to accelerate. She knew that sometimes servant doors—doors that led onto the back stairs, allowing servants to silently slip in and out of bedchambers—existed in many old manors. And often these doors were hidden to keep from marring the décor of the room—wallpapered to look exactly like the walls until they were opened. She pushed against the seam hidden along the slat of wooden trim . . . and felt it bounce back, as though she'd triggered a spring latch. She sucked in a breath, looked behind her to make sure her door was still closed, then pushed again. The four-foot section of wall popped ajar, opening toward her. A waft of cool, musty air met her nose.

She had found it! Found . . . something, at least.

Once again she looked over her shoulder, and then, on second thought, crossed to her door and turned the key in the lock.

Pausing to slip on her shoes and tie on her dressing gown with shaky hands, she returned to the hidden door. What would she find inside? Was there really treasure worth the lives it had cost and ruined?

As her fingers came to rest on the hidden door again, someone rapped soundly on her bedchamber door, causing her to gasp, jump back, and press a hand to her heart.

"Who is it?" she called, voice high, shutting the door and making sure the wall panel appeared undisturbed.

A muffled male voice responded. It didn't sound like her father's voice, but surely Miles would not come to her bedchamber at night. Or would he?

On impulse, she set a ladder-back chair in front of the hidden door as quietly as she could, wincing as it scraped the floor. Yes, the chair helped the wall look less noticeably bare.

"Coming! Just tying on my dressing gown . . ." She hurried over and unlocked the door. Since she already wore her dressing gown over her nightdress, she silently asked forgiveness for the lie.

She opened the door several inches. Miles stood there, waiting expectantly.

"What is it, Mr. Pembrooke?"

His gaze swept her nightclothes, and his brows rose. "Forgive me. I didn't think you'd be dressed for bed already. It is still quite early."

He was right. So perhaps his call wasn't so audacious after all.

"I hope you aren't ill," he added.

"I was just . . . tired."

"You look positively flushed." He reached out and pressed a hand to her forehead. "Are you sure you've no fever?" The act pushed the door open farther, and she noticed his gaze dart about the room.

"No, I'm fine. Thank you." She took a half step back from his hand. "Was there something you wanted?"

His gaze hovered on the wardrobe. "Done some rearranging, I see."

Abigail hesitated, then asked, "And how would you know that? I don't recall your being in my room before."

"Your father gave me a tour that first evening, when you were at the ball."

"Ah. What a keen memory you have. I've only moved a few things about. Making the room more comfortable. I hope you are not offended?"

"Not at all. Why should I be?" His eyes swept the exposed wall. "Find anything interesting?"

"Excuse me?"

"Sometimes long-lost treasures show up when one moves things that haven't been touched for decades."

"A great deal of dust, Mr. Pembrooke. That is all I have found."

That was true. So far at least.

"Tut, tut, Miss Abigail. I have asked you to call me Miles. We are family, after all."

That again. "I shall endeavor to remember, *Miles.*"

"That's better." He reached out again and tweaked her nose, a fond smile curving his lips and revealing the space between his front teeth.

"I suppose I shouldn't ask to come in?" he pouted. "Though I hear a whole tribe of Chapmans spent time in here earlier today."

"Oh, and who told you that?"

He shrugged. "I forget which of the servants mentioned it. Duncan . . . or Polly, perhaps."

"Kitty is quite taken with the dolls' house. Her brothers kept us company."

"And helped move furniture?"

"While they were here, yes." *Wonderful,* Abigail thought sarcastically. Word had reached Duncan and Miles already. "But that was during the daylight hours," she added. "It would be quite a different matter for you to come in now. Alone."

"Because I am a man, you mean?"

"Well . . . yes, I suppose."

Another thin smile curved his lips. "I am glad you are aware of that fact. We are not *so* closely related, after all."

Footsteps paused outside her room, and Louisa appeared. "Oh. Mr. Pembrooke."

Miles stepped back from the door. "Another fair cousin. How delightful. I was only checking on your dear sister. When she retired so early I feared she might be ill."

"I wondered the same." Louisa looked at her, something sparking in her eyes that Abigail hadn't seen in years—that old conspiratorial gleam when they had teamed up as sisters, covering for each other with their parents. She feared Louisa would suspect a liaison, finding their houseguest at her door at night, Abigail in her nightclothes, no less. But that wasn't what that look said. It told her she understood.

Louisa said, "Excuse me, Mr. Pembrooke. But I simply must speak to my sister alone. Girl talk. You understand."

He nodded amiably. "Oh yes, yes, perfectly. Well, no, not at all, really. But I shall go just the same and bid you both good night." He bowed and swept down the passage.

With a relieved sigh, Abigail ushered her sister inside and closed the door behind her.

"Thank you."

"Are you quite all right, Abby? You were thoroughly distracted at dinner. I doubt you heard half of what we said. And barely reacted at all when I told you we met the Morgans and saw Gilbert when we stopped at Hunts Hall."

"Sorry. I've been . . . preoccupied."

"Not with our *dear cousin,* I hope."

"No."

Louisa patted the bed. "Good. Well, I saved you from that man, so now you need to repay me by listening."

"Very well." Abigail climbed back in bed, and Louisa sat beside her.

"I wasn't eager to visit Hunts Hall when Papa suggested it," Louisa began, "for I met Andrew Morgan in London you see, a few weeks ago. And I . . . Well, he was quite rude to me, truth be told. I hate to say something so unneighborly, but there it is."

"Really? I am surprised," Abigail said. "I have only met him a few times, but he was quite kind and perfectly polite. And a friend of Mr. Chapman's."

"Yes, well. I am ready to forgive him everything, now I've seen his house." Louisa winked. "Don't look so scandalized. I am only teasing. I will say that once Papa formally introduced me as his daughter and your sister, his demeanor changed toward me. So perhaps things in London were all a simple . . . misunderstanding. Or he feels quite mortified by his treatment of me, now he knows who I am. That we are to be neighbors, I mean."

"What do you mean by 'his treatment' of you? What did he do?"

Louisa shrugged. "Since he seems determined to put it behind us, I shall endeavor to do the same. Give him the benefit of the doubt."

Abigail narrowed her eyes, studying her sister's averted face. Wondering what she wasn't telling her. She must own a share in the wrong, if wrong it was, to be so reticent to repeat it.

Louisa added, "I will say Gilbert was more polite as well. I was quite shocked at how cold he was the first time I saw him here."

Abigail asked gently, "What happened between the two of you?"

"Oh . . . well. I think he felt snubbed when he returned from Italy. But what was I to do? So many gentlemen wishing to dance with me and pay calls . . . I couldn't spend all my time with Gilbert. Even if he is a family friend."

"Family friend?" Abigail asked. "Are you sure he wasn't more than that?" Her sister's memory seemed to be shifting to suit her own purposes.

Louisa looked down, pulling at a loose thread of her frock. "I thought he might be before he left for Italy. That's why I gave him a lock of my hair. But apparently I was wrong."

"If you gave him a lock of your hair but then couldn't be bothered to give him a dance or the time of day, is it any wonder if he is cool toward you now?"

"Oh, he'll forgive me. Men always do. Just look at Andrew Morgan."

Wariness pinched Abigail's stomach. She said gently, "Louisa, I think you should know. Mr. Morgan admires someone else."

"Does he? Who?"

Abigail thought it wiser not to mention Miss Chapman. She knew too well how much her sister liked a challenge. And she didn't want to give Louisa any reason to dislike Mr. Chapman's dear sister.

"Just . . . be careful, Louisa. Men aren't playthings, you know."

She smiled coyly. "No? Then why do I so enjoy playing with them?"

"Louisa! Do you know how wanton that sounds?"

Her sister nudged her. "Don't be such a prude. I am only teasing my sister. Not talking to a man—or your clergyman." Louisa's eyes sparkled with interest. "Is he *your* clergyman?" she asked.

Had her little sister not noticed the clergyman's reaction to *her*?

Abigail's cheeks heated. "No. He is no such thing." Did she even want him to be? After the way he had reacted to the sight of her sister? And especially now that Gilbert was in the neighborhood, and seeking her out, and declaring how blind he'd been?

They talked for a long time, and Abigail felt her heart begin to thaw toward her younger sister. When Louisa finally yawned and rose to go to her own bed, it was late, and Abigail was tired. She decided not to open the door again that night and risk someone hearing her rummaging about and becoming suspicious. She could imagine Miles at the door, or loitering in the passage, listening to her every move.

She blew out her candle and settled in, darkness and weariness descending quickly. She would fall asleep any second, she was sure. But then she heard something.

The house made many sounds and groans, but this was one she had not heard before. A low moaning *creeeeak* . . . Her gaze flew to the hidden door and her heart thumped painfully hard. The door was opening. . . .

She stared, unable to move, unable even to cry out. A ghostly white hand appeared, gripping the edge. The door inched open, creak by creak, and there in the cavernous black cave beyond stood a man in a long hooded cape, his face shadowed and invisible.

Her mouth fell open, in a silent scream.

Then he stepped forward and a shaft of moonlight revealed what lay beneath that hood. A skull with sightless eyes.

"Huhhhn . . . !" She awoke with a start, gasping and eyes flying wide. Scrambling, she sat up, retreating back against her headboard, staring wildly at the crypt-like door, only to see the feminine rosebud-papered wall. Quiet. Undisturbed. Modest in its newly exposed state.

With a heavy sigh of relief and disgust at herself, she slumped back against her pillows. But it was quite some time before sleep claimed her once again.

Chapter 25

*I*n the morning Abigail awoke, for a moment forgetting. Then her eyes fell on the newly bared wall, and her heart thumped in anticipation. She eagerly climbed from bed, opened her own shutters, and began washing for the day.

Polly came in to help her dress, her face oddly alight. "Thought you should know, miss. The parson is in the morning room, waiting to see you. He told me not to disturb you until you were quite ready to come down—didn't want to rush you." She shook her head. "Never known a gentleman to call so early."

Abigail's pulse rate accelerated. He was there already? Had he read her mind? "I'm glad you told me. Here, let's do the rose day dress instead. Far fewer fastenings."

"Very well, miss. Though he did say not to hurry."

"That's all right. I hate to keep the parson waiting."

"And your hair, miss?"

She was tempted to leave it down, recalling his fingers touching her hair that first night in the sickroom, but she blinked away the memory. "Just a simple coil, if you please."

As soon as she was ready, Abigail hurried downstairs, slowing her steps as she neared the morning room. When she entered, he looked up from a newspaper and stood, setting the paper aside.

"Good morning, Mr. Chapman. I hope you have not been waiting long."

"Not at all. Please forgive the early hour of my call. I have a full day of appointments and commitments ahead of me, so this was the only time I could stop by. I am afraid my curiosity has been nipping at me all night. I keep thinking we may have missed something. I slept very poorly, I don't mind telling you."

"As did I." She lowered her voice. "I dreamt the door opened and someone came out. A . . . skeleton." She shivered.

"Door?" His eyebrows rose.

She looked behind her, then stepped nearer. "Yes. I found a seam along the trim and a spring latch before I went to bed."

His eyes widened. "Have you been inside?"

She shook her head. "I haven't even *looked* inside yet. I kept getting interrupted, and then I lost my courage. And I . . . didn't really want to go in alone."

She forced herself to meet his gaze, and for a moment neither said anything. Then she looked over her shoulder into the empty hall. "None of my family are up and about yet."

He added helpfully, "I saw Mr. Pembrooke from the parsonage window, leaving on his morning ride."

She pulled a face. "Too bad we don't have Kitty here as an excuse."

He nodded. "Or as chaperone."

"So . . . it wouldn't be a good idea for you to come upstairs with me now."

Again he nodded. "You are quite right."

He looked so solemn, so parson-like, that she felt a grin quiver on her lips. Seeing it, his eyes sparkled, and an answering grin lifted his mouth.

Two minutes later, Abigail led the way upstairs and across the gallery on tiptoe. William Chapman followed behind, all stealth. A bubble of mirth tickled her stomach. They were like two naughty children, sneaking around on some mischievous errand. She thought briefly of Gilbert and their childhood together and felt a pang of guilt.

She quickly shook it off, picked up the candle lamp still burning in the dim corridor, and let him into her room, quietly shutting the door behind them.

She trusted William Chapman fully. And so, she believed, did her father. But that didn't mean he would approve of finding the two of them alone in her bedchamber. And to lock her door when a man was with her? She could not bring herself to do it. Instead she lugged her dressing stool in front of her door. It would at least give them a little warning if someone entered.

Crossing the room, Abigail's heart beat a little too fast, but she didn't feel nearly as anxious as she had the night before, about to open the hidden door for the first time by herself. William's presence was comforting. Even if he had disappointed her with his reaction to Louisa, she was glad he was with her at this moment.

She handed him the candle lamp and placed her hand on the seam. Glancing at William for reassurance, she took a deep breath and pushed the same spot along the trim, triggering the spring latch.

Again that waft of stale, musty air met Abigail's nose. The door creaked open, reminding her of her dream. Seeing no skeleton, she released the breath she'd been holding.

"Good heavens . . ." Mr. Chapman murmured beside her.

She'd expected a completely dark room but was surprised to find a shaft of sunlight filtering in through a small window. She had thought the windows on the tower had been covered over, but here was one that had been left intact. Through the murky glass she could see why—the window looked out onto another exterior wall a few feet away and was therefore not visible from the ground—nothing to be noted by the window-tax man, or by someone searching for a secret room.

Stepping inside and pulling the door closed behind them, Abigail surveyed the square chamber. Thick pipes ran along one wall, draped in cobwebs. The other two walls held floor-to-waist-high shelves stacked with dusty boxes and crates and bundled papers. An old square of carpet covered the floor. No stairway, as in the sketch, but she hadn't really expected one, as she'd never found formal plans for stairs in the former water tower.

In one corner, several framed portraits leaned against the wall. Turning, she saw another large portrait had been hung on the back of the door. Sunlight illuminated the image, and Abigail gasped.

Beside her William turned to see what had caught her attention and sucked in a breath as well.

The formal portrait was of a woman in attire from decades past, a ruby necklace at her throat. Her hair was golden brown, her eyes large and gentle, her face serene, lovely, and startlingly familiar.

It was the face of Leah Chapman.

"What in the world . . . ?" Abigail breathed.

"Merciful God . . ." William murmured beside her. "It's Leah."

She gaped at him. "How can that be? The painting has clearly been here for years. But yes"—she returned her gaze to the portrait—"the woman looks just like her."

"It's understandable," he whispered. "It's her mother."

Again she turned to gape at him. "What?"

He nodded, his eyes full of awe and riveted to the portrait. "That's Elizabeth Pembrooke—Leah's real mother."

Abigail stared at him. Her mind was too busy to form a reply, whirling with impressions and snippets of things Mac and William and even Leah herself had told her in passing about Robert Pembrooke and his family, supposedly all now deceased.

She thought of the portrait of Robert Pembrooke in the mistress's bedchamber. This was definitely its mate, painted at the same general time period, in the same style, and likely by the same artist. Had it been hidden away by Robert Pembrooke as a painful reminder of his losses, or by someone after his death?

She thought of the graves in the churchyard, recalled seeing flowers on the one marked *Eleanor Pembrooke, Beloved Daughter*. And in one of the old journal pages she'd sent, Harriet had mentioned putting flowers on Eleanor's grave. "But . . . you all told me Robert Pembrooke's daughter was dead."

"I believed she was. I was too young to be fully aware of all that happened in those days following Robert Pembrooke's death. I only recently found out the truth about Leah myself."

"But . . . Why? How?"

"Before I say anything more, I must ask you to keep this to yourself for now. As much as I loathe the deception, it is not my right to reveal the truth to the world. Especially not until we can be perfectly certain all danger to her is past."

Suddenly from somewhere nearby came the sound of a slamming door. Abigail jumped and grabbed William's arm. William quickly lay a calming hand on her shoulder. "Shh . . ."

Then came the even nearer sound of someone knocking on her bedchamber door. Her gaze flew to William's. What should they do? Should they remain hidden inside? Abigail was tempted to do just that, but what if Miles or Duncan or whoever it was came inside and searched the room? She hated the thought of the two of them being caught like cornered rats. But neither did she want to open her bedchamber door while William Chapman was there in plain sight.

"You stay here," she whispered. "I'll see who it is."

He nodded, and she slipped from the secret room, carefully closing the door behind her.

Taking a deep breath, she crossed the room, pressing damp palms to her skirt. She moved aside the stool, put on a smile, and opened the door.

Miles Pembrooke stood there in his riding clothes. Gloves and stick in hand.

"I thought you left for your ride," she said. "You're back early."

"I spied dark clouds on the horizon and suspected a storm brewing. So I hurried home."

Abigail glanced out her window at the clear day, a gentle breeze swaying the tree branches and sunshine shimmering through the leaves. "Looks very pleasant to me."

"Looks can be deceiving, Miss Foster. In fact, I thought I saw Mr. Chapman walking over as I rode out . . ." His gaze swept the room over her shoulder. "He is not with you?"

She glanced around her bedchamber. "Just me, as you see. Though he was here earlier."

"Ah. I am sorry to have missed him."

"Are you? I am sure he will be happy to receive you if you stop by the parsonage later. Though he did mention he'd be away on appointments most of the day." *Appointments!* For which he was likely already late. . . . She had to get rid of Miles Pembrooke and sneak Mr. Chapman out of the house without anyone noticing.

Louisa appeared in the corridor at that moment, looking pretty and fresh in one of her new day dresses. "Good morning."

Miles turned, bowed, and then beamed at her. "Miss Louisa, how lovely you look this morning."

"Thank you." She looked from one to the other, her smile thin. "Back at my sister's door already, Mr. Pembrooke? I can't say I like that."

"Yes, well . . . Abigail's room is very . . . popular."

Louisa's brow puckered at that, but she said pleasantly, "I was just on my way down to breakfast. Have you two already eaten, or will you join me?"

Miles smiled. "I would love to join you, Miss Louisa. May I call you Louisa . . . ?"

Thank goodness for her sister and her ability to manage men, Abigail thought, sending Louisa a secret smile over Miles's shoulder. Shutting her door behind her, Abigail followed them down the passage and out into the gallery. When they began descending the stairs, Abigail remained at the railing. "You two go ahead," Abigail called down to them. "I remembered something I need to . . . finish first."

When the two had disappeared down the stairs, Abigail returned to her room. Nerves jangling, her mind whirled through possible ways to sneak Mr. Chapman out of her bedchamber now that her family was beginning to rise. Especially when she'd deceived Mr. Pembrooke, carefully wording her reply to suggest Mr. Chapman had already left.

She quietly opened the door to the secret room, eager to ask what he might suggest.

But the room was empty.

Befuddled and feeling foolish, Abigail looked inside her wardrobe and under her bed just to be sure, but no. He was definitely gone.

Thank heavens, Abigail sighed in relief. The parson was faster than she would have given him credit for. He must have slipped from her room as soon as she left with Miles and Louisa and gone down the back stairs without her noticing. She hoped he knew his way belowstairs and out the servants' entrance. She also hoped he didn't give Polly a fright or earn himself a tongue lashing from Mrs. Walsh for daring to enter her domain. But no, the housekeeper doted on him and no doubt happily aided—or at least overlooked—his escape.

Chapter 26

To avoid making Miles even more suspicious, Abigail joined him and Louisa for breakfast as promised. During the meal, she felt Miles's gaze on her often and did her best to enter into the conversation as though nothing unusual were going on. Father joined them, and the two men chatted a long while. Finally Abigail was able to excuse herself.

She returned to the secret room and closed its hidden door behind her. Stepping to the nearest shelf, she tripped over an upturned corner of carpet. She bent to straighten it, then began looking more closely at the things left piled on the shelves. The bandboxes, which she very much hoped did not contain hats. Stacks of paper and what looked like a jeweler's box. She felt like an intruder. Nearly like a thief. Tenant or not, these things were not meant for her eyes.

As she stood there hesitating, the hidden door behind her creaked open. Heart leaping, she gasped and whirled.

There stood Leah Chapman.

Abigail sputtered, "Leah! You frightened me. Come in and shut the door. Did William tell you we found it?"

Leah nodded, avoiding her eyes.

Abigail studied her expression. She said tentatively, "But you . . . already knew where it was, didn't you."

Leah's chest rose and fell in a deep breath, then she looked directly at her. "Yes. I played here as a child. My first father showed it to me, and helped me transform this forgotten storeroom into a secret hideaway. He and I were the only two who knew about it, as far as I know."

"And Mac?"

Leah's gaze flitted around the room. "Not until I showed him where it was. We hid here that night when . . ."

When her words trailed away, Abigail prompted, "The night the valet returned to report that your . . . Robert Pembrooke had been killed?"

Leah nodded again and turned, her focus landing on the portrait on the back of the door. She stilled, arrested, mouth falling slack. Then she stepped nearer to look at it more closely.

Seen together now, Abigail could see differences in the two faces. But even so, the resemblance was remarkable.

"Mamma . . ." Leah breathed. And Abigail for the first time fully grasped that the living, breathing woman before her, whom she knew as Leah Chapman—Mac and Kate's daughter and William's sister—was in fact Eleanor Pembrooke.

She tried the name on her tongue. "Eleanor . . ."

Leah turned sharply, her eyes meeting Abigail's, then softening into vague focus somewhere beyond her. "No one has called me that in years. It barely seems like my name anymore."

She looked at the shelves, the small window, then pointed to the child-size chair and cushions on the floor. "Oh, the hours I spent here, reading and playing dolls . . ." She pressed her eyes closed. "If only all of my moments here had been as pleasant . . ."

Abigail asked, "Can you tell me what happened that night?"

Leah shrugged. "I can try. I was only eight years old at the time, but the scenes are still very real in my mind. And now and again over the years, I have begged Papa to fill in the missing blanks for me, which he has done very reluctantly. Even so, he could tell it better."

"But Mac won't tell me, will he?"

Again Leah shrugged. "Probably not." She gazed toward the

ceiling, apparently gathering her thoughts, then began, "My father was away in Town. With Mamma passed away, he'd decided to sell the London house, and took several servants along to help him pack up the place. He'd planned to close up the manor here for a few weeks and had given the other servants time off. I was supposed to go with him, but at the last moment, I came down with a cold.

"Father sent Mac for the physician, who proclaimed me in no danger but said a quiet time at home would be wise. I begged Father to let me go with him, but since he had recently lost Mamma and the baby to illness, he insisted he would take no chances with my health and I would remain at home. I had outgrown a nurse, and my governess had only recently left us, so I was left in the care of our steward and housekeeper.

"My illness was God's merciful providence, Pa . . . Mac declared later, for had I been with my father, I might have met with the same fate. The official report was that he had been killed by thieves, but by the time the authorities brought the news of his death, we already knew the truth."

She paused for breath, then continued, "Mrs. Hayes's sister had fallen ill, so Mac and I were alone in the manor—me in my bed, and him downstairs somewhere—when Father's valet came home unexpectedly in the wee hours of the morning. . . ."

As Leah described the scene, it came to life in Abigail's mind, like a play in a theatre.

The front door banged open like a gunshot. Hearing it, young Eleanor left her bed and crept out of her room, standing at the stair rail to see what the matter was. Her father's valet crossed the hall below, his face ill-white, nearly green. His cravat and waistcoat were stained, his usually pristine boots muddied. Had he galloped all the way from Town?

From between the spindles she saw their steward rush into the hall, frowning thunderously. "Good heavens, Walter. What is the matter? Where is the master?"

"He's coming!" Walter cried. "He's coming!"

"Who's coming—the master?"

"No! His brother. The master's dead!" Walter's voice cracked. "Here . . . read this. He wrote this before he . . ." The valet's words trailed away. He handed over a note, and the steward read it.

Grim-faced, Mac tucked it inside an inner pocket. "I'll gather her things directly."

"No, there isn't time. We mustn't be here when he arrives. None of us. But especially her."

"I just need a few minutes. . . ." Mac started up the stairs.

Not wishing to be found eavesdropping, Eleanor retreated into her bedchamber.

"Do what you must, but hurry!" the valet called after him.

Mac entered her bedchamber and knelt before her. "Your father is dead, lass," he said. "I'm sorry—and sorry to say it so bluntly, but there's no time to waste."

Pain lanced her chest and tears filled her eyes. "Not Papa too."

"I'm afraid so."

Breathing hard, the valet scurried into the room, arms spread like a hen's wings to shepherd her chicks to safety. "Hurry. Gather a few things and let's go."

But no sooner had Mac risen to his feet than the front door downstairs banged open once more.

The valet's face stretched into a mask of terror. "No. He's here." He slowly backed from the room. "You hide her. I shall do what I can to distract him." He swallowed, his Adam's apple convulsing up and down his long thin neck.

The steward nodded gravely. "You're a good man, Walter." Then Mac turned to her. "We need to hide, lass."

"From whom?" she asked, eyes wide.

He grimaced. "Your uncle, I'm afraid. You are the last person to stand between him and Pembrooke Park. If he finds us, he will not hesitate to kill us both."

Her heart lurched. Her family . . . all dead. Would she be next? She feared she would be sick. But she composed herself and lifted her chin, determined to behave as her parents would wish her to.

Like the little lady of the manor her father declared her, after her mother passed on.

A voice she didn't recognize called from downstairs. "Hello! Anybody home?" Eleanor shuddered. Was it really the uncle she had never met—a man who would not hesitate to kill her?

She knew of only one place to hide. But did her uncle know about it as well? He might, she feared, having grown up at Pembrooke Park.

Taking the steward's large damp hand in her smaller one, she stepped to the wall and, pressing the invisible latch, opened the hidden door. Beside her, the man sucked in a sharp breath of surprise. She led him inside and closed the door most of the way behind them. They stood there together, listening at the crack. She smelled dust, sweat, and fear and hoped she would not sneeze and give away their hiding place. For a moment, the only sound she heard was Mac's breathing in the darkness.

Through the narrow crack, she could see across her bedchamber and out into the corridor beyond, lit with wall sconces. But she didn't see anyone.

Her uncle's voice sounded again from downstairs. "Ah . . . there you are."

"I didn't see . . . anything, sir," Walter said, his voice strained, its pitch higher than usual. She guessed he stood at the top of the stairs.

"I think you did," the other man said, his voice low and menacing.

She heard a heavy tread mount the wooden stairs.

"Who have you told?" the man asked.

The valet's voice rose in protest. "There is no one here, sir. No one to tell. What with the mistress and daughter passed on and the house all but closed up."

"They're all dead?"

"Yes. Died in the typhus epidemic last year."

"How convenient. But then . . . upon what errand did you race, hell-bent, back here?" It sounded as if the man now stood with Walter at the top of the stairs.

"I . . ."

"What did my brother tell you to do—what was his last request? Tell me. If you value your life."

Silence, followed by the echoing *snap* of a gun being cocked.

"Last chance . . ."

Panicked, Walter said, "He . . . he wanted us to . . . to hide his treasure."

"Ah! And where is it?"

"Upon my life, sir, I do not know. He wasn't able to tell me."

"Unfortunately, I believe you."

"No!" Walter screamed. An awful scream. Then came a sickening *fwank* of metal on bone. Then a thud, followed by a series of thuds, like a branch caught in the spokes of a wagon wheel: *thum-thump-thum-thump.* Walter falling down the stairs, she guessed. She wanted to run out and help—at the same time she wanted to hide forever. Mac grasped her hand, hard, likely feeling the same.

The heavy footsteps didn't descend the stairs; instead they proceeded up the corridor. One door was thrown open across the gallery, then another, then the door to the room next to hers. She jumped at the sounds, louder and louder, nearer and nearer. With trembling fingers, she pulled the hidden door closed all the way, praying, *God, please don't let him know about this room. . . .*

Would he really kill her? Kill them both? The man beside her obviously believed it. Fear, anger, disbelief gripped her—there was only one thing to do. *Our Father in heaven, help us,* she prayed. *Deliver us from evil!*

She had never been afraid of the dark, but she was afraid of being alone. And if she survived that night, that was exactly what she would be.

Leah sighed and sat down on the cushions on the floor.

The lights went out on the stage in Abigail's mind, but she knew she would imagine the horrific scene for a long time to come.

Leah continued more lightly, "At all events, my uncle didn't find us. After he left, we slipped back into my room. Mac gathered a few things and took me to Grandmamma's cottage and hid me there until he could decide what to do. He met with the housekeeper. Apparently she and the other servants agreed to say I had died with my mother, to keep my identity secret from my uncle. To save me."

She expelled a breath. "All my life, my adoptive parents have warned me over and over again to stay away from Pembrooke Park. Not to reveal my true name or identity to anyone. Not even to William. Even after Pembrooke Park was abandoned, I could not feel safe. After all, Papa would remind me, we never knew when my uncle or his offspring might return. . . ."

Leah shook her head. "William tells me that I must trust God will protect me eternally, even if not on this earth. But I have to say, it's this earth I most worry about." She managed a weak chuckle.

Abigail's mind whirled with questions. She snatched one from the air and asked, "Where did 'Leah' come from?"

"Oh, who can say how family pet names evolve. . . ." Leah considered, then explained, "My father, my first father, called me Ellie—short for Eleanor. When I came to live with the Chapmans, little William took to calling me by the second syllable of Ellie: Lee, which became Leah." She shrugged. "Papa thought it best for me to go by another name to help keep me hidden until the danger had passed. Papa . . . that is how I think of Mac now."

"Understandable, after so many years."

"Yes. Mac Chapman has filled the role of father far longer, and in many ways better, than Robert Pembrooke ever did, no matter how high a pedestal Papa insists on placing him on. Don't misunderstand me, I loved my father and mother, and was devastated by their deaths. But my father, like many men, was often absent—gone to Town for business or pleasure, or off riding or hunting. I simply didn't spend much time with him.

"Mac is the best of men, and has been an excellent father to me, if a bit overprotective. And in all truth, I don't remember my first father very well." She glanced again at the portrait. "And less so my mother. Though she and I were very close, she died about a year before my father. This is the first time I've seen her likeness in twenty years."

"William mentioned he only recently found out, and I haven't told a soul—don't worry."

She nodded. "William was so young when it all happened. Too young to be trusted with such an important secret. Mac and Kate made arrangements to send me away to school just before my uncle and his family took up residence in the house, to foster the ruse that Eleanor had died in the same epidemic that killed my mother."

Abigail said, "But the grave in the churchyard has your name on it. . . ."

She nodded. "My infant sister died a few days before my mother. But headstones take a long time to quarry and carve. Especially that year, with so many dead in the epidemic and such a long list of headstones to prepare. . . .

"Mac allowed people to believe the infant had been buried in the same casket with my mother, as was often done in the case of newborns. Mamma—Kate—argued against it, I recall, but Papa insisted on having the headstone carved with my name. We could always replace it, he said. Rectify the mistake if and when the danger was passed and I could reclaim my rightful name and rightful place as Robert Pembrooke's daughter and heir."

Abigail shook her head. "How you must have detested our coming and moving in to your home. . . ."

"Not at all! You mistake me, Abigail. It has saddened me to see my family home sitting empty and slowly decaying all these years, despite Papa's efforts to keep the roof sound and vandals away. I am glad you are here. And I am glad you've lifted the lid on this long stewing pot. It was only a matter of time before it all boiled over, or scorched and burned. . . ."

She shook her head as though to dispel the notion. "I have been content with my lot, Abigail. Truly. There are times I wish I might lighten Mamma's load or see the Chapmans living here in Pembrooke Park in style and ease, compared to that crowded old cottage. But they would never want to live here. And I'm not certain I would either, even if it were mine free and clear and safe. Don't feel sorry for me, I beg of you. I don't." She smiled bravely, charming dimples framing her gentle mouth. "Well, not often, at any rate."

"But surely some people knew, or guessed, who you really were?"

"Of course. After all, Mac and Kate Chapman had announced the birth of their firstborn son four years before. But when I returned from school after a year away, they told anyone who asked that I was an orphan of relatives in the north that they were raising as their own. William grew up believing that story, more or less. I don't think he was ever lied to directly—though many lies of omission, yes. Papa felt no remorse about lying to outsiders, though. He would have done anything to protect me. Some of our neighbors knew or recognized me as a Pembrooke. But with the man we all believed guilty of killing my father living right here in Pembrooke Park—all were willing to keep our secret, apparently.

"How Mac worried over the years, coddling this neighbor or that with loose lips or a tendency to drink too much, or growing old and forgetful. . . . But, thankfully, his worst fears have never come to pass. At least . . . so far."

Abigail thought of Mrs. Hayes. Did this explain Mac's visits and gifts?

Leah glanced at the hidden door behind them. "Papa won't be happy when he hears you know about me. But William and I agree we must tell him. He has every right to know."

Abigail nodded, a tremor of dread pinching her gut at the thought of Mac's anger.

"William has ridden to Hunts Hall to tell him, if he can find him around the estate. I think I shall wait to look through the rest of these things until he's with me. Or at least, until he knows that I'm in here with you." Leah expelled a breath of amazement at the thought.

"I understand." Abigail led the way back into the bedchamber, carefully closing the hidden door behind them. She looked around the room with new eyes. "How strange to think this is your room . . ."

"*Was* my room. Twenty years ago."

"That's why you cried—when you watched Kitty play with the dolls' house. It's yours."

"I don't know why I cried, exactly."

Abigail shook her head in bemusement and said gently, "You have many valid reasons to choose from."

"Perhaps. But I choose not to dwell on them. Now, would you mind terribly if I returned later, after I have talked to Papa?"

"Not at all. You are welcome any time. More than welcome. This is your home. Your room."

"Shh . . . Enough of that."

"Very well. For now." Abigail went to the bedside table and opened the drawer. "But in the meantime, you might wish to read these." She handed Leah the ribbon-tied bundle of letters and journal pages she'd received from Harriet Pembrooke.

Leah glanced at them, saw Abigail's own name written on the letters, and lifted questioning eyes to her face.

"Your friend 'Jane' has been writing to me these many weeks. And I think she'd want you to see them."

Early the next morning, Duncan knocked on her door and announced that Miss Chapman had come to call. Opening the door a crack, Abigail asked the manservant to send up her guest, as she was not yet fully dressed.

A few minutes later, she opened the door for Leah and shut it softly behind her. "I thought Mac would be coming with you."

"He is. He'll be here any moment, I imagine. He let himself in through the servants' entrance but insisted I go to the front door as a proper lady. He's probably helping himself to one of Mrs. Walsh's sausages as we speak."

"I thought you might return last night."

"We considered it. But he thought it would be more difficult to explain to your family."

"Ah."

"I hope we're not too early."

"No. Just give me one minute . . ."

Abigail sat at the dressing table and began gathering her long hair. She had shooed Polly away earlier, saying she would take care of her own hair that morning. In case the Chapmans made an early morning call, she wanted to be alone as soon as possible. Now she hurriedly twisted the hair into a coil atop her head. Holding it in place with one hand, she reached for the pins with the other.

Leah came and stood behind her. "Let me help you."

Leah picked up the pins and made quick work of securing Abigail's hair.

A soft scratching at the door alerted them, and Leah walked over and opened it, gesturing for Mac to enter. She returned to the dressing table and pushed in the last pin.

His voice low and regretful, Mac said, "You were meant to be a lady, my dear, not a lady's maid."

"Papa . . . I offered to help. And how many times have I told you I don't mind a little work."

Abigail rose, ran a self-conscious hand over her hair, and forced herself to meet Mac's gaze. She was relieved not to see anger there, only caution and concern.

"How many of Mrs. Walsh's sausages did you eat?" Leah asked him wryly.

"Only two."

"Ah. Cutting back, I see."

"I told her Miss Foster mentioned having trouble with her door and I'd said I'd take a look at it. I ran into Duncan on the way up and told him the same."

Abigail nodded. "Good thinking."

She hoped Duncan wouldn't become suspicious with all these visitors to her room, as Miles had.

This time, Abigail locked her bedchamber door and then gestured for the two of them to enter the secret room whenever they were ready. They left the door partway open for her, but she hung back, not wanting to intrude on their private moment, yet undeniably curious.

For several moments a heavy silence hung in the air of the secret room. Then she heard Mac's voice, throaty and rough, "You look so much like her. Much more so now than when I hung this here. Turns out I was right to do so."

Abigail stood just to the side of the door, watching the scene through the opening, knowing she probably shouldn't but unable to look away.

Leah asked, "You took it down from Father's room and hung it here?"

Mac nodded. "I feared the resemblance would eventually give you away."

"It's good to see her again."

He glanced at Leah. "I'm sorry the painting's been kept from you. Sorry so many things rightfully yours have been kept from you. I hope you know everything I did, I did to protect you."

"I do know, Papa." She pressed his hand.

Reassured, Mac looked again at the painting. "I didn't know if Clive had been acquainted with Elizabeth Pembrooke. The brothers had been estranged for years, but I feared if he'd met her, he would remember, being as beautiful as she was. It was the main reason we sent you to school for that year. To give time for his memory to fade. His and our neighbors' as well."

The words were out of Abigail's mouth before she could stop them. "It was a courageous thing to do—to hide Robert Pembrooke's daughter right under his brother's nose."

Mac opened the door wider. "Courageous? To hide?" He shook his head, lip curled. "I don't think so. And I can't take credit for the idea. I never would have presumed to remove her from the house, to send her away, and then to raise her as my own in our wee cottage, had Robert Pembrooke not asked it of me."

Abigail felt her brow furrow and joined them inside. "What do you mean?"

Mac turned to one of the shelves. "I left it hidden here. The note he sent with his valet. God rest their souls. . . ."

He picked up a cigar tin from the lowest shelf, blew the dust off the cover, and carried it to the window ledge. There he opened the lid and from the bottom of a stack of invoices and receipts pulled forth a small notebook entitled *Household Accounts*. "I folded it within this, knowing it would not appeal to a man like Clive Pembrooke, even if he ever found this room."

From within the account book, he extracted a piece of paper, unfolded it, and handed it to Leah. "Written by your father, right before he died."

Hands trembling, Leah read the letter, her eyes filling with tears as she did so. Then she handed it to Abigail to read.

Abigail hesitated. "Are you certain?"

Leah nodded, and pulled a handkerchief from her sleeve.

Abigail read the note written in a hurried, erratic hand. And guessed the dark brown stain on one corner might be Robert Pembrooke's own blood.

Mac,
> *Protect Eleanor or he will kill her.*
> *Let him have the house, anything he wants,*
> *but hide my treasure.*

> > *—R. Pembrooke*

Ellie,
> *I love you more than life. Never forget.*

> > *—Papa*

"How I wished that Mr. Pembrooke had identified his attacker," Mac said. "Given me something I could take to the magistrates to use against Clive. Solid evidence. But considering he was near death, it's a miracle he was able to write this much. And a testament of his love for you, my dear, that you were foremost in his mind. His last, most precious, thought."

Mac looked at Abigail. "Leah told you about that night . . . ?"

Abigail nodded solemnly.

Leah explained, "Only up until the part where Uncle Pembrooke left and you took me to Grandmamma's cottage."

He nodded thoughtfully and filled in some of the details. "Eventually, we heard the front door slam closed, and for a time, all was quiet. Assuming Clive had fled the scene of the crime, I tiptoed back through Ellie's room and went down to check on poor Walter, but as I feared, he was dead. I took advantage of the empty house, gathered a few things for Ellie, and then left the manor, taking her to my mother-in-law's cottage. Thinking she would be safer there than in my own, in case Clive came looking.

"Then I waited and watched the manor from a distance, just in case. Soon a gig approached with Mr. Brown at the reins and Clive Pembrooke riding that big black of his alongside. I admit I was surprised.

"A few minutes later, I entered the house, claiming to have heard a carriage and that I was coming to check on the place. I found Mr. Brown and Clive Pembrooke standing over Walter Kelly's body. Clive Pembrooke was all cool civility, all concern and grief over Walter's fate, theorizing the young man had fallen down the stairs in his hurry to answer the door. Of course there was nothing Mr. Brown could do for him. He was already dead—had died honorably, protecting his young mistress.

"The surgeon left to summon the undertaker. While Clive and I waited for him to come and remove the poor man's body, Clive told me he had come to Pembrooke Park with the news he'd heard in London, that Robert Pembrooke was dead—killed by thieves who broke into the London house."

Here, Mac looked at Abigail and interjected, "Lies, all of it."

Then he continued, "Clive said he'd seen the valet's horse out front, lathered and exhausted, and assumed he'd come on the same mission. He asked me why the man would ride so far in such a hurry. Whom had he meant to tell if the house was empty?

"I told him, 'The housekeeper and me, I suppose. He wouldn't know that she had gone to sit at her sister's sickbed. And of course the rector and all the parish would want to know the news—the most significant news to grieve our parish since the death of Mrs. Pembrooke.'"

"Clive said, 'His wife and daughter died, I believe I heard.'"

"'Yes,' I said. 'Taken in the typhus epidemic that claimed so many.'"

"Then Clive said, all casual-like, 'The poor man muttered something before I went for the surgeon. Perhaps it will make more sense to you than it did to me. He said his master had sent him home to hide his treasure.'"

Mac gave Abigail another sidelong glance. "That part of his story was true. Clive looked at me then with his snakelike eyes. Genial and venomous all at once. He asked me, 'What did he mean by that? Had my brother some treasure I don't know about?'"

"I shrugged and answered as casually as I could, 'I suppose there must be some family jewels or something of that sort, though I don't know the particulars. But I hardly think this is the time to worry about such things. Not when two men are dead.'"

"I suppose it was a risk, speaking to him like that. But it was how I would have spoken to him under other circumstances. And I feared he would guess that I knew what he'd done if I acted servile or timid."

"It seemed to convince him, for he continued on with his act of innocence in full confidence that the only witness against him—or so he thought—was dead."

Mac turned to Leah. "Had it not been for you, my dear, or your father's plea that I act quickly to hide and protect you, I shudder to think what I might have done, likely confronting him then and there—accusing him of killing both men, and likely ending up a third victim." He shook his head. "Even so, how guilty I've felt. Perhaps I should have confronted him, called in the law, and tried to avenge Robert Pembrooke, to obtain justice, weak evidence or not."

"No, Papa." Leah laid a hand on his arm. "As Mamma and I

have always tried to tell you—you did what Robert Pembrooke asked of you. You protected me. And likely saved your own life and perhaps even the lives of your wife and son in the bargain."

He nodded. "I know. But I can't help think I could have done things differently. Handled it more wisely. Found some way to guarantee your future and not merely your safety."

"Do you think I care about the house? About the money?" She shook her head. "No, I would not have chosen to go through all I have, but you did not steal my life. You gave me a new one. You gave me the best mother, the best father, the best brothers and sister I could hope for. A loving, loyal family far better than I deserve."

"But you are Robert Pembrooke's daughter. You deserve better." Mac paused, glanced at Abigail as if just then remembering she was there, and continued his story.

"When the other servants came back from London or from holiday, what news awaited them. Their master and his daughter were both believed dead. The new master had gone to collect his family and would be returning at some point to take over Pembrooke Park. That's when I moved the portrait and hid the letter and family Bible and some of the jewels. Fortunately, his absence also gave Mrs. Hayes and me time to warn and coach the servants we thought we could trust, and to replace those we weren't sure of.

"The old rector was reticent to lie, until I showed him the note in Robert Pembrooke's own hand. He suggested we go to the law, but I knew, without the testimony of Walter, we had insufficient evidence. I would obey my master. I would let Clive have Pembrooke Park but not let on that Eleanor was still alive. Eventually, the rector agreed and noted her earlier 'death' in the parish record, in case Mr. Pembrooke came to check. And he did, eventually. Clive waited a 'respectable' fortnight before returning with his family to claim his brother's house as his own, Robert barely in his grave.

"By then, we had sent Ellie to school for a year in the north near my sister—far away and safe, in case he came searching or threatened someone until they gave up the information. Later, when he asked me, I told Clive that my wife and I had two children, one who was away at school at the time.

"Of course, many of the servants and our neighbors knew that the girl was not really ours. But they were ready to keep our secret in unspoken bond against the usurper, Robert Pembrooke's killer. When the need arose, we said she was the daughter of relatives in the north, recently orphaned." He shrugged. "We are a small community. Far from city laws and legalities. There were few to question except the one we were most determined not to tell. Her own uncle.

"So yes, while younger people or those new to the parish don't know, some of the older folks knew or at least suspected who Leah really was. The servants may have whispered among themselves about Miss Eleanor's fate but never said anything to Mr. Pembrooke, as far as I know. Though he did check the parish records, as I said, so perhaps he'd heard some rumor she still lived."

He shook his head. "The rumor may even have fostered Eliza Smith's mistaken belief that she was that daughter."

Abigail wondered if the same rumor had fueled Harriet's hope that a closer heir of Robert Pembrooke's still lived.

"You may wonder why I continued to work for the man," Mac went on. "I feared to leave would be to risk Clive's wrath and his suspicions. But I detested him—detested working for him. How relieved I was when he and his family abandoned the house two years later."

Mac glanced around the room once more. "I don't think Clive had ever heard of a secret room—just went all over the house and grounds searching for a hiding place. He helped himself to some gold and silver in the family safe, having found the key in his brother's desk. He dressed his wife in Elizabeth Pembrooke's jewelry, and took to wearing Robert Pembrooke's signet ring, once it had been returned to the estate after his funeral. I made no effort to stop him. But even that didn't quench his desire for more, his certainty that there must be a treasure worth far more—a pearl of great price—hidden elsewhere. And in a sense, he was right." He looked at Leah fondly. "Thank God he never found you. And he never shall, as long as it is in my power to prevent it."

Abigail said, "But surely after all this time . . . If he meant to come back for Pembrooke Park, or for Eleanor, he would have done so by now."

Mac's eyes glinted cold and hard, like glass. "He might have been transported or imprisoned and unable to return as yet. Or sent his son Miles to continue his quest." He shook his head. "Until I find solid evidence that Clive Pembrooke is well and truly dead, I shall never feel our Leah is safe to resume her rightful name and place."

Mac went to the jeweler's box on another shelf. "I also hid away a few of your mother's things for you, Leah." He ducked his head. "Sorry—it's how I think of you now."

"Never be sorry, Papa. It is how I think of myself as well. I like the name, truly."

"I hoped it would only be temporary—that I could give these to you long before now. I wanted you to have a few family heirlooms once you were able to reclaim your home." He opened the box, swirling a work-worn finger through dainty gold chains and pearls before handing it to her. "There are also several pieces of jewelry still in your mother's room. And a fine gold snuffbox and ruby cravat pin left in the master bedroom after Clive Pembrooke and his family left. Never understood why they didn't take more with them. But I had secreted away these few things for you, for when you grew to womanhood."

"I am nearly nine and twenty, Papa," she said, amber eyes sparkling. "I think that moment has come and gone."

"But there's something else I really wanted you to have." Lifting the lid from a bandbox, he pulled forth a hat ornamented with flaccid, dusty feathers, a tiny stuffed bird that had lost its beak, and a spray of silk hydrangeas. In truth, Abigail thought it the ugliest hat she had ever seen. She glanced awkwardly at Leah, to gauge her reaction.

Leah pasted on a smile. "It is quite . . . something."

"Don't be polite, lass. Even I can see it's hideous. It was awful twenty years ago, and time and dust have not improved it."

He turned the hat over and reached inside. "That's why I chose it." He pulled from it a small hinged box, set the hat aside, and opened the lid, exposing a velvet-lined jewel case. Inside glistened a ruby necklace and matching earrings. The jewels Elizabeth Pembrooke wore in the portrait.

"I wanted you to have these, especially. Another reason to hide the portrait."

"They're beautiful," Leah breathed, lightly fingering the deep-red gems. She looked up at Mac, eyes shimmering with tears. "Thank you, Papa."

He ducked his head again and sent a self-conscious glance at Abigail before saying almost shyly to Leah, "I like hearing you call me by that name, though I suppose I should give you leave to call me Mac now, as everyone else does."

Leah shook her head, the motion causing one fat tear to escape her eye and roll down her cheek. "I am not everyone else. I am your daughter. One of your four children. And I always shall be."

Abigail's heart twisted to see answering tears brighten Mac Chapman's eyes, and his stern chin tremble.

Chapter 27

O n Sunday, Abigail, Louisa, and their parents attended
church together. On the way over, Abigail noticed Mamma
wrap both hands around Papa's arm as they walked side
by side. He bent his head near hers, and she chuckled at something
he said. Abigail's heart lightened. Maybe her family's change of
circumstance and the move to Pembrooke Park was having some
benefit after all.

Ahead she saw Leah entering the church, the greengrocer's little
girl hanging on one hand, the blacksmith's youngest tugging on
the other. Abigail thought of Leah's gift baskets and her teaching,
and her quiet, humble service, and felt tears prick her eyes. She
wondered what Leah—Eleanor—would be like now had she grown
up at Pembrooke Park in privilege her whole life. Would she have
done so much, served so many regardless of her upbringing? Maybe,
but somehow Abigail doubted it. Another benefit—another good
thing from a bad situation. *"Good from bad,"* William had once
said. *"God excels at that."*

Yes, Abigail silently agreed. *He does.*

As usual, Louisa enjoyed all the attention that came her way,
especially sitting in the front box. Gilbert sat with the Morgans
across the aisle, as did Rebekah Garwood. The rector, Mr. Mor-

ris, was in church that morning as well, and assisted in officiating the service. He was accompanied by his nephew, who had just matriculated from Christ Church College. The rector introduced the young man with obvious fondness and pride.

After church Louisa made a beeline for Mr. Chapman, thanking him for his sermon. He smiled in reply, and Abigail's stomach soured. He was perfectly polite to Abigail and her parents as they thanked him and passed through the door, but Abigail noticed he did not quite meet her gaze. She wondered why. Was he distancing himself because of Gilbert, or because he now preferred another woman? Did he fear he had given her the wrong impression during their foray into the secret room—worry she might think he was romantically interested in her again, assuming he ever had been?

In the churchyard, Abigail waited while Louisa spoke sweetly with two adolescent girls who gaped in awe at her beauty and fashionable attire. Behind them the Morgans exited, Andrew and his father talking earnestly to William, while Mrs. Morgan gave him a brittle smile and remained aloof. Beside her, Rebekah Garwood looked striking in her fitted morning gown and smart black hat, her figure already remarkably good for having recently borne a child. She smiled up into Mr. Chapman's face, asking him about some verse he had quoted. He answered, and she thanked him, briefly laying her gloved hand on his sleeve. Abigail was probably the only person who noticed.

Or was she? Mrs. Peterman sidled up to Abigail, her disapproving gaze on the pair. "First you, then your sister, and now a recent widow." She sniffed and shook her head. "I shall be glad when Mr. Morris's nephew comes into possession of his uncle's living. He'll put an end to such ungodly flirtations."

"Oh, and what makes you think that?"

"Look at him!" She gestured toward the gangly young man. "No girls will be fawning over him. And he, I daresay, will remain too busy writing good long sermons to have time for females for a year or two. And by then, the women of the parish will have found him a plain, practical wife."

"Yes," Abigail murmured in wry wistfulness. "The practical ones are usually plain."

When the last of his parishioners had exited, William disappeared from the doorway. A few minutes later, he exited as well, having removed his vestments. He paused to help a fallen toddler who had scratched his knee, and reunited the scamp with his mother. Then, seeing her watching him, William raised a hand and walked her way.

Abigail steeled herself, unsure what to expect.

"Hello, Miss Foster."

She nodded. "Mr. Chapman."

"Mamma was just saying you haven't been to our house in some time. I tried to tell her you've been busy, what with your family here now and . . . all. Even so, she has charged me with inviting you over again. Might you and your sister come over for tea this afternoon? Perhaps you might sing for Grandmamma and Miss Louisa might play. I understand she is very accomplished."

It was Louisa he wished to see most of all, she guessed. "Yes, well. Louisa might, but I don't know that I will have the time."

He winced and asked tentatively, "Are you angry with me about something, Miss Foster?"

"No."

"Have I done something to offend you or disappoint you?"

Abigail didn't want to lie, but nor did she want to tell him the truth. Besides, the truth was he'd done nothing wrong. It was her problem, not his.

When she hesitated, he asked, "Is this about . . . your sister?"

Taken aback, she darted a glance at him, then looked away, feeling her neck heat. How had he divined the answer? Were her feelings, her petty jealousy, so transparent?

He added, "Or because of Mr. Scott?"

She blinked in confusion. She would have thought he'd be relieved that Gilbert was showing interest in her. That it might assuage his guilt and give him the freedom to pursue Louisa or Rebekah Garwood, as he probably wanted to.

Gilbert appeared at her elbow. "Hello, Abby." He smiled at her and took her hand, tucking it under his arm. "I'll walk you home."

Belatedly, he acknowledged Mr. Chapman. "Good sermon, Parson. Nice and short."

"Thank you. By the way, I saw the new wing at Hunts Hall. Well done. Nice and short."

Gilbert's face colored. "They only wanted the one level—there's to be a conservatory. But we are also adding a two-story addition to the rear and—"

Abigail interrupted, "Mr. Chapman is only teasing you, Gilbert."

"Oh," Gilbert said dully.

She said in consolatory tones, "He isn't used to your teasing yet, as I am."

Mr. Chapman pulled a face. "Sorry. It's one of my persistent weaknesses, I'm afraid." He looked at her. "But not the only one."

That night, Abigail sat on a large rock, a natural step down from the riverbank, and dangled her feet in the water, idly peeling the bark from a stick in her hands. The moon shone bright, glistening on the lazy current. The air was still, without a breath of wind. And only the chirring of frogs and the occasional flying insect kept her company. The summer night was warm. Too warm. She'd been unable to sleep in her stifling room, with her stifling thoughts and doubts about both Gilbert and William. Must every man she admired prefer her sister? Perhaps she should accept it, and be grateful any man would be interested in her at all, once Louisa made it clear she did not return his attentions. But the thought made her feel ill. Would she wonder at every family gathering for the rest of her life if her husband was eyeing Louisa wistfully, wishing he had married her instead?

She tossed the stick upriver, with a satisfying *plunk*, wishing she could toss away her doubts as easily. But sure enough, the current brought it back to her.

"Hello?"

She sucked in a breath at the unexpected call, then turned her head and saw William approaching. "Oh, Mr. Chapman, you startled me."

"And who else would you expect to find in my spot?"

"Your spot? I didn't know it was anyone's spot. I shall leave you." She scrambled to her feet and up the bank.

He forestalled her, saying, "Miss Foster. I was only teasing. I am glad to find you here."

He was dressed in breeches and untucked shirt, she noticed. A towel in hand.

"I did not come here with the design of meeting you," she said, feeling defensive. "I was simply warm and thought the water would cool me."

"As did I."

"I only met you at the river once after all, and that was weeks ago. And not here but there under that tree . . ." She nodded vaguely a few yards ahead, then searched the ground. "Now, where did I put my shoes?"

He laid a hand on her arm, stilling her. "Miss Foster . . . are you still angry with me?"

"I am not angry."

He tucked his chin, and raised his eyebrows, giving her a doubtful look.

"I am not angry," she repeated. "But . . ."

"But what? I realize that with Mr. Scott back in your life, you may wish to spend less time with me, but I don't think there's call for animosity."

"No, of course not."

"Here," he said, spreading his towel on the bank, fortunately larger than the last one he'd brought. "Sit, and let's talk."

"But your swim . . ."

"Can wait."

They sat on the bank, sharing the towel but not quite touching. He began, "You can't deny you have changed toward me. I don't know if it has something to do with your sister being here now. Or more likely, I suppose, Mr. Scott . . ."

Abigail again recalled William Chapman's dumbfounded expression when he'd first seen Louisa. And then seeing them together that day in the churchyard . . .

"No," she whispered. "Not Gilbert." She shook her head, not able to meet his eyes. The moonlight would reveal too much. Her insecurity. Her jealousy.

"Then . . . ?"

She swallowed and quietly admitted, "I saw how you looked at Louisa when Mamma introduced her."

She felt his gaze on her profile. Then he sighed. "I am sorry. Truly. I tried to be as polite as possible to her then and since. Not to show anything else in my expression or in my words, to reveal what I knew, and how I felt."

How he felt? Lord, have mercy. Help me through this! He had *fallen* for Louisa. It was more than passing desire or admiration. He had *feelings* for her.

"It was obvious," Abigail said. "To me, at least."

"Hopefully not to her. I haven't wanted to say anything. Even though I wondered if I should. For her sake. And yours. But I was afraid to offend you. You are her sister, after all."

"As I am very much aware."

"You must wonder how it began, how I even discovered who she was. . . ."

No, not really, she thought. It likely began the way it always did. Men making complete cakes of themselves over Louisa.

He went on, "You might remember Louisa asking if we had met before. Saying I looked familiar to her . . . ?"

Abigail nodded, vaguely recalling the exchange.

William continued, "I said we had not met, and that was true— we had not been introduced. But I had seen her before."

This was news to Abigail. "Oh? When?"

"You remember that I spent several days with Andrew Morgan in London?"

Yes, Abigail did remember. And what long, lonely, tiresome days they had been.

She nodded, and he continued.

"Andrew insisted I needed a rest after the fire, so I went with him to Town, as I had done once or twice while we were at school together. Mr. Morris agreed to take my services for me while I was away, eager to show his nephew his future living, I imagine.

"In London, Andrew dragged me to the most crowded, noisiest rout I had ever attended, held at some wealthy acquaintance's home. While we were there, one of his highborn friends said something very cutting about a certain young woman in attendance. I did not hear her name over all the noise and music, but I did see her quite clearly, laughing loudly and flirting with an officer and a dandy at once. This man pointed her out and said, 'Careful, gents, the minx may look an angel, but she is the biggest flirt in London, so determined to net a titled man that she is willing to do *anything* to trap him.' The insinuation was perfectly clear."

Was he talking about Louisa? Surely not! Even so, Abigail's stomach sickened as he spoke and her cheeks heated. Oh, the mortification! What a crude and cruel thing to say, if unsubstantiated. If true, well, heaven help them all.

"I left soon after, much to Andrew's disappointment. I confess I thought very little about it, or about the girl, not praying for her or her family as I should have done. But when I saw her here, I recognized her instantly. And to learn she is your sister . . . Well, I was stunned speechless.

"I still don't know what I said at the time, hopefully something polite and coherent. And I hope you will forgive me for repeating the scurrilous accusations now, to you. But if Louisa has acted in a manner to expose herself to such talk, it could very well damage her reputation and yours, so perhaps it is better that you know.

"She did seek me out in the churchyard once, and I tried to offer a word of counsel, but I don't think I got through to her. I suppose I should have gone right to your father with the report and offered a gentle warning. But I would hate to rouse his wrath against Louisa or the men in question if it might be addressed another way, with less damage to . . . everyone."

For several moments, Abigail said nothing, her mind struggling to reconfigure what she thought she had seen, with this new information. She was relieved and upset all at once. Her heart felt sick and exalted in turns. *Oh, Louisa! Foolish, foolish girl.* Abigail could very well believe her sister capable of such flirtatious behavior, thinking her beauty and charm made her immune to the normal rules of propriety.

William looked at her in concern, and grimaced. "Apparently I judged wrong in telling you. Please believe my motives good even if my decision poor."

She turned to face him. "No. You were right to tell me. It explains several things . . . things she has said about Andrew Morgan and her reluctance to visit Hunts Hall, so apparently some unpleasantness along these lines passed between them. I will speak to her. Perhaps she is unaware of the extent of her breach of propriety. Hopefully her reputation is not damaged beyond repair."

"Likely she didn't realize," William agreed kindly. "She is very young, after all."

"Yes. She did write in one of her letters that all the attention from gentlemen had gone quite to her head."

"Understandable. And you were not there to guide her. Along with your mother, of course."

"I don't know that I would have been an effective guide, even had I been there. I am no great expert in deflecting the admiration of multiple suitors."

He lifted one auburn eyebrow. "Are you not? For I can count at least three admirers at present. And that is only here in tiny Easton."

Abigail ducked her head, her cheeks now heating for a far different reason. "Careful, Parson, you don't want all that flattery to go to *my* head."

"I don't fear that for a moment, Abigail Foster. You are far too modest for that, sensible, lovely girl."

Pleasure and relief washed over her.

Even as concern for her sister nipped at her breastbone, Abigail's thoughts whirled now on a far happier axis. William Chapman did not admire Louisa. And even if he thought her sister pretty, which was undeniable, he was not smitten with her. In fact he saw her as a wayward young girl to be set upon the right course, not as a woman to court or love or marry. *Thank you, God!* Abigail thought, not bothering to stifle the smile that curved her lips.

"What's made you smile, Miss Foster? I am relieved you are not angry with me, but what have I said to so amuse you?"

Dare she tell him the truth? Would his respect for her dim if she revealed her insecurity? Besides, it didn't change the fact that she had no dowry and didn't deserve an educated, devoted, handsome clergyman paid far less than he was worth.

He sat up straight and looked at her in bewilderment. "Wait a minute . . . Don't tell me you feared I'd fallen under her spell?"

Abigail shrugged. "It had crossed my mind. You should have seen your face when you saw her! Gaping like a hooked fish, all wide-eyed and tongue-tied."

He shook his head. "And here I thought you'd guessed the truth of my dismay, or had somehow wrongly heard that I had been among those speaking ill of her."

Abigail was embarrassed to recall her earlier words about how *obvious* his reaction had been when he'd laid eyes on Louisa. She had been completely wrong! She had seen what she'd feared—no, what she'd expected to see.

"So that's why you've been, shall we say, chilly of late," he said. "I was afraid it had something to do with Mr. Scott. I saw him embrace you in the library and assumed, well . . ." His sentence trailed away on a shrug.

Mr. Scott. Odd that she had barely thought of him during their entire conversation. No wonder Gilbert had been irritated with and cold toward Louisa—if she had acted the wanton flirt with multiple gentlemen at every event of the season.

"And here all along you assumed I admired your sister." He

tsked and took her hand in his. "My dear Abigail, I thought you knew me better than that."

She managed a wobbly smile and said quietly, "I once thought I knew Gilbert Scott better than that as well."

He looked at her, suddenly serious. "I thought the scales had fallen from his eyes at last where you and Louisa were concerned. That he had become disillusioned with Louisa and . . . enamored with you."

Yes, Gilbert had certainly changed toward her. But would his feelings for her last once his disillusionment and anger with Louisa faded? She said, "He's asked to court me, but I'm not certain how I feel."

William squeezed her hand. "Well, I am quite certain how I feel about—"

She met his gaze, hope rising in her breast, but William winced and looked away. "But unfortunately, I am not in a position to do anything about those feelings." He expelled a ragged breath. "You are so appealing, Miss Foster, every bit as beautiful as your sister—more so, to me—that I almost lost my head. I want nothing more than to let this romantic current sweep us along. This chance meeting. This moonlit night. Your tantalizing bare toes . . ."

He managed a grin, but it fell away nearly as soon as it formed. He shook his head. "But that would be unfair to you. Dishonest even. For the truth is, my current income barely supports me. And with Mr. Morris's nephew waiting in the wings, I cannot realistically hope my situation will improve anytime soon. If ever. It would be wrong of me to ask you to wait without a clear hope of a future. Especially with Mr. Scott in your life once again—waiting in the wings as well."

Her hope plummeted. Yes. How much better for him to marry a wealthy widow like Rebekah Garwood. And she could marry Gilbert. That should make everyone happy. Then why did she feel like crying instead?

His eyes widened as he watched her. "You look so sad."

"Do I? That's . . . silly. I'm fine." She forced a smile, which only served to push a hot tear from each eye.

"I'm fine too," he whispered. He leaned near and touched a finger to her cheekbone, tracing the tear. Then he leaned nearer yet and brushed his lips against her cheek.

Abigail's heart pounded. Her chest tightened until she found it painful to breathe. Every particle of her being longed to reach for him. To lift her face. To press her mouth to his. Dare she? Was this her last chance? Would she regret not doing so for the rest of her life?

She turned toward him. He stilled, inches away. She slowly raised her eyes to his, willing him to see all she felt but could not say aloud.

"Abigail . . ." he breathed, his eyes lowering to her mouth.

She reached up a shaky hand and laid her palm against his face, her finger brushing his earlobe. The skin smooth above his cheekbone and beginning to bristle near his jaw. She lifted her thumb, caressing the groove along his mouth, then traced his upper lip.

He half sighed, half groaned.

"William," she whispered, liking the feel of his given name on her tongue.

He stared at her. "Say it again," he whispered back, voice tight.

"Wi—" But she had no more puckered her lips to form the W than his mouth pressed to hers. Firmly, warmly, deliciously. She tentatively returned the pressure, and he angled his head to kiss her more deeply.

Her pulse raced, every nerve quivering to life. Her first kiss. Not with Gilbert Scott, as she'd always dreamed and hoped. But with William Chapman, a man who had just said he could not marry her.

He broke the kiss as if reading her thoughts, and rested his forehead against hers, catching his breath.

"Miss Foster, forgive me. I—"

"Shh . . . I know."

She heard distant footsteps crunching on gravel and sucked in a breath, afraid to be discovered alone with a man at night. She looked past his shoulder, and what she saw frightened her even more.

A figure in a long hooded cloak furtively crossed the drive carrying a lantern, its flame turned down low.

William turned to follow her gaze and instantly stiffened. He began to rise, but Abigail grasped his arm. She didn't want him to go rushing headlong into danger, to confront whomever it was without a weapon, not to mention without shoes or coat.

He looked at her in question, seeming torn, but allowed her to stop him. "You're right. I would never want to expose you to scandal."

That wasn't what she was most worried about. But she did not correct him, glad he was safe.

They watched the figure disappear around the side of the manor. Headed where? Finally, he could restrain himself no longer and rose, pulling her easily to her feet. "You slip back inside through the front. I'm going to follow him around back—make sure he isn't on his way to the cottage."

"William, be careful."

He gave her one last regretful look and said very gently, "Perhaps you ought to call me Mr. Chapman from now on."

He didn't say it to hurt her, she knew. But it hurt, just the same.

Pausing long enough to make sure Miss Foster entered the manor safely, William then ran around the corner. Brutus started barking in the distance, increasing William's alarm. He ran all the way to his parents' cottage and found his father already at the front door, lantern in hand, hollering at the dog.

Seeing him, Mac asked, "What is it, Will?"

"The man in the hooded cloak . . ." William panted to catch his breath. "I saw him coming this way."

His father's jaw clenched. "Here. You take the lantern. I'm getting a gun."

Thus armed, the two men searched the area, the cottage itself, and the outbuildings. They found the door to the old gamekeeper's lodge ajar but no evidence of anyone lurking about. Eventually, they ended their search and called it a night, Mac taking extra ammunition into the cottage with him, and double bolting the woodshed, where he kept his rifle and fowling pieces. He offered a gun to William as well, but he declined. However, then and there,

William decided that the next time Miss Foster was out, he would pay a quiet visit to Pembrooke Park. Just to be safe.

Finally, father and son parted ways, though William doubted either of them would get much sleep that night.

The disturbance did have one benefit—it distracted William from his regret over Miss Foster. At least for a time. Before tonight, he had all but decided to bow out of Miss Foster's life. But after that kiss . . . heaven help him, it would take every ounce of strength he had to do so. *Thy will be done. But please, God, have mercy on your besotted servant. . . .*

Chapter 28

The following day, Eliza Smith came to call, face pale, eyes damp and red. Without preamble, she began unfastening the E pin from her fichu. "I should never have accepted this."

"Did Duncan give it to you?" Abigail asked.

Eliza nodded. "He didn't see it as stealing. He thought I was entitled to some memento—some . . . recompense." The latch snagged on the muslin, and she worked to free it. "He believed me, you see, about who my father was. He said there were two pins and one wouldn't be missed. Robert Pembrooke must have had the matching pins made for his wife and daughter. I thought that's why Mamma had given me an E name. That perhaps it had been his suggestion, like Eleanor and baby Emma. His quiet way of acknowledging me privately if not publicly. But no. I was fooling myself." She yanked the pin free, taking several threads with it.

Her chin trembled. "But now . . . Mac's told me the truth. I didn't want to believe him, but I know him to be an honest man. It's just that . . . Auntie told me several times that my father lived in Pembrooke Park. That's where Mamma met him. And that much was true. But the man wasn't Robert Pembrooke, it was the butler. It's his mother's house we live in now. He signed it over to Mamma before he left town. Left us." Tears filled her eyes.

Abigail said gently, "I'm sorry you grew up without a father, Eliza. But it's your life now, to do with as you will."

Eliza shook her head. "I've struggled for so long to make something of myself, to have something to show for my supposed heritage . . . and for what?" She thrust the pin toward Abigail. "Here, take it."

Abigail accepted the pin. "But look at the good that's come of that striving," she soothed. "You've pushed yourself to succeed. You singlehandedly support yourself and your aunt. That is an accomplishment to feel proud of—one few women can boast of."

"Proud is the last thing I feel."

"Well then, *I* am proud of you. Proud to know you. You are quite a good writer, Miss E. P. Brooks, if I do say so myself."

Eliza looked up at her in wary surprise.

"You *are* someone, Eliza. Someone valuable—just as you are. God has blessed you with gifts, and talents, and abilities." Abigail squeezed her hand. "Make the most of them."

Mr. Chapman stopped by the house later that afternoon. Abigail's heart rose to see him at her door, but her happiness was quickly dampened by the look on his face.

"Good afternoon, Miss Foster." His dull eyes belied his fleeting smile.

"What happened last night?" she whispered. "Did you find that man?"

He shook his head. "No. No sign of him. But that's not why I'm here. You haven't seen my father, have you?"

"No. Not since yesterday. Why?"

He rubbed the back of his neck. "He has gone out to look for Mr. Morgan's hound again. Mamma expected him back by now." He sighed. "No doubt checking fences or something, to make the best use of his time while he's out."

"Sounds like your father. Never one to idle."

"Exactly." He gave a little chuckle, but it sounded flat to Abigail's ears.

"I'm sure he'll be back soon," Abigail assured him.

"No doubt you're right, and I shall feel a fool for worrying."

She smiled gently and said, "Our parson is very fond of quoting the verse 'Fear thou not; for I am with thee. . . .'"

"Sounds a wise man, your parson." He managed a grin, then pressed a hand to his midriff. "Just can't shake this feeling that something is wrong." Again he tried to joke it off. "That's what I get for eating my own cooking again today."

An hour later, after dinner with her family, Abigail walked over to the Chapman cottage to see if Mac had returned and found William saddling the carriage horse. Nearby, the dog kennel was empty and silent.

"No sign of him?"

He shook his head, all joking and laughter gone from his eyes. "No. And there's a storm brewing in the west. Not like him to be gone so long, not without sending word to Mamma. He knows she'll worry. The rest of us too."

"What can I do? Give me someplace to look."

He looked at her skeptically. "On foot?"

"I am a good walker. Or I could ask Miles to ride out with you."

He tossed back the stirrup leather and tightened the cinch. "No need to involve Mr. Pembrooke, Miss Foster. No offense. But perhaps you might walk through the village and ask at the inn and shops if anyone has seen him, or knows where he was headed."

"Of course I will. What about Hunts Hall? Would someone there know which direction he went?"

"I hope so. I plan to ride there first. And if they don't know, God help me."

A gust of wind jerked the bonnet from Abigail's head. Clutching at the ribbons, she frowned up at the churning grey sky. "Are you sure you should ride out in this alone?"

"If Andrew is willing, I'll take him along. But either way, I'm going. I think Papa found the dog somewhere in Black's Wood last time. But it's a huge area to cover, and I—"

"Wait!" Abigail grabbed his arm as the memory struck her. "That night I sat with you while Mac was out late searching. I think he said something about a ravine. . . ."

William stilled. "Snake Ravine?"

"Yes! That's it."

He grasped her by both shoulders and pressed a sound kiss to her cheek. "God bless you, Abigail."

He already has. . . . She cupped her cheek as though to capture a butterfly, and watched him canter away.

The rain began to fall. Of course it did. William tried not to grumble, but the cold rain matched his mood and dragged it lower. It would not make his search any easier. Was his father all right? William's spirit remained troubled. Was his own conscience smiting him for some reason? Or was the Holy Spirit actually nudging him to hurry?

In reply, he urged the horse into a gallop across the field. He had to stop at two gates to let the horse through—this old boy was no jumper. And neither was he.

He reached the southern tip of Black's Wood and followed the road through the scrubby forest, bordered on one side by a winding stream. As he rode farther, the stream narrowed and deepened into a ravine, the current now a mere trickle at the bottom of a steep rocky cut, the thirsty roots of pine and black oaks fingering through the soil of the bank, clawing for water.

William rode carefully along the rim, looking this way and that, but saw no sign of his father or his telltale tartan hat.

"Papa!" he called out. "Mac!" He paused to listen but heard nothing save the wind whistling and the pine trees swaying in reply. Overhead a hawk shrieked and circled. At least it wasn't a vulture.

Deep in the wood, the sky, already grey on the rainy evening, darkened even more, the faint daylight blocked now by the canopy of trees. As the wood grew more dense, riding on horseback became increasingly difficult.

He was about to dismount and continue on foot, when he saw his father's horse ahead, its rein tied to a branch. Pulse racing, William urged his horse faster.

Suddenly a dog barked, and his horse lurched in a violent side-step. Caught unawares, William slid from the saddle, losing his toehold in the stirrups and his grip on the rain-slick reins. He fell, hit angled ground, and rolled, down, down, into the ravine.

Branches scratched his face, and his knee and shoulders banged against rock before he came to a stop against a mound of leaves and dirt, which thankfully stopped his fall before he reached the muddy stream. For a moment he lay there, stunned breathless, then began a mental inventory of his limbs. Nothing seemed broken. He reached out and laid his hand on the mound to push himself into a sitting position. His hand rested on something hard, a rock or stout branch. He glanced down and recoiled instantly, snatching his hand back—it had been resting on a skeletal bone.

Another bark startled him, and suddenly Brutus bounded over, wagging his tail and licking William's cheek. Meanwhile Toby, the Morgans' hound, sniffed the mound, then lay down and began gnawing on something. A leg bone, perhaps? William shuddered at the thought, relieved that most of the skeleton was covered by silt and leaves.

"Stop that, boy," he commanded and gingerly rose. His knee throbbed, as did his shoulder, but he thanked God he was otherwise unhurt.

"William . . . ?" came a reedy call. His father's voice.

"Papa!" William shouted, wheeling about. A muddy hand lifted from the underbrush on the other side of the water. William leapt across the narrow stream and bounded over, heart hammering.

Please let him be all right. . . .

His father lay on the ground, hat missing, coat askew and mud streaked. His hair, normally neatly combed back, fell in damp disarray around his pale face.

"Am I glad to see you, lad."

"What happened?" William crouched beside his father. "Where are you hurt?"

Mac raised himself on one elbow with a grimace. "Fell down the blasted ravine chasing after that hound. I sprained my ankle, I'm afraid. I might have hobbled home with a stick, if that's all it was, but I think I may have cracked a rib or two in the bargain."

"Thank God I found you."

"I do indeed." He looked beyond William at the sniffing dogs pawing at the mound across the ravine.

"Intended to come down and investigate what has that dog all worked up. I called and called but he wouldn't leave his find, whatever it is. Now Brutus has the scent as well. Some animal, I take it?"

William grimaced. "I'm afraid not. It's a human skeleton."

His father gaped at him. "Human?"

"Yes. I, um, met him when I fell."

"Sorry, lad. That can't have been pleasant. Help me over there, so I can have a look."

"But, Papa, we need to get you home. It's getting dark. Perhaps I should go straightaway for Mr. Brown."

A strange light sparked in his father's green eyes. "First let me see it."

"I'm afraid I'll hurt you worse, trying to move you."

"Come on now. I've lain here too long as it is. Damp through from lying on the ground."

"Oh, very well." William half pulled, half levered him to his feet and maneuvered his arm around his shoulder. His father bit his lip to stifle a cry, his fair complexion paling all the more.

"Lean on me, Papa."

Mac managed a terse nod, and William noticed the sweat breaking out on his forehead and his rigid countenance. The pain was evidently bad indeed. William tried to be gentle as he helped him across the stream, bearing as much of the man's weight as he could, apologizing when he stumbled over a rock.

"There." William nodded toward the mound of dirt. A bony hand protruded from one end and a leg bone from the other.

"Let me down here. I'll rest a minute," Mac said, panting.

William complied, and his father sat on a fallen log.

"No wonder the dog returned," William said. "Poor soul, whoever it is. We shall have to see that he gets a decent burial."

Mac solemnly nodded, but then his eyes narrowed and he leaned forward in his sitting position, focusing on something. Suddenly heedless of his pain or injuries, he lurched forward into a crouch and crawled the few feet between him and the skeleton.

"Look at this. . . ." Mac brushed away leaves and pine needles from the area around the hand. "What do you see?" he asked, his voice hushed in breathless anticipation, as though afraid to believe his eyes.

William crouched beside his father, looking to see what had captured his attention.

"Good heavens," he breathed.

For the skeletal hand held a rusted pistol.

"And this . . ." Mac picked up a stick and pried up the finger bones.

"Papa, I don't think you should touch it."

"Look. Do you not see what this is? Tell me I am not imagining it, that I am not crazy."

William looked at the finger bones. "It's a ring."

"Yes. By God, it is. And not just any ring. This is Robert Pembrooke's signet ring. Do you know what this means?"

Before William could fashion a reply, his father looked up at him, eyes glinting. "It means we've finally found Clive Pembrooke."

As darkness fell, William managed to get his father up on his horse for the slow, painful ride home. Brutus bounded alongside, with Toby tethered behind, less willing to leave the ravine.

Hours later, after Mr. Brown had treated and bound Mac's injuries and reassured the family, William sat alone at his father's bedside.

"You did it, lad. You found Clive Pembrooke, when no one else could. Can you imagine?" Mac slowly shook his head. "All these years, right there in Snake Ravine. While we worried he'd return any day."

William bit back the urge to say *"Didn't I tell you so?"* That after all this time, it was foolish to live in fear, to keep Leah living in its shadow. But he asked God to help him control his tongue. Now wasn't the time to gloat over being right.

"Ask your sister to join us. No, wait." His father chewed his lip, eyes troubled. "She may resent me. Forcing her to keep her identity secret all this time, while her house, her inheritance, her future prospects deteriorated more and more each day. But I did it for her good. Her safety."

William sighed. "I know you did, Papa. And Leah knows it too."

"To think—there all along. All the wasted years . . ."

"Will you tell Miles Pembrooke?"

Mac looked up, eyes pensive. "Perhaps it would be better coming from a clergyman. You might offer comfort, though I doubt the lad has any reason to mourn the news of his father's death."

"He was still his father, whatever else he might have been. Or done."

"Perhaps you're right. Mr. Brown would tell him, I am sure. Or the constable . . ."

"I shall do it, Papa." William rose. "And Leah?"

Mac sat up straighter in bed, wincing at the pain of his wrapped ribs. "I shan't shirk my duty. Ask her to come in."

A thought struck William. "Papa . . ."

"Yes?"

William hesitated to even mention it, not when his father was finally ready to give up his choke hold on Leah's life, to let her live at last, to be who she was meant to be. But still the thought niggled at him. He winced, then said, "If Clive Pembrooke has been dead all these years, then who did I see in the hooded green cloak?"

After sending Leah in to speak with their father, William walked over to Pembrooke Park, knowing Miss Foster would be awake, worried and wondering. And he was determined to fulfill his duty to Miles Pembrooke as kindly as he could.

Duncan sullenly showed him into the drawing room, where Miles and Miss Foster sat.

"I come bearing news," William began, hat in hand.

She said, "My family has gone up to bed. But Miles kindly waited up with me."

Miles rose. "But now I shall leave you—"

"No, stay, Mr. Pembrooke," William said. "The news affects you even more than it does Miss Foster."

Miles paused and waited where he was, but did not reclaim his seat.

"Your father—is he all right?" Miss Foster asked, face strained.

"Yes. He will be. He took a bad fall while walking along a ravine and sprained his ankle and bruised a few ribs. Painful, but it could have been far worse."

She expelled a ragged breath. "Thank God. I've been so worried."

William explained to Miles, "Thankfully Miss Foster remembered my father mention Snake Ravine, so I knew where to look and found him before he had suffered overlong from exposure.

"Mr. Brown assures us of a complete recovery, provided we keep him from taking a chill. Mother has him under a mountain of bedclothes and in woolens, as you can imagine. He was grumbling about all the fuss before I left, so I know he'll be well."

William looked at Abigail again, hoping his expression communicated the deep gratitude he felt but could not adequately express with Miles Pembrooke standing there.

Then he solemnly faced Miles. "In looking for my father, Mr. Pembrooke, I'm afraid I also found yours. . . . That is, his remains."

"What?" Miles roared.

William winced. Why could he not have thought of a more graceful way to say it? "At the bottom of the ravine. I hate to be indelicate, but it is clear he has been there for many years. Mr. Brown and the constable have removed the . . . uh, bones with the utmost care, I assure you."

"Then how did you identify him?" Miles asked, face contorted. "You must be mistaken. You cannot know it was him."

William held his challenging gaze. "He was wearing the Pembrooke signet ring."

Miles flopped down on the chair, face pale. He swallowed, then sputtered, "Can you tell how . . . how he . . . died?"

"The constable assumes he fell from his horse, much as I did today when looking for my father along that steep ravine."

"Oh, Mr. Chapman," Miss Foster exclaimed. "Are you all right?"

"I am. A little sore of body and pride, but otherwise perfectly well."

Miles protested, "How is it you escaped unhurt, but my father supposedly died from such a fall?"

William said gently, "Brown guesses he either broke his neck or hit his head on a rock when he fell from his horse."

"But my father was an excellent rider."

"Perhaps he was pursuing someone at breakneck speed and wasn't heedful of the danger," William said. "Especially if he rode after dark, or during a rainstorm, as I did today."

"How can you know that? It's only supposition. Perhaps someone stole that ring from my father and fell to his death while fleeing the crime."

"I suppose it's possible. But we found something else besides the ring."

"Oh?" Miles seemed to hold his breath.

William nodded. "A double-barrel flintlock pistol. My father recalls Clive Pembrooke having such a gun. He liked that he could take two shots before reloading, though yes, such guns are common enough."

Miles shook his head. "I want to see him with my own eyes. Or I shall never believe it."

"You and my father, sir, had that in common."

Miles rose. "Where have they taken him?"

"The undertaker's in Caldwell."

"I will go there directly."

William offered, "Shall I go with you, Mr. Pembrooke?"

Miles turned, hesitated, and then surprised them all by saying, "Yes. Please. If you would, Parson."

"I will stay here," Miss Foster said awkwardly. "And inform my family."

"No, of course you must not go," Miles said. "A lady like yourself. To see such a gruesome thing." He shuddered.

"Will you tell your sister yourself?" she asked. "Will she wish to see him as well?"

"I don't know. I doubt it. But then, I doubt she'll believe it either, otherwise."

"She is staying at Hunts Hall this week," Miss Foster said. "If you like, I shall—"

"Is she?" Miles interrupted, eyes narrowing. "I did not realize you two had become acquainted." He turned to William. "Might we stop there on the way? I'd like her to hear it from me."

"Of course," William agreed.

Miles said, "If you will give me a few minutes, I shall go and fetch my hat and gloves."

William nodded.

Miles bowed to Miss Foster, turned, and left the room.

When they were alone, William said to Abigail, "I am sorry to bring such a report to your door."

"You were right to do so. It was kind of you to tell Miles yourself and offer to accompany him on such an unpleasant errand."

He lowered his eyes a moment. "I cannot claim purely selfless motives in coming to tell him. I admit I wanted to see his reaction firsthand. To know whether he was grieved or relieved. And whether the news came as a surprise."

She cocked her head to one side. "He certainly seemed surprised. How could he have known?"

William shrugged. "If he killed his father or saw it done. Or if he was among those Clive Pembrooke was pursuing with those double barrels."

Miss Foster shook her head. "He couldn't have killed him. He was only a boy at the time. Besides, I thought you said the constable and Mr. Brown guess the death was caused by the fall."

"A guess is all it is. But something tells me Miles knows more about it than he lets on."

Chapter 29

*T*he next day Molly found Abigail in the library and told her a Mrs. Webb was waiting for her in the hall but refused to be shown into the drawing room.

"Thank you, Molly."

Abigail returned the quill to its holder and hurried out. In the hall, she found Harriet Webb standing, hands clasped, looking around and slowly shaking her head. "I told myself I would never set foot in this place again." She spread her arms, disbelief and self-deprecation in her expression. "Yet here I am. . . ."

"Come into the drawing room and sit down," Abigail said warmly.

"The morning room is far enough, if you don't mind."

"Of course not." Abigail led the way and opened the door for her. "How are you? Did Miles come to see you?"

"Yes. I still haven't slept."

"Did you go with him to . . . Caldwell?"

"I did. I didn't want to but knew I must . . . to finish the story. I thought of writing to you again. But instead, I decided I would come and see you in person."

"I'm glad you did. Here. Sit down. Shall I ring for tea?"

"No. Nothing for me." She pulled a grim smile. "Other than a listening ear."

Abigail sat across from her. "Gladly."

Harriet swallowed and lifted her eyes as though searching her memory. "About a week before we left here, Mother told us to quietly begin gathering our possessions—just a few special things that meant a great deal to us, and only three or four changes of clothing. Nothing obvious, that our father would notice until after we were gone. After Father and the gamekeeper left for a hunting trip, Mother met with the housekeeper. I don't know exactly what she said to her, but I gather she told her to let all the servants go. She was probably afraid what my father might do to anyone foolish enough to be in arm's reach when he returned and discovered us gone."

"She also told Mrs. Hayes to lock up the place after we left. To lock it up exactly as she found it—not to linger and risk being here when Father returned."

So, Abigail realized, that's why she had found the rooms left as though they had been abruptly abandoned.

Pain glittered in Harriet's eyes as she continued. "We were planning to leave the next day. Mac and the servants had left already. Only Mrs. Hayes remained to lock up after us. Father wasn't expected home for two days. We thought we had plenty of time. But we were wrong. He came home earlier than expected. . . ."

Harriet shivered and slowly shook her head. "The boys and I were already in our beds, though I knew I wouldn't sleep a wink. Mamma was still downstairs, packing a few last-minute things and drinking tea to calm her nerves. What happened next is something of a blur . . . a nightmare. The door slamming. My father shouting. My mother crying . . ."

Harriet bit her lip. "I heard a blow, heard Mamma shriek and fall, and knew he had struck her. My brother Harold shoved Miles into my room and told me to lock the door. I thought about hiding in the secret room but instead remained glued to the door, listening. Harold ran downstairs to try to protect Mamma, I knew. What a coward I felt standing there, doing nothing to help. I remember thinking Father would kill Mamma *and* Harold, and then come upstairs for Miles and me. I tried to pray but felt so hopeless, I couldn't. Finally, I tiptoed out of my room, telling Miles to wait inside. I had to see what was happening, even as I dreaded it. From the stair rail, I looked down and saw Harold and Father struggling in the hall below. Father had a stranglehold on Harold's neck, and Harold was turning red, suffocating . . . Mother lay sprawled on the floor nearby, pleading and sobbing. Harold began to turn blue. I wanted to do something—to at least shout at Father, tell him to stop—but I was frozen in terror. Useless.

"Suddenly a gunshot rent the air, and Father and Harold fell as one. I turned in stupefied shock and stared, unable to believe what I was seeing. There stood my little brother, a pistol in his outstretched hands—a weapon Father kept under his bed in case of intruders. The gun was not large, but it looked huge in Miles's hands. He was only twelve years old at the time. He stood there, pistol still leveled, smoking, until his arms began to shake, and then his whole body.

"Mother crawled over and rolled Father's body away to get to her son. Only then did we see the awful truth. Miles had meant to shoot our father. But the bullet had gone through him and into Harold."

"Oh no!" Abigail exclaimed. "Poor Miles!"

"Poor Miles, yes. He'd meant to save his brother. But poor Harold. The bullet lodged in his abdomen after passing through Father's side. Both were alive but were losing blood fast. Harold looked very bad indeed. Father was stunned out of his senses for a time, and Mamma sprang into action. She ran out to the stable to find the gamekeeper, who'd gone hunting with Father. She found him unsaddling the horses and asked him to ready the traveling coach. She returned to the house and commanded Miles and me to bring down our things, Harold's valise as well. We did so, terrified though we were.

"The gamekeeper came into the house. He took one look at

Harold, then at my mother's bruised face, and offered to help us get away. I wasn't sure if we should trust him. He was in Father's employ, after all. But Mother must have felt we had little choice and gratefully accepted. The man helped her carry Harold out to the coach and even offered to drive. We had planned to hire horses and a postilion, but there was no time to make such arrangements. We left Father there, on the floor, not knowing if he would live or die. But Mother was determined to take Harold to a surgeon as soon as we were safely away."

Harriet slowly shook her head, eyes distant in memory. "The first few miles were sheer torture, poor Harold crying out at every jarring bump and turn." Her voice cracked. "But then he grew quiet, and that was even worse."

Tears filled Abigail's eyes to hear the pain in Harriet's voice, though the woman's eyes remained stoically dry.

"Suddenly the gamekeeper yelled down to us from the coachman's bench. 'A rider! Galloping fast!'"

Mother cried and braced Harold as the driver urged the horses to speed, cracking his whip and shouting. I reminded myself that Father's horse would be tired having just returned from a distant hunt. At least I hoped so. I remember praying then, as I'd failed to do before. "Please let us get away. Don't let him catch us."

"But the gamekeeper shouted that he was gaining on us. So much for prayer, I thought. I strained my ears and heard the beating of hooves. But then a minute later, I heard them no more. Perhaps in my fear, I only imagined him that close. Perhaps it had only been the rumble of thunder."

Abigail suggested, "Or perhaps God answered your prayer after all."

Harriet shrugged. "If so, then why didn't he answer my prayer to spare Harold?"

"I don't know. He . . . died in the carriage?"

Harriet nodded. "He breathed his last as we were crossing the bridge into Bristol. We stopped to bury him there. I was afraid it would give Father time to change horses and catch up with us. To kill us all.

But the gamekeeper escorted Mother into a disreputable-looking public house, and she came out a quarter of an hour later—her hand no longer bearing a wedding ring but instead a gun.

"'Let him come,' she said grimly. And I knew she would not hesitate to use that gun if need be.'"

Harriet paused to gather her thoughts. "Miles sat silent and stone-faced throughout the entire journey. Mamma, in her grief, all but ignored him. Perhaps by her silence, her neglect in absolving Miles from guilt, he felt she held him responsible for his brother's death. I tried to tell him it wasn't his fault, but I don't think he really heard me. Later, when Miles's odd demeanor continued, Mamma did try to talk to him, but by then the impression was set, and it didn't seem to do any good." Harriet's brow furrowed, then she visibly shook off her troubled thoughts.

"The gamekeeper had a wife and child in Ham Green, not far from Caldwell—therefore he couldn't be gone for long. So we left him at a coaching inn with enough money to see him home. We hoped my father would not learn of his absence before he could safely rejoin his family. But if asked, he could honestly say we'd gone on without him and he didn't know where we were headed. Of course, I don't think Mamma knew either. Before he left, he taught Miles how to handle the reins, and Miles himself drove until we reached the next village and found a postilion to hire.

"We kept moving for days. Staying only one night in any one place, until the money Mamma had been squirreling away began to run low. Every day she read all the newspapers she could find, in coffee houses or from refuse bins, or buying them if she couldn't procure them another way. But we never saw a word in print about my father. We knew that if he died, the news would be reported. So we assumed he still lived, probably at Pembrooke Park.

"After some time had passed, Mamma finally wrote a letter to the gamekeeper using the name Thomas, asking for news of 'his employer' and directing him to write back in care of a Welsh inn.

"I still have his reply," Harriet said, tugging open her cinched reticule. "I thought about sending it to you earlier, but doubted it would make any sense to you." She extracted a letter from the bag. "Here."

The yellowed paper was addressed cryptically to H. J. Thomas, in care of the Bell, Newport, Wales.

> *To whom it may concern,*
>
> *I am in receipt of your inquiry. My employment is, at present, of an uncertain nature.*
>
> *The estate where I have been serving is currently closed and shuttered. Abandoned, by all appearances. I've had no word from my employer. Nor has anyone of my acquaintance seen or heard from any of the family. It is assumed that they have gone off together for some reason. The carriage is gone, as was my master's horse. However, the horse returned riderless a few days later, and I have taken the liberty of selling it in payment of wages owing. I trust the mistress would approve.*
>
> *Even so, I judge it premature to consider a return to a previous situation at present. It might be wise for all parties to remain where they are for now.*
>
> *I hope this satisfies your inquiry.*
>
> > *Sincerely,*
> > *JD, Ham Green, Caldwell*

Abigail looked up. "It's written in a bit of a code, isn't it? In case the letter was intercepted?"

"Yes. The gamekeeper was more clever than I would have given him credit for. He knew what my father was capable of, after all, and had his wife and child to think of. And as my father's fate was uncertain, he wrote to tell us basically, to stay where we were."

Harriet sighed. "I confess I thought, even hoped, my father was dead. But Mamma . . ." She shook her head. "She was unwilling to risk it. Afraid he was biding his time somewhere, plotting his revenge. So we stayed in Wales, using the name Thomas, hoping to avoid being found. Only Miles kept the Pembrooke surname.

But he left us to join the navy when he was still very young. We didn't see him for years."

"And what do you think now?" Abigail asked gently. "Do you believe it is your father Mr. Chapman found at the bottom of the ravine?"

Harriet nodded. "I do think it's him. The ring. The pistol. Where they found him . . . But remember, I have wanted to believe him dead for a long, long time."

"And Miles?"

Harriet hesitated. "He didn't react with the relief I expected. He was . . . strange about it. He had tears in his eyes, even as he muttered something quite disrespectful to the dead. . . . Not that I blame him, but still I found his reaction unsettling, I admit."

"Is it such a surprise that he should feel torn?" Abigail asked. "He was a boy who shot his father, and probably still wishes his father would forgive him, and love him, and value him. . . ." Abigail swallowed, realizing she was prattling on. "After all, he cannot know whether his shot ended his life, or the exhausted horse, or the ravine itself, or all of the above. . . ."

"I told Miles again and again he has no need to feel guilty."

"Saying the words and believing oneself forgiven are very different things." Abigail knew this from firsthand experience.

"Yes, you're right. That's why I've felt I needed to do something, to make restitution."

"And you have, but remember that God is merciful. You are not responsible for your father's wrongdoing."

She managed a humorless smile. "The Old Testament contradicts you, Miss Foster. Perhaps you ought to read the Book of Numbers. . . ."

"Numbers 14, perhaps?" Abigail said, naming one of the verses referenced in the miniature book.

"Ah! You found one of my clues! You cannot know how satisfying that is. Did you find the one about Cain and Abel as well?"

Abigail nodded.

"I wrote them down while we were packing to leave. My small attempt to hint at the truth—and how I felt about it." Harriet smiled, then sobered. "I have thought about what you told me, Miss Foster. And I will continue to consider your words."

Abigail thought for a moment. Hadn't Duncan mentioned something about the gamekeeper—that he had died? She asked, "Did you ever hear from the gamekeeper again?"

Harriet shook her head. "No. But I recently asked Mr. Morgan's man if he knew anything about the old Pembrooke gamekeeper. He told me the man died only last year but is survived by his wife and son."

A sense of foreboding prickling her skin, Abigail asked, "What was his name?"

For a moment, Harriet met her gaze, then said evenly, "James Duncan."

After Harriet left, Abigail went to find Duncan, looking in his usual haunts. He wasn't in his room or in the servants' hall. Entering the lamp room, she found it empty as well.

From the corner of her eye, she saw something and turned back. A hefty wad of faded green material lay bunched on a stool in the corner. Frowning, she stepped closer and picked up one edge of the moth-eaten, musty wool with two pincher fingers. She stilled, nerves prickling. Was this the hooded cloak she had seen someone lurking around in? She felt something hard through the material. Laying down the cloak, she patted until she found an inner pocket. Inside was an old copper lamp base.

Footsteps echoed in the passage and Abigail dropped her find and whirled, feeling illogically guilty.

In the threshold, Mrs. Walsh drew up short at the sight of her. "Oh. Hello, miss. Where's Duncan?"

"That's what I want to know."

Abigail asked Polly and Molly as well, but no one had seen him all day.

She went to find Miles instead, but he wasn't in his room either, nor in the library or drawing room. Finally she wandered out to the stables, and there found Miles sitting in the straw of an empty stall—sleeves rolled up, forearms on his knees, hair rumpled and specked with straw. He looked twelve years old all over again.

"Miles . . ." she said, relieved to find him but concerned at his state.

He looked up at her with haunted eyes, reminding her of Harriet's description of the little girl staring up at her window with haunted eyes. A girl whose father had also met a violent end.

"What are you doing out here all alone?" she asked gently. "I was worried about you."

"Were you? Dear Cousin Abigail . . ." He patted the straw beside him.

Pushing aside concerns for her skirt, she sat. "Harriet was just here."

"Did she tell you?" he asked softly, not meeting her eyes. "About . . . everything?"

"I think so, yes."

He nodded, appearing relieved.

He stared at the stall wall and said, "Harold was good. You wouldn't know it to look at him—foul-tempered and sullen most of the time. But he stood up to Father, put himself between him and Mother, or me, time and time again. And ended up black and blue for his trouble. And I . . . killed him." His chin trembled. "A good man. Barely more than a boy himself. And I killed him. Unforgivable."

"It wasn't your fault, Miles. You were trying to *save* him. You were only an innocent boy."

He shook his head. "Don't make me out to be innocent, Miss Foster. I know myself too well. I am no innocent. I meant to kill my father." His voice shook. "And I came here fully intending to take all I could . . . until I became acquainted with you and your kind father." Again he shook his head. "No. Don't try to make me an innocent."

Abigail's heart burned within her. "I couldn't, Miles. Only Christ can make an innocent out of a guilty man. That's what He did when He died a criminal's death on the cross." She took his hand in hers. "God loves you, Miles. Ask Him to forgive you, and He will, once and for all."

Miles stared blindly ahead and nodded vaguely. They sat in silence for several minutes, his hand in hers.

Then Miles pulled a handkerchief from his pocket and wiped his eyes and dabbed his nose. "Well, at least finding his remains should finally settle things with the courts."

Abigail hesitated. "Actually . . ."

He looked at her. "What?"

She bit her lip. It wasn't her secret to tell. And who knew how distraught Miles might become at the news that neither he nor his sister was rightful heir to Pembrooke Park and its treasures?

Instead she squeezed his hand once more. "I'm just glad you're all right."

Abigail and Leah walked through the grove between the Chapmans' cottage and Pembrooke Park. Abigail had told her what she learned from Harriet, and how both she and Miles had reacted to the news that their father's remains had been found. Leah for her part, reacted calmly to the news—relieved but in no hurry to proclaim her identity to the world. In fact, she had decided to leave the ruby necklace and most of the mementoes in the secret room for the time being—and leave everything else the way it was too.

"Let's give Harriet and Miles time to come to terms with their father's fate," she said, "before springing this on them too."

Abigail spied someone in the distance, through the trees, and drew up short. Duncan sat just inside the doorway of the old gamekeeper's lodge. "There's Duncan. I want to ask him about his father."

Leah held back, and whispered, "I don't want to face him right now. I know I've hurt him, but he refuses to stop trying to make me feel guilty for breaking things off."

Abigail looked at her in understanding. "You wait here, then."

Leah nodded, looking relieved.

Abigail walked toward the open lodge door. Duncan sat on a wooden chair, tipped back on two legs, idly smoking a cigar and sipping from a bottle of brandy—her father's brandy, she guessed.

"I didn't know anyone came here," she began casually, hoping to put him off his guard. "It's the old gamekeeper's lodge, is it not?"

He nodded. "I come here now and again to think."

"Ah." She said, "Your father was gamekeeper to Clive Pembrooke, I understand."

"That's right, and to his brother before him." He glanced around the dusty room with its low, beamed ceiling. "My father lived in this hovel as a young man, before he married my mother and had me."

"You grew up in Ham Green?"

"That's right," he said with pride. "In a far better house than this. My father made a good living as gamekeeper, and I was to have his place one day, but life, I've learnt, is not fair."

She said, "And I learnt recently of a great service your father performed for Mrs. Pembrooke and her children."

"Helping them get away from her husband, you mean? Not sure Mr. Pembrooke would have agreed with you."

"What did your father tell you about Clive Pembrooke?"

Duncan set down the bottle and crossed his arms over his chest. "Not much."

"Did he tell you about his determination to find a treasure he believed hidden in the house?"

He shrugged. "Everyone knows that."

"Is that why you're here? A little lifting and polishing your small price to pay for access to Pembrooke Park?"

"I'm the one getting paid." He gave her a cheeky grin.

"Getting paid to treasure hunt. Not bad work, if you can get it."

"There is more than one way to pursue treasure," he said philosophically, taking a puff on his cigar and watching the smoke rise. "If one door gets slammed in your face, you try another."

Ah, Abigail thought. He liked to talk in riddles like his gamekeeper father. She interpreted, "Like the door Mac Chapman slammed in your face?"

Anger glinted in his eyes. "Perhaps."

She asked, "Did you ever even admire Leah Chapman? Or were you courting Eliza all along?"

He lifted his chin. "Yes, I did admire her. But she wouldn't have me. Laid me low for weeks, I don't mind telling you. It's why Pa finally told me . . . who she really was. Thought it might take the sting out. I hadn't been rejected by Leah Chapman, humble steward's daughter. I'd been rejected by Eleanor Pembrooke, heiress of Pembrooke Park." He sneered. "But somehow, that did *not* make me feel better. In fact, it had the opposite effect. I admired her before I knew, but I don't see any shame in admitting it added to her appeal. In fact, I wanted her more than ever. And the life I could have had, had she not been blinded by prejudice. Mac influenced her, I know. She might have accepted me, if not for him. Always devilish proud of his Pembrooke connection, Mac was." He shook his head, a bitter twist to his lips. "So he sent me on my way. And the young parson took his side against me."

"And so you thought you'd pursue another Pembrooke 'connection' in Eliza—is that it?"

He pulled a face. "Eliza has nothing to do with it. Even if Robert Pembrooke was her father, an illegitimate chit gets nothing, unless he recognized her in his will. Which of course he didn't."

"So you decided to work here instead."

He shrugged. "Why not? I had planned to work here since boyhood, though as independent gamekeeper with my own lodgings, not a house-bound drudge. Those plans were spoiled when Pembrooke Park closed, so I've had to make the best of it. It's up to me to support my mother now my father's gone. He worked close with Clive Pembrooke, see. Told me how sure the man was that there was a sizeable treasure hidden away. My father half believed him. And so did I."

"And what have you found so far in your late-night searches? Beyond that pin you gave Eliza?"

"Now, don't look daggers at me like that," Duncan said. "It was only a trifle. And it's not as though you weren't conducting your own search, ey, miss? I'm not blind, ya know."

When she made no reply, he smirked and puffed again on his cigar.

"So, yes. I felt ill used by the Chapmans," he went on. "Robbed for the second time of what might have been my destiny. How it chafed—toting and carrying for your lot, when I might have been lord of the manor myself, with Eleanor as my bride. . . ."

His eyes grew fondly distant for a moment, then hardened once more. "So I figured, if I found the treasure in the course of my work, well, I had it coming, hadn't I? A little recompense for my heartache."

Leah appeared in the doorway beside her, and Duncan's chair tipped forward onto all four legs with a bang.

Leah said, "My father recommended you for this post as all the recompense he felt he ever owed you, even though he had concerns about your character and engaging you went against his better judgment. He felt bad for disappointing you where I'm concerned, but he also did so out of respect for your father, whom he greatly esteemed. He hoped in time, you would follow in his footsteps. Become the honorable, hardworking man Jim Duncan was."

Duncan's nostrils flared, but Leah continued resolutely, "I didn't reject you because you were beneath my station. I rejected you because you are lazy and meanspirited and greedy."

His lip curled. "And that's supposed to make me feel better?"

Leah shook her head. "No. It's the truth. It's supposed to make you want to become a better man."

After that, Abigail walked Leah home, leaving Duncan stewing in the lodge. She returned to Pembrooke Park and went belowstairs again, wanting to have the cloak in hand when she next confronted Duncan. She considered giving it to Mac instead and allow him to ask the questions after he recovered from his injuries. . . .

But when she reached the lamp room, the cloak was gone.

The following week, Abigail sat with her family in the drawing room. She and Louisa played a halfhearted game of draughts while their mother embroidered a cushion and their father read his mail.

Abruptly, Papa muttered an oath and tossed down the letter he had received from Uncle Vincent.

"Not again."

"Now what, my dear?" Concern etched lines across Mamma's pretty face.

"Your brother asks that I come to London again, as soon as possible. Something about another investment. So help me, if he tries to—"

"There, there, my dear. I am certain he's learnt his lesson."

"Are you? That makes one of us. I pray this isn't to do with more backlash from the last debacle. . . ."

Abigail's stomach knotted at the thought.

He rubbed an agitated hand over his face. "I suppose I must go. He says it's important."

"Why don't we all go?" Mamma said. "It would only be for a few days, would it not?"

"Yes, let's do!" Louisa interjected. "I long for London and to see all my friends."

Abigail spoke up. "I'll stay, if you don't mind. There is a lot going on, and I want to be here."

"A lot going on?" Louisa echoed. "Here? You have been in the rustics too long, Abigail."

Her parents soon agreed, however, realizing it would be rude to abandon their houseguest, and perhaps unwise to abandon the house.

That night, Louisa took her aside. "Are you certain you should stay here alone? With Miles, I mean?"

"Thank you for worrying about me, but I shall be fine," Abigail said. She hoped she would be, at any rate. After all, she had nothing he wanted—no treasure.

Two days later, Abigail again bid farewell to her parents and Louisa.

Not long after they had left, she saw Mac riding his horse across the bridge, Brutus bounding alongside. He was on his way home from Hunts Hall, she guessed, surprised he had returned to his duties so quickly after his recent injuries. She waved and hurried across the drive to him. "May I talk with you a moment," she asked.

He halted and, ignoring her protests, dismounted. "Aye. Do you mind if we walk while we do? I need to stretch my stiff legs."

"I don't mind at all," she said. "But are you sure you should be walking on that ankle?"

"Only a sprain," he insisted. "It's bound tight." He pulled down the stout branch tied to his saddle and used it for support as he walked toward his cottage, leading the horse by its reins.

She walked alongside. She wanted to talk to him about Duncan, but first she apprised him of her family's departure and her decision to remain behind while they visited London for a few days.

He sent her a glinting glance. "Perhaps it's time you learnt to shoot a gun, Miss Foster. I could teach you, if you like."

She was surprised by the offer, and what it implied.

They reached the clearing, and Abigail glanced up at the cottage. Beside her, Mac sucked in a sharp breath and tensed. Miles sat on the bench in the little front garden, rubbing a cloth over a gun. One of Mac's guns, she supposed, as she had seen Mac oiling his collection in the nearby woodshed on previous occasions.

Mac called, "I am not in the habit of finding strangers at my door, helping themselves to my guns."

Miles replied casually, "Then you ought not leave them lying about for strangers to find."

Was his manner as friendly as it outwardly appeared, Abigail wondered. Or subtly threatening? It was difficult to tell.

Releasing his horse, Mac pushed through the gate. "I was called away whilst cleaning it," he said defensively, "and left it in harmless pieces."

"So I guessed. But it was the work of a moment to put it back together. Not for a novice, perhaps. But the navy did teach me something useful, in the end." Miles tilted his head, observing Mac's crude cane with interest. "Apparently I've started a fashion here." He smirked. "Fine stick."

Mac squared his shoulders. "To what do I owe the honor of your visit to my humble cottage, Mr. Pembrooke?"

"That's right." Miles looked around. "This is my first visit. I have been remiss . . . Oh no, that's right—I've never been invited."

"Is this a social call, then?"

"If you like."

Irritation flashed over Mac's face. "What do you want, Miles?"

Miles looked at him closely and said, "Mac, I know Robert Pembrooke confided in you."

"That's right," Mac said, eyeing him warily. "He did. And proud I am of that fact. He was the best of men, Robert Pembrooke was."

"I shall have to take your word for it." Miles smiled thinly. "Though my father did best him in the end."

Mac frowned. "What are you getting at? If you dare make light of what your father did to him, to us all, I'll—"

Miles held up his palm in consolation. "Now, now. No need to get riled. Are you sure you're Scottish and not Irish, *Red*?"

Miles grinned as though he'd made a great joke, but Abigail saw Mac fist his hands.

"So if Robert Pembrooke confided so much in you, his trusted steward," Miles continued, "then you must know where it is." He added cheerfully, "You can tell me, now that we know my father is dead. He can't take anything else from your revered Robert Pembrooke. Can no longer get his bony hands on his house or his riches."

Mac looked at Miles as he might size up an unfamiliar dog. Friendly . . . or dangerous? "True," he allowed.

"So, where is it?" Miles urged. "Where is Robert Pembrooke's treasure?"

"Here I am," Leah said, stepping outside.

Miles turned to her in surprise. "Miss Chapman . . . ?"

"No."

His brows rose. "No?"

She shook her head. "My name is Eleanor Pembrooke, daughter of Robert and Elizabeth Pembrooke. Your first cousin."

Miles scowled. "I don't believe you. You're dead. That is . . . she's dead."

"No. I am very much alive. Mac hid me from your father. Protected me all these years."

His eyes narrowed. "Prove it."

"Very well."

"Leah . . ." Mac warned. "You don't have to do this."

"It's all right, Papa. I want to. It's time." She looked at Miles. "Give me one moment." She retreated into the house and came back out a minute later.

She said, "Here's the letter my father sent home with his valet after your father stabbed him. He wrote it with his last breath, his last bit of strength."

Miles snatched it from her.

As he read it, his eyes widened. "Yes! You see . . . It's right here! *Give him the house, anything he wants, but hide my treasure.* This proves it! My father was right all along—there is a treasure. Show me where it is."

When no one moved, Miles glared at Mac. "I know how you idealized the man, so I am certain you obeyed this command, as you did in everything."

"That's right. I did."

"So where is it? Where is Robert Pembrooke's treasure?"

Leah slowly shook her head. "There is no treasure. Not really. It was my father's pet name for me. He called me 'my treasure.'"

"I don't believe you." His eyes narrowed. "If you're Eleanor Pembrooke, then who's buried in her grave in the churchyard?"

"My baby sister, who died of the same fever that took my mother."

"But my father checked the parish records when he heard some rumor one of Robert's children was still alive."

Mac nodded. "The old rector agreed to change the records. To protect Eleanor."

Miles looked at Leah. "We did wonder when you came home from school. Harriet said you looked nothing like Mac or William, though a bit like Kate Chapman, perhaps. But we never guessed . . ."

Returning his gaze to her adoptive father, Miles laid the gun on his knee and clapped lazily. "Bravo, Mac. That is quite a feat. And what do you get out of it? Fifty percent of the treasure?"

"Nothing of the kind."

"You're wrong, Miles," Leah said. "It isn't like that."

"Does Harri know of your claim?"

"Not yet," Leah said. "Though I plan to tell her."

He rose, taking up his ebony stick. "Don't bother. I shall ride over to Hunts Hall right now and tell her myself. I want to see her face when she hears. She told me she had a feeling we'd find another heir—even wished the rumor was true and one of Robert Pembrooke's children still lived."

He looked at Abigail, eyes glinting. "Apparently all this time I've been wooing the wrong cousin. . . ."

Miles turned his smile on Leah like a weapon. "And you, Le— Eleanor. Do you know where the secret room is?"

"Leah . . ." Mac warned under his breath.

"I do," Leah acknowledged, chin high.

His eyes widened. "Where is it?"

"I shall be happy to show it to you . . . tomorrow. You want to go and speak to your sister first, and I . . . shall collect a few personal keepsakes."

"Nothing too valuable, I trust?" His eyes glittered suspiciously.

"As you will see, there is not a great deal of value in there. Mostly family papers. A few portraits. Things that will mean more to me than to you."

"If you say so."

Abigail thought he might demand to go in immediately, or to extract a promise that she remove no valuables until he'd had the chance to search the room. But he did not.

Instead he drew himself up, handing Mac his gun at last. "Well." He consulted his pocket watch. "I had better hurry over to Hunts Hall if I hope to beg a dinner invitation." He wagged his eyebrows comically, but after the tense scene, no one smiled.

Leah and Abigail waited until he had disappeared into the stables and ridden off before making haste to Pembrooke Park.

Chapter 30

*L*eah wanted time to cull personal letters, her mother's portrait, and the ruby necklace before giving over the rest to Miles's frantic search. Abigail offered to help her, briefly wondering if there was still hope of claiming that reward, now that the jewels had been reunited with their rightful owner. Harriet had hinted as much, but somehow she doubted it.

They donned bibbed aprons and set to work inside the secret room—closing the door in case any servants entered the bedchamber. Leah gathered the family Bible, necklace, and a few other things and set them in a pile on one shelf. Then they carefully took down the portrait of Elizabeth Pembrooke from the back of the door and set it nearby. The nail the portrait had hung on clinked to the floor.

Abigail glanced up and was surprised to see the tiniest pinprick of light. "Look! It's left a hole." She stood on tiptoe and put her eye to it. "You can see into the bedchamber—a little."

But Leah's focus remained on the contents of the shelves in the hidden room.

"How can I help?" Abigail asked, joining her.

"I don't want to miss anything personal. Letters between my parents, or to me."

"I understand."

Each took a stack and began reading through the correspondence. Leah spread a lap rug on the cushions and reclined back on
them with a handful of letters. Abigail could easily imagine little
Ellie snug in her private hideaway, reading a favorite book.

Abigail sat less comfortably on the child-size chair.

"Are you sure you don't want to trade?" Leah offered.

"No, I'm fine."

"Good." Leah grinned. "I doubt my backside would fit in that
chair nowadays."

They continued to read, the silence broken by the occasional
rustle of paper or birdcall outside the window.

Abigail then heard something else, from the other side of the
door.

Leah must have sensed her unnatural stillness, for she glanced
up at her. "What?"

"Shh . . . Someone's out there. In my . . . our . . . bedchamber."

"Who?" Leah asked.

Abigail rose and started to crack open the door but then remembered the nail hole. She raised herself on tiptoe and looked
through it once more. At first she didn't see anyone. She could see
only a narrow shaft of the room—her side table and the edge of
the bed. But then a figure walked past and opened the drawer of
her side table.

"It's Miles," she whispered, perplexed. There hadn't been time
for him to ride out to Hunts Hall and back, let alone to talk with
Harriet. Had he come back hoping to catch them entering the secret room—catch them in the act of extracting all the "treasure"?

Miles sat on the edge of her bed and lifted a stack of letters
onto his lap—the letters Harriet had sent her anonymously. Letters
about the past, about coming to Pembrooke Park, about the girl
with the haunted eyes, about her increasingly violent father, her
troubled brother, and the secret room . . .

Oh no. How would Miles react? Should she bolt from the room
and snatch them away? She certainly couldn't overpower the man
if he refused to hand over the letters. And in so doing, she would

reveal their hiding place. And Eleanor's treasures. And they weren't ready to do that yet. Besides, the letters were written by his own sister. They were his business, in some ways, more than hers.

Would Harriet wish Miles to read them? Probably not. But at the moment Abigail could think of no way to forestall him without revealing the secret room to him.

"What is he doing?" Leah whispered anxiously.

"Reading the letters you returned."

Leah's mouth formed a silent O as she, too, thought through the implications.

There was little in the letters Miles didn't already know or hadn't lived through himself. If he read through them all—and found the one in which Harriet mentioned finding the secret room at last, even then the letter did not specify where it was. There was no great risk to them. If anything, reading them would likely spur him to seek out his sister, as he'd claimed he'd do earlier. Abigail did not like the thought of driving a wedge between brother and sister. To cause problems for Harriet. But better for Harriet, than for vulnerable Leah . . .

As Abigail watched, Miles lifted the glass off her bedside lamp, set it aside, and then fed the corner of one of the letters into its flame. Abigail gasped. "He's burning one of them. . . ." She wondered which. Maybe the one in which Harriet had accused him of lighting a fire in the dolls' house and blaming their brother.

Miles carried the letter toward the hearth, then returned empty-handed to read another.

Abigail watched for a few moments longer, then stepped away from the peephole and tiptoed back to her chair.

"Let's see how long he stays," she whispered. They would wait him out and keep their secret to themselves for a little while longer.

She sat down and picked up another box to sort through. Then she lifted the family Bible onto her lap and looked at the names written in the front leaves, tracing her fingers down the long list of births and deaths until she reached Eleanor's birth date. Eight years later came the birth of *Baby Emma*. Her birth and death dates a poignantly brief span, followed by the death of her mother, Elizabeth. Abigail traced the entries but found no notice of Eleanor's fictional death. Nor of Robert Pembrooke's death, which had been all too real.

Leah glanced over Abigail's shoulder and said, "No wonder Mac hid the Bible in here." She picked up another letter from her stack and resumed her reading.

Abigail read for a while longer as well, and then leaned her head back against the wall. Her thoughts drifted to William as she idly glanced around the room. How strange to find herself there with Eleanor, Robert Pembrooke's "treasure." Her gaze rested on the rusted water pipes against the far wall. What was that verse William had quoted? *"Lay not up for yourselves treasures upon earth, where moth and rust doth corrupt. . . ."*

Sometime later, Abigail looked up and wondered what time it was. From the small window, she saw fading daylight in orangey twilight hues. She'd lost track of time as she'd read a series of love letters between Leah's great-grandparents—distant relatives of Abigail as well. Even so, she wouldn't have expected to see the sunset from this east-facing window.

She glanced at the cushions beside her and noticed Leah had fallen asleep, a letter lying on her chest. Abigail closed her eyes and listened for movement in the next room. Was Miles still there? She heard a low roar but couldn't identify the sound. She took a long breath and suddenly stilled. What was that smell? She sniffed the air again. Smoke.

She frowned. Was Miles still burning letters? Or had Polly come in to lay a fire for the evening? Abigail's neck ached from bending over letters for so long. She rose on stiff legs and tiptoed to the peephole. She didn't see Miles. But she couldn't see the whole room from her vantage point.

She laid her palm on the panel and gingerly opened it a slit. Suddenly heat penetrated her skin, and she snatched it back. The door was hot. What on earth . . . ? Then through the crack she saw . . . Her heart banged against her ribs. The dolls' house engulfed in flames. As she stared, disbelieving, fire seemed to leap from the carpet before the hearth to the nearby window curtain. Then orange-red flames whipped up her bed-curtains.

Panic gripped her.

Miles. Had the letters he'd burnt fallen to the floor by accident? Or had he set the fire intentionally—somehow knowing Leah was there and meaning to snuff out her life, to follow in his father's footsteps and do away with the rightful owner of Pembrooke Park? *Please, God, no . . .*

Nerves zinging to high alert, she whirled to her companion.

"Leah? Leah, wake up!"

Leah groggily turned her face away. Was the smoke affecting her already? Abigail crouched beside her and shook her shoulder. "Leah! Get up. The room is on fire."

Leah's eyes opened, and Abigail's words penetrated, chasing the dazed look away.

"Fire? Where?" Panicked, Leah lumbered to her feet, and Abigail gripped her arm to help steady her.

"In the bedchamber. We have to get out. Now."

She yanked the lap robe from the cushion and told Leah to cover her nose and mouth. Lifting her foot, she pushed open the hot door with her shoe. The room beyond was now nearly engulfed in flames. Their way to the door blocked—the carpet runner between them and the door burned like a pathway of hot coals, and fire licked its way hungrily up the doorframe.

Pulse pounding, Abigail whirled to look at the nearest window. Though high above the ground, they would likely survive the fall, far better than remaining trapped as they were.

She glanced back at the window inside the secret room, but it was so small, and let out only to the steep roof, not to safety. Hardly an appealing escape route, even if they could squeeze through. Was the whole house on fire? Or just her room?

Oh, God, help us! Abigail prayed.

Flames leapt toward the bedchamber window, consuming the frilly curtains and cutting off that final way of escape. The fire billowed and roared closer. Abigail leapt back, the fumes slamming the hidden door and barely missing her face. Abigail turned and met Leah's wide eyes.

"What now?" Leah breathed.

Abigail thought a moment, then prised open the small window, a welcome breeze rushing in to cool the stifling air within. If she yelled from it, would anyone hear her? What could they do about it, even if they heard her calls? Abigail's mind whirled, searching desperately for a way out. To hatch an escape plan.

To hatch . . . The word echoed in her mind, and she pictured the old building plans for the water tower. She and Leah now stood in one level of that tower, finished into a storeroom at some later date after the water tower had been abandoned. She recalled the rough sketch of stairs. Her assumption that the sketch represented a possible set of servants' stairs, never completed. But what if they were never meant to be permanent stairs. While workmen were building the tower they had likely used a series of ladders to ascend and descend from one level to the next. Might they still be there?

Clutching the desperate thread of hope, Abigail threw back one end of the square carpet covering the floor.

"What are you doing?" Leah asked.

Abigail studied the wood. No obvious hole or hatch cover—but wait . . . there. A seam. She fell to her knees and tried to tug it up, but even her small fingers were too big.

"Find something I can prise this up with."

Leah searched the room, then snatched up the nail that had hung the portrait. "Try this."

Abigail slid it into the seam and tried to prise up the hatch, if hatch it was. Nothing. She came at it along the opposite seam, but it didn't give. "Find something longer, to use as a lever."

From the bedchamber beyond came the sound of breaking glass—windows shattering from the heat. Would the sound draw help in time? Or would it allow in wind that would fuel the fire into a frenzy?

William saw Miles Pembrooke leaving the manor, walking in the direction of his family's cottage. Unease instantly nipped at him.

"Mr. Pembrooke!" He strode over to meet the man.

"Ah, Mr. Chapman. Perhaps you know. I have been looking for Miss Foster and your sister without success. The servants tell me they saw the two ladies enter the manor an hour ago but haven't seen them since. And I can't find them anywhere. Have you seen them?"

"No," William answered in mild surprise, having seen the girls enter the house from his own window.

Suddenly the front door banged open and Polly ran out, waving her arms. "Fire! The house is on fire!"

"Where?" William called, hoping for a simple kitchen fire.

"Upstairs! I saw it from the landing!"

William's heart lurched. Panic gripped him and in turn he gripped Miles's arm. "Did you check Miss Foster's room?"

"I did, yes. But no one was there."

"But what about . . . the secret room?"

Miles stared at him. "How could I check that, when I don't know where it is?"

William's stomach clenched. Were Leah and Abigail even aware of the fire? He said, "I wager that's where they are."

Miles paled. "Is the secret room anywhere near Miss Foster's bedchamber?"

"Yes—opens right into it."

"God, no . . . The room was empty. I made sure, before I . . ."

"Before you . . . what? Good lord, Miles. What did you do?"

Abigail forced that nail, then a tin lid, then any other object she could find into that seam until her fingernails had broken to the quick and her hands bled. Desperate, she pounded the boards with her fists and let out a frustrated cry.

Leah grabbed one bloodied hand, staying her futile beating.

Abigail's eyes snapped to hers and saw the calm, tear-filled eyes of her friend, the brave resignation as she slowly shook her head.

"It's no good, Abigail."

"We can't give up."

"We must be ready to meet our Maker. I am not afraid to die—if it is our time to go."

"It's not our time." Abigail beat the boards with her free hand once more.

Leah grasped that hand as well. "I pray not. But if it is, we need to be ready."

For a moment, Abigail paused in her frenetic efforts and held Leah's clear, resolute gaze. Then she closed her eyes and prayed, "Lord, please save us. Please pluck us from the fire or protect us from the fiery furnace. I know you can do anything. But if you will otherwise, please let us wake up with you in heaven. I know I don't deserve it. But in your Son's name, I ask you to save us both. Here on earth, if at all possible. And if not, for eternity. We—"

A pounding interrupted her prayer, hammering the air and shaking the floor beneath them. Was the tower about to collapse? Would they be buried alive before smoke or fire did them in? Abigail braced herself and squeezed Leah's hand. Any fate seemed better than that wicked scorching fire.

Over the roar of the encroaching flames, Abigail heard a muffled voice. Was she imagining it?

Leah said, "Shh. Listen."

Abigail, already on her hands and knees, bent forward and laid her ear on the floor.

"Abigail! Leah!" she heard faintly.

"We're here!" she shouted, mouth close to the wood. "We're here!"

"Back away from the hatch!" came the shout—William's voice. Tense and harsh and, oh, so welcome.

"All right. We're clear!" Abigail called.

Bang, came the first blow. Then another. A sledgehammer? An axe?

Crack! A flash of silvery metal sliced through one of the planks. Then again. Two bent nails went pinging across the floor and landed near their feet.

Behind them, the door of the secret room wavered, then burst into flames, and a wave of heat rushed into the small room.

"William, hurry!" Leah cried. "The fire is getting closer!"

More grunts and blows, more splintered wood. The cadence changed, as did the pace. Two men wielding tools at once, Abigail guessed.

She dared another glance over her shoulder. The fire had entered the secret room like an evil intruder. It lapped at the shelves and seared the walls, moving toward Elizabeth Pembrooke's portrait among Leah's gathered things.

Leah stared at it, eyes filling with tears, but she made no protest.

Abigail's back felt so hot she feared her frock would burst into flames. The portrait was too big to carry, but she swiped up the ruby necklace and tucked it into her apron pocket. Then she grasped Leah's hand and pulled her to the far wall, on the other side of the hatch. As far as they could go.

With a final crack, the hatch whined from its hinges and fell downward. Below someone grunted and called a warning, followed by the clatter of falling planks. Through the ragged hole, Abigail saw the sweaty, sooty, anxious faces of William and Mac Chapman.

"Leah!" Mac called. "Are you all right?"

Leah glanced fearfully at the flames whipping toward them. "The fire is almost upon us!"

"Come down." William braced the rickety ladder-steps from the level below. "Hurry."

"But, Abigail . . ."

"I'm right behind you," Abigail insisted. "Go!"

Leah sat on the floor and hung down her legs. William reached up and guided her feet to the top rungs while Mac steadied the ladder.

Abigail glanced behind her. The fire consumed a bandbox of family papers and began licking the frame of Mrs. Pembrooke's portrait.

Suddenly a figure appeared through the flames—a figure in a hooded cloak. Was this the grim reaper come for her? *Dear Jesus, no!* The coat smoked, sputtered, and sparked as its wearer ran through the inferno and launched itself through the burning door as though through a circus ring of fire. The figure dove toward her, arms outstretched. Abigail shrieked in horror and jumped back. The figure landed face-first on the floor of the secret room with a shuddering thud. The cloak was dripping wet—doused against the flames.

The head lifted and the hood fell back, revealing a black-streaked face, awful, yet familiar.

"Miles?"

"Abigail!" he cried. "I never meant to . . . I didn't know you were in here. Honest, I didn't!"

"Miles, we have to get out now!"

He looked up, near his outstretched hands. His focus caught on the ruby necklace spilling from her pocket onto the floor like a red snake.

"I came to rescue you . . ." he said, then his eyes landed on the sparkling rubies once more.

The flames lashed closer and closer, the heat nearly overwhelming her senses. But even before the flames reached her, the smoke did. Abigail coughed and placed her handkerchief over her nose and mouth.

"Abigail, hurry!" William called from below. "Cover your mouth. Stay low!"

Inside the secret room, Miles began digging through the boxes.

"Miles, come on! Let's go—it's not worth your life." She stretched out her hand to him, beseeching him. "Come with me, Miles. Now."

He looked briefly at her hand, but then he reached for the rubies instead.

The fire flared, catching his cloak on fire and scalding her ankle. Her petticoat hem burst into flames.

"William!" she cried, whirling back to the hatch.

He stood at the base of the ladder, face fierce and set.

"Jump, Abigail. Quick."

She dropped to her haunches at the edge of the hatch, smacking her petticoat with her hand, hoping to smother the fire before her whole dress went up in flames and her with it.

She propped her hand on the floor to brace herself, only to snatch back her burning hand, and half-fell half-dropped onto the ladder. She flailed for a handhold as the rotted rungs collapsed and she fell onto William. The force of the collision drove him backward, to the edge of the open hatch below, but he caught himself before momentum sent them both tumbling down it.

She looked up through the hatch above in time to see Elizabeth Pembrooke begin to burn and curl and melt.

"I'll go up for it," Mac said, starting to shimmy back up the ladder brace.

Leah caught his arm. "Papa, don't! I'd rather have you alive than an oil painting of someone I barely remember."

Abigail sucked in a breath and cried, "Miles is up there!"

William gaped in shock. "No . . ."

Abigail grabbed the axe and raised it high—slamming it against the old water pipe. Seeing her intention, William took the axe from her and sliced into the pipe, knocking off the valve with one blow. Water burst forth like a high-pressure fountain, murky, smelly, and wonderful. The rank water flooded the floor and cascaded through the hatch below. It wouldn't save the secret room, but it might buy them time to escape.

The floor above wavered and orange-red flames leeched through the wood.

Over the roar, Mac called, "We've got to get out of here before the whole place goes."

Abigail frantically searched the hatch opening once more, willing Miles to appear there. "Miles!" she cried.

Nothing.

William grabbed the ladder brace. "I'll go."

The floor above them began to collapse, peeling away like bark.

Mac grabbed his arm tight. "No, son. It's too late."

William winced and breathed, "God have mercy on his soul. . . ."

They escaped through the next hatch, just as the burning floor above crashed down over it.

Rung by rung, they descended each angled ladder of the tower until they reached the bottom. In the dim cellar-like space stood a door and a low archway. From a distance came the faint sound of the church bell ringing.

Mac reached for the door. "Let's go."

"No," William said sharply. "That leads into the old wine cellar. We want to get out of the house, not back into it. This way." He pointed to the low half circle that looked like the arched entrance to a cave.

"What is it?" Leah asked.

"A drain tunnel. Watch your heads."

Ducking low, and trying not to scrape their heads on spider webs, bat dung, and who knew what else, they plodded, bent over, through the murky tunnel. After what seemed like hundreds of yards, though probably far less, Abigail glanced up and saw a crescent of light ahead. William explained in choppy breaths that this was where the excess rainwater from the cistern once flowed out into the garden and fishpond.

They emerged from the tunnel in a tiled drainage area at the back of the garden behind the house.

Mac embraced Leah, stroking her hair and murmuring over and over again, "It's all right, lass. You're safe now."

Leah panted, "I never even knew there was a hatch. I suppose Father covered it to keep me from falling when I was little."

"No doubt you're right," Mac said. "He only wanted to protect you. And so did I. . . ."

Abigail glanced up at William. Saw that he was looking not at his sister but at her, with concern and something else glimmering in his eyes.

"Thank God you're safe." He wrapped his arms around her and held her close. Abigail closed her eyes and leaned into his solid chest. He murmured against her hair, "I don't know what I would have done had anything happened to you and Leah. I treasure you both."

From the other side of the manor, the calls of neighbors and the clank of buckets and water cans reached them. The sounds of people nearing made Abigail aware that she stood in William Chapman's embrace. He seemed to realize it at the same moment and pulled back.

His eyes searched her face. "Are you certain you're all right?"

"Yes. I am well, thanks to you."

He managed a sad, weary smile. "Did I not tell you, back when you suspected me of being a treasure hunter, that had I really wanted to get inside Pembrooke Park, I could have done so at any time?"

She nodded and gestured toward the tunnel. "But . . . how did you know?"

"I grew up not one hundred yards from this spot. I know every acre of this estate and the woods between it and our cottage."

"And I am very glad of it." Her smile faltered. "Is that how you so quickly disappeared from the secret room when Miles interrupted us?" When he nodded she asked, "But who nailed the hatch shut?"

William pulled a regretful face. "I did. Last week. I didn't want any man in a hooded cloak slipping into your room as easily as I slipped out of it. Forgive me. I never dreamed—"

"Of course you didn't. It's not your fault, William. You didn't start the fire. . . ."

Abigail looked back at the house, cringing at the billowing black smoke and angry flames lashing out her bedchamber window. "Poor Miles . . ."

"Yes." William grimaced and slowly shook his head.

As the shock began to fade, her hand began to throb. She held it up to look at it, murmuring, "I've burnt my hand."

He took it gently in his, both of them studying the red puckered flesh, mottled white. Concern quickly filled his eyes. "We had better get you to Mr. Brown directly."

As they walked toward the front of the house, a traveling chaise and horses rumbled through the gate, and William saw with mixed emotions that the vehicle conveyed his friend Andrew Morgan, his sister Rebekah, as well as Mr. Scott. He didn't recognize the chaise but had heard Mr. Scott had been given the use of his employer's fine carriage for his regular trips from London to Hunts Hall.

"Word reached us about the fire," Andrew called. "We've come to help."

"And to make sure you were all right," Rebekah added, eyes wide in concern as she laid a hand on William's sleeve.

Mr. Scott hurried to Abigail's side, embraced her tightly, and inspected her hand.

William stepped forward. "I was just about to take her to the local surgeon."

Mr. Scott shook his head, an angry twist to his mouth. "No, I will. And then I'll take her to our family physician in London."

He led her to the carriage. There she paused in its doorway, looking over her shoulder at William, her expression weary and regretful and resigned. He didn't blame her. After all, nothing had changed. He was in no position to protest her departure. No position to make her an offer, to ask for her hand, her poor burnt hand. . . .

She was far better off with Mr. Scott, he told himself, even as the thought lanced his soul. From the corner of his eye, he felt his father's and sister's concerned looks but dared not meet them.

Through the gate came a gig and wagons overflowing with servants and tenants from Hunts Hall, arriving to help.

William thanked Andrew and joined the line. But a part of his heart left in a fine carriage, as it carried away the woman he loved.

Thunder rumbled and rain began to fall, and around him friends and neighbors thanked God. The rain would help their efforts to fight the fire. The rain would cool the hot, weary workers of the fire brigade and wash away sweat and even tears as it did so.

Chapter 31

A month later, Abigail stood in the window of Aunt Bess's townhouse, looking out at the damp cobblestones below, busy with passing carriages, carts, and well-dressed pedestrians. How strange to be back in London, she reflected, when she had planned to remain in Pembrooke Park for a twelvemonth at least. At one time Abigail had privately hoped to renew the lease indefinitely, assuming Mr. Arbeau and Harriet Pembrooke were in agreement, for she had grown fond of the house and countryside, the village and her neighbors. Especially a certain neighbor and his family. Of course, that was before she'd learned Leah's true identity, and before the fire.

The searchers had found Miles Pembrooke's body among the rubble of the ruined tower, rubies still clutched in his hand—reminiscent of the way his father had been found, a pistol clutched in his. Harriet had Miles buried in the Bristol churchyard, next to their beloved mother and brother. For though damaged by the experiences of his childhood, he was her brother, and she had loved him. Abigail had as well.

The fire destroyed most of the west wing, rendering Pembrooke Park even less habitable than when she and her father had first arrived. So Abigail had little choice but to remain in London with her family, sharing the cramped quarters and uneasy hospitality of Aunt Bess's townhouse.

But her family's unexpected change in situation had not ended there. To the surprise of everyone, Uncle Vincent's last remaining investment had actually been a great success, paying out a good deal of money. And with it, he repaid his brother-in-law a large portion of what he had lost in the failed banking venture. Their former home was not for sale, which wasn't surprising, having only recently been purchased. And Abigail, her practical nature reasserting itself, managed to convince her father not to buy or let a house in one of the most elite and expensive squares as before, but a fashionable, though more modest home in Cavendish Square. They would move in next week.

They had seen little of Gilbert since their return, as he'd been assigned to a new project in Greenwich. His sister, Susan Lloyd, however, invited Abigail over for tea, wanting to hear all about her experiences in Easton and about the fire. Her old friend's astute, well-informed questions demonstrated a surprising familiarity with the area and the players involved. Abigail grew suspicious. She asked Susan how she knew so much about it, and Susan confessed the writer from Caldwell, E. P. Brooks, had sent a story based on what she claimed were true events. Could Abigail corroborate the account before they printed it? Unfortunately, Abigail could.

Abigail's mother and sister had decided Miles was too distant a relation to publicly mourn. But Abigail and her father dressed in mourning for several weeks. She was glad she was wearing black when Harriet paid a call soon after she returned to London, dressed in full mourning for her brother. She delivered the long-promised reward in person, pressing Abigail to accept it, when she would have refused. Then Harriet asked Abigail to tell her everything that had happened the day of the fire—insisting she not spare her feelings.

Abigail swallowed and told Harriet about Miles reading the

letters, seeing him carry the letter he'd burnt toward the hearth, and being convinced the fire had been accidental, emphasizing his heroic return when William told him she and Leah were likely trapped in the house, his quick thinking in wearing the soaked hooded cloak to reach them. His words, *"I didn't know you were in here. Honest I didn't! I came to rescue you. . . ."*

"He tried to rescue us, Harriet," Abigail repeated earnestly. "He risked his own life to reach us. He made mistakes, but I honestly believe he intended us no harm. He tried to save us, but in the end he could not. I am so sorry we were not able to get him out of there with us."

Harriet slowly nodded, her mouth trembling. "You have no doubt portrayed my brother in a more heroic light than he deserved." Tears shone in her eyes at last. "But I thank you for it, just the same."

Once the Fosters moved into their new house, their old neighbors, the Scotts, decided to host a party to celebrate their return to London and their return to fortune. Thrilled at the prospect, Louisa pored over fashion prints in search of a new gown and hairstyle and went out with Mamma to visit their favorite *modiste*. Everyone hoped Gilbert would return from Greenwich in time for the party.

Abigail soon found herself relegated to the task of organizing their new home—interviewing and hiring staff, and meeting with the new housekeeper and cook to review menus and approve orders for the larder, linens, etc. Abigail had offered Mrs. Walsh, Polly, and Molly positions with them in London, but all decided to remain in Easton, with its family ties and the hope of future employment if and when Pembrooke Park was repaired. She had no idea of Duncan's plans, nor did she care.

Mamma and Louisa happened to meet Gilbert's mother and sister while they were out, and came home with the news that Andrew Morgan was in town and would join their party. Mamma said, "An invitation has also been extended to the rector—I gather Mr. Morgan is acquainted with him from Caldwell. We met him one Sunday, did we not?"

"Yes, briefly." Abigail wondered if Mr. Morris had come to Town with his nephew or on his own. She was relieved to hear his health had improved enough to allow him to travel. Or perhaps he came to Town seeking a second opinion from a London physician.

The day of the party arrived, and Louisa spent nearly the entire afternoon bathing and getting ready. Abigail had a new dress for the occasion as well. To her credit, Mamma had insisted *both* girls should have new gowns.

But late that afternoon Abigail was called into the housekeeper's parlor to witness a disciplinary lecture between the older woman and a young maid caught flirting with a footman from next door.

"Shall I give her the sack, miss?" the housekeeper asked.

After everything Abigail had experienced in Pembrooke Park, with Miles and even disrespectful Duncan, this seemed to her a petty offense, but she hesitated to undermine their new housekeeper—especially in front of one of the woman's subordinates. She said with gentle respect, "I . . . don't think that's necessary, Mrs. Wilkins. Not on her first infraction. We all make mistakes, don't we? Especially when we are in a new situation."

"That's it, miss," the girl said eagerly, reminding her of Molly. "I didn't know what I was doin' was so wrong. Honest I didn't."

Which led the housekeeper to coolly request that Miss Foster write all the house rules and post them in the servants' hall as soon as may be, to avoid future excuses of ignorance.

Abigail forced a smile and said she would get to it straightaway.

By the time she was able to extricate herself from the goings-on belowstairs, it was well past six. Her mother and father were already dressed, talking companionably in the vestibule while they awaited their daughters and the hired carriage.

Abigail entered the hall in time to see Louisa descend the stairs, looking stunning as usual in a gown of peach satin. Mamma stopped talking, watching with maternal pride as her beautiful daughter came down the stairs.

"I'm sorry the jeweler wasn't able to repair the necklace in time, my dear."

Louisa lifted her chin. "So am I."

"But the coral looks very well on you, all the same," Mamma soothed.

Abigail had originally thought the emerald necklace would look well with her own new gown but had given way when Louisa begged to wear it, trying on the gems with her new gown and enthusing over how elegant she looked, and somehow breaking the clasp in the bargain.

"The emeralds would have looked well on Abigail too," her father put in. And Abigail was touched by his loyalty.

Her mother noticed her then.

"Abigail! You're not even dressed."

"Sorry. Mrs. Wilkins needed me. Some crisis belowstairs."

"I do hope everything is all right," her father said.

"Oh yes. Nothing to worry about. But I am sorry to hold you up."

"We shall go and then send the carriage back for you," he suggested. "You can come over when you're ready, all right?"

"It won't take Abigail long to slip into a dress and repin her hair," Louisa said. "But . . . I suppose it would be rude if we were *all* late. You don't mind, Abigail, do you?"

Abigail hesitated, feeling herself snapping back into the old pattern like a missing mosaic tile from the floor. "No, of course not. You three go ahead."

"Thank you, Abigail." Her mother's smile shone with genuine gratitude.

You see, Abigail told herself, *you are appreciated. Useful . . . in your way.* That was something.

As her family left, Abigail took herself upstairs, passing Mary, the upper housemaid who usually helped her dress and pinned her hair.

"I was just going down to my supper, miss," she said. "But if you want me to do your hair, I can wait."

Abigail hesitated, torn. She forced a smile and said, "That's all right. You go on. Don't miss your supper on my account, I can repin my own hair. No need for anything special."

"Thank you, miss." The girl smiled, bobbed a little curtsy, and hurried down the stairs.

Abigail could arrange her own hair, but she could not get into her new gown on her own. Not with all the fastenings and seed-pearl buttons at the back of the bodice. She sighed. Perhaps she would just make do with her old ivory dress. She might even return the new gown, as she'd never worn it. Madame LeClair would have no trouble selling the beautiful thing, and they could put the credit toward Louisa's large balance.

Abigail went to her closet and regarded the ivory dress. Nothing special. Nothing wrong with it either.

Leaving the gown where it was, Abigail walked to her dressing stool and sat down heavily upon it. Maybe she would simply claim fatigue and stay home. She was tired from all the tasks and supervision of the last few weeks. No one would blame her, and her family would make her excuses. . . .

Then words William Chapman had said whispered on the edges of her mind. *"You are every bit as beautiful as your sister. More so, to me. I treasure you. . . ."*

Oh, William . . . she thought fondly. How she missed him. Even if he exaggerated her charms. She had thought he might write to her, but he had apparently seen her move to London as an opportunity for a clean break. Leah *had* written a few times—at least their friendship would continue, even if her relationship with William would not. After all, nothing had changed between them.

Marcel, her mother's lady's maid, scratched at the door and entered, her often stern face bright and a parcel in her hands. "Mademoiselle! Zee jeweler has returned your necklace just in time! You must wear eet tonight!"

Abigail shook her head. "Louisa wanted to wear it, but . . . In any case, I'm thinking of staying home."

"No, mademoiselle. You should go."

"Oh. I don't know."

Abigail opened the hinged case and looked at the sparkling emeralds within, winking at her.

"I treasure you. . . ."

Suddenly, Abigail stood. "You know what, Marcel. I will go. But I must ask you to help me. I know I have refused in the past, but Mary has gone to her dinner, and I shall make it worth your while."

"No, no, mademoiselle. No need. It will be my pleasure, I promise you. How long I have wished to get my hands on zat beautiful hair of yours! Sit, sit!"

———

Dressed in uncomfortable evening clothes of his least favorite color, black, William Chapman surveyed the people mingling in the drawing room with sinking disappointment. Miss Foster was not among them. Perhaps he ought not to have come with Andrew. Maybe he could still bow out.

Charles Foster saw him from across the room, and a sincere smile lit the older man's handsome face as he made his way over. "Mr. Chapman! What a pleasure to see you again. I didn't realize you were in Town."

"Yes. Staying with Mr. Morgan for a few days. The Scotts were kind enough to extend their invitation to me as well."

"We heard Mr. Morris was coming, but not you."

"Mr. Morris? No, sir, he is not—"

Mr. Foster interrupted, brow puckered. "But I am quite certain Mrs. Scott mentioned the rector of our former parish would be attending. . . ."

"Ah, yes. You see, I have recently been granted the living. Mr. Morris, you may not have heard, passed on a fortnight ago."

"Oh, no. I had not heard. I'm sorry. But I thought his nephew was angling for the living."

"He was. But the owner of Pembrooke Park—in whose benefice the living lies—grants it to the man of her choosing. And Eleanor

Pembrooke chose me." He gave a self-deprecating grin. "I suppose you think it terribly unfair."

"Not at all—you mistake me. I think your sister an excellent woman and an excellent judge of character. She chose wisely and well. Allow me to offer my sincerest and heartiest congratulations."

Charles Foster offered his hand, and William shook it.

"Thank you, sir. I plan to hire young Mr. Morris as my curate, to help conduct services in outlying churches of the parish and in visiting the sick."

"Well again, congratulations. The rest of my family will be happy to hear the news as well. Though I am afraid Abigail may not be joining us."

"Oh?" William hoped his disappointment wasn't too obvious, especially with Gilbert Scott in attendance. Had she entered into an understanding with Mr. Scott during the intervening weeks? He'd not had leave to write to her but thought she would have mentioned it in one of her letters to his sister. He prayed he wasn't too late.

"Yes, I'm afraid we've kept her quite busy arranging the house-keeping and things for the new place. Quite worn off her feet. Louisa wagers she will be too tired to come."

"I am sorry to hear it. I had hoped to see her before I left Town." There was something he very much wished to say to her.

Mr. Foster excused himself to go and find his wife.

A few moments later Louisa Foster and Gilbert Scott approached.

"Mr. Chapman!" Louisa beamed. "What a pleasant surprise to see you here."

William bowed. "Miss Louisa. Mr. Scott."

"I've been talking to Andrew Morgan and hear congratulations are in order," Gilbert said.

"Thank you, yes. I am very grateful for the opportunity."

Louisa said, "Too bad Abigail isn't here—she will be so sorry to have missed you."

"Yes, I am sorry to have missed her as well." *More sorry than you know.*

The door opened behind them, and a butler announced in an affected voice, "Miss Foster."

Heart leaping, William turned. The smile instantly lifting his mouth fell away. He blinked and stared again, his heart beating erratically. Here she was, Miss Abigail Foster. The girl of his fondest memories and fonder dreams, yet somehow altered. Head high, posture erect as she entered the room, her gaze slowly sweeping the assembled company. She met the varyingly pleased and surprised looks with a gentle smile and stopped to greet her host and hostess.

She wore a luminous green-and-white gown with a beguiling neckline and a ribbon sash under her bosom which accentuated the fullness above and slenderness below. Her hair was piled in a high mound of soft curls, flattering her delicate features and making her eyes seem larger. Twin spirals danced along each cheek, emphasizing her fine cheekbones and the heart shape of her face. Her dark eyes shone like chocolate, her small lips pleasingly pink. He drew in a ragged breath. Had he actually kissed those lips once upon a time? His chest tightened at the memory.

At her neck sparkled an emerald necklace which drew his attention to her long pale neck, the fine delicate collarbones he'd give anything to kiss . . .

Stop it, he told himself. But his thoughts refused to yield. This was the woman he loved. The woman he wished to marry. To be one with. Such feelings were not wrong; they were a gift. But did she feel the same? He glanced at Gilbert Scott standing to his right. He, too, had stopped and stared, not dragging his gaze from Abigail for all her sister's tugging on his arm.

Did Abigail still nurture feelings for the man? William's happiness dimmed at the thought.

Unaccustomed to having so many people looking at her, Abigail took a deep breath and reminded herself she was among friends. She glimpsed Louisa leaving Gilbert's side to talk with Andrew Morgan. And there were her parents, and Susan and

Edward Lloyd. She did not yet see Mr. Morris but, then, wasn't all that eager to do so.

Her mother and father walked forward to welcome her.

He took her hands. "My dear, you look beautiful."

Abigail smiled, self-conscious but pleased at his praise. "Thank you, Papa."

"I am glad you decided to come," her mother said. "I began to fear you had worn yourself out and would stay home. I am sorry I left all of that to you. It is only that you are so capable. But I shall endeavor not to shift my responsibilities to you in future. It isn't fair to you."

"Thank you, Mamma."

Her mother's eyes fastened on the gemstones. "I see the jeweler delivered the necklace at last."

"Yes, Marcel brought it up to me not long after you left."

"Louisa will be disappointed."

Abigail met her mother's look with a gentle one of her own but made no offer to remove the necklace. And no apology.

Her sister would have many other chances to wear it, Abigail knew. Tonight was her turn.

Louisa approached, gaze riveted on the necklace. "You are wearing it?"

"Yes. The jeweler delivered it after you left. Marcel brought it up to me."

"And did your hair as well, I see."

"Yes," Abigail acknowledged, calmly holding her sister's gaze and ignoring the slight irritation glittering in her fair eyes.

"Well . . ." Louisa seemed torn between vexation and reluctant admiration. "It looks very well with your new dress, I own."

"Thank you, Louisa."

"In fact, I don't mind saying you look very pretty tonight, Abigail."

"Thank you. That means a great deal, coming from the most beautiful girl in the room."

The two sisters shared a tentative smile, and then Louisa pressed her hand. "I'd best not keep Mr. Morgan waiting. He says he has news to share."

Yes, Abigail thought. But not the news her sister probably hoped for.

When Louisa walked away, William took a deep breath and approached Abigail. How elegant the well-dressed creature looked. It made him miss the bedraggled girl in mud-spattered wool cape with damp hair falling from its pins. But he couldn't deny she looked beautiful.

"Miss Foster. How pleased I am to see you. I began to fear I'd begged an invitation in vain."

Her eyes widened in surprise. "Mr. Chapman. William. I am pleased to see you as well. I'd heard someone from Easton was attending, but I dared not hope it was you." She gave him a soft smile. "Had I known, I would have come sooner."

His heart warmed. "Then I am very glad indeed I begged that invitation."

Her smile widened. "Andrew Morgan is here as well, I see."

"Yes. I am in Town as his guest. He is here purchasing wedding clothes."

"Wedding clothes?"

"Yes. He and Leah—excuse me, I shall never grow accustomed to calling her Eleanor—are recently engaged and soon to be married. I thought you knew."

"I hoped, but I had not yet heard the news."

"No doubt my sister has written to you and I have stolen her surprise. She shall box my ears when I get home."

"I think she would forgive you anything." She added, "Have his parents come round to the idea, now that they know who Leah is?"

"Yes. Though, after Leah's brush with death, I don't think anything would have stopped Andrew from making his feelings known—and making up for lost time."

"I am glad to hear it."

"Miss Foster, speaking of making up for lost time, I wonder if I might have a private word . . . ?"

Her dark brows rose. "Of . . . course."

Gilbert Scott suddenly appeared between them. "Abby, how beautiful you look. I almost didn't recognize you when you came in."

"Thank you, Gilbert."

"And Mr. Chapman. When Miss Pembrooke is ready to discuss refurbishments for Pembrooke Park, tell her I would be honored to offer my services."

"Thank you, Mr. Scott. But I believe my sister hopes to gather Miss Foster's ideas first, before proceeding and hiring a builder. We also plan to implement her scheme for the parsonage."

William noticed her quick look of surprise and pleasure.

"Ah. Well. Of course." Scott conceded, "Abby has always had an excellent eye."

"Not always," Abigail allowed. "But I think I recognize excellence now when I see it." She looked at William with shining eyes.

Mr. Scott looked from one to the other. "Abby, Louisa insists we have dancing after dinner. Do say you'll dance with me. For old times' sake."

She smiled at her old friend, but then she lifted her gaze to William, her dark eyes meeting, melding with his.

"Actually, I fear I may be engaged," she said. "Is that not right, Mr. Chapman?"

William felt his chest expand with hope and pleasure. "You are engaged for the entire evening," he said earnestly. "And for every evening after that, if I have my way."

At his words, Abigail's whole body thrummed in anticipation. She tucked her hand under his arm. "Then indeed you shall."

Without removing his gaze from hers, William Chapman said, "If you will excuse us, Mr. Scott?"

Not waiting to hear Gilbert's reply, William led her out of the drawing room and into the quiet vestibule, her heart beating hard with each step. She fleetingly recalled coming upon Louisa and Gilbert in this very vestibule last year. And now it was her turn to stand there in a private tête-à-tête.

William turned and solemnly faced her. "Miss Foster. Abigail. I know I said I was in no position to marry. That it would be wrong to ask you to wait until my situation improved—"

"I've thought about that," Abigail interrupted. "But I don't care about the living. I care about you."

He stepped nearer. "You don't know how happy that makes me." His blue eyes shone. "But then I gather you haven't heard . . ."

"Heard what?"

"Mr. Morris has passed on."

She felt her smile falter. "I am sorry to hear it. And his nephew?"

"Leah—Eleanor—has granted the living to me."

"Ohhh . . ." Abigail breathed, thoughts whirling. Perhaps she should have foreseen that possibility, but she had not.

He took her hand in his. "Will you marry me, dearest loveliest Abigail?"

The question sent a thrill of pleasure through Abigail, and she gazed at him in wonder. "Of course I shall. Nothing would make me happier. For I love you with all my heart."

Flushed with happiness, she wished she had some token of her love to give him. A miniature, a lover's eye, a lock of hair set in a ring. She had none of these things, so she took his face in her hands and drew his head down, pressing her mouth to his in a passionate kiss.

And judging from his reaction, the gift was very much appreciated.

A short while later, they caught their breaths and rejoined the others for dinner. Abigail barely tasted her food, but she enjoyed the company, and the warm congratulations that flowed around them. That evening, she danced every dance and, if her future husband could be believed, outshone every woman there.

She had said yes to William Chapman even before she learned

he had a valuable living. She had said yes to a life of working alongside the man she loved. A life different than the one she'd once imagined—but oh so right. Together they would serve the parish, and God, and each other. Together they would build a practical, happy life.

Abigail realized anew she had never needed a treasure to make herself worthy. How thankful she was to be treasured by God, and the man who loved her.

Epilogue

*W*illiam and I stood, hand in hand, watching as the foundation was laid for a large addition to the parsonage. The rebuilding has also begun on Pembrooke Park. True to her word, Leah asked for my opinion on what should be done to the manor house during the refurbishment. She had thought about pulling the place down and being done with it. Washing her hands forever of her childhood home. But she decided in the end that to truly make peace with her past, she had to first embrace it, embrace her role as heiress of Pembrooke Park and lady of the manor. I think she will do credit to the role and be a wonderful patroness of the village and church.

She and Andrew talked at length about what was best to do. He is to have Hunts Hall one day, after all, and the two could reside there instead. But as his parents are sure to remain there as long as they live, Andrew and Leah have decided they will rebuild Pembrooke Park and live in it together as husband and wife for the time being.

Even though Mrs. Morgan seems to approve of "dear Eleanor" now that her true origins are known, Leah prefers to live nearer her family. She says the Chapmans will always be the family of her heart—Mac, Kate, Kitty, and Jacob. And William of course. Her family feeling and affection now extend to me as well, I'm pleased to say. And I treasure our friendship. It is such a joy to see her well and truly happy. The fears of the past gone. The secrets and hiding with it.

She is free to be who she really is and loved for who she really is. And really, isn't that what we all want?

Gilbert remains a dear friend, though relations between us are not what they once were. How could they be, when the piece of my heart I'd long ago given him is now fully, soundly in William's possession? Even so, we are cordial, and I wish him every success in his future. He has yet to marry. For his sake, I wish he would.

Louisa, I think, has learnt the error of her flirtatious ways— praise be to God. She was disappointed that Andrew Morgan married Leah, and that Gilbert has not renewed his addresses. She's had no offers—well, no offers of marriage from honorable gentlemen, that is, though all sorts of other offers abound. Realizing this, she has become more circumspect in her behavior—quieter and more modest. And I think it suits her well. She is still quite the most beautiful woman of my acquaintance, and now, day by day, her heart begins to match her outward appearance. Blessed will be the man who wins that heart at last.

And Harriet Pembrooke Webb? My breath still catches a little when I think of her and all she has lost. Her parents. Her elder brother. And more recently, her younger brother—her last remaining relative . . . Or so she thought.

I received one last letter from her shortly before I moved back to Easton as William's wife.

Dear Abigail,

Thank you for your recent letter and your continuing condolences regarding Miles. That you remember him fondly means more to me than you know. I still grieve my brother— all my family, really—even as I rejoice over the wondrous fact that my secret friend is back in my life. And more wonderful yet, that she is, indeed, more than a friend—my own first cousin. Have I not long wished that Pembrooke Park had a deserving heir? And I cannot conceive of a more deserving heir than Eleanor.

It gave me great satisfaction to relinquish my role as executor, and hand the reins of stewardship to Robert Pembrooke's daughter. I find solace in the knowledge that I have made some sort of restitution for the sins of my father. Despite the fact that you and the Reverend Mr. William Chapman have assured me I need not do so.

"Christ has made the ultimate restitution beyond what you or I or any person could do," he often reminds me.

I humbly agree, and I thank God for it every day. But now that Pembrooke Park is in Eleanor's hands, I sleep better every night.

I have sold my London house and taken a place in Caldwell. Many is the afternoon my cousin and I meet in the sunny spot between the potting shed and walled garden. We have carried away the old rubbish, trimmed the grass, and placed a small wrought-iron table and chairs there, graced by that same colorful glass jar, filled with a fresh bouquet of flowers every week or so.

Now and again, if one of us can't make it, we leave each other notes in the old hiding place behind the loose brick, rearranging the time, or simply letting the other know we were thinking of her.

And so you see, our private, mismatched friendship continues. We meet nearly every week when the weather is fine. We take tea, talk about our homes and families, the books we are reading. We no longer need to escape into a world of make-believe. But even so, how pleasant to escape for an hour or two into the company of a treasured friend.

When we are in that secret place, we sometimes slip and call each other by our old nicknames, Lizzie and Jane.

Once you have taken up residence here, you must join

us sometime, Abigail. No one else would we invite into our special place. But you, dear girl, are always welcome, for it is thanks to you that we have found each other again. For that, you have my eternal gratitude and affectionate friendship. And I know I speak for, em, Lizzie as well.

I look forward to joining them there soon.

Ah, the weary wonder of this life. Of faith. And family. And friends. The truest treasures we can ever know or possess.

Author's Note

*P*embrooke Park is a fictional estate inspired by Great Chalfield Manor in Wiltshire, England, a fifteenth-century country house surrounded by extensive gardens and a moat. For many months, I kept photos of the manor and the adjacent church on my bulletin board and grew quite attached to the place. My friend Sara and I had the pleasure of visiting Great Chalfield in person while this book was being edited, and how lovely it is, with its great hall, oriel windows, and topiary houses. We met several gracious, helpful people there and enjoyed a history-rich tour of the manor, which is often used as a film location. The exterior and grounds were much as I'd imagined them, though the interior is quite a bit different than my depiction of Pembrooke Park.

Sara and I also attended an Evensong service at the Church of All Saints there, where the Reverend Andrew Evans delivered a beautiful sermon that touched us both. (Though it was perhaps a shade longer than those William Chapman delivered.) If you have the opportunity to travel to England, I hope you will visit Great Chalfield Manor. In the meantime, stop by my website or the National Trust site to see photos of this historical manor and church.

The Secret of Pembrooke Park is my longest book to date, written in less time than usual. I would not have been able to accomplish this without help from several people:

Authors Susan May Warren and Michelle Lim, who helped me brainstorm and plot the book during a weekend retreat with our local chapter of American Christian Fiction Writers.

My husband and sons, who had to make do—and frozen pizza and taco runs—while I was racing toward deadlines.

My sister-friend and first reader, Cari Weber, who provided valuable feedback and a listening ear.

Fellow author Michelle Griep, who provided laser-sharp and encouraging feedback as well.

Amy Boucher Pye—London vicar's wife, editor, author, and speaker—who read the book to help me avoid errors in describing Church of England services as well as other British gaffes. And her husband, the Reverend Nicholas Pye, who answered her questions as needed. Any remaining errors are mine.

Pastor Ken Lewis, for helping me refine Mr. Chapman's sermons.

Sara Ring, for serving as brave driver, photographer, and fun fellow traveler.

My agent, Wendy Lawton, whose love of antique dollhouses surpasses my own. Thanks for cheering me on.

My editorial team at Bethany House Publishers, especially Charlene Patterson, Karen Schurrer, and Raela Schoenherr. I appreciate your editorial support and friendship.

And you, my readers. Thank you for your enthusiasm about my books and for sharing them with your friends and book clubs.

What a blessing this writing career has been. I'm thankful for each and every one of you!

Discussion Questions

1. What secrets in the book did you figure out early on? Anything you guessed wrong? What happening or plot twist took you most by surprise?

2. Did your first impression of any character turn out to be wrong? Have you had a similar experience in real life (realizing your first impression of someone—good or bad—was not at all accurate)?

3. When Abigail, and later William, saw the figure in the hooded green cloak, who do you think it was? The same person who wore it in the climactic scene, or someone else?

4. Did you ever think you were meant to marry one person, only to discover in hindsight he wasn't the person God intended for you after all? What would you tell a young person pining for someone who doesn't return his or her affections?

5. Did you grow up feeling like a favored child, or an overlooked child, or did your parents make a point of treating their offspring equally? What is your view of Mr. and Mrs. Foster's parenting style in this regard? What would you say to someone who feels he or she is living in a sibling's shadow?

6. Do you think Abigail chose the right man? Did you vacillate or feel torn about which man she should end up with?

7. Did you feel any sympathy for Miles? Like him at all? Wish the author had given him a different ending—or do you think he got the ending he deserved?

8. What about Harriet? What did you think about her desire to make restitution for the wrongdoings of her father? What is your view of the verse: "The Lord is longsuffering, and of great mercy, forgiving iniquity and transgression, and by no means clearing the guilty, visiting the iniquity of the fathers upon the children unto the third and fourth generation" (Numbers 14:18)?

9. Abigail is tempted to believe she needs a large dowry—a treasure—to make herself valuable, and worthy of a man's love. Have you ever struggled with a similar feeling of insecurity? In the end, Abigail learns ". . . she had never needed a treasure to make herself worthy. How thankful she was to be treasured by God, and the man who loved her." Can you relate?

10. Do you agree or disagree with this concluding line? "Ah, the weary wonder of this life. Of faith. And family. And friends. The truest treasures we can ever know or possess." Is there anything you would omit or add?

Julie Klassen loves all things Jane—*Jane Eyre* and Jane Austen. A graduate of the University of Illinois, Julie worked in publishing for sixteen years and now writes full time. Three of her books, *The Silent Governess*, *The Girl in the Gatehouse*, and *The Maid of Fairbourne Hall*, have won the Christy Award for Historical Romance. She has also won the Midwest Book Award and Christian Retailing's BEST Award, and has been a finalist in the Romance Writers of America's RITA Awards, Minnesota Book Awards, and ACFW's Carol Awards. Julie and her husband have two sons and live in a suburb of St. Paul, Minnesota.

For more information, visit www.julieklassen.com.

More From Julie Klassen

To learn more about Julie and her books, visit julieklassen.com.

With the help of the lovely Miss Midwinter, can London dancing master Alec Valcourt unravel old mysteries and bring new life to the village of Beaworthy—and to one widow's hardened heart?

The Dancing Master

Emma and her father have come to the Cornish coast to tutor the youngest sons of a baronet—but all is not as it seems. When mysterious things begin to happen and danger mounts, can she figure out which brother to blame...and which to trust with her heart?

The Tutor's Daughter

To escape marrying a dishonorable man, Margaret Macy temporarily disguises herself as a housemaid. Soon entangled in intrigues both above *and* below-stairs, will she sacrifice a chance at love in order to preserve her secret?

The Maid of Fairbourne Hall

Fiction You May Also Enjoy

Washington, D.C., 1891. United in a quest to cure tuberculosis, physician Trevor McDonough and statistician Kate Livingston must overcome past secrets and current threats to find hope for their cause—and their hearts.

With Every Breath by Elizabeth Camden
elizabethcamden.com

Based on the books of Ezra and Nehemiah! After years of exile in Babylon, faithful Jews Iddo and Zechariah are among the first to return to Jerusalem. After the arduous journey, they—and the women they love—struggle to rebuild their lives in obedience to the God who beckons them home.

Return to Me, THE RESTORATION CHRONICLES #1
lynnaustin.org

A powerful retelling of the story of Esther! In 1944, blond-haired and blue-eyed Jewess Hadassah Benjamin will do all she can to save her people—even if she cannot save herself.

For Such a Time by Kate Breslin
katebreslin.com

◆ BETHANYHOUSE